ELLERY QUEEN'S
EYEWITNESSES

ELLERY QUEEN'S
EYEWITNESSES

Edited by ELLERY QUEEN

The Dial Press

Davis Publications, Inc.
380 Lexington Avenue, New York, N.Y. 10017

COPYRIGHT NOTICES AND ACKNOWLEDGMENTS

Grateful acknowledgment is hereby made for permission to reprint the following:

The Sweet Corn Murder by Rex Stout; copyright © 1962 by Rex Stout; first published in the Saturday Evening Post; reprinted by permission of A. Searle Pinney, executor of the author's estate.

The Glory Hunter by Brian Garfield; © 1977 by Brian Garfield; reprinted by permission of the author.

Death at the Excelsior by P. G. Wodehouse; copyright 1976 by the estate of P. G. Wodehouse; from THE UNCOLLECTED WODEHOUSE; reprinted by permission of Scott Meredith Literary Agency, Inc.

Counting Steps by David Ely; © 1978 by David Ely; reprinted by permission of International Creative Management.

Her Heart's Home by Mary McMullen; © 1977 by Mary McMullen; reprinted by permission of Marie Rodell-Frances Collin Literary Agency.

Raffles and the Unique Bequest by Barry Perowne; © 1978 by Philip Atkey; reprinted by permission of the author.

Something Like Murder by John Lutz; © 1978 by John Lutz; reprinted by permission of the author.

Dover Without Perks by Joyce Porter; © 1978 by Joyce Porter; reprinted by permission of Curtis Brown Associates, Ltd.

The de Rougemont Case by Nigel Morland; © 1978 by Nigel Morland; reprinted by permission of the author.

The Birthday Killer by Hugh Pentecost; © 1978 by author; reprinted by permission of Brandt & Brandt Literary Agents, Inc.

4

"Q"

CONTENTS

INTRODUCTION

Dear Reader:

The dictionary definition reads:

eyewitness. n. One who sees an object or act; especially one who testifies what he has seen.

Part of the dictionary definition for "see" reads:

see. v.t. To perceive by the eye. To behold as if with the eye in imagination.

Thus, there is an inner eye, a mind's eye, and by extension, a mind's-eyewitness.

Let us examine the concept of a mind's-eyewitness. In real life not every crime has an eyewitness, in the sense of an objective or disinterested bystander. But in fiction every crime has many impartial eyewitnesses. These omnipresent multiwitnesses of crime fiction are the readers—you.

Sometimes, as mind's-eyewitnesses, you "see" the crime planned, in every detail; "see" it committed step by step; "see" it investigated stage by stage; "see" its aftermath, the ultimate failure or triumph of the detectors.

But how reliable is this "seeing"? If called upon, how accurate would your mind's-eye testimony be? It is well known that in real life the testimony of most eyewitnesses, even unprejudiced ones, is

8

not dependable. Remember the test a college professor gave his first-term law students: in the midst of the professor's lecture the door of the classroom burst open, a man rushed in with a gun in his hand, crouched and fired three blanks into the teacher's body, the victim fell to the floor, the assailant turned and fled.

What actually happened? Exactly what did the students see and hear? As it developed, few students agreed on the particulars. Some saw the intruder as tall and thin, others insisted he was short and stout. His hair—black, grizzled, and at least one student remembered the gunman as bald. The attacker's suit?—grey, brown, possibly blue. In which hand did he hold the gun? Half said right, half said left. Number of shots?—only one, no two, or were there three? Would eyewitness-readers of crime fiction be in more agreement or in less? Beware your role as a mind's-eyewitness, or if you prefer reading the tougher tales, as a private-eyewitness. Take the advice of this old-timer at the mystery-reading game: keep your senses keen, note the observable facts, follow through on every clue.

But *caveat lector:* the motto of all who hesitate to accept the testimony of eyewitnesses is this: "The deaf man heard the dumb man say that the blind man saw the lame man run" . . .

Now, settle yourself comfortably, prop up the pillows, have drinks and snacks handy, turn this page—and become a mind's-eyewitness to tantalizing mysteries and exciting crimes and detections . . .

ELLERY QUEEN

Rex Stout

The Sweet Corn Murder

When the doorbell rang that Tuesday evening in September and I stepped to the hall for a look and through the one-way glass saw Inspector Cramer on the stoop, bearing a fair-sized carton, I proceeded to the door, intending to open it a couple of inches and say through the crack, "Deliveries in the rear."

Inspector Cramer was uninvited and unexpected, we had no case and no client, and we owed him nothing, so why pretend he was welcome?

But by the time I reached the door I had changed my mind. Not because of him. He looked perfectly normal—big and burly, round red face with bushy gray eyebrows, broad heavy shoulders straining the sleeve seams of his coat. It was the carton. It was a used one, the right size, the cord around it was the kind McLeod used, and the NERO WOLFE on it in blue crayon was McLeod's style of printing.

Having switched the stoop light on, I could observe those details as I approached, so I swung the door open and asked politely, "Where did you get the corn?"

I suppose I should explain a little. Usually Wolfe comes closest to being human after dinner, when we leave the dining room to cross the hall to the office, and he gets his bulk deposited in his favorite chair behind his desk, and Fritz brings coffee; and either Wolfe opens his current book or, if I have no date and am staying in, he starts a conversation.

The topic may be anything from women's shoes to the importance of the new moon in Babylonian astrology. But that evening he had taken his cup and crossed to the big globe over by the bookshelves and stood twirling the globe, scowling at it, probably picking a place he would rather be.

For the corn hadn't come. By an arrangement with a farmer named Duncan McLeod up in Putnam County, every Tuesday from July 20 to October 5, sixteen ears of just-picked corn were delivered. They were roasted in the husk, and we did our own shucking as we ate—four ears for me, eight for Wolfe, and four in the kitchen for Fritz. The corn had to arrive no earlier than 5:30 and no later than 6:30. That day it hadn't arrived at all and Fritz had had to do some stuffed eggplant, so Wolfe was standing scowling at the globe when the doorbell rang.

And now here was Inspector Cramer with the carton. Could it possibly be it? It was. Handing me his hat to put on the shelf, he tramped down the hall to the office, and when I entered he had put the carton on Wolfe's desk and had his knife out to cut the cord, and Wolfe, cup in hand, was crossing to him.

Cramer opened the flaps, took out an ear of corn, and said, "If you were going to have this for dinner, I guess it's too late."

Wolfe moved to his elbow, turned the flap to see the inscription, his name, grunted, circled around the desk to his chair, and sat. "You have your effect," he said. "I am impressed. Where did you get it?"

"If you don't know, maybe Goodwin does." Cramer shot a glance at me, went to the red-leather chair facing the end of Wolfe's desk, and sat. "I've got some questions for you and for him, but of course you want grounds. You would. At a quarter past five, four hours ago, the dead body of a man was found in the alley back of Ruster-man's restaurant. He had been hit in the back of the head with a piece of iron pipe which was there on the ground by the body. The station wagon he had come in was alongside the receiving platform of the restaurant, and in the station wagon were nine cartons containing ears of corn."

Cramer pointed. "That's one of them, your name on it. You get one like it every Tuesday. Right?"

Wolfe nodded. "I do. In season. Has the body been identified?"

"Yes. Driver's license and other items in his pockets, including cash, eighty-some dollars. Kenneth Faber, twenty-eight years old. Also men at the restaurant identified him. He had been delivering the corn there the past five weeks, and then he had been coming on here with yours. Right?"

"I don't know."

"The hell you don't. If you're going to start that kind—"

I cut in. "Hold it. Stay in the buggy. As you know, Mr. Wolfe is up in the plant rooms from four to six every day except Sunday. The corn usually comes before six, and either Fritz or I receive it. So Mr. Wolfe doesn't know, but I do. Kenneth Faber has been bringing it the past five weeks. If you want—"

I stopped because Wolfe was moving. Cramer had dropped the ear of corn onto Wolfe's desk, and Wolfe had picked it up and felt it, gripping it in the middle, and now he was shucking it. From where

I sat, at my desk, the rows of kernels looked too big, too yellow, and too crowded.

Wolfe frowned at it, muttered, "I thought so," put it down, stood up, reached for the carton, said, "You will help, Archie," took an ear, and started shucking it. As I got up Cramer said something but was ignored.

When we finished we had three piles, as assorted by Wolfe. Two ears were too young, six were too old, and eight were just right. He returned to his chair, looked at Cramer, and declared, "This is preposterous."

"So you're stalling," Cramer growled.

"No. Shall I expound it?"

"Yeah. Go ahead."

"Since you have questioned men at the restaurant, you know that the corn comes from a man named Duncan McLeod, who grows it on a farm some sixty miles north of here. He has been supplying it for four years, and he knows precisely what I require. It must be nearly mature, but not quite, and it must be picked not more than three hours before it reaches me. Do you eat sweet corn?"

"Yes. You're stalling."

"No. Who cooks it?"

"My wife. I haven't got a Fritz."

"Does she cook it in water?"

"Sure. Is yours cooked in beer?"

"No. Millions of American women, and some men, commit that outrage every summer day. They are turning a superb treat into mere provender. Shucked and boiled in water, sweet corn is edible and nutritious; roasted in the husk in the hottest possible oven for forty minutes, shucked at the table, buttered and salted, nothing else, it is ambrosia. No chef's ingenuity and imagination have ever created a finer dish. American women should themselves be boiled in water. Ideally the corn—"

"How much longer are you going to stall?"

"I'm not stalling. Ideally the corn should go straight from the stalk to the oven, but of course that's impractical for city dwellers. If it's picked at the right stage of development it is still a treat for the palate after twenty-four hours, or even forty-eight; I have tried it. But look at this." Wolfe pointed to the assorted piles. "This is preposterous. Mr. McLeod knows better. The first year I had him send two dozen ears, and I returned those that were not acceptable. He knows what I require, and he knows how to choose it without opening the husk. He is supposed to be equally meticulous with the supply for the restaurant, but I doubt if he is—they take fifteen to twenty dozen. Are they serving what they got today?"

"Yes. They've admitted that they took it from the station wagon even before they reported the body." Cramer's chin was down and his eyes were narrowed under the eyebrow hedge. "You're the boss at that restaurant."

Wolfe shook his head. "Not the boss. My trusteeship, under the will of my friend Marko Vukcic when he died, will end next year. You know the arrangement; you investigated the murder; you may remember that I brought the murderer back from Yugoslavia."

"Yeah. Maybe I never thanked you." Cramer's eyes came to me. "You go there fairly often—not to Yugoslavia, to Rusterman's. How often?"

I raised one brow. That annoys him because he can't do it. "Oh, once a week, sometimes twice. I have privileges, and it's the best restaurant in New York."

"Sure. Were you there today?"

"No."

"Where were you at five-fifteen this afternoon?"

"In the Heron sedan which Mr. Wolfe owns and I drive. Five fifteen? Grand Concourse, headed for the East River Drive."

"Who was with you?"

"Saul Panzer."

He grunted. "You and Wolfe are the only two men alive Panzer would lie for. Where had you been?"

"Ball game. Yankee Stadium."

"What happened in the ninth inning?" He flipped a hand. "To hell with it. You'd know all right, you'd see to that. How well do you know Max Maslow?"

I raised the brow again. "Connect it, please."

"I'm investigating a murder."

"So I gathered. And apparently I'm a suspect. Connect it."

"One item in Kenneth Faber's pockets was a little notebook. One page had the names of four men written in pencil. Three of the names had checkmarks in front of them. The last one, no checkmark, was Archie Goodwin. The first one was Max Maslow. Will that do?"

"I'd rather see the notebook."

"It's at the laboratory." His voice went up a notch. "Look, Goodwin. You're a licensed private detective."

I nodded. "But that crack about who Saul Panzer would lie for.

Okay, I'll file it. I don't know any Max Maslow and have never heard the name before. The other two names with checkmarks?"

"Peter Jay. J-A-Y."

"Don't know him and never heard of him."

"Carl Heydt." He spelled it.

"That's better. Couturier?"

"He makes clothes for women."

"Including a friend of mine, Miss Lily Rowan. I have gone with her a few times to his place to help her decide. His suits and dresses come high, but I suppose he'd turn out a little apron for three Cs."

"How well do you know him?"

"Not well at all. I call him Carl, but you know how that is. We have been fellow weekend guests at Miss Rowan's place in the country a couple of times. I have seen him only when I have been with Miss Rowan."

"Do you know why his name would be in Faber's notebook with a checkmark?"

"I don't know and I couldn't guess."

"Do you want me to connect Susan McLeod before I ask you about her?"

I had supposed that would be coming as soon as I heard the name Carl Heydt, since the cops had had the notebook for four hours and had certainly lost no time making contacts. Saving me for the last, and Cramer himself coming, was of course a compliment, but more for Wolfe than for me.

"No, thanks," I told him. "I'll do the connecting. The first time Kenneth Faber came with the corn, six weeks ago today, the first time I ever saw him, he told me Sue McLeod had got her father to give him a job on the farm. He was very chatty. He said he was a free-lance cartoonist, and the cartoon business was in a slump, and he wanted some sun and air and his muscles needed exercise, and Sue often spent weekends at the farm and that would be nice. You can't beat that for a connection. Go ahead and ask me about Susan McLeod."

Cramer was eying me. "You're never slow, are you, Goodwin?"

I gave him a grin. "Slow as cold honey. But I try hard to keep up."

"Don't overdo. How long have you been intimate with her?"

"Well. There are several definitions for 'intimate.' Which one?"

"You know damn well which one."

My shoulders went up. "If you won't say, I'll have to guess." The shoulders went down. "If you mean the very worst, or the very best, depending on how you look at it, nothing doing. I have known her three years, having met her when she brought the corn one day. Have you seen her?"

"Yes."

"Then you know how she looks, and much obliged for the compliment. She has points. I think she means well, and she can't help it if she can't keep the come-on from showing because she was born with it. She didn't pick her eyes and voice, they came in the package. Her talk is something special. Not only do you never know what she will say next; she doesn't know herself. One evening I kissed her, a good healthy kiss, and when we broke she said, 'I saw a horse kiss a cow once.' But she's a lousy dancer, and after a show or prizefight or ball game I want an hour or two with a band and a partner.

"So I haven't seen much of her for a year. The last time I saw her was at a party somewhere a couple of weeks ago. I don't know who her escort was, but it wasn't me. As for my being intimate with her, meaning what you mean, what do you expect? I haven't, but even if I had I'm certainly not intimate enough with you to blab it. Anything else?"

"Plenty. You got her a job with that Carl Heydt. You found her a place to live, an apartment that happens to be only six blocks from here."

I cocked my head at him. "Where did you get that? From Carl Heydt?"

"No. From her."

"She didn't mention Miss Rowan?"

"No."

"Then I give her a mark. You were at her about a murder, and she didn't want to drag in Miss Rowan. One day, the second summer she was bringing the corn, two years ago, she said she wanted a job in New York and asked if I could get her one. I doubted if she could hold a job any friend of mine might have open or might make room for, so I consulted Miss Rowan, and she took it on. She got two girls she knew to share their apartment with Sue—it's only five blocks from here, not six—she paid for a course at the Midtown Studio—Sue has paid her back—and she got Carl Heydt to give Sue a tryout at modeling.

"I understand that Sue is now one of the ten most popular models in New York and her price is a hundred dollars an hour, but that's hearsay. I haven't seen her on a magazine cover. I didn't get her a job or a place to live. I know Miss Rowan better than Sue does; she won't mind my dragging her in. Anything else?"

"Plenty. When and how did you find out that Kenneth Faber had shoved you out and taken Sue over?"

"Nuts." I turned to Wolfe. "Your Honor, I object to the question on the ground that it is insulting, impertinent, and disgusticulous. It assumes not only that I am shovable but also that I can be shoved out of a place I have never been."

"Objection sustained." A corner of Wolfe's mouth was up a little. "You will rephrase the question, Mr. Cramer."

"The hell I will." Cramer's eyes kept at me. "You might as well open up, Goodwin. We have a signed statement from her. What passed between you and Faber when he was here a week ago today?"

"The corn. It passed from him to me."

"So you're a clown. I already know that. A real wit. What else?"

"Well, let's see." I screwed my lips, concentrating. "The bell rang and I went and opened the door and said, quote, 'Greetings. How's things on the farm?' As he handed me the carton he said, 'Lousy, thank you, hot as hell and I've got blisters.' As I took it I said, 'What's a few blisters if you're the backbone of the country?' He said, 'Go soak your head,' and went, and I shut the door and took the carton to the kitchen."

"That's it?"

"That's it."

"Okay." He got up. "You don't wear a hat. You can have one minute to get a toothbrush."

"Now listen." I turned a palm up. "I can throw sliders in a pinch, and do, but this is no pinch. It's close to bedtime. If I don't check with something in Sue McLeod's statement, of course you want to work on me before I can get in touch with her, so go ahead, here I am."

"The minute's up. Come on."

I stayed put. "No. I now have a right to be sore, so I am. You'll have to make it good."

"You think I won't?" At least I had him glaring. "You're under arrest as a material witness. Move!"

I took my time getting up. "You have no warrant, but I don't want to be fussy." I turned to Wolfe. "If you want me around tomorrow, you might give Parker a ring."

"I shall." He swiveled. "Mr. Cramer. Knowing your considerable talents as I do, I am sometimes dumfounded by your fatuity. You were so bent on baiting Mr. Goodwin that you completely ignored the point I was at pains to make." He pointed at the piles on his desk. "Who picked that corn? Pfui!"

"That's *your* point, " Cramer rasped. "Mine is who killed Kenneth Faber. Move, Goodwin."

At twenty minutes past eleven Wednesday morning, standing at the curb on Leonard Street with Nathaniel Parker, I said, "Of course in a way it's a compliment. Last time the bail was a measly five hundred. Now twenty grand. That's progress."

Parker nodded. "That's one way of looking at it. He argued for fifty thousand, but I got it down to twenty. You know what that means. They actually—here's one."

A taxi headed in to us and stopped. When we were in and I had told the driver Eighth Avenue and Thirty-fifth Street, and we were rolling, Parker resumed, leaning to me and keeping his voice down. The legal mind. Hackies are even better listeners than they are talkers, and that one could be a spy sicked on us by the District Attorney.

"They actually," Parker said, "think you may have killed that man. This is serious, Archie. I told the judge that bail in the amount that was asked would be justified only if they had enough evidence to charge you with murder, and he agreed. As your counsel, I must advise you to be prepared for such a charge at any moment. I didn't like Mandel's attitude. By the way, Wolfe told me to send my bill to you, not him. He said this is your affair and he isn't concerned. I'll make it moderate."

I thanked him. I already knew that Assistant District Attorney Mandel, and maybe Cramer too, regarded me as a real candidate for the big one. Cramer had taken me to his place, Homicide South, and after spending half an hour on me had turned me over to Lieutenant Rowcliff and gone home. Rowcliff had stood me for nearly an hour—I had him stuttering in fourteen minutes, not a record—and had then sent me under convoy to the D.A.'s office, where Mandel had taken me on, obviously expecting to make a night of it.

Which he did, with the help of a pair of dicks from the D.A.'s Homicide Bureau. He had of course been phoned by both Cramer and Rowcliff, and it was evident from the start that he didn't merely think I was holding out on details that might be useful, to prevent either bother for myself or trouble for someone else; he had me tagged as a real prospect. Naturally I wanted to know why, so I played along. I hadn't with Cramer because he had got me sore in front of Wolfe, and I hadn't with Rowcliff because playing along is impossible with a double-breasted baboon, but with Mandel I could.

Of course he was asking the questions, him and the dicks, but the trick is to answer them in such a way that the next question, or maybe one later on, tells you something you want to know, or at least gives you a hint. That takes practise, but I had had plenty, and it makes it simpler when one guy pecks away at you for an hour or so and then backs off, and another guy starts in and goes all over it again.

For instance, the scene of the crime—the alley and receiving platform at the rear of Rusterman's. Since Wolfe was the trustee, there was nothing about that restaurant I wasn't familiar with. From the side street it was only about fifteen yards along the narrow alley to the platform, and the alley ended a few feet farther on at the wall of another building.

A car or small truck entering to deliver something had to back out. Knowing, as I had, that Kenneth Faber would come with the corn sometime after five o'clock, I could have walked in and hid under the platform behind a concrete post with the weapon in my hand, and when Faber drove in, got out, and came around to open the tailgate he would never know what hit him.

If I could have done that, who couldn't? I would have had to know one other thing, that I couldn't be seen from the windows of the restaurant kitchen because the glass had been painted on the inside so boys and girls couldn't climb onto the platform to watch Leo boning a duck or Felix stirring goose blood into a Sauce Rouennaise.

In helping them get it on the record that I knew all that, I learned only that they had found no one who had seen the murderer in the alley or entering or leaving it, that Faber had probably been dead five to ten minutes when someone came from the kitchen to the platform and found the body, and that the weapon was a piece of two-inch galvanized iron pipe sixteen and five-eighths inches long, threaded male at one end and female at the other, old and battered. Easy to hide under a coat. Where it came from might be discovered by one man in ten hours, or by a thousand men in ten years.

Getting those details was nothing, since they would be in the morning papers, but regarding their slant on me I got some hints that the papers wouldn't have. Hints were the best I could get, no facts to check, so I'll just report how it looked when Parker came to spring me in the morning.

They hadn't let me see Sue's statement, but there must have been something in it, or something she had said, or something someone else, maybe Carl Heydt or Peter Jay or Max Maslow, had said, either to her or to the cops. Or possibly something Duncan McLeod, Sue's father, had said. That didn't seem likely, but I included him because I saw him.

When Parker and I entered the anteroom on our way out he was there on a chair in the row against the wall, dressed for town, with a necktie, his square deep-tanned face shiny with sweat. I crossed over and told him good morning, and he said it wasn't, it was a bad morning, a day lost and no one to leave to see to things. It was noplace for a talk, with people there on the chairs, but I might at least have asked him who had picked the corn if someone hadn't come to take him inside.

So when I climbed out of the taxi at the corner and thanked Parker for the lift and told him I'd call him if and when, and walked the block and a half on Thirty-fifth Street to the old brownstone, I was worse off than when I had left, since I hadn't learned anything really useful, and no matter how Parker defined "moderate," the cost of a twenty-grand bond is not peanuts. I couldn't expect to pass the buck to Wolfe, since he had never seen either Kenneth Faber or Sue McLeod, and as I mounted the seven steps to the stoop and put my key in the lock I decided not to try to.

The key wasn't enough. The door opened two inches and stopped. The chain bolt was on. I pushed the button, and Fritz came and slipped the bolt; and his face told me something was stirring before he spoke. If you're not onto the faces you see most of, how can you expect to tell anything from strange ones?

As I crossed the sill I said, "Good morning. What's up?"

He turned from closing the door and stared. "But Archie. You look terrible."

"I feel worse. Now what?"

"A woman to see you. Miss Susan McLeod. She used to bring—"

"Yeah. Where is she?"

"In the office."

"Where is he?"

"In the kitchen."

"Has he talked with her?"

"No."

"How long has she been here?"

"Half an hour."

"Excuse my manners. I've had a night."

I headed for the end of the hall, the swinging door to the kitchen, pushed it open, and entered. Wolfe was at the center table with a glass of beer in his hand. He grunted. "So. Have you slept?"

"No."

"Have you eaten?"

I got a glass from the cupboard, went to the refrigerator and got milk, filled the glass, and took a sip. "If you could see the bacon and eggs they had brought in for me and I paid two bucks for, let alone taste it, you'd never be the same. You'd be so afraid you might be hauled in as a material witness you'd lose your nerve. They think maybe I killed Faber. For your information, I didn't."

I sipped the milk. "This will hold me till lunch. I understand I have a caller. As you told Parker, this is my affair and you are not concerned. May I take her to the front room? I'm not intimate enough with her to take her up to my room."

"Confound it," he growled. "How much of what you told Mr. Cramer was flummery?"

"None. All straight. But he's on me and so is the D.A. and I've got to find out why." I sipped milk.

He was eying me. "You will see Miss McLeod in the office."

"The front room will do. It may be an hour. Two hours."

"You may need the telephone. The office."

If I had been myself I would have given that offer a little attention, but I was somewhat pooped. So I went, taking my half a glass of milk. The door to the office was closed and, entering, I closed it again.

She wasn't in the red-leather chair. Since she was there for me, not for Wolfe, Fritz had moved up one of the yellow chairs for her, but hearing the door open and seeing me she had sprung up, and by the time I had shut the door and turned she was to me, gripping my arms, her head tilted back to get my eyes.

If it hadn't been for the milk I would have used my arms for one of their basic functions, since that's a sensible way to start a good frank talk with a girl. That being impractical, I tilted my head forward and kissed her. Not just a peck. She not only took it, she helped, and her grip on my arms tightened, and I had to keep the glass plumb by feel since I couldn't see it. It wouldn't have been polite for me to quit, so I left it to her.

She let go, backed up a step, and said, "You haven't shaved."

I crossed to my desk, sipped milk, put the glass down, and said,

"I spent the night at the District Attorney's office, and I'm tired, dirty, and sour. I could shower and shave and change in half an hour."

"You're all right." She plumped onto the chair. "Look at me."

"I am looking at you." I sat. "You'd do fine for a before-and-after vitamin ad. The before. Did you get to bed?"

"I guess so, I don't know." Her mouth opened to pull air in. Not a yawn, just helping her nose. "It couldn't have been a jail because the windows didn't have bars. They kept me until after midnight asking questions, and one of them took me home. Oh, yes, I went to bed, but I didn't sleep, but I must have, because I woke up. Archie, I don't know what you're going to do to me."

"Neither do I." I drank milk, emptying the glass. "Why, have you done something to me?"

"I didn't mean to."

"Of course not."

"It came out. You remember you explained it for me one night."

I nodded. "I said you have a bypass in your wiring. With ordinary people like me, when words start on their way out they have to go through a checking station for an okay, except when we're too mad or scared or something. You may have a perfectly good checking station, but for some reason, maybe a loose connection, it often gets bypassed."

She was frowning. "But the trouble is, if I haven't got a checking station I'm just plain dumb. If I do have one, it certainly got bypassed when the words came out about my going to meet you there yesterday."

"Meet me where?"

"On Forty-eighth Street. There at the entrance to the alley where I used to turn to deliver the corn to Rusterman's. I said I was to meet you there at five o'clock and we were going to wait there until Ken came because we wanted to have a talk with him. But I was late, I didn't get there until a quarter past five, and you weren't there, so I left."

I kept my shirt on. "You said that to whom?"

"To several people. I said it to a man who came to the apartment, and in that building he took me to downtown I said it to another man, and then to two more, and it was in a statement they had me sign."

"When did we make the date to meet there? Of course they asked that."

"They asked everything. I said I phoned you yesterday morning and we made it then."

"It's just possible that you *are* dumb. Didn't you realize they would come to me?"

"Why, of course. And you would deny it. But I thought they would think you just didn't want to be involved, and I said you weren't there, and you could probably prove you were somewhere else, so that wouldn't matter, and I had to give them some reason why I went there and then came away without even going in the restaurant to ask if Ken had been there."

She leaned forward. "Don't you see, Archie? I couldn't say I had gone there to see Ken, could I?"

"No. Okay, you're not dumb." I crossed my legs and leaned back. "You *had* gone there to see Ken?"

"Yes. There was something—about something."

"You got there at a quarter past five?"

"Yes."

"And came away without even going in the restaurant to ask if Ken had been there?"

"I didn't— Yes, I came away."

I shook my head. "Look, Sue. Maybe you didn't want to get me involved, but you have, and I want to know. If you went there to see Ken and got there at a quarter past five, you *did* see him. Didn't you?"

"I didn't see him alive." Her hands on her lap, very nice hands, were curled into fists. "I saw him dead. I went up the alley and he was there on the ground. I thought he was dead, but, if he wasn't, someone would soon come out and find him, and I was scared. I was scared because I had told him just two days ago that I would like to kill him. I didn't think it out, I didn't stop to think, I was just scared. I didn't realize until I was several blocks away how dumb *that* was."

"Why was it dumb?"

"Because Felix and the doorman had seen me. When I came I passed the front of the restaurant, and they were there on the sidewalk, and we spoke. So I couldn't say I hadn't been there and it was dumb to go away, but I was scared. When I got to the apartment I thought it over and decided what to say, about going there to meet you, and when a man came and started asking questions I told him about it before he asked." She opened a fist to gesture. "I did think about it, Archie. I did think it couldn't matter to you, not much."

That didn't gibe with the bypassing-the-checking-station theory, but there was no point in making an issue of it. "You thought wrong," I said, not complaining, just stating a fact. "Of course they asked you why we were going to meet there to have a talk with Ken, since he would be coming here. Why not here instead of there?"

"Because you didn't want to. You didn't want to talk with him here."

"I see. You really thought it over. Also they asked what we wanted to talk with him about. Had you thought about that?"

"Oh, I didn't have to. About what he had told you, that I thought I was pregnant and he was responsible."

That was a little too much. I goggled at her, and my eyes were in no shape for goggling. "He had told *me* that?" I demanded. "When?"

"You know when. Last week. Last Tuesday when he brought the corn. He told me about it Saturday—no, Sunday. At the farm."

I uncrossed my legs and straightened up. "I may have heard it wrong. I may be lower than I realized. Ken Faber told you on Sunday that he had told me on Tuesday that you thought you were pregnant and he was responsible? Was that it?"

"Yes. He told Carl too—you know, Carl Heydt. He didn't tell me he had told Carl, but Carl did. I think he told two other men too—Peter Jay and Max Maslow. I don't think you know them. That was when I told him I would like to kill him, when he told me he had told you."

"And that's what you told the cops we wanted to talk with him about?"

"Yes. I don't see why you say I thought wrong, thinking it wouldn't matter much to you, because you weren't there. Can't you prove you were somewhere else?"

I shut my eyes to look it over. The more I sorted it out, the messier it got. Mandel hadn't been fooling when he asked the judge to put a fifty-grand tag on me; the wonder was that he hadn't hit me with the big one.

I opened my itching eyes and had to blink to get her in focus. "For a frame," I said, "it's close to perfect, but I'm willing to doubt if you meant it. I doubt if you know the ropes well enough, and why pick on me? I am not a patsy. But whether you meant it or not, what are you here for? Why bother to come and tell me about it?"

"Because—I thought— don't you understand, Archie?"

"I understand plenty, but not why you're here."

"But don't you see, it's my word against yours. They told me last

night that you denied that we had arranged to meet there. I wanted
to ask you—I thought you might change that, you might tell them
that you denied it just because you didn't want to be involved, that
you had agreed to meet me there but you decided not to go, and
they'll have to believe you because of course you were somewhere
else. Then they won't have any reason not to believe me."

She put out a hand. "Archie—will you? Then it will be all right."

"Holy saints. You think so?"

"Of course it will. The way it is now they think either I'm lying
or you're lying, but if you tell them—"

"Shut up!"

She gawked at me; then all of a sudden she broke. Her head went
down and her hands up to cover her face. Her shoulders started to
tremble and then she was shaking all over. If she had sobbed or
groaned or something I would have merely waited it out, but there
was no sound effect at all, and that was dangerous. She might crack.

I went to Wolfe's desk and got the vase of orchids, *Dendrobium
nobile* that day, removed the flowers and put them on my desk pad,
went to her, got fingers under her chin, forced her head up, and
sloshed her good. The vase holds two quarts. Her hands came down
and I sloshed her again, and she squealed and grabbed for my arm.
I dodged, put the vase on my desk, went to the bathroom, which is
over in the corner, and came back with a towel. She was on her feet,
dabbing at her front.

"Here," I said, "use this."

She took it and wiped her face. "You didn't have to do that," she
said.

"The hell I didn't." I got another chair and put it at a dry spot,
went to my desk, and sat. "It might help if someone did it to me.
Now listen. Whether you meant it or not, I am out on an extremely
rickety limb. Ken did not tell me last Tuesday that you thought you
were pregnant and he was responsible, he told me nothing whatever,
but whether he lied to you or you're lying to the cops and me, they
think he did.

"They also think or suspect that you and I have been what they
call intimate. They also expect you to say under oath that I agreed
to meet you at the entrance of that alley yesterday at five o'clock,
and I can't prove I wasn't there. There's a man who will say he was
with me somewhere else, but he's a friend of mine and he often
works with me when Mr. Wolfe needs more help, and the cops don't

have to believe him and neither would a jury. I don't know what else the cops have or haven't got, but any time now—"

"I didn't lie to you, Archie." She was on the dry chair, gripping the towel. A strand of wet hair dropped over her eye and she pushed it back. "Everything I told—"

"Skip it. Any time now, any minute, I may be hauled in on a charge of murder, and then where am I? Or suppose I somehow made it stick that I did not agree to meet you there, that you're lying to them, and I wasn't there. Then where will *you* be? The way it stands, the way you've staged it, today or tomorrow either you or I will be in the jug with no out. So either I—"

"But Archie, you—"

"Don't interrupt. Either I wriggle off by selling them on you—and by the way, I haven't asked you." I got up and went to her. "Stand up. Look at me." I extended my hands at waist level, open, palms up. "Put your hands on mine, palms down. No, don't press, relax, just let them rest there. Damn it, relax! Right. Look at me. Did you kill Ken?"

"No."

"Again. Did you kill him?"

"No, Archie!"

I turned and went back to my chair. She came a step forward, backed up, and sat. "That's my private lie detector," I told her. "Not patented. Either I wriggle off by selling them on you, and it would take some wriggling, which is not my style, or I do a job that *is* my style—I hope.

"As you know, I work for Nero Wolfe. First I see him and tell him I'm taking a leave of absence—I hope a short one. Then you and I go someplace where we're sure we won't be interrupted, and you tell me things, a lot of things, and no fudging. Where I go from there depends on what you tell me. I'll tell *you* one thing now, if you—"

The door opened and Wolfe was there. He crossed to the corner of his desk, faced her, and spoke. "I'm Nero Wolfe. Will you please move to this chair?" He indicated the red-leather chair by a nod, circled around his desk, and sat. He looked at me. "A job that is your style?"

Well. As I remarked when he insisted that I see her in the office, if I hadn't been pooped I would have given that offer a little attention. If I had been myself I would have known, or at least suspected, what he intended. I suppose he and I came as close to trusting each other as any two men can, on matters of joint concern, but as he had told

Parker, this was my affair, and I was discussing it with someone in his office, keeping him away from his favorite chair, and I had just told him that nothing of what I had told Cramer was flummery. So he had gone to the hole in the alcove.

I looked back at him. "I said I hope. What if I heard the panel open and steered clear?"

"Pfui. Clear of what?"

"Okay. Your trick. But I think she has a right to know."

"I agree." Sue had moved to the red-leather chair, and he swiveled. "Miss McLeod. I eavesdropped, without Mr. Goodwin's knowledge. I heard all that was said, and I saw. Do you wish to complain?"

She had fingered her hair back, but it was still a sight. "Why?" she asked.

"Why did I listen? To learn how much of a pickle Mr. Goodwin was in. And I learned. I have intruded because the situation is intolerable. You are either a cockatrice or a witling. Whether by design or stupidity, you have brought Mr. Goodwin to a desperate pass. That is—"

I broke in. "It's my affair. You said so."

He stayed at her. "That is his affair, but now it threatens me. I depend on him. I can't function properly, let alone comfortably, without him. He just told you he would take a leave of absence. That would be inconvenient for me but bearable, even if it were rather prolonged, but it's quite possible that I would lose him for good, and that would be a calamity. I won't have it. Thanks to you, he is in grave jeopardy." He turned. "Archie. This is now our joint affair. By your leave."

I raised both eyebrows. "Retroactive? Parker and my bail?"

He made a face. "Very well. Intimate or not, you have known Miss McLeod three years. Did she kill that man?"

"No and yes."

"That doesn't help."

"I know it doesn't. The 'no' because of a lot of assorted items, including the lie-detector test I just gave her, which of course you would hoot at if you hooted. The 'yes,' chiefly because she's here. Why did she come? She says to ask me to change my story and back hers up, that we had a date to meet there. That's a good deal to expect, and I wonder.

"If she killed him, of course she's scared stiff and she might ask anybody anything, but if she didn't, why come and tell me she went in the alley and saw him dead and scooted? I wonder. On balance, one will get you two that she didn't. One item for 'no,' when a man gets a girl pregnant her normal procedure is to make him marry her, and quick. What she wants most and has got to have is a father for the baby, and not a dead father. She certainly isn't going to kill him unless—"

"That's silly," Sue blurted, "I'm not pregnant."

I stared. "You said Ken told you he told me."

She nodded. "Ken would tell anybody anything."

"But you thought you were?"

"Of course not. How could I? There's only one way a girl can get pregnant, and it couldn't have been that with me because it's never happened."

Like everybody else, I like to kid myself that I know why I think this or do that, but sometimes it just won't work, and that was once. I don't mean why I believed her about not being pregnant and how she knew she couldn't be; I do know that; it was the way she said it and the way she looked. I *had* known her three years. But since, if I believed her on that, I had to scrap the item I had just given Wolfe for "no" on her killing Faber, why didn't I change the odds to even money?

I pass. I could cook up a case—for instance if she was straight on one thing, about not being pregnant and why not, she was probably straight on other things too—but who would buy it? It's even possible that every man alive, of whom I am one, has a feeling down below that an unmarried girl who knows she *can't* be pregnant is less apt to commit murder than one who can't be sure. I admit that a good private detective shouldn't have feelings down below, but have you any suggestions?

Since Wolfe pretends to think I could qualify on the witness stand as an expert on attractive young women, of course he turned to me and said, "Archie?" and I nodded yes. An expert shouldn't back and fill, and as I just said, I believed her on the pregnancy issue. Wolfe grunted, told me to take my notebook, gave her a hard eye for five seconds, and started in.

An hour and ten minutes later, when Fritz came to announce lunch, I had filled most of a new notebook and Wolfe was leaning back with his eyes shut and his lips tight. It was evident that he was going to have to work. She had answered all his questions with no apparent fumbling, and it still looked very much as if either I was going to ride the bumps or she was. Or possibly both.

As she told it, she had met Ken Faber eight months ago at a party at the apartment of Peter Jay. Ken had been fast on the follow-up, and four months later, in May, she had told him she would marry him someday—say in two or three years, when she was ready to give up modeling—if he had shown that he could support a family.

From the notebook: "I was making over eight hundred dollars a week, ten times as much as he was, and of course if I got married I couldn't expect to keep that up. I don't think a married woman should model anyway because if you're married you ought to have babies, and there's no telling what that will do to you, and who looks after the babies?"

In June, at his request, she had got her father to give him a job on the farm, but she had soon regretted it. From the notebook: "Of course he knew I went to the farm weekends in the summer, and the very first weekend it was easy to see what his idea was. He thought it would be different on the farm than in town, it would be easy to get me to do what he wanted, as easy as falling off a log.

"The second week it was worse, and the third week it was still worse, and I was seeing what he was really like and I wished I hadn't said I would marry him. He accused me of letting other men do what I wouldn't let him do, and he tried to make me promise I wouldn't date any other man, even for dinner or a show.

"Then the last week in July he seemed to get some sense and I thought maybe he had just gone through some kind of phase or something, but last week, Friday evening, he was worse than ever all of a sudden, and Sunday he told me he had told Archie Goodwin that I thought I was pregnant and he was responsible, and of course Archie would pass it on, and if I denied it no one would believe me, and the only thing to do was to get married right away.

"That was when I told him I'd kill him. Then the next day, Monday, Carl—Carl Heydt—told me that Ken had told him the same thing, and I suspected he had told two other men, on account of things they had said, and I decided to go there Tuesday and see him. I was going to tell him he had to tell Archie and Carl it was a lie, and anybody else he had told, and if I had to I'd get a lawyer."

If that was straight, and the part about Carl Heydt and Peter Jay and Max Maslow could be checked, that made it more like ten to one that she hadn't killed him. She couldn't have ad-libbed it; she would have had to go there intending to kill him, or at least bruise him, since she couldn't have just happened to have with her a piece of two-inch pipe sixteen inches long. Say twenty to one.

But if she hadn't who had? Better than twenty to one, not some thug. There had been eighty bucks in Ken's pockets, and why would a thug go up that alley with the piece of pipe, much less hide under the platform with it? No. It had to be someone out for Ken specifically who knew that spot, or at least knew about it, and knew he would come there, and when.

Of course it was possible the murderer was someone Sue had never heard of and the motive had no connection with her, but that would make it really tough, and there she was, and Wolfe got all she had—or at least everything she would turn loose of. She didn't know how many different men she had had dates with in the twenty months she had been modeling—maybe thirty. More in the first year than recently; she had thought it would help to get jobs if she knew a lot of men, and it had, but now she turned down as many jobs as she accepted.

When she said she didn't know why so many men wanted to date her Wolfe made a face, but I knew she really meant it. It was hard to believe that a girl with so much born come-on actually wasn't aware of it, but I knew her, and so did my friend Lily Rowan, who *is* an expert on women.

She didn't know how many of them had asked her to marry them; maybe ten; she hadn't kept count. Of course you don't like her; to like a girl who says things like that, you'd have to see her and hear her, and if you're a man you wouldn't stop to ask whether you liked her or not. I frankly admit that the fact that she couldn't dance had saved me a lot of wear and tear.

From the time she had met Ken Faber she had let up on dates, and in recent months she had let only three other men take her places. Those three had all asked her to marry them, and they had stuck to it in spite of Ken Faber. Carl Heydt, who had given her her first modeling job, was nearly twice her age, but that wouldn't matter if she wanted to marry him when the time came. Peter Jay, who was something important in a big advertising agency, was younger, and Max Maslow, who was a fashion photographer, was still younger.

She had told Carl Heydt that what Ken had told him wasn't true, but she wasn't sure that he had believed her. She couldn't remember exactly what Peter Jay and Max Maslow had said that made her think that Ken had told them too; she hadn't had the suspicion until Monday, when Carl had told her what Ken had told him. She had told no one that she was going to Rusterman's Tuesday to see Ken.

All three of them knew about the corn delivery to Rusterman's and Nero Wolfe; they knew she had made the deliveries for two summers and had kidded her about it; Peter Jay had tried to get her to pose in a cornfield, in an evening gown, for a client of his. They knew Ken was working at the farm and was making the deliveries.

From the notebook, Wolfe speaking: "You know those men quite well. You know their temperaments and bents. If one of them, enraged beyond endurance by Mr. Faber's conduct, went there and killed him, which one? Remember it was not a sudden fit of passion, it was planned. From your knowledge of them, which one?"

She was staring. "They didn't."

"Not 'they.' One of them. Which?"

She shook her head. "None of them."

Wolfe wiggled a finger at her. "That's twaddle, Miss McLeod. You may be shocked at the notion that someone close to you is a murderer; anyone would be; but you may not reject it as inconceivable. By your foolish subterfuge you have made it impossible to satisfy the police that neither you nor Mr. Goodwin killed that man except by one procedure: demonstrate that someone else killed him, and identify him. I must see those three men, and, since I never leave my house on business, they must come to me. Will you get them here? At nine o'clock this evening?"

"No," she said. "I won't."

He glared at her. If she had been merely a client, with nothing but a fee at stake, he would have told her to either do as she was told or clear out; but the stake was an errand boy it would be a calamity to lose—me—as he had admitted in my hearing. So he turned the glare off and turned a palm up.

"Miss McLeod. I concede that your refusal to think ill of a friend is commendable. I concede that Mr. Faber may have been killed by someone you have never heard of with a motive you can't even conjecture—and by the way, I haven't asked you: do you know of anyone who might have had a ponderable reason for killing him?"

"No."

"But it's possible that Mr. Heydt does, or Mr. Jay or Mr. Maslow. Even accepting your conclusion that none of them killed him, I must see them. I must also see your father, but separately—I'll attend to that. My only possible path to the murderer is the motive, and one or more of those four men, who knew Mr. Faber, may start me on it. I ask you to have those three here this evening. Not you with them."

She was frowning. "But you can't—you said identify him. How can you?"

"I don't know. Perhaps I can't, but I must try. Nine o'clock?"

She didn't want to, even after the concessions he had made, but she had to admit that we had to get some kind of information from somebody, and who else was there to start with? So she finally agreed, definitely, and Wolfe leaned back with his eyes shut and his lips tight, and Fritz came to announce lunch.

Sue got up to go, and when I returned after seeing her to the door and out, Wolfe had crossed to the dining room and was at the table. Instead of joining him, I stood and said, "Ordinarily I would think I was well worth it, but right now I'm no bargain at any price. Have we a program for the afternoon?"

"No. Except to telephone Mr. McLeod."

"I saw him at the D.A.'s office. Then I'm going up and rinse off. I think I smell. Tell Fritz to save me a bite in the kitchen."

I went to the hall and mounted the two flights to my room. During the forty minutes it took to do the job I kept telling my brain to lay off until it caught up, but it wouldn't. It insisted on trying to analyze the situation, with the emphasis on Sue McLeod. If I had her figured wrong, if she was it, it would almost certainly be a waste of time to try to get anything from three guys who were absolutely hooked, and if there was no program for the afternoon I had damn well better think one up. If it would be a calamity for Wolfe to lose me for good, what would it be for me?

By the time I stepped into the shower the brain had it doped that the main point was the piece of pipe. She had not gone into that alley toting that pipe; that was out. But I hadn't got that point settled conclusively by Cramer or Mandel, and I hadn't seen a morning paper. I would consult *The Times* when I went downstairs. But the brain wanted to know now, and when I left the shower I dried in a hurry, went to the phone on the bedtable, dialed the *Gazette,* got Lon Cohen, and asked him.

Of course he knew I had spent the night downtown and he wanted a page or two of facts, but I told him I was naked and would catch cold, and how final was it that whoever had conked Faber had brought the pipe with him? Sewed up, Lon said. Positively. The pipe was at the laboratory, revealing—maybe—its past to the scientists, and three or four dicks with color photos of it were trying to pick up its trail. I thanked him and promised him something for a headline if and when. So that was settled.

As I went to a drawer for clean shorts the brain started in on Carl Heydt, but it was darned little to work on, and by the time I tied my tie it was buzzing around trying to find . place to land.

Downstairs Wolfe was still in the dining room, but I went on by to the kitchen, got at my breakfast table with *The Times,* and was served by Fritz with what do you think? Corn fritters. There had been eight perfectly good ears, and Fritz hates to throw good food away. With bacon and homemade blackberry jam they were ambrosia, and in *The Times* report on the Faber murder Wolfe's name was mentioned twice and mine four times, so it was a fine meal.

I had finished the eighth fritter and was deciding whether to take on another one and a third cup of coffee when the doorbell rang, and I got up and went to the hall for a look. Wolfe was back in the office, and I stuck my head in and said, "McLeod."

He let out a growl. True, he had told Sue he must see her father and was even going to phone to ask him to come in from the country, but he always resents an unexpected visitor, no matter who. Ignoring the growl, I went to the front and opened the door, and when McLeod said he wanted to see Mr. Wolfe, with his burr on the *r,* I invited him in, took his Sunday hat, a dark-gray antique fedora in good condition, put it on the shelf, and took him to the office. Wolfe, who is no hand-shaker, told him good afternoon and motioned to the red-leather chair.

McLeod stood. "No need to sit," he said. "I've been told about the corn and I came to apologize. I'm to blame, and I'd like to explain how it happened. I didn't pick it; that young man did. Kenneth Faber."

Wolfe grunted. "Wasn't that heedless? I telephoned the restaurant this morning and was told that theirs was as bad as mine. You know what we require."

He nodded. "I ought to by now. You pay a good price, and I want to say it'll never happen again. I'd like to explain it. A man was coming Thursday with a bulldozer to work on a lot I'm clearing, but Monday night he told me he'd have to come Wednesday instead, and I had to dynamite a lot of stumps and rock before he came.

"I got at it by daylight yesterday and I thought I could finish in time to pick the corn, but I had some trouble and I had to leave the corn to that young man. I had showed him and I thought he knew.

So I've got to apologize and I'll see it don't happen again. Of course I'm not expecting you to pay for it."

Wolfe grunted. "I'll pay for the eight ears we used. It was vexatious, Mr. McLeod."

"I know it was." He turned and aimed his gray-blue eyes, with their farmer's squint, at me. "Since I'm here I'm going to ask you. What did that young man tell you about my daughter?"

I met his eyes. It was a matter not only of murder, but also of my personal jam that might land me in the jug any minute, and all I really knew of him was that he was Sue's father and he knew how to pick corn.

"Not a lot," I said. "Where did you get the idea he told me anything about her?"

"From her. This morning. What he told her he told you. So I'm asking you, to get it straight."

"Mr. McLeod," Wolfe cut in. He nodded at the red-leather chair. "Please sit down."

"No need to sit. I just want to know what that young man said about my daughter."

"She has told you what he said he said. She has also told Mr. Goodwin and me. We have spoken with her at length. She came shortly after eleven o'clock this morning to see Mr. Goodwin and stayed two hours."

"My daughter Susan? Came here?"

"Yes."

McLeod moved. In no hurry he went to the red-leather chair, sat, focused on Wolfe, and demanded, "What did she come for?"

Wolfe shook his head. "You have it wrong side up. That tone is for us, not you. We may or may not oblige you later; that will depend. The young man you permitted to pick my corn has been murdered, and because of false statements made by your daughter to the police, Mr. Goodwin may be charged with murder. The danger is great and imminent. You say you spent yesterday dynamiting stumps and rocks. Until what hour?"

McLeod's set jaw made his deep-tanned seamed face even squarer.

"My daughter doesn't make false statements," he said. "What were they?"

"They were about Mr. Goodwin. Anyone will lie when the alternative is intolerable. She may have been impelled by a desperate need to save herself, but Mr. Goodwin and I do not believe she killed that man. Archie?"

I nodded. "Right. Any odds you want to name."

"And we're going to learn who did kill him. Did you?"

"No. But I would have, if—" He let it hang.

"If what?"

"If I had known what he was saying about my daughter. I told them that, the police. I heard about it from them, and from my daughter, last night and this morning. He was a bad man, an evil man. You say you're going to learn who killed him, but I hope you don't. I told them that too. They asked me what you did, about yesterday, and I told them I was there in the lot working with the stumps until nearly dark and it made me late with the milking. I can tell you this, I don't resent you thinking I might have killed him, because I might."

"Who was helping you with the stumps?"

"Nobody, not in the afternoon. He was with me all morning after he did the chores, but then he had to pick the corn and then he had to go with it."

"You have no other help?"

"No."

"Other children? A wife?"

"My wife died ten years ago. We only had Susan. I told you, I don't resent this, not a bit. I said I would have killed him if I'd known. I didn't want her to come to New York, I knew something like this might happen—the kind of people she got to know and all the pictures of her. I'm an old-fashioned man and I'm a righteous man, only that word righteous may not mean for you what it means for me. You said you might oblige me later. What did my daughter come here for?"

"I don't know." Wolfe's eyes were narrowed at him. "Ask her. Her avowed purpose is open to question. This is futile, Mr. McLeod, since you think a righteous man may wink at murder. I wanted—"

"I didn't say that. I don't wink at murder. But I don't have to want whoever killed Kenneth Faber to get caught and suffer for it. Do I?"

"No. I wanted to see you. I wanted to ask you, for instance, if you know a man named Carl Heydt, but since—"

"I don't know him. I've never seen him. I've heard his name from my daughter; he was the first one she worked for. What about him?"

"Nothing, since you don't know him. Do you know Max Maslow?"

"No."

"Peter Jay?"

"No. I've heard their names from my daughter. She tells me about people; she tries to tell me they're not as bad as I think they are, only their ideas are different from mine. Now this has happened, and I knew it would, something like this. I don't wink at murder and I don't wink at anything sinful."

"But if you knew who killed that man or had reason to suspect anyone, you wouldn't tell me—or the police."

"I would not."

"Then I won't keep you. Good afternoon, sir."

McLeod stayed put. "If you won't tell me what my daughter came here for I can't make you. But you can't tell me she made false statements and not say what they were."

Wolfe grunted. "I can and do. I will tell you nothing." He slapped the desk. "Confound it, after sending me inedible corn you presume to come and make demands on me? Go!"

McLeod's mouth opened and closed again. In no hurry he got up. "I don't think it's fair," he said. "I don't think it's right." He turned to go and turned back. "Of course you won't be wanting any more corn."

Wolfe was scowling at him. "Why not? It's only the middle of September."

"I mean not from me."

"Then from whom? Mr. Goodwin can't go scouring the countryside with this imbroglio on our hands. I want corn this week. Tomorrow?"

"I don't see— There's nobody to bring it."

"Friday, then?"

"I might. I've got a neighbor— Yes, I guess so. The restaurant too?"

Wolfe said yes, he would tell them to expect it, and McLeod turned and went. I stepped to the hall, got to the front ahead of him to hand him his hat, and saw him out. When I returned to the office Wolfe was leaning back, frowning at the ceiling. As I crossed to my desk and sat I felt a yawn coming, and I stopped it.

A man expecting to be tagged for murder is in no position to yawn, even if he has had no sleep for thirty hours. I had my nose fill the order for more oxygen, swiveled, and said brightly, "That was a big help. Now we know about the corn."

Wolfe straightened up. "Pfui. Call Felix and tell him to expect a delivery on Friday."

"Yes, sir. Good. Then everything's jake."

"That's bad slang. There is good slang and bad slang. How long will it take you to type a full report of our conversation with Miss McLeod, yours and mine, from the beginning?"

"Verbatim?"

"Yes."

"The last half, more than half, is in the notebook. For the first part I'll have to dig, and though my memory is as good as you think it is, that will be a little slower. Altogether, say four hours. But what's the idea? Do you want it to remember me by?"

"No. Two carbons."

I cocked my head. "Your memory is as good as mine—nearly. Are you actually telling me to type all that stuff just to keep me off your neck until nine o'clock?"

"No. It may be useful."

"Useful how? As your employee I'm supposed to do what I'm told, and I often do, but this is different. This is our joint affair now—trying to save you from the calamity of losing me. Useful how?"

"I don't know!" he bellowed. "I say it *may* be useful, if I decide to use it. Can you suggest something that may be more useful?"

"Offhand, no."

"Then *if* you type it, two carbons."

I got up and went to the kitchen for a glass of milk. I might or might not start on it before four o'clock, when he would go up to the plant rooms for his afternoon session with the orchids.

At five minutes past nine that evening the three men whose names had had checkmarks in front of them in Kenneth Faber's little notebook were in the office, waiting for Wolfe to show. They hadn't come together; Carl Heydt had arrived first, ten minutes early, then Peter Jay, on the dot at nine, and then Max Maslow. I had put Heydt in the red-leather chair, and Jay and Maslow on two of the yellow ones facing Wolfe's desk. Nearest me was Maslow.

I had seen Heydt before, of course, but you take a new look at a man when he becomes a homicide candidate. He looked the same as ever—medium height with a slight bulge in the middle, round face with a wide mouth, quick dark eyes that kept on the move.

Peter Jay, the something important in a big advertising agency, tall as me but not as broad, with more than his share of chin and thick dark mane that needed a comb, looked as if he had the regulation ulcer, but it could have been just the current difficulty.

Max Maslow, the fashion photographer, was a surprise. With the twisted smile he must have practised in front of a mirror, the trick haircut, the string tie dangling, and the jacket with four buttons buttoned, he was a screwball if I ever saw one, and I wouldn't have supposed that Sue McLeod would let such a specimen hang on. I admit it could have been just that his ideas were different from mine, but I like mine.

Wolfe came. When there is to be a gathering he stays in the kitchen until I buzz on the house phone, and then he doesn't enter, he makes an entrance. Nothing showy, but it's an entrance. A line from the door to the corner of his desk just misses the red-leather chair, so with Heydt in the chair he would have had to circle around his feet and also pass between Heydt and the other two; and he detoured to his right, between the chair and the wall, to his side of the desk, stood, and shot me a glance.

I pronounced their names, indicating who was which, and he gave them a nod, sat, moved his eyes from left to right and back again, and spoke.

"This can be fairly brief," he said, "or it can go on for hours. I think, gentlemen, you would prefer brevity, and so would I. I assume you have all been questioned by the police and by the District Attorney or one of his assistants?"

Heydt and Maslow nodded, and Jay said yes. Maslow had his twisted smile on.

"Then you're on record, but I'm not privy to that record. Since you came here to oblige Miss McLeod, you should know our position, Mr. Goodwin's and mine, regarding her. She is not our client; we are under no commitment to her; we are acting solely in our own interest. But as it now stands we are satisfied that she didn't kill Kenneth Faber."

"That's damn nice of you," Maslow said. "So am I."

"Your own interest?" Jay asked. "What's your interest?"

"We're reserving that. We don't know how candid Miss McLeod has been with you, any or all of you, or how devious. I will say only that, because of statements made to the police by Miss McLeod, Mr. Goodwin is under heavy suspicion, and that because she knew the suspicion was unfounded she agreed to ask you gentlemen to come to see me. To lift the suspicion from Mr. Goodwin we must find out where it belongs, and for that we need your help."

"My God," Heydt blurted, "*I* don't know where it belongs."

The other two looked at him, and he looked back. There had been a feel in the atmosphere, and the looks made it more than a feel.

Evidently each of them had ideas about the other two, but of course
it wasn't as simple as that if one of them had killed Faber, since he
would be faking it. Anyhow, they all had ideas and they were itching.
"Quite possibly," Wolfe conceded, "none of you knows. But it is
not mere conjecture that one of you has good reason to know. All of
you knew he would be there that day at that hour, and you could
have gone there at some previous time to reconnoiter. All of you had
an adequate motive—adequate, at least, for the one it moved: Mr.
Faber had either debased or grossly slandered the woman you
wanted to marry.

"All of you had some special significance in his private thoughts
or plans; your names were in his notebook, with checkmarks. You
are not targets chosen at random for want of better ones; you are
plainly marked by circumstances. Do you dispute that?"

Maslow said, "All right, that's our bad luck."

Heydt, biting his lip, said nothing.

Jay said, "It's no news that we're targets. Go on from there."

Wolfe nodded. "That's the rub. The police have questioned you,
but I doubt if they have been importunate; they have been set at
Mr. Goodwin by Miss McLeod. I don't know—"

"That's your interest," Jay said. "To get Goodwin from under."

"Certainly. I said so. I—"

"He has known Miss McLeod longer than we have," Maslow said.
"He's the hero type. He rescued her from the sticks and started her
on the path of glory. He's her hero. I asked her once why she didn't
marry him if he was such a prize, and she said he hadn't asked her,
Now you say she has set the police on him. Permit me to say I don't,
believe it. If they're on him they have a damn good reason. Also
permit me to say I hope he *does* get from under, but not by making
me the goat. I'm no hero."

Wolfe shook his head. "As I said, I'm reserving what Miss McLeod
has told the police. She may tell you if you ask her. As for you
gentlemen, I don't know how curious the police have been about you.
Have they tried seriously to find someone who saw one of you in
that neighborhood Tuesday afternoon?

"Of course they have asked you where you were that afternoon,
that's mere routine, but have they properly checked your accounts?
Are you under surveillance? I doubt it; and I haven't the resources
for those procedures. I invite you to eliminate yourselves from consideration if you can. The man who killed Kenneth Faber was in
that alley, concealed under that platform, shortly after five o'clock

yesterday afternoon. Mr. Heydt. Can you furnish incontestable evidence that you weren't there?"

Heydt cleared his throat. "If I could, I don't have to furnish it to you. It seems to me—oh, what the hell. No, I can't."

"Mr. Jay?"

"Incontestable, no." Jay leaned forward, his chin out. "I came here because Miss McLeod asked me to, but if I understand what you're after I might as well go. You intend to find out who killed Faber and pin it on him. To prove it wasn't Archie Goodwin. Is that it?"

"Yes."

"Then count me out. I don't want Goodwin to get it, but neither do I want anyone else to. Not even Max Maslow."

"That's damn nice of you, Pete," Maslow said. "A real pal."

Wolfe turned to him. "You, sir. Can you eliminate yourself?"

"Not by proving I wasn't there." Maslow flipped a hand. "I must say, Wolfe, I'm surprised at you. I thought you were very tough and cagey, but you've swallowed something. You said we all wanted to marry Miss McLeod. Who fed you that? I admit I do, and as far as I know Carl Heydt does, but not my pal Pete. He's the pay-as-you-go type. I wouldn't exactly call him a Casanova, because Casanova never tried to score by talking up marriage, and that's Pete's favorite gambit. I could name—"

"Stand up." It was his pal Pete, on his feet, with fists, glaring down at him.

Maslow tilted his head back. "I wouldn't, Pete. I was merely—"

"Stand up or I'll slap you out of the chair."

Of course I had plenty of time to get there and in between them, but I was curious. It was likely that Jay, not caring about his knuckles, would go for the jaw, and I wanted to see what effect it would have on the twisted smile.

My curiosity didn't get satisfied. As Maslow came up out of the chair he sidestepped, and Jay had to turn, hauling his right back. He started it for Maslow's jaw by the longest route, and Maslow ducked, came on in, and landed with his right at the very best spot for a bare fist. A beautiful kidney punch.

As Jay started to bend, Maslow delivered another one to the same spot, harder, and Jay went down. He didn't tumble, he just wilted. By then I was there. Maslow went to his chair, sat, breathed, and fingered his string tie. The smile was intact, maybe twisted a little more.

He spoke to Wolfe. "I hope you didn't misunderstand me. I wasn't suggesting that I think he killed Faber. Even if he did I wouldn't want him to get it. On that point we're pals. I was only saying I don't see how you got your reputation if you— You all right, Pete?"

I was helping Jay up. A kidney punch doesn't daze you, it just makes you sick. I asked him if he wanted a bathroom, and he shook his head, and I steered him to his chair. He turned his face to Maslow, muttered a couple of vulgar words, and belched.

Wolfe spoke. "Will you have brandy, Mr. Jay? Whiskey? Coffee?" Jay shook his head and belched again.

Wolfe turned. "Mr. Heydt. The others have made it clear that if they have information that would help to expose the murderer they won't divulge it. How about you?"

Heydt cleared his throat. "I'm glad I don't have to answer that," he said. "I don't have to answer it because I have no information that would help. I know Archie Goodwin and I might say we're friends. If he's really in a jam I would want to help if I could. You say Miss McLeod has said something to the police that set them on him, but you won't tell us what she said."

"Ask her. You can give me no information whatever?"

"No."

Wolfe's eyes moved right, to the other two, and back again. "I doubt if it's worth the trouble," he said. "Assuming that one of you killed that man, I doubt if I can get at him from the front; I must go around. But I may have given you a false impression, and if so I wish to correct it. I said that to lift the suspicion from Mr. Goodwin we must find out where it belongs, but that isn't vital, for we have an alternative.

"We can merely shift the suspicion to Miss McLeod. That will be simple, and it will relieve Mr. Goodwin of further annoyance. We'll discuss it after you leave, and decide. You gentlemen may view the matter differently when Miss McLeod is in custody, charged with murder, without bail, but that is your—"

"You're a damn liar." Peter Jay.

"Amazing." Max Maslow. "Where *did* you get your reputation? What do you expect us to do, kick and scream or go down on our knees?"

"Of course you don't mean it." Carl Heydt. "You said you're satisfied that she didn't kill him."

Wolfe nodded. "I doubt if she would be convicted. She might not even go to trial; the police are not blockheads. It will be an ordeal for her, but it will also be a lesson; her implication of Mr. Goodwin

may not have been willful, but it was inexcusable." His eyes went
to Maslow. "You have mentioned my reputation. I made it and I
don't risk it rashly. If tomorrow you learn that Miss McLeod has
been arrested and is inaccessible, you may—"

" 'If.' " That crooked smile.

"Yes. It is contingent not on our power but on our preference. I
am inviting you gentlemen to have a voice in our decision. You have
told me nothing whatever, and I do not believe that you have nothing
whatever to tell. Do you want to talk now, to me, or later, to the
police, when that woman is in a pickle?"

"You're bluffing," Maslow said. "I call." He got up and headed for
the hall. I got up and followed him out, got his hat from the shelf,
and opened the front door; and as I closed it behind him and started
back down the hall here came the other two. I opened the door again,
and Jay, who had no hat, went by and on out, but Heydt stood there.
I got his hat and he took it and put it on.

"Look, Archie," he said. "You've got to do something."

"Check," I said. "What, for instance?"

"I don't know. But about Sue—my God, he doesn't mean it, does
he?"

"It isn't just a question of what he means, it's also what I mean.
Damn it, I'm short on sleep, and I may soon be short on life, liberty,
and the pursuit of happiness. Get the news every hour on the hour.
Pleasant dreams."

"What did Sue tell the police about you?"

"No comment. My resistance is low and with the door open I might
catch cold. If you don't mind?"

He went. I shut the door, put the chain bolt on, returned to the
office, sat at my desk, and said, "So you thought it might be useful."

He grunted. "Have you finished it?"

"Yes. Twelve pages."

"May I see it?"

Not an order, a request. At least he was remembering that it was
now a joint affair. I opened a drawer, got the original, and took it
to him. He inspected the heading and the first page, flipped through
the sheets, took a look at the end, dropped it on his desk, and said,
"Your notebook, please." I sat and got my notebook and pen.

"There will be two," he said, "one for you and one for me. First
mine. Heading in caps, affidavit by Nero Wolfe. The usual State of
New York, County of New York. The text: I hereby depose that the
twelve foregoing typewritten pages attached hereto, comma, each

page initialed by me, comma, are a full and accurate record of a conversation that took place in my office on September thirteenth, nineteen sixty-one, by Susan McLeod, comma, Archie Goodwin, comma, and myself, semicolon; that nothing of consequence has been omitted or added in this typewritten record, semicolon; and that the conversation was wholly impromptu, comma, with no prior preparation or arrangement. A space for my signature, and, below, the conventional formula for notarizing. The one for you, on the same sheet if there is room, will be the same with the appropriate changes."

I looked up. "All right, it wasn't just to keep me off your neck. Okay on the power. But there's still the if on the preference. She didn't kill him. She came to me and opened the bag. I'm her hero. She as good as told Maslow that she'd marry me if I asked her. Maybe she could learn how to dance if she tried hard, though I admit that's doubtful. She makes a lot more than you pay me, and we could postpone the babies. You said you doubt if she would be convicted, but that's not good enough. Before I sign that affidavit I would need to know that you won't chuck the joint affair as soon as the heat is off of me."

"Rrrhhh," he said.

"I agree," I said, "it's a damn nuisance. It's entirely her fault, she dragged me in without even telling me, and if a girl pushes a man in a hole he has a right to wiggle out, but you must remember that I am now a hero. Heroes don't wiggle. Will you say that it will be our joint affair to make sure she doesn't go to trial?"

"I wouldn't say that I will make sure of anything whatever."

"Correction: that you will be concerned?"

He took air in, all the way, through his nose, and let it out through his mouth. "Very well. I'll be concerned." He glanced at the twelve pages on his desk. "Will you bring Miss Pinelli to my room at five minutes to nine in the morning?"

"No. She doesn't get to her office until nine-thirty."

"Then bring her to the plant rooms at nine-forty with the affidavit." He looked at the wall clock. "You can type it in the morning. You've had no sleep for forty hours. Go to bed."

That was quite a compliment, and I was appreciating it as I mounted the stairs to my room. Except for a real emergency he will permit no interruptions from nine to eleven in the morning, when he is in the plant rooms, but he wasn't going to wait until he came down to the office to get the affidavit notarized.

As I got into bed and turned the light off I was considering whether to ask for a raise now or wait till the end of the year, but before I made up my mind I didn't have a mind. It was gone.

I never did actually make up my mind about passing the buck to Sue. I was still on the fence after breakfast Thursday morning when I dialed the number of Lila Pinelli, who adds maybe two bucks a week to the take of her secretarial service in a building on Eighth Avenue by doubling as a notary public. Doing the affidavits didn't commit me to anything; the question was, what then?

So I asked her to come, and she came, and I took her up to the plant rooms. She was in a hurry to get back, but she had never seen the orchids, and no one alive could just breeze on by those benches, with everything from the neat little *Oncidiums* to the big show-offs like the *Laeliocattleyas*. So it was after ten o'clock when we came back down and I paid her and let her out, and I went to the office and put the document in the safe.

As I say, I never did actually make up my mind; it just happened. At ten minutes past eleven Wolfe, having come down at eleven as usual, was at his desk looking over the morning crop of mail, and I was at mine sorting the germination slips he had brought, when the doorbell rang. I stepped to the hall for a look, turned, and said, "Cramer. I'll go hide in the cellar."

"Confound it," he growled. "I wanted— Very well."

"There's no law about answering doorbells."

"No. We'll see."

I went to the front, opened up, said good morning, and gave him room. He crossed the sill, took a folded paper from a pocket, and handed it to me. I unfolded it, and a glance was enough, but I read it through. "At least my name's spelled right," I said. I extended my hands, the wrists together. "Okay, do it right."

"You'd clown in the chair," he said. "I want to see Wolfe."

He marched down the hall and into the office. Very careless. I could have scooted on out and away, and for half a second I considered it, but I wouldn't have been there to see the look on his face when he found I was gone. When I entered the office he was lowering his fanny onto the red-leather chair and putting his hat on the stand beside it. Also he was speaking.

"I have just handed Goodwin a warrant for his arrest," he was saying, "and this time he'll stay."

I stood. "It's an honor. Anyone can be banged by a bull or a dick. It takes me to be pinched by an Inspector twice in one week."

His eyes stayed at Wolfe. "I came myself," he said, "because I want to tell you how it stands. A police officer with a warrant to serve is not only allowed to use his discretion, he's supposed to. I know damn well what Goodwin will do—he'll clam up, and a crowbar wouldn't pry him open. Give me that warrant, Goodwin."

"It's mine. You've served it."

"I have not. I just showed it to you." He stretched an arm and took it. "When I was here Tuesday night," he told Wolfe, "you were dumfounded by my fatuity. So you said in your fancy way. All you cared about was who picked that corn. I came myself to see how you feel now. Goodwin will talk if you tell him to. Do you want me to wait in the front room while you discuss it? Not all day, say ten minutes. I'm giving you a—"

He stopped to glare. Wolfe had pushed his chair back and was rising, and of course Cramer thought he was walking out. It wouldn't have been the first time. But Wolfe headed for the safe, not the hall. As he turned the handle and pulled the door open, there I was. If he had told me to bring it instead of going for it himself, I could have stalled while I made up my mind, even with Cramer there; but as I have said twice before I never did actually make up my mind.

I merely went to my desk and sat. I owed Sue McLeod nothing. If either she or I was going to be cooped, there were two good reasons why it should be her: she had made the soup herself, and I wouldn't be much help in the joint affair if I was salted down. So I sat, and Wolfe got it from the safe, went and handed it to Cramer, and spoke. "I suggest that you look at the affidavits first. The last two sheets."

Over the years I have made a large assortment of cracks about Inspector Cramer, but I admit he has his points. Having inspected the affidavits, he went through the twelve pages fast, and then he went back and started over and took his time. Altogether, more than half an hour; and not once did he ask a question or even look up. And when he finished, even then no questions.

Lieutenant Rowcliff or Sergeant Purley Stebbins would have kept at us for an hour. Cramer merely gave each of us a five-second-straight hard look, folded the document, put it in his inside breast pocket, rose and came to my desk, picked up the phone, and dialed. In a moment he spoke.

"Donovan? Inspector Cramer. Give me Sergeant Stebbins." In another moment: "Purley? Get Susan McLeod. Don't call her, get her.

Go yourself. I'll be there in ten minutes and I want her there fast. Take a man along. If she balks, wrap her up and carry her." He cradled the phone, went and got his hat, and marched out.

Of all the thousand or more times I have felt like putting vinegar in Wolfe's beer, I believe the closest I ever came to doing it was that Thursday evening when the doorbell rang at a quarter past nine, and after a look at the front I told him that Carl Heydt, Max Maslow, and Peter Jay were on the stoop, and he said they were not to be admitted.

In the nine and a half hours that had passed since Cramer had used my phone to call Purley Stebbins I had let it lie. I couldn't expect Wolfe to start any fur flying until there was a reaction, or there wasn't, say by tomorrow noon, to what had happened to Sue. However, I had made a move on my own.

When Wolfe had left the office at four o'clock to go up to the plant rooms, I had told him I would be out on an errand for an hour or so, and I had taken a walk, to Rusterman's, thinking I might pick up some little hint.

I didn't. First I went out back for a look at the platform and the alley, which might seem screwy, since two days and nights had passed and the city scientists had combed it, but you never know. I once got an idea just running my eye around a hotel room where a woman had spent a night six months earlier. But I got nothing from the platform or alley except a scraped ear from squeezing under the platform and out again, and after talking with Felix and Joe and some of the kitchen staff I crossed it off.

No one had seen or heard anyone or anything until Zoltan had stepped out for a cigarette (no smoking is allowed in the kitchen) and had seen the station wagon and the body on the ground.

I would have let it ride that evening, no needling until tomorrow noon. When Lily Rowan phoned around seven o'clock and said Sue had phoned her from the D.A.'s office that she was under arrest and had to have a lawyer and would Lily send her one, and Lily wanted me to come and tell her what was what, I would have gone if I hadn't wanted to be on hand if there was a development. But when the development came Wolfe told me not to let it in.

I straight-eyed him. "You said you'd be concerned."

"I am concerned."

"Then here they are. You tossed her to the wolves to open them up, and here—"

"No. I did that to keep you out of jail. I am considering how to
deal with the problem, and until I decide there is no point in seeing
them. Tell them they'll hear from us."

The doorbell rang again. "Then I'll see them. In the front room."

"No. Not in my house." He went back to his book.

Either put vinegar in his beer or get the Marley .32 from my desk
drawer and shoot him dead, but that would have to wait; they were
on the stoop. I went and opened the door enough for me to slip
through, did so, bumping into Carl Heydt, and pulled the door shut.
"Good evening," I said. "Mr. Wolfe is busy on an important matter
and can't be disturbed. Do you want to disturb me instead?"

They all spoke at once. The general idea seemed to be that I would
open the door and they would handle the disturbing.

"You don't seem to realize," I told them, "that you're up against
a genius. So am I, only I'm used to it. You were damn fools to think
he was bluffing. You might have known he would do exactly what
he said."

"Then he did?" Peter Jay. "He did it?"

"We did. I share the glory. We did."

"Glory, hell." Max Maslow. "You know Sue didn't kill Ken Faber.
He said so."

"He said we were satisfied that she didn't. We still are. He also
said that we doubt if she'll be convicted. He also said that our interest
was to get me from under, and we had alternatives. We could either
find out who killed Faber, for which we needed your help; or, if you
refused to help, we could switch it to Sue.

"You refused, and we switched it, and I am in the clear, and here
you are. Why? Why should he waste time on you now? He is busy
on an important matter; he's reading a book entitled *My Life in
Court,* by Louis Nizer. Why should he put it down for you?"

"I can't believe it, Archie." Carl Heydt had hold of my arm. "I
can't believe you'd do a thing like this—to Sue—when you say she
didn't—"

"You never can tell, Carl. There was that woman who went to the
park every day to feed the pigeons, but she fed her husband arsenic.
I have a suggestion. This is Mr. Wolfe's house and he doesn't want
you in it, but if you guys have changed your minds, at least two of
you, about helping to find out who killed Faber, I'm a licensed detective too and I could spare a couple of hours. We can sit here on
the steps, or we can go somewhere—"

"And you can tell us," Maslow said, "what Sue told the cops that got them on you. I may believe that when I hear it."

"You won't hear it from me. That's not the idea. *You* tell *me* things. I ask questions and you answer them. If I don't ask them, who will? I doubt if the cops or the D.A. will; they've got too good a line on Sue. I'll tell you this much, they know she was there Tuesday at the right time, and they know that she lied to them about about what she was there for and what she saw. I can spare an hour or two."

They exchanged glances, and they were not the glances of buddies with a common interest. They also exchanged words and found they agreed on one point: if one of them took me up they all would. Peter Jay said we could go to his place and they agreed on that too, and we descended to the sidewalk and headed east. At Eighth Avenue we flagged a taxi with room for four. It was ten minutes to ten when it rolled to the curb at a marquee on Park Avenue in the Seventies.

Jay's apartment, on the fifteenth floor, was quite a perch for a bachelor. The living room was high, wide, and handsome, and it would have been an appropriate spot for our talk, since it was there that Sue McLeod and Ken Faber had first met; but Jay took us on through to a room, smaller but also handsome, with chairs and carpet of matching green, a desk, bookshelves, and a TV-player cabinet. He asked us what we would drink but got no orders, and we sat.

"All right, ask your questions," Maslow said. The twisted smile.

He was blocking my view of Heydt, and I shifted my chair. "I've changed my mind," I said. "I looked it over on the way, and I decided to take another tack. Sue told the police, and it was in her signed statement, that she and I had arranged to meet there at the alley at five o'clock, and she was late, she didn't get there until five-fifteen, and I wasn't there, so she left. She had to tell them she was there because she had been seen in front of the restaurant, just around the corner, by two of the staff who know her."

Their eyes were glued on me. "So you weren't there at five-fifteen," Jay said. "The body was found at five-fifteen. So you had been and gone?"

"No. Sue also told the police that Faber had told her on Sunday that he had told me on Tuesday that she was pregnant and he was responsible. He had told you that, all three of you. She said that was why she and I were going to meet there, to make Faber swallow his lies. So it's fair to say she set the cops on me, and it's no wonder they turned on the heat. The trouble—"

"Why not?" Maslow demanded. "Why isn't it still on?"

"Don't interrupt. The trouble was, she lied. Not about what Faber had told her on Sunday he had told me on Tuesday; that was probably *his* lie; he probably had told her that, but it wasn't true; he had told me nothing on Tuesday. That's why your names in his notebook had checkmarks but mine didn't; he was going to feed us that to put the pressure on Sue, and he had fed it to you but not me. So that was his lie, not Sue's. Hers was about our arranging to meet there Tuesday afternoon to have it out with Faber. We hadn't arranged anything. She also—"

"So *you* say." Peter Jay.

"Don't interrupt. She also lied about what she did when she got there at five-fifteen. She said she saw I wasn't there and left. Actually she went down the alley, saw Faber's body there on the ground with his skull smashed, panicked, and blew. The time thing—"

"So *you* say." Peter Jay.

"Shut up. The time thing is only a matter of seconds. Sue says she got there at five-fifteen, and the record says that a man coming from the kitchen discovered the body at five-fifteen. Sue may be off half a minute, or the man may. Evidently she had just been and gone when the man came from the kitchen."

"Look, pal." Maslow had his head cocked and his eyes narrowed. "Shut up? Go soak your head. Who's lying, Sue or you?"

I nodded. "That's a fair question. Until noon today, a little before noon, they thought I was. Then they found out I wasn't. They didn't just guess again, they found out, and that's why they took her down and they're going to keep her. Which—"

"How did they find out?"

"Ask them. You can be sure it was good. They were liking it fine, having me on a hook, and they hated to see me flop off. It had to be good, and it was. Which brings me to the point. I think Sue's lie was part truth. I think she *had* arranged with someone to meet her there at five o'clock.

"She got there fifteen minutes late and he wasn't there, and she went down the alley and saw Faber dead, and what would she think? That's obvious. No wonder she panicked. She went home and looked it over. She couldn't deny she had been there because she had been seen. If she said she had gone there on her own to see Faber, alone, they wouldn't believe she hadn't gone in the alley, and they certainly *would* believe she had killed him.

"So she decided to tell the truth, part of it, that she had arranged to meet someone and she got there late and he wasn't there and she had left—leaving out that she had gone in the alley and seen the body. But since she thought that the man she had arranged to meet had killed Faber she couldn't name him; but they would insist on her naming him. So she decided to name me. It wasn't so dirty really; she thought I could prove I was somewhere else, having decided not to meet her. I couldn't, but she didn't know that." I turned a palm up. "So the point is, who had agreed to meet her there?"

Heydt said, "That took a lot of cutting and fitting, Archie."

"You were going to ask questions," Maslow said. "Ask one we can answer."

"I'll settle for that one," I said. "Say it was one of you, which of course I *am* saying. I don't expect him to answer it. If Sue stands pat and doesn't name him and it gets to where he has to choose between letting her go to trial and unloading, he might come across, but not here and now. But I do expect the other two to consider it.

"Put it another way: if Sue decided to jump on Faber for the lies he was spreading around and to ask one of you to help, which one would she pick? Or still another: which one of you would be most likely to decide to jump Faber and ask Sue to join in? I like the first one better because it was probably her idea." I looked at Heydt. "What about it, Carl? Just a plain answer to a plain question. Which one would she pick? You?"

"No. Maslow."

"Why?"

"He's articulate and he's tough. I'm not tough, and Sue knows it."

"How about Jay?"

"My God, no. I hope not. She must know that nobody can depend on him for anything that takes guts."

Jay left his chair, and his hands were fists as he moved. Guts or not, he certainly believed in making contact. Thinking that Heydt probably wasn't as well educated as Maslow, I got up and blocked Jay off, and darned if he didn't swing at me, or start to. I got his arm and whirled him and shoved, and he stumbled but managed to stay on his feet. As he turned, Maslow spoke.

"Hold it, Pete. I have an idea. There's no love lost among us three, but we all feel the same about this Goodwin. He's a persona non

grata if I ever saw one." He got up. "Let's bounce him. Not just a
nudge, the bum's rush. Care to help, Carl?"

Heydt shook his head. "No, thanks. I'll watch."

"Okay. It'll be simpler if you just relax, Goodwin."

I couldn't turn and go, leaving my rear open. "I hope you won't
tickle," I said, backing up a step.

"Come in behind, Pete," Maslow said, and started, slow, his elbows
out a little and his open hands extended and up some. Since he had
been so neat with the kidney punch he probably knew a few tricks,
maybe the armpit or the apple, and with Jay on my back I would
have been a setup, so I doubled up and whirled, came up bumping
Jay, and gave him the edge of my hand, as sharp as I could make
it, on the side of his neck, the tendon below the ear.

It got exactly the right spot and so much for him, but Maslow had
my left wrist and was getting his shoulder in for the lock, and in
another tenth of a second I would have been meat. The only way to
go was down, and I went, sliding off his shoulder and bending my
elbow into his belly, and he made a mistake. Having lost the lock,
he reached for my other wrist. That opened him up, and I rolled into
him, brought my right arm around, and had his neck with a knee
in his back.

"Do you want to hear it crack?" I asked him, which was bad
manners, since he couldn't answer. I loosened my arm a little. "I
admit I was lucky. If Jay had been sideways you would have had
me."

I looked at Jay, who was on a chair, rubbing his neck. "If you
want to play games you ought to take lessons. Maslow would be a
good teacher." I unwound my arm and got erect. "Don't bother to
see me out," I said and headed for the front.

I was still breathing a little fast when I emerged to the sidewalk,
having straightened my tie and run my comb through my hair in
the elevator. My watch said twenty past ten. Also in the elevator
I had decided to make a phone call, so I walked to Madison Avenue,
found a booth, and dialed one of the numbers I knew best.

Miss Lily Rowan was in and would be pleased to have me come
and tell her things, and I walked the twelve blocks to the number
on 63rd Street where her penthouse occupies the roof.

Since it wasn't one of Wolfe's cases with a client involved, but a
joint affair, and since it was Lily who had started Sue on her way
at my request, I gave her the whole picture. Her chief reactions were
(a) that she didn't blame Sue and I had no right to, I should feel

flattered; (b) that I had to somehow get Sue out of it without in-
volving whoever had removed such a louse as Kenneth Faber from
circulation; and (c) that if I did have to involve him she hoped to
heaven it wasn't Carl Heydt because there was no one else around
who could make clothes that were fit to wear, especially suits.

She had sent a lawyer to Sue, Bernard Ross, and he had seen her
and had phoned an hour before I came to report that she was being
held without bail and he would decide in the morning whether to
apply for a writ.

It was after one o'clock when I climbed out of a cab in front of the
old brownstone on West 35th Street, mounted the stoop, used my
key, went down the hall to the office and switched the light on, and
got a surprise. Under a paperweight on my desk was a note in Wolfe's
handwriting. It said:

AG: Saul will take the car in the morning, probably for
most of the day. His car is not presently available.   NW

I went to the safe, manipulated the knob, opened the door, got the
petty-cash book from the drawer, flipped to the current page, and
saw an entry:

9/14 SP exp AG 100

I put it back, shut the door, twirled the knob, and considered.
Wolfe had summoned Saul, and he had come and had been given an
errand for which he needed a car. What errand, for God's sake? Not
to drive to Putnam County to get the corn that had been ordered for
Friday; for that he wouldn't need to start in the morning, he wouldn't
need a hundred bucks for possible expenses, and the entry wouldn't
say "exp AG." It shouldn't say that anyway since I wasn't a paying
client; it should say "exp JA" for joint affair.

And if we were going to split the outlay I should damn well have
been consulted beforehand. But up in my room, as I took off and put
on, what was biting me was the errand. In the name of the Almighty
Lord what and where was the errand?

Wolfe eats breakfast in his room from a tray taken up by Fritz,
and ordinarily I don't see him until he comes down from the plant
rooms at eleven o'clock. If he has something important or complicated for me he sends word by Fritz for me to go up to his room; for
something trivial he gets me on the house phone. That Friday morning there was neither word by Fritz nor the buzzer, and after a late
and leisurely breakfast in the kitchen, having learned nothing new
from the report of developments in the morning papers on the Sweet

Corn Murder, as the *Gazette* called it, I went to the office and opened the mail.

If Wolfe saw fit to keep Saul's errand strictly private, he could eat wormy old corn boiled in water before I'd ask him. I decided to go out for a walk and was starting for the kitchen to tell Fritz when the phone rang. I got it, and a woman said she was the secretary of Mr. Bernard Ross, counsel for Miss Susan McLeod, and Mr. Ross would like very much to talk with Mr. Wolfe and Mr. Goodwin at their earliest convenience. He would appreciate it if they would call at his office today, this morning if possible.

I would have enjoyed telling Wolfe that Bernard Ross, the cele-brated attorney, didn't know that Nero Wolfe, the celebrated detec-tive, never left his house to call on anyone whoever, but since I wasn't on speaking terms with him I had to skip it. I told the sec-retary that Wolfe couldn't but I could and would, went and told Fritz I would probably be back for lunch, put a carbon copy of the twelve-page conversation with affidavits in my pocket, and departed.

I did get back for lunch, just barely. Including the time he took to study the document I had brought, Ross kept me a solid two hours and a half. When I left he knew nearly everything I did, but not quite; I omitted a few items that were immaterial as far as he was concerned—for instance, that Wolfe had sent Saul Panzer some-where to do something. Since I couldn't tell him where, to do what, there was no point in mentioning it.

I would have preferred to buy my lunch somewhere, say at Rus-terman's, rather than sit through a meal with Wolfe, but he would be the one to gripe, not me, if he didn't know where I was. Entering his house, and hearing him in the dining room speaking to Fritz, I went first to the office, and there on my desk under a paperweight were four sawbucks. Leaving them there, I went to the dining room and said good morning, though it wasn't.

Wolfe nodded and went on dishing shrimps from a steaming cas-serole. "Good afternoon. That forty dollars on your desk can be re-turned to the safe. Saul had no expenses and I gave him sixty dollars for his six hours."

"His daily minimum is eighty."

"He wouldn't take eighty. He didn't want to take anything, since this is our personal affair, but I insisted. This shrimp Bordelaise is without onions but has some garlic. I think an improvement, but Fritz and I invite your opinion."

"I'll be glad to give it. It smells good." I sat. That was by no means the first time the question had arisen whether he was more pig-headed than I was strong-minded. I was supposed to explode. I was supposed to demand to know where and how Saul had spent the six hours, and he would then be good enough to explain that he had got an idea last night in my absence, and, not knowing where I was, he had had to call Saul. So I wouldn't explode. I would eat shrimp Bordelaise without onions but with garlic and like it.

Obviously, whatever Saul's errand had been, it had been a wash-out, since he had returned, reported, and been paid off. So it was Wolfe's move, since he had refused to see the three candidates when they came and rang the bell, and I would not explode. Nor would I report on last night or this morning unless and until he asked for it.

Back in the office after lunch, he got settled in his favorite chair with *My Life in Court,* and I brought a file of cards from the cabinet and got busy with the germination records. At one minute to four he put his book down and went to keep his date with the orchids. It would have been a pleasure to take the Marley .32 from the drawer and plug him in the back.

I was at my desk, looking through the evening edition of the *Gazette* that had just been delivered, when I heard a noise I couldn't believe. The elevator. I looked at my watch: half past five. That was unprecedented. He never did that. Once in the plant rooms he stuck there for the two hours, no matter what. If he had a notion that couldn't wait he buzzed me on the house phone, or Fritz if I wasn't there. I dropped the paper and got up and stepped to the hall. The elevator jolted to a stop at the bottom, the door opened, and he emerged.

"The corn," he said. "Has it come?"

For Pete's sake. Being finicky about grub is all right up to a point, but there's a limit. "No," I said. "Unless Saul brought it."

He grunted. "A possibility occurred to me. When it comes—if it comes—no. I'll see for myself. The possibility is remote, but it would be—"

"Here it is," I said. "Good timing." A man with a carton had appeared on the stoop. As I started to the front the doorbell rang, and as I opened the door Wolfe was there beside me. The man, a skinny little guy in pants too big for him and a bright-green shirt, spoke. "Nero Wolfe?"

"I'm Nero Wolfe." He was on the sill. "You have my corn?"

"Right here." He put the carton down and let go of the cord.

"May I have your name, sir?"

"My name's Palmer. Delbert Palmer. Why?"

"I like to know the names of men who render me a service. Did you pick the corn?"

"Hell, no. McLeod picked it."

"Did you pack it in the carton?"

"No, he did. Look here, I know you're a detective. You just ask questions from habit, huh?"

"No, Mr. Palmer. I merely want to be sure about the corn. I'm obliged to you. Good day, sir." He bent over to slip his fingers under the cord, lifted the carton, and headed for the office. Palmer told me distinctly, "It takes all kinds," turned, and started down the steps, and I shut the door.

In the office Wolfe was standing eying the carton, which he had put on the seat of the red-leather chair. As I crossed over he said without looking up, "Get Mr. Cramer."

It's nice to have a man around who obeys orders no matter how batty they are and saves the questions for later. That time the questions got answered before they were asked. I went to my desk, dialed Homicide South, and got Cramer, and Wolfe, who had gone to his chair, took his phone.

"Mr. Cramer? I must ask a favor. I have here in my office a carton which has just been delivered to me. It is supposed to contain corn, and perhaps it does, but it is conceivable that it contains dynamite and a contraption that will detonate it when the cord is cut and the flaps raised. My suspicion may be groundless, but I have it.

"I know this is not your department, but you will know how to proceed. Will you please notify the proper person without delay? . . . That can wait until we know what's in the carton . . . Certainly. Even if it contains only corn I'll give you all relevant information . . . No, there is no ticking sound. If it does contain explosive there is almost certainly no danger until the carton is opened . . . Yes, I'll make sure."

He hung up, swiveled, and glared at the carton. "Confound it," he growled, "again. We'll get some somewhere before the season ends."

The first city employee to arrive, four or five minutes after Wolfe hung up, was one in uniform. Wolfe was telling me what Saul's errand had been when the doorbell rang, and since I resented the interruption I trotted to the front, opened the door, saw a prowl car at the curb, and demanded rudely, "Well?"

"Where's that carton?" he demanded back.

"Where it will stay until someone comes who knows something."
I was shutting the door but his foot was there.

"You're Archie Goodwin," he said. "I know about you. I'm coming
in. Did you yell for help or didn't you?"

He had a point. An officer of the law doesn't have to bring a search
warrant to enter a house whose owner has asked the police to come
and get a carton of maybe dynamite. I gave him room to enter, shut
the door, took him to the office, pointed to the carton, and said, "If
you touch it and it goes off we can sue you for damages."

"You couldn't pay me to touch it," he said. "I'm here to see that
nobody does."

He glanced around, went over by the big globe, and stood, a good
fifteen feet away from the carton. With him there, the rest of the
explanation of Saul's errand had to wait, but I had something to
look at to pass the time—a carbon copy, one sheet, which Wolfe had
taken from his desk drawer and handed me, of something Saul had
typed on my machine during my absence Thursday evening.

The second city employee to arrive, at ten minutes to six, was
Inspector Cramer. When the bell rang and I went to let him in, the
look on his face was one I had seen before. He knew Wolfe had
something fancy by the tail, and he would have given a month's pay
before taxes to know what. He tramped to the office, saw the carton,
turned to the cop, got a salute but didn't acknowledge it, and said,
"You can go, Schwab."

"Yes, sir. Stay out front?"

"No. You won't be needed."

Fully as rude as I had been, but he was a superior officer. Schwab
saluted again and went. Cramer looked at the red-leather chair. He
always sat there, but the carton was on it. I moved up one of the
yellow ones, and he sat, took his hat off, dropped it on the floor, and
asked Wolfe, "What is this, a gag?"

Wolfe shook his head. "It may be a bugaboo, but I'm not crying
wolf. I can tell you nothing until we know what's in the carton."

"The hell you can't. When did it come?"

"One minute before I telephoned you."

"Who brought it?"

"A stranger. A man I had never seen before."

"Why do you think it's dynamite?"

"I think it may be. I reserve further information until—"

I missed the rest because the doorbell rang and I went. It was the bomb squad, two of them. They were in uniform, but one look and you knew they weren't flatties—if nothing else, their eyes. When I opened the door I saw another one down on the sidewalk, and their special bus, with its made-to-order enclosed body, was double-parked in front.

I asked, "Bomb squad?" and the shorter one said, "Right," and I convoyed them to the office. Cramer, on his feet, returned their salute, pointed to the carton, and said, "It may be just corn. I mean the kind of corn you eat. Or it may not. Nero Wolfe thinks not. He also thinks it's safe until the flaps are opened, but you're the experts. As soon as you know, phone me here. How long will it take?"

"That depends, Inspector. It could be an hour, or ten hours—or it could be never."

"I hope not never. Will you call me here as soon as you know?"

"Yes, sir."

The other one, the taller one, had stooped to press his ear against the carton and kept it there. He raised his head, said, "No comment," eased his fingers under the carton's bottom, a hand at each side, and came up with it. I said, "The man who brought it carried it by the cord," and got ignored. They went, the one with the carton in front, and I followed to the stoop, watched them put it in the bus, then I returned to the office. Cramer was in the red-leather chair, and Wolfe was speaking.

"But if you insist, very well. My reason for thinking it may contain an explosive is that it was brought by a stranger. My name printed on it was as usual, but naturally such a detail would not be overlooked. There are a number of people in the metropolitan area who have reason to wish me ill, and it would be imprudent—"

"My God, you can lie."

Wolfe tapped the desk with a fingertip. "Mr. Cramer. If you insist on lies you'll get them. Until I know what's in that carton. Then we'll see." He picked up his book, opened to his place, and swiveled to get the light right.

Cramer was stuck. He looked at me, started to say something, and vetoed it. He couldn't get up and go because he had told the Bomb Squad to call him there, but an Inspector couldn't just sit. He took a cigar from a pocket, looked at it, put it back, arose, came to me, and said, "I've got some calls to make." Meaning he wanted my chair, which was a good dodge since it got *some* action; I had to move.

He stayed at the phone nearly half an hour, making four or five calls, none of which sounded important, then got up and went over to the big globe and started studying geography. Ten minutes was enough for that and he switched to the bookshelves. Back at my desk, leaning back with my legs crossed, my hands clasped behind my head, I noted which books he took out and looked at.

Now that I knew who had killed Ken Faber, little things like that were interesting. The one he looked at longest was *The Coming Fury* by Bruce Catton. He was still at that when the phone rang. I turned to get it, but by the time I had it to my ear he was there. A man asked for Inspector Cramer and I handed it to him and permitted myself a grin as I saw Wolfe put his book down and reach for his phone. He wasn't going to take hearsay, even from an Inspector.

It was a short conversation; Cramer's end of it wasn't more than twenty words. He hung up and went to the red-leather chair. "Okay," he growled. "If you had opened that carton they wouldn't have found all the pieces. You didn't think it was dynamite, you knew it was. Talk."

Wolfe, his lips tight, was breathing deep. "Not me," he said. "It would have been Archie or Fritz, or both of them. And of course my house. The possibility occurred to me, and I came down, barely in time. Three minutes later . . . Pfui. That man is a blackguard."

He shook his head, as if getting rid of a fly. "Well. Shortly after ten o'clock last evening I decided how to proceed, and I sent for Saul Panzer. When he came—"

"Who put that dynamite in that carton?"

"I'm telling you. When he came I had him type something on a sheet of paper and told him to drive to Duncan McLeod's farm this morning and give it to Mr. McLeod. Archie. You have the copy,"

I took it from my pocket and went and handed it to Cramer. He kept it, but this is what it said:

MEMORANDUM FROM NERO WOLFE

TO DUNCAN MCLEOD

I suggest that you should have in readiness acceptable answers to the following questions if and when they are asked:

1. When did Kenneth Faber tell you that your daughter was pregnant and he was responsible?

2. Where did you go when you drove away from your farm Tuesday afternoon around two o'clock—perhaps a little later—and returned around seven o'clock, late for milking?

3. Where did you get the piece of pipe? Was it on your premises?

4. Do you know that your daughter saw you leaving the alley Tuesday afternoon? Did you see her?

5. Is it true that the man with the bulldozer told you Monday night that he would have to come Wednesday instead of Thursday?

There are many other questions you may be asked; these are only samples. If competent investigators are moved to start inquiries of this nature, you will of course be in a difficult position, and it would be well to anticipate it.

Cramer looked up and aimed beady eyes at Wolfe. "You knew last night that McLeod killed Faber."

"Not certain knowledge. A reasoned conclusion."

"You knew he left his farm Tuesday afternoon. You knew his daughter saw him at the alley. You knew—"

"No. Those were conclusions." Wolfe turned a palm up. "Mr. Cramer. You sat there yesterday morning and read a document sworn to by Mr. Goodwin and me. When you finished it you knew everything that I knew, and I have learned nothing since then. From the knowledge we shared I had concluded that McLeod had killed Faber. You haven't. Shall I detail it?"

"Yes."

"First, the corn. I presume McLeod told you, as he did me, that he had Faber pick the corn because he had to dynamite some stumps and rock."

"Yes."

"That seemed to me unlikely. He knows how extremely particular I am, and also the restaurant. We pay him well, more than well; it must be a substantial portion of his income. He knew that young man couldn't possibly do that job. It must have been something more urgent than stumps and rocks that led him to risk losing such desirable customers. Second, the pipe. It was chiefly on account of the pipe that I wanted to see Mr. Heydt, Mr. Maslow, and Mr. Jay. Any man—"

"When did you see them?"

"They came here Wednesday evening, at Miss McLeod's request. Any man, sufficiently provoked, might plan to kill, but very few men would choose a massive iron bludgeon for a weapon to carry through the streets. Seeing those three, I thought it highly improbable that any of them would. But a countryman might, a man who does rough work with rough and heavy tools."

"You came to a conclusion on stuff like that?"

"No. Those details were merely corroborative. The conclusive item came from Miss McLeod. You read that document. I asked her—I'll quote from memory. I said to her, 'You know those men quite well. You know their temperaments. If one of them, enraged beyond endurance by Mr. Faber's conduct, went there and killed him, which one? It wasn't a sudden fit of passion, it was planned. From your knowledge of them, which one?' How did she answer me?"

"She said, 'They didn't.' "

"Yes. Didn't you think that significant? Of course I had the advantage of seeing and hearing her."

"Sure it was significant. It wasn't the reaction you always get to the idea that some close friend has committed murder. It wasn't shock. She just stated a fact. She *knew* they hadn't."

Wolfe nodded. "Precisely. And I saw and heard her. And there was only one way she could know they hadn't, with such certainty in her words and voice and manner: She knew who had. Did you form that conclusion?"

"Yes."

"Then why didn't you go on? If she hadn't killed him herself but knew who had, and it wasn't one of those three men—isn't it obvious?"

"You slipped that in, if she hadn't killed him herself. Why hadn't she?"

A corner of Wolfe's mouth went up. "There it is, your one major flaw: a distorted conception of the impossible. You will reject as inconceivable such a phenomenon as a man being at two different spots simultaneously, though any adroit trickster could easily contrive it; but you consider it credible that that young woman—even after you had studied her conversation with Mr. Goodwin and me—that she concealed that piece of pipe on her person and took it there with the intention of crushing a man's skull with it. Preposterous. That *is* inconceivable."

He waved it away. "Of course that's academic, now that that wretch has betrayed himself by sending me dynamite instead of corn, and the last step to my conclusion was inevitable. Since she knew who had killed Faber but wouldn't name him, and it wasn't one of those three, it was her father; and since she was certain—I heard and saw her say, 'They didn't'—she had seen him there. I doubt if he knew it, because—But that's immaterial. So much for—"

He stopped because Cramer was up, coming to my desk. He picked up the phone, dialed, and in a moment said, "Irwin? Inspector Cramer. I want Sergeant Stebbins." After another moment: "Purley? Get Carmel, the sheriff's office. Ask him to get Duncan McLeod and hold him, and no mistake . . . Yes, Susan McLeod's father. Send two men to Carmel and tell them to call in as soon as they arrive. Tell Carmel to watch it, McLeod is down for murder and he may be rough . . . No, that can wait. I'll be there soon—half an hour, maybe less."

He hung up, about-faced to Wolfe, and growled, "You knew all this Wednesday afternoon, two days ago."

Wolfe nodded. "And you have known it since yesterday morning. It's a question of interpretation, not of knowledge. Will you please sit? As you know, I like eyes at my level. Thank you. Yes, as early as Wednesday afternoon, when Miss McLeod left, I was all but certain of the identity of the murderer, but I took the precaution of seeing those three men that evening because it was just possible that one of them would disclose something cogent.

"When you came yesterday morning with that warrant, I gave you that document for two reasons: to keep Mr. Goodwin out of jail, and to share my knowledge with you. I wasn't obliged to share also my interpretation of it. Any moment since yesterday noon I have rather expected to hear that Mr. McLeod had been taken into custody, but no."

"So you decided to share your interpretation with him instead of me."

"I like that," Wolfe said approvingly. "That was neat. I prefer to put it that I decided not to decide. Having given you all the facts I had, I had met my obligation as a citizen and a licensed private detective. I was under no compulsion, legal or moral, to assume the role of a nemesis. It was only conjecture that Faber had told Mr. McLeod that he had debauched his daughter, but he had told others, and McLeod must have had a potent motive, so it was highly probable. If so, the question of moral turpitude was moot, and I would not rule on it.

"Since I had given you the facts, I thought it only fair to inform Mr. McLeod that he was menaced by a logical conclusion from those facts; and I did so. I used Mr. Panzer as my messenger because I chose not to involve Mr. Goodwin. He was unaware of the conclusion

I had reached, and if I had told him there might have been disagreement regarding the course to take. He can be—uh—difficult."

Cramer grunted. "Yeah. He can. So you deliberately warned a murderer. Telling him to have answers ready. Nuts. You expected him to lam."

"No. I had no specific expectation. It would have been idle to speculate, but if I had, I doubt if I would have expected him to scoot. He couldn't take his farm along, and he would be leaving his daughter in mortal jeopardy. I didn't consciously speculate, but my subconscious must have, for suddenly, when I was busy at the potting bench, it struck me.

"Saul Panzer's description of McLeod's stony face as he read the memorandum; the stubborn ego of a self-righteous man; dynamite for stumps and rocks; corn; a closed carton. Most improbable. I resumed the potting. But conceivable. I dropped the trowel and went to the elevator, and within thirty seconds after I emerged in the hall the carton came."

"Luck," Cramer said. "Your damn incredible luck. If it had made mincemeat of Goodwin you might have been willing to admit for once—okay, it didn't." He got up. "Stick around, Goodwin. They'll want you at the D.A.'s office, probably in the morning." To Wolfe: "What if that phone call had said the carton held corn, just corn? You think you could have talked me off, don't you?"

"I could have tried."

"By God. Talk about stubborn egos." Cramer shook his head. "That break you got on the carton. You know, any normal man, if he got a break like that, coming down just in the nick of time, what any normal man would do, he would go down on his knees and thank God. Do you know what you'll do? You'll thank *you*. I admit it would be a job for you to get down on your knees, but—"

The phone rang. I swiveled and got it, and a voice I recognized asked for Inspector Cramer. I turned and told him, "Purley Stebbins," and he came and took it. The conversation was even shorter than the one about the carton, and Cramer's part was only a dozen words and a couple of growls. He hung up, went and got his hat, and headed for the hall, but a step short of the door he stopped and turned.

"I might as well tell you," he said. "It'll give you a better appetite for dinner, even if it's not corn. About an hour ago Duncan McLeod sat or stood or lay on a pile of dynamite and it went off. They'll want to decide whether it was an accident or he did it. Maybe you can help them interpret the facts." He turned and went.

One day last week there was a party at Lily Rowan's penthouse. She never invites more than six to dinner—eight counting her and me—but that was a dancing party and around coffee time a dozen more came and three musicians got set in the alcove and started up. After rounds with Lily and three or four others, I approached Sue McLeod and offered a hand.

She gave me a look. "You know you don't want to. Let's go outside."

I said it was cold, and she said she knew it and headed for the foyer. We got her wrap—a fur thing which she probably didn't own, since topflight models are offered loans of everything from socks to sable—went back in, on through, and out to the terrace. There were evergreens in tubs, and we crossed to them for shelter.

"You told Lily I hate you," she said. "I don't."

"Not 'hate,'" I said. "She misquoted me or you're misquoting her. She said I should dance with you and I said when I tried it a month ago you froze."

"I know I did." She put a hand on my arm. "Archie. It was hard, you know it was. If I hadn't got my father to let him work on the farm—it was my fault, I know it was—but I couldn't help thinking if you hadn't sent him that—letting him know you knew—"

"I didn't send it, Mr. Wolfe did. But I would have. Okay, he was your father, so it was hard. But no matter whose father he was, I'm not wearing an armband for the guy who packed dynamite in that carton."

"Of course not. I know. Of course not. I tell myself I'll have to forget it . . . but it's not easy." She shivered. "Anyway, I wanted to say I don't hate you. You don't have to dance with me, and you know I'm not going to get married until I can stop working and have babies, and I know you never are, and even if you do, it will be Lily, but you don't have to stand there and let me *really* freeze, do you?"

I didn't. You don't have to be rude, even with a girl who can't dance, and it was cold out there.

"Q"

Brian Garfield

The Glory Hunter

On the evening when the kid came to kill him, the man returned from the day's labor at his usual time.

The man and the woman went out each morning from the ruined fort to the cliff. It was about a half-mile walk. They worked side by side inside the mountain.

In the course of four years of work they had tunneled deep into the quartz. Hardrocking was not easy work, especially for a man and a woman both in their fifties and neither of them very large in size; but they accepted the arduous work because it had a goal and the goal was in sight.

Inside the tunnel they would crush the rock together and shovel it into the wooden dumpcart. They would wheel the cart out of the tunnel and dump it into the sluice that the man had designed in the second year to replace the rocker-box they'd begun with. The sluice carried water at high speed. This was water that came down through a wooden flume from a creek 70 yards above them, above the top of the low cliff. The floor of the sluice was rippled with wooden barriers; these were designed to separate the particles and retain the heaviest ones—the gold flakes—while everything else washed away downstream.

It was a good lode and during the four years they had washed a great deal of gold out of the mountain, flake by flake. Most of it was hidden in various caches. When they made the forty-mile muleback ride to Florence Junction for stocking up, they would take only enough gold dust to pay for their purchases; the town knew they had a claim back in the Superstitions but from the amount they spent it appeared they were barely making ends meet. They had never been invaded by gold-rush crowds.

They'd started working the claim when the man was 51 and the woman 48 and he figured to quit when he was 56, at which time they should have enough money to live handsomely in one of those big new gabled houses over in San José or Palo Alto or San Francisco. They'd be able to afford all the genteel things. In the meantime they worked hard to pay for it, pitting their muscles and pickaxes against the hard skeleton of the mountain.

The mountain was called Longshot Bluff because it was topped by a needle-shaped pinnacle like the spike on a Prussian helmet; from up there you could command everything in sight with an unobstructed circle of fire and because of the altitude you could make a bullet travel an extremely long distance.

The cavalry, back in 1879, had chased a small band of warriors onto the mountain and the Apaches had taken up positions on top of the spire. There were only five Apaches; there were 40 soldiers in the troop but the Indians barricaded themselves and there was no way the army could get at them. A siege had ensued and finally the Apaches were starved out.

After that the army built the little outpost on a hilltop about a mile out from the base of Longshot Bluff. Troops had occupied the post for five years; then the Indian wars came to an end and the camp was abandoned. It was the ruins of this fort that the man and the woman used as their home.

The abandoned camp had no stockade around it; the simple outpost consisted merely of a handful of squat adobes built around a flat parade ground. There had been a post-and-rail corral, but travelers had consumed the rails for firewood over the twelve years since the camp had been decommissioned by the army. The man and the woman had kept their four mules loose-hobbled for the first few weeks of their residence; after that they let the animals graze at will because this had become home and the mules had nowhere else to go.

When you sat on the veranda after supper, as the man and the woman often did, you faced the east. You looked down a long easy hardpan slope dotted with a spindle tracery of desert growth—catclaw and ocotillo, manzanita and cholla and sage. The foot of the slope was nearly a half-mile away.

At that point you saw the low cliff where the man and the woman had drilled their mining tunnel. Beyond it lofted the abrupt mass of Longshot Bluff. The pinnacle was perhaps 800 feet higher than the fort. From this angle the spire appeared as slender as a lance, sharp enough to pierce the clouds. It stood, as the crow flies, perhaps three miles from the veranda.

They came in from work in the late afternoon and the man packed his pipe on the veranda while he waited for supper. Over on the southern slope of Longshot Bluff he saw briefly the movement of an approaching horseman. From the window the woman must have seen it as well; she appeared on the veranda. "He'll be too late for supper unless we wait on him."

"Then we'll wait on him," the man said.

It would take the rider at least an hour to get here and it would be about 45 minutes short of sunset by then. But the man went inside immediately and opened the threadbare carpetbag that he kept under the bed.

The woman said, "I hope he's not another glory hunter." She said it without heat; when the man glanced at her she cracked her brief gentle smile.

He unwrapped his revolver from the oiled rags that protected it. The revolver was a single-action Bisley model with a 7½-inch barrel, caliber .45 Long Colt. It had been designed for match target competition and the Colt people had named it after the shooting range at Bisley in England where marksmen met every year to decide the championship.

The man put the revolver in his waistband and snugged it around until it didn't abrade his hipbone.

On his way to the door he glanced at the woman. She was, he thought, a woman of rare quality. When he'd met her she'd been working in a brothel in Leadville. After they'd known each other a few years the man had said, "We're both getting kind of long in the tooth," and they'd both left their previous occupations and gone out together looking for gold.

At the door he said, "I'll be back directly," and walked down toward the cliff.

He covered the distance briskly; it took some 15 minutes and when he reached the mouth of the tunnel he ran the empty ore cart out past the sluice and pushed it up onto a little hump of rocky ground. In the debris of the tailings dump he found two cracked half-gallon jugs they'd discarded. He set the jugs on two corners of the ore cart; they balanced sturdily and nothing short of a direct blow would knock them off.

Then he walked back up toward the fort, but he moved more slowly now, keeping to cover because it wasn't certain just when the approaching horseman would come into sight down along the far end of the base of the mountain.

The man laid up in a clump of manzanita about 30 feet from the veranda and kept his eye on the little stand of cottonwoods a mile away. That was where the creek flowed off the mountain. The creek went underground there but you could trace the line of its passage out onto the desert plain by the deep green row of mesquite and scrub sycamore. The rider would appear somewhere along there; he'd have to cross the creek.

After a little while the visitor came across the creek and rode along the slope toward the ruined fort.

Coming in straight up, the man observed; but still he didn't show himself.

Halfway up to the house the horseman drew his rifle out of the saddle scabbard and laid it across his pommel, holding it that way with one hand as he approached without hurry.

The man lay in the brush and watched.

He saw that the rider was just a kid. Maybe 18, maybe 20. A leaned-down kid with no meat on him and a hungry narrow face under the brim of a pretentious black hat.

The horse went by not ten feet from the man's hiding place. Just beyond, the kid drew rein, not riding any closer to the fort.

"Hello the house. Anybody home?"

The man stood up behind him. "Right back here. Drop the rifle first. Then we'll talk."

The man was braced for anything; the kid might be a wild one. The man had the Bisley Colt cocked in his fist. The kid's head turned slowly until he picked up the man in the corner of his vision; evidently he saw and recognized the revolver because he let the rifle slide to the ground.

"Now the belt gun," the man said, and the kid stripped off his gunbelt and let it drop alongside the rifle. The kid eased his horse off to one side away from the weapons and the man said, "All right, you can speak your piece."

"Ain't rightly fair coming up from behind me like that," the kid said.

He had a surprisingly deep voice.

"Well you came calling on me with a rifle across your saddle-bow."

"Place like this, how do I know what to expect? Could be rattlers in there. Place could be crawling with road agents for all I know."

"Well, that's all right, son. You won't need your weapons. You want to come inside and share a bit of supper?"

The kid looked uncertainly at the man's Bisley revolver. The man walked over to the discarded weapons and picked them up. Then he uncocked the revolver and put it back in his waistband. He went up to the house and the woman came out onto the veranda and shaded her eyes to look at the visitor. She smiled a welcome, but when she glanced at the man he saw the knowledge in her face.

The kid had come to kill the man, right enough. All three of them knew it, but nobody said anything.

The kid ate politely; somebody had taught him manners. The woman said, to make conversation, "You hail from Tucson?"

"No, ma'am. Laramie, Wyoming."

"Long way off," the man said.

"I reckon."

After supper the three of them sat on the veranda. The sun was behind the house and they were in shadow; another ten minutes to sundown. The hard slanting light struck the face of Longshot Bluff and made the spire look like a fiery signal against the dark sky beyond it. The man got his pipe going to his satisfaction, broke the match, and contemplated the kid who had come to kill him. "How much they paying you for my scalp, son?"

"What?"

"The last one they sent, it was two thousand dollars they offered him."

"Mister, I ain't quite sure what you're talking about."

"That's a powerful grudge they're carrying, two thousand dollars' worth. It happened a long while back, you know."

The woman said, "But I suppose two thousand dollars looks like the world of money to a young man like you."

The man said, "It's not legal any more, you know, son. No matter what they told you. There was a fugitive warrant out on me from the state of Wyoming, but that was some years back. The statute of limitations expired three years ago."

"I'm sorry, mister, I just ain't tracking what you mean."

"The cattlemen up there were hiring range detectives like me to discourage homesteaders," the man explained. "This one cattleman had an eager kind of streak in him. I told him to keep out of the way but he had to mess in things. Got in the way of a bullet. My bullet, I expect, although I've never been whole certain about that.

"Anyhow, that cattleman's been in a wheelchair ever since. Accused me of backshooting him, said I'd sold out to the homestead crowd. It wasn't true, of course, but it's what he believes. All he does is sit in that wheelchair and brood over it. He's sent seven bounty men after me, one time or another. He just keeps sending them. Reckon he won't give it up till one of us dies of old age. You're number eight now. Maybe you want to think on that—think about the other seven that came after me, pretty good professionals some of them. I'm still here, son."

The kid just watched him, not blinking, no longer protesting innocence.

The man said, "That fellow in the wheelchair, how much did he offer you?"

The kid didn't answer that. After a moment the woman said, "You probably want the money for some good purpose, don't you, young fellow?"

"Ma'am, I expect anybody could find his own good purpose to turn money to if he had it."

"You got a girl back in Laramie, Wyoming?" she asked.

"Yes, ma'am."

"Fixing to marry her?"

"That's right, ma'am."

"On two thousand dollars you'd have a right good start," she said.

"That would be true, ma'am," the kid said with great courtesy.

"Well, I hope you make your way proper in the world," she said, "but you ain't likely to do that here. You do a sight of hunting, I imagine, from the look of that rifle you carry. You must have seen buck antelope square off a time or two. The young buck tries to get the better of the old buck, tries to displace him in the herd. Rarely happens. I expect you know that. The old buck knows all the tricks that the young buck still needs to learn. That's why you're setting on this porch now without a gun."

The man's pipe had gone out. He struck another match and indulged himself in the ritual of spreading the flame around the bowl. Then he said, "If you ain't ready to give it up, son, I'll take your weapons out there on the desert in the morning and then let you go out and get them and we'll finish this thing between us. If that's the way you want it."

The kid looked at him and uncertainty crept into his young face.

The man said, "The only weapon I own is this Bisley revolver here. Of course you may think you can outrange me with that forty-four-forty rifle of yours. You may think that, but I reckon as how you'd be mistaken."

The light was beginning to fade, but he still had another 15 or 20 minutes of light good enough for shooting. The wind had died; that was what he had waited for. He went inside the house and got the kid's rifle and brought it out onto the veranda. The kid watched him while the man worked the lever-action, jacking out the cartridges one by one until the rifle was empty.

Then the man picked up one of the cartridges off the floor and wiped it clean with his hand and chambered it into the rifle. He locked the breech shut and looked at the kid.

"Now I've put one load into this rifle of yours. I'm going to let you shoot it, if you like, but not at me. You can aim it down there toward the cliff. If I see that rifle start to swing toward me I'll just have to shoot you."

The kid, baffled, just stared at him.

The man pointed off toward the cliff. You could see the little ore cart down there; you could, if you had good eyesight, make out the two jugs perched on it.

"You see those jugs on the ore cart, son?"

"Yes, sir, if that's what they are."

"Half-gallon clay jugs. You think you can hit those with that rifle?"

The kid stood up and went to the rail of the veranda. He peered down the slope. "That's an awful long way off," he said, half to himself.

"Pret' near half a mile," the man agreed. "Six, seven hundred yards anyhow."

The kid said, "I don't know as how even Wild Bill Hickok could have made a shot like that, sir."

"Well, you can try it if you like."

"I don't see the point."

The man handed the rifle to the woman. Then he drew out his Bisley revolver and stepped over to the pillar that supported the veranda roof.

"I'll show you why," he said, and lifted his left arm straight out from the shoulder and braced his palm against the pillar. Then he twisted his body a little and set his feet firm, and holding the Bisley revolver in his right fist he lowered it until his two wrists were crossed, the left one supporting the right one—the shooter's-rest position. He cocked the revolver and fired it once, almost with careless speed.

Down below at the cliff all three of them plainly saw one of the clay jugs hurtle off its perch on the corner of the ore cart. The jug struck the rocky ground and shattered.

The kid's eyes, big and round, came around slowly to rest on the man. "Lordy. Seven hundred yards—with a *handgun?*"

The man cocked his Bisley revolver again and held it in his right hand pointed more or less at the kid. The woman walked behind the kid and held the rifle out over the railing, pointing it toward the cliff. She was proffering it to the kid. "Go ahead," she said. "You try."

Slowly the kid took the rifle from her. He was careful to make no sudden motions. He got down on one knee and braced his left forearm against the porch railing to steady his aim. He took his time. The man saw him look up toward the sky, trying to judge the elevation and the windage and the range. The kid adjusted the rear sight of the rifle twice before he snugged down to take serious aim.

Finally he was ready and the man saw the kid's finger begin to whiten on the trigger as he squeezed. The kid was all right, the man thought. Knew what he was doing. But then that had been clear from the start—when the kid hadn't tried something foolish at the moment when the man had taken him by surprise back there on the horse. The kid was wise enough to know you didn't fight when the other man had the drop.

The kid squeezed the trigger with professionally unhurried skill and the rifle thundered. The man was watching the cliff and saw the white streak appear on the rocks where the bullet struck.

"Not bad," the man said. "You only missed by about ten feet."

"Lordy," the kid said. He handed the empty rifle back to the woman.

Then the man took his position again and fired a single shot from his Bisley revolver.

They saw the remaining jug shatter.

The light began to fade. The man said, "I did that to show you the first one wasn't a fluke."

The kid swallowed. "I expect I'm kind of overmatched." He wiped his mouth. "I take it right kindly you did it this way. I mean you could've proved the same thing by using me instead of those jugs." He sat down slowly. "You was right. But that old man in the wheelchair, he showed me a warrant. He said it was all fair and legal. He even showed me where it said dead-or-alive."

The woman said, "Likely he didn't show you the date on that warrant, though, did he?"

"I don't recollect that he did, no, ma'am."

The man said, "If you ask at the courthouse when you get home you'll find out those charges expired three years ago."

In the morning they watched the kid ride away to the north. The man packed his Bisley revolver away after he cleaned it. Then he took the woman's hand and they went down to the cliff to start the day's work.

The man picked up the shards of the broken jugs and tossed them on the tailings pile. "It's a good thing he's that young. If he'd been older he'd have known for a fact that you just can't make a shot that far with a handgun. But a fellow that young, you can trick him because he believes what he sees."

The woman smiled. "Well, it wasn't exactly a trick. You still had to aim rock-steady. And figure the wind."

"I waited until there wasn't no wind. If the air's moving you can't do a trick like that."

He'd set up for it four years ago because he'd known they'd keep coming after him. He'd been counting on the statute of limitations; he hadn't reckoned, at the time, on that old man being so obsessed that he'd keep sending bounty men forever. But the trick still worked.

He'd done it by figuring the shot in reverse. He'd made a little notch on the pillar of the veranda and that was where he aimed the revolver from. He'd taken aim at the left side of the spire on top of Longshot Bluff. Then he'd taken aim at the right side of it. Then he'd gone down the hill and marked the spots where the two bullets had struck. After that, all he had to do was set up his two targets on exactly those spots. If there wasn't any wind, all you had to do was aim at one side of the spire or the other. You'd hit the same spots every time.

It had fooled the kid, of course, because it hadn't occurred to the kid that there was a fixed aiming point. The kid had had to guess the drop of his bullet over a seven-hundred-yard range. He'd guessed pretty close, matter of fact, but it hadn't been close enough.

The man was pleased with it. Because all the time he'd been a gun-handler by profession he'd managed to do it without ever killing a man. He'd arrested a lot of them and he'd shot a few, but none of them fatally. He wasn't about to let a bitter old fool in a wheelchair make a killer out of him at this time of his life.

"Q"

P. G. Wodehouse

Death at the Excelsior

The room was the typical bedroom of the typical boardinghouse, furnished, insofar as it could be said to be furnished at all, with a severe simplicity. In contained two beds, a pine chest of drawers, a strip of faded carpet, and a wash basin. But there was that on the floor which set this room apart from a thousand rooms of the same kind. Flat on his back, with his hands tightly clenched and one leg twisted oddly under him and with his teeth gleaming through his gray beard in a horrible grin, Captain John Gunner stared up at the ceiling with eyes that saw nothing.

Until a moment before, he had had the little room all to himself. But now two people were standing just inside the door, looking down at him. One was a large policeman, who twisted his helmet nervously in his hands. The other was a tall gaunt old woman in a rusty black dress, who gazed with pale eyes at the dead man. Her face was quite expressionless.

The woman was Mrs. Pickett, owner of the Excelsior boardinghouse. The policeman's name was Grogan. He was a genial giant, a terror to the riotous element of the waterfront, but obviously ill at ease in the presence of death. He drew in his breath, wiped his forehead, and whispered, "Look at his eyes, ma'am!"

Mrs. Pickett had not spoken a word since she had brought the policeman into the room, and she did not do so now. Constable Grogan looked at her quickly. He was afraid of Mother Pickett, as was everybody else along the waterfront. Her silence, her pale eyes, and the quiet decisiveness of her personality cowed even the tough old salts who patronized the Excelsior. She was a formidable influence in that little community of sailormen.

"That's just how I found him," said Mrs. Pickett. She did not speak loudly, but her voice made the policeman start.

He wiped his forehead again. "It might have been apoplexy," he hazarded.

Mrs. Pickett said nothing. There was a sound of footsteps outside, and a young man entered, carrying a black bag.

"Good morning, Mrs. Pickett. I was told that—good Lord!" The young doctor dropped to his knees beside the body and raised one of the arms. After a moment he lowered it gently to the floor and shook his head in grim resignation.

"He's been dead for hours," he announced. "When did you find him?"

"Twenty minutes back," replied the old woman. "I guess he died last night. He never would be called in the morning. Said he liked to sleep on. Well, he's got his wish."

"What did he die of, sir?" asked the policeman.

"It's impossible to say without an examination," the doctor answered. "It looks like a stroke, but I'm pretty sure it isn't. It might be a coronary attack, but I happen to know his blood pressure was normal, and his heart sound. He called in to see me only a week ago and I examined him thoroughly. But sometimes you can be deceived. The inquest will tell us."

He eyed the body almost resentfully. "I can't understand it. The man had no right to drop dead like this. He was a tough old sailor who ought to have been good for another twenty years. If you want my honest opinion—though I can't possibly be certain until after the inquest—I should say he had been poisoned."

"How would he be poisoned?" asked Mrs. Pickett quietly.

"That's more than I can tell you. There's no glass about that he could have drunk it from. He might have got it in capsule form. But why should he have done it? He was always a pretty cheerful sort of man, wasn't he?"

"Yes, sir," said the constable. "He had the name of being a joker in these parts. Kind of sarcastic, they tell me, though he never tried it on me."

"He must have died quite early last night," said the doctor. He turned to Mrs. Pickett. "What's become of Captain Muller? If he shares this room he ought to be able to tell us something."

"Captain Muller spent the night with some friends at Portsmouth," said Mrs. Pickett. "He left right after supper, and hasn't returned."

The doctor stared thoughtfully about the room, frowning.

"I don't like it. I can't understand it. If this had happened in India I should have said the man had died from some form of snake bite. I was out there two years, and I've seen a hundred cases of it. The poor devils all looked just like this. But the thing's ridiculous. How could a man be bitten by a snake in a Southampton waterfront boardinghouse? Was the door locked when you found him, Mrs. Pickett?"

Mrs. Pickett nodded. "I opened it with my own key. I had been calling to him and he didn't answer, so I guessed something was wrong."

The constable spoke, "You ain't touched anything, ma'am? They're always very particular about that. If the doctor's right and there's been anything up, that's the first thing they'll ask."

"Everything's just as I found it."

"What's that on the floor beside him?" the doctor asked.

"Only his harmonica. He liked to play it of an evening in his room. I've had some complaints about it from some of the gentlemen, but I never saw any harm, so long as he didn't play it too late."

"Seems as if he was playing it when—it happened," Constable Grogan said. "That don't look much like suicide, sir."

"I didn't say it was suicide."

Grogan whistled. "You don't think—"

"I'm not thinking anything—until after the inquest. All I say is that it's queer."

Another aspect of the matter seemed to strike the policeman. "I guess this ain't going to do the Excelsior any good, ma'am," he said sympathetically.

Mrs. Pickett shrugged.

"I suppose I had better go and notify the coroner," said the doctor.

He went out, and after a momentary pause the policeman followed. Constable Grogan was not greatly troubled with nerves, but he felt a decided desire to be where he could not see the dead man's staring eyes.

Mrs. Pickett remained where she was, looking down at the still form on the floor. Her face was expressionless, but inwardly she was tormented and alarmed. It was the first time such a thing as this had happened at the Excelsior, and, as Constable Grogan had suggested, it was not likely to increase the attractiveness of the house in the eyes of possible boarders. It was not the threatened pecuniary loss which was troubling her. As far as money was concerned, she could have lived comfortably on her savings, for she was richer than most of her friends supposed. It was the blot on the escutcheon of the Excelsior, the stain on its reputation, which was tormenting her.

The Excelsior was her life. Starting many years before, beyond the memory of the oldest boarder, she had built up a model establishment. Men spoke of it as a place where you were fed well, cleanly housed, and where petty robbery was unknown.

Such was the chorus of praise that it is not likely that much harm could come to the Excelsior from a single mysterious death, but Mother Pickett was not consoling herself with that.

She looked at the dead man with pale grim eyes. Out in the hallway the doctor's voice further increased her despair. He was talking to the police on the telephone, and she could distinctly hear his every word.

The offices of Mr. Paul Snyder's Detective Agency in New Oxford Street had grown in the course of a dozen years from a single room to an impressive suite bright with polished wood, clicking typewriters, and other evidences of success. Where once Mr. Snyder had sat and waited for clients and attended to them himself, he now sat in his private office and directed eight assistants.

He had just accepted a case—a case that might be nothing at all or something exceedingly big. It was on the latter possibility that he had gambled. The fee offered was, judged by his present standards of prosperity, small. But the bizarre facts, coupled with something in the personality of the client, had won him over. He briskly touched the bell and requested that Mr. Oakes should be sent in to him.

Elliott Oakes was a young man who both amused and interested Mr. Snyder, for though he had only recently joined the staff, he made no secret of his intention of revolutionizing the methods of the agency. Mr. Snyder himself, in common with most of his assistants, relied for results on hard work and common sense. He had never been a detective of the showy type. Results had justified his methods, but he was perfectly aware that young Mr. Oakes looked on him as a dull old man who had been miraculously favored by luck.

Mr. Snyder had selected Oakes for the case in hand principally because it was one where inexperience could do no harm, and where the brilliant guesswork which Oakes preferred to call his inductive reasoning might achieve an unexpected success.

Another motive actuated Mr. Snyder. He had a strong suspicion that the conduct of this case was going to have the beneficial result of lowering Oakes's self-esteem. If failure achieved this end, Mr. Snyder felt that failure, though it would not help the agency, would not be an unmixed ill.

The door opened and Oakes entered tensely. He did everything tensely, partly from a natural nervous energy, and partly as a pose. He was a lean young man, with dark eyes and a thin-lipped mouth, and he looked quite as much like a typical detective as Mr. Snyder looked like a comfortable and prosperous stockbroker.

"Sit down, Oakes," said Mr. Snyder. "I've got a job for you."

Oakes sank into a chair like a crouching leopard and placed the tips of his fingers together. He nodded curtly. It was part of his pose to be keen and silent.

"I want you to go to this address"—Mr. Snyder handed him an envelope—"and look around. The address is of a sailors' boarding-house down in Southampton. You know the sort of place—retired sea captains and so on live there. All most respectable. In all its history nothing more sensational has ever happened than a case of suspected cheating at halfpenny nap. Well, a man has died there."

"Murdered?" Oakes asked.

"I don't know. That's for you to find out. The coroner left it open. 'Death by Misadventure' was the verdict, and I don't blame him. I don't see how it could have been murder. The door was locked on the inside, so nobody could have got in."

"The window?"

"The window was open, granted. But the room is on the second floor. Anyway, you may dismiss the window. I remember the old lady saying there were bars across it, and that nobody could have squeezed through."

Oakes's eyes glistened. "What was the cause of death?" he asked.

Mr. Snyder coughed. "Snake bite," he said.

Oakes's careful calm deserted him. He uttered a cry of astonishment. "Why, that's incredible!"

"It's the literal truth. The medical examination proved that the fellow had been killed by snake poison—cobra, to be exact, which is found principally in India."

"Cobra!"

"Just so. In a Southampton boardinghouse, in a room with a door locked on the inside, this man was stung by a cobra. To add a little mystification to the limpid simplicity of the affair, when the door was opened there was no sign of any cobra. It couldn't have got out through the door, because the door was locked. It couldn't have got out of the window, because the window was too high up, and snakes can't jump. And it couldn't have got up the chimney, because there was no chimney. So there you have it."

He looked at Oakes with a certain quiet satisfaction. It had come to his ears that Oakes had been heard to complain of the infantile nature of the last two cases to which he had been assigned. He had even said that he hoped someday to be given a problem which should be beyond the reasoning powers of a child of six. It seemed to Mr. Snyder that Oakes was about to get his wish.

"I should like further details," said Oakes, a little breathlessly.

"You had better apply to Mrs. Pickett, who owns the boarding-house," Mr. Snyder said. "It was she who put the case in my hands. She is convinced that it is murder. But if we exclude ghosts, I don't see how any third party could have taken a hand in the thing at all. However, she wanted a man from this agency, and was prepared to pay for him, so I promised her I would send one. It is not our policy to turn business away."

He smiled wryly. "In pursuance of that policy I want you to go and put up at Mrs. Pickett's boardinghouse and do your best to enhance the reputation of our agency. I would suggest that you pose as a ship's chandler or something of that sort. You will have to be something maritime or they'll be suspicious of you. And if your visit produces no other results, it will, at least, enable you to make the acquaintance of a very remarkable woman. I commend Mrs. Pickett to your notice. By the way, she says she will help you in your investigations."

Oakes laughed shortly. The idea amused him.

"It's a mistake to scoff at amateur assistance, my boy," said Mr. Snyder in the benevolently paternal manner which had made a score of criminals refuse to believe him a detective until the moment when the handcuffs snapped on their wrists. "Crime investigation isn't an exact science. Success or failure depends in a large measure on applied common sense and the possession of a great deal of special information. Mrs. Pickett knows certain things which neither you nor I know, and it's just possible that she may have some stray piece of information which will provide the key to the entire mystery."

Oakes laughed again. "It is very kind of Mrs. Pickett," he said, "but I prefer to trust to my own methods." Oakes rose, his face purposeful. "I'd better be starting at once," he said. "I'll send you reports from time to time."

"Good. The more detailed the better," said Mr. Snyder genially. "I hope your visit to the Excelsior will be pleasant. And cultivate Mrs. Pickett. She's worthwhile."

The door closed, and Mr. Snyder lighted a fresh cigar. Dashed young fool, he thought and turned his mind to other matters.

A day later Mr. Snyder sat in his office reading a typewritten report. It appeared to be of a humorous nature, for, as he read, chuckles escaped him. Finishing the last sheet he threw his head back and laughed heartily. The manuscript had not been intended by its author for a humorous effect. What Mr. Snyder had been reading was the first of Elliott Oakes's reports from the Excelsior. It read as follows:

"I am sorry to be unable to report any real progress. I have formed several theories which I will put forward later, but at present I cannot say that I am hopeful.

"Directly I arrived I sought out Mrs. Pickett, explained who I was, and requested her to furnish me with any further information which might be of service to me. She is a strange silent woman, who impressed me as having very little intelligence. Your suggestion that I should avail myself of her assistance seems more curious than ever now that I have seen her.

"The whole affair seems to me at the moment of writing quite inexplicable. Assuming that this Captain Gunner was murdered, there appears to have been no motive for the crime whatsoever. I have made careful inquiries about him, and find that he was a man of 55; had spent nearly 40 years of his life at sea, the last dozen in command of his own ship; was of a somewhat overbearing disposition, though with a fund of rough humour; he had travelled all over the world, and had been a resident of the Excelsior for about ten months. He had a small annuity, and no other money at all, which disposes of money as the motive for the crime.

"In my character of James Burton, a retired ship's chandler, I have mixed with the other boarders, and have heard all they have to say about the affair. I gather that the deceased was by no means popular. He appears to have had a bitter tongue, and I have not met one man who seems to regret his death. On the other hand, I have heard nothing which would suggest that he had any active and violent enemies. He was simply the unpopular boarder—there is always one in every boardinghouse—but nothing more.

"I have seen a good deal of the man who shared his room—another sea captain named Muller. He is a big silent person, and it is not easy to get him to talk. As regards the death of Captain Gunner he can tell me nothing. It seems that on the night of the tragedy he was away at Portsmouth. All I have got from him is some information as to Captain Gunner's habits, which leads nowhere.

"The dead man seldom drank, except at night when he would take some whisky. His head was not strong, and a little of the spirit was enough to make him semi-intoxicated, when he would be hilarious and often insulting. I gather that Muller found him a difficult room-mate, but he is one of those placid persons who can put up with anything. He and Gunner were in the habit of playing draughts together every night in their room, and Gunner had a harmonica which he played frequently. Apparently he was playing it very soon before he died, which is significant, as seeming to dispose of any idea of suicide.

"As I say, I have one or two theories, but they are in a very nebulous state. The most plausible is that on one of his visits to India—I have ascertained that he made several voyages there—Captain Gunner may in some way have fallen foul of the natives. The fact that he certainly died of the poison of an Indian snake supports this theory. I am making inquiries as to the movements of several Indian sailors who were here in their ships at the time of the tragedy.

"I have another theory. Does Mrs. Pickett know more about this affair than she appears to? I may be wrong in my estimate of her mental qualities. Her apparent stupidity may be cunning. But here again, the absence of motive brings me up against a dead wall. I must confess that at present I do not see my way clearly. However, I will write again shortly."

Mr. Snyder derived the utmost enjoyment from the report. He liked the substance of it, and above all he was tickled by the bitter tone of frustration which characterized it. Oakes was baffled, and his knowledge of Oakes told him that the sensation of being baffled was gall and wormwood to that high-spirited young man. Whatever might be the result of this investigation, it would teach him the virtue of patience.

He wrote his assistant a short note:

"Dear Oakes,

"Your report received. You certainly seem to have got the hard case which, I hear, you were pining for. Don't build too much on plausible motives in a case of this sort. Fauntleroy, the London murderer, killed a woman for no other reason than that she had thick ankles. Many years ago I myself was on a case where a man murdered an intimate friend because of a dispute about a bet. My experience is that five murderers out of ten act on the whim of the moment, without anything which, properly speaking, you could call a motive at all.

Yours very cordially,
Paul Snyder

P.S. I don't think much of your Pickett theory. However, you're in charge. I wish you luck."

Young Mr. Oakes was not enjoying himself. For the first time in his life the self-confidence which characterized all his actions seemed to be failing him. The change had taken place almost overnight. The fact that the case had the appearance of presenting the unusual had merely stimulated him at first. But then doubts had crept in and the problem had begun to appear insoluble.

True, he had only just taken it up, but something told him that, for all the progress he was likely to make, he might just as well have been working on it steadily for a month. He was completely baffled. And every moment which he spent in the Excelsior boardinghouse made it clearer to him that that infernal old woman with the pale eyes thought him an incompetent fool. It was that, more than anything, which made him acutely conscious of his lack of success.

His nerves were being sorely troubled by the quiet scorn of Mrs. Pickett's gaze. He began to think that perhaps he had been a shade too self-confident and abrupt in the short interview which he had had with her on his arrival.

As might have been expected, his first act, after his brief interview with Mrs. Pickett, was to examine the room where the tragedy had taken place. The body was gone, but otherwise nothing had been moved.

Oakes belonged to the magnifying-glass school of detection. The first thing he did on entering the room was to make a careful examination of the floor, the walls, the furniture, and the window sill. He would have hotly denied the assertion that he did this because it looked well, but he would have been hard put to it to advance any other reason.

If he discovered anything, his discoveries were entirely negative and served only to deepen the mystery. As Mr. Snyder had said, there was no chimney, and nobody could have entered through the locked door.

There remained the window. It was small, and apprehensiveness, perhaps, of the possibility of burglars had caused the proprietress to make it doubly secure with two iron bars. No human being could have squeezed his way through.

It was late that night that he wrote and dispatched to headquarters the report which had amused Mr. Snyder . . .

Two days later Mr. Snyder sat at his desk, staring with wide unbelieving eyes at a telegram he had just received. It read as follows:

HAVE SOLVED GUNNER MYSTERY. RETURNING. OAKES.

Mr. Snyder narrowed his eyes and rang the bell.

"Send Mr. Oakes to me directly he arrives," he said.

He was pained to find that his chief emotion was one of bitter annoyance. The swift solution of such an apparently insoluble problem would reflect the highest credit of the agency, and there were picturesque circumstances connected with the case which would make it popular with the newspapers and lead to its being given a great deal of publicity.

Yet, in spite of all this, Mr. Snyder was annoyed. He realized now how large a part the desire to reduce Oakes's self-esteem had played with him. He further realized, looking at the thing honestly, that he had been firmly convinced that the young man would not come within a mile of a reasonable solution of the mystery. He had desired only that his failure would prove a valuable educational experience for him. For he believed that failure at this particular point in his career would make Oakes a more valuable asset to the agency.

But now here Oakes was, within a ridiculously short space of time, returning to the fold, not humble and defeated, but triumphant. Mr. Snyder looked forward with apprehension to the young man's probable demeanor under the intoxicating influence of victory.

His apprehensions were well grounded. He had barely finished the third of the series of cigars which, like milestones, marked the progress of his afternoon, when the door opened and young Oakes entered. Mr Snyder could not repress a faint moan at the sight of him. One glance was enough to tell him that his worst fears were realized.

"I got your telegram," said Mr. Snyder.

Oakes nodded. "It surprised you, eh?" he asked.

Mr. Snyder resented the patronizing tone of the question, but he had resigned himself to be patronized, and managed to keep his anger in check.

"Yes," he replied, "I must say it did surprise me. I didn't gather from your report that you had even found a clue. Was it the Indian theory that turned the trick?"

Oakes laughed tolerantly. "Oh, I never really believed that preposterous theory for one moment. I just put it in to round out my report. I hadn't begun to think about the case then—not really think."

Mr Snyder, nearly exploding with wrath, extended his cigar case. "Light up and tell me all about it," he said, controlling his anger.

"Well, I won't say I haven't earned this," said Oakes, puffing away. He let the ash of his cigar fall delicately to the floor—another action which seemed significant to his employer. As a rule his assistants, unless particularly pleased with themselves, used the ashtray.

"My first act on arriving," Oakes said, "was to have a talk with Mrs. Pickett. A very dull old woman."

"Curious. She struck me as rather intelligent."

"Not on your life. She gave me no assistance whatever. I then examined the room where the death had taken place. It was exactly as you described it. There was no chimney, the door had been locked on the inside, and the one window was too high up. At first sight it looked extremely unpromising. Then I had a chat with some of the other boarders. They had nothing of any importance to contribute. Most of them simply gibbered. I then gave up trying to get help from the outside and resolved to rely on my own intelligence."

He smiled triumphantly. "It is a theory of mine, Mr. Snyder, which I have found valuable, that in nine cases out of ten remarkable things don't happen."

"I don't quite follow you there," Mr. Snyder interrupted.

"I will put it another way, if you like. What I mean is that the simplest explanation is nearly always the right one. Consider this case. It seemed impossible that there should have been any reasonable explanation of the man's death. Most men would have worn themselves out guessing at wild theories. If I had started to do that, I should have been guessing now. As it is—here I am. I trusted to my belief that nothing remarkable ever happens, and I won out."

Mr. Snyder sighed softly. Oakes was entitled to a certain amount of gloating, but there could be no doubt that his way of telling a story was downright infuriating.

"I believe in the logical sequence of events. I refuse to accept effects unless they are preceded by causes. In other words, with all due respect to your possibly contrary opinions, Mr. Snyder, I simply decline to believe in a murder unless there was a motive for it. The first thing I set myself to ascertain was—what was the motive for the murder of Captain Gunner? And after thinking it over and making every possible inquiry, I decided that there was no motive. Therefore, there was no murder."

Mr. Snyder's mouth opened, and he obviously was about to protest. But he appeared to think better of it and Oakes proceeded: "I then tested the suicide theory. What motive was there for suicide? There was no motive. Therefore, there was no suicide."

This time Mr. Snyder spoke. "You haven't been spending the last few days in the wrong house by any chance, have you? You will be telling me next that there wasn't any dead man."

Oakes smiled. "Not at all. Captain John Gunner was dead, all right. As the medical evidence proved, he died of the bite of a cobra. It was a small cobra which came from Java."

Mr. Snyder stared at him. "How do you know?"

"I do know, beyond any possibility of doubt."

"Did you see the snake?"

Oakes shook his head.

"Then, how in heaven's name—"

"I have enough evidence to make a jury convict Mr. Snake without leaving the box."

"Then suppose you tell me this. How did your cobra from Java get out of the room?"

"By the window," replied Oakes impassively.

"How can you possibly explain that? You say yourself that the window was too high up."

"Nevertheless, it got out by the window. The logical sequence of events is proof enough that it was in the room. It killed Captain Gunner there and left traces of its presence outside. Therefore, as the window was the only exit, it must have escaped by that route. Somehow it got out of that window."

"What do you mean—it left traces of its presence outside?"

"It killed a dog in the back yard behind the house," Oakes said. "The window of Captain Gunner's room projects out over it. It is full of boxes and litter and there are a few stunted shrubs scattered about. In fact, there is enough cover to hide any small object like the body of a dog. That's why it was not discovered at first. The maid at the Excelsior came on it the morning after I sent you my report while she was emptying a box of ashes in the yard. It was just an ordinary stray dog without collar or license. The analyst examined the body and found that the dog had died of the bite of a cobra."

"But you didn't find the snake?"

"No. We cleaned out that yard till you could have eaten your breakfast there, but the snake had gone. It must have escaped through the door of the yard, which was standing ajar. That was a couple of days ago, and there has been no further tragedy. In all likelihood it is dead. The nights are pretty cold now, and it would probably have died of exposure."

"But I just don't understand how a cobra got to Southampton," said the amazed Mr. Snyder.

"Can't you guess it? I told you it came from Java."

"How did you know it did?"

"Captain Muller told me. Not directly, but I pieced it together from what he said. It seems that an old shipmate of Captain Gunner's was living in Java. They corresponded, and occasionally this man would send the captain a present as a mark of his esteem. The last present he sent was a crate of bananas. Unfortunately, the snake must have got in unnoticed. That's why I told you the cobra was a small one. Well, that's my case against Mr. Snake, and short of catching him with the goods, I don't see how I could have made out a stronger one. Don't you agree?"

It went against the grain for Mr. Snyder to acknowledge defeat, but he was a fair-minded man, and he was forced to admit that Oakes did certainly seem to have solved the impossible.

"I congratulate you, my boy," he said as heartily as he could. "To be completely frank, when you started out, I didn't think you could do it. By the way, I suppose Mrs. Pickett was pleased?"

"If she was, she didn't show it. I'm pretty well convinced she hasn't enough sense to be pleased at anything. However, she has invited me to dinner with her tonight. I imagine she'll be as boring as usual, but she made such a point of it I had to accept."

For some time after Oakes had gone, Mr. Snyder sat smoking and thinking, in embittered meditation. Suddenly there was brought the card of Mrs. Pickett, who would be grateful if he could spare her a few moments. Mr. Snyder was glad to see Mrs. Pickett. He was a student of character, and she had interested him at their first meeting. There was something about her which had seemed to him unique, and he welcomed this second chance of studying her at close range.

She came in and sat down stiffly, balancing herself on the extreme edge of the chair in which a short while before young Oakes had lounged so luxuriously.

"How are you, Mrs. Pickett?" said Mr. Snyder genially. "I'm very glad that you could find time to pay me a visit. Well, so it wasn't murder after all."

"Sir?"

"I've been talking to Mr. Oakes, whom you met as James Burton," said the detective. "He has told me all about it."

"He told *me* all about it," said Mrs. Pickett dryly.

Mr. Snyder looked at her inquiringly. Her manner seemed more suggestive than her words.

"A conceited, headstrong young fool," said Mrs. Pickett.

It was no new picture of his assistant that she had drawn. Mr. Snyder had often drawn it himself, but at the present juncture it surprised him. Oakes, in his hour of triumph, surely did not deserve this sweeping condemnation.

"Did not Mr. Oakes's solution of the mystery satisfy you, Mrs. Pickett?"

"No."

"It struck me as logical and convincing," Mr. Snyder said.

"You may call it all the fancy names you please, Mr. Snyder. But Mr. Oakes's solution was not the right one."

"Have you an alternative to offer?"

Mrs. Pickett tightened her lips.

"If you have, I should like to hear it."

"You will—at the proper time."

"What makes you so certain that Mr. Oakes is wrong?"

"He starts out with an impossible explanation and rests his whole case on it. There couldn't have been a snake in that room because it couldn't have gotten out. The window was too high."

"But surely the evidence of the dead dog?"

Mrs. Pickett looked at him as if he had disappointed her. "I had always heard *you* spoken of as a man with common sense, Mr. Snyder."

"I have always tried to use common sense."

"Then why are you trying now to make yourself believe that something happened which could not possibly have happened just because it fits in with something which isn't easy to explain?"

"You mean that there is another explanation of the dead dog?" Mr. Snyder asked.

"Not *another*. What Mr. Oakes takes for granted is not an explanation. But there is a common-sense explanation, and if he had not been so headstrong and conceited he might have found it."

"You speak as if you had found it," said Mr. Snyder.

"I have." Mrs. Pickett leaned forward as she spoke, and stared at him defiantly.

Mr. Snyder started. "*You* have?"

"Yes."

"What is it?"

"You will know before tomorrow. In the meantime try and think it out for yourself. A successful and prosperous detective agency like yours, Mr. Snyder, ought to do something in return for a fee."

There was something in her manner so reminiscent of the school-teacher reprimanding a recalcitrant pupil that Mr. Snyder's sense of humor came to his rescue. "We do our best, Mrs. Pickett," he said. "But you mustn't forget that we are only human and cannot guarantee results."

Mrs. Pickett did not pursue the subject. Instead, she proceeded to astonish Mr. Snyder by asking him to swear out a warrant for the arrest of a man known to them both on a charge of murder.

Mr. Snyder's breath was not often taken away in his own office. As a rule he received his clients' communications calmly, strange as they often were. But at her words he gasped. The thought crossed his mind that Mrs. Pickett might be mentally unbalanced.

Mrs. Pickett was regarding him with an unfaltering stare. To all outward appearances she was the opposite of unbalanced. "But you can't swear out a warrant without evidence," he told her.

"I have evidence," she replied firmly.

"Precisely what kind of evidence?" he demanded.

"If I told you now you would think that I was out of my mind."

"But, Mrs. Pickett, do you realize what you are asking me to do? I cannot make this agency responsible for the arbitrary arrest of a man on the strength of a single individual's suspicions. It might ruin me. At the least it would made me a laughingstock."

"Mr. Snyder, you may use your own judgment whether or not to swear out that warrant. You will listen to what I have to say, and you will see for yourself how the crime was committed. If after that you feel that you cannot make the arrest I will accept your decision. I know who killed Captain Gunner," she said. "I knew it from the beginning. But I had no proof. Now things have come to light and everything is clear."

Against his judgment Mr. Snyder was impressed. This woman had the magnetism which makes for persuasiveness.

"It—it sounds incredible." Even as he spoke, he remembered that it had long been a professional maxim of his that nothing was incredible, and he weakened still further.

"Mr. Snyder, I ask you to swear out that warrant."

The detective gave in. "Very well," he said.

Mrs. Pickett rose. "If you will come and dine at my house tonight I think I can prove to you that it will be needed. Will you come?"

"I'll come," promised Mr. Snyder.

Mr. Snyder arrived at the Excelsior and shortly after he was shown into the little private sitting room where he found Oakes, the third guest of the evening unexpectedly arrived.

Mr. Snyder looked curiously at the newcomer. Captain Muller had a peculiar fascination for him. It was not Mr. Snyder's habit to trust overmuch to appearances. But he could not help admitting that there was something about this man's aspect, something odd—an unnatural aspect of gloom. He bore himself like one carrying a heavy burden. His eyes were dull, his face haggard. The next moment the detective was reproaching himself with allowing his imagination to run away with his calmer judgment.

The door opened and Mrs. Pickett came in.

To Mr. Snyder one of the most remarkable points about the dinner was the peculiar metamorphosis of Mrs. Pickett from the brooding silent woman he had known to the gracious and considerate hostess.

Oakes appeared also to be overcome with surprise, so much so that he was unable to keep his astonishment to himself. He had come prepared to endure a dull evening absorbed in grim silence, and he found himself instead opposite a bottle of champagne of a brand and year which commanded his utmost respect. What was even more incredible, his hostess had transformed herself into a pleasant old lady whose only aim seemed to be to make him feel at home.

Beside each of the guest's plates was a neat paper parcel. Oakes picked his up and stared at it in wonderment. "Why, this is more than a party souvenir, Mrs. Pickett," he said. "It's the kind of mechanical marvel I've always wanted to have on my desk."

"I'm glad you like it, Mr. Oakes," Mrs. Pickett said, smiling. "You must not think of me simply as a tired old woman whom age has completely defeated. I am an ambitious hostess. When I give these little parties, I like to make them a success. I want each of you to remember this dinner."

"I'm sure I will."

Mrs. Pickett smiled again. "I think you all will. You, Mr. Snyder." She paused. "And you, Captain Muller."

To Mr. Snyder there was so much meaning in her voice as she

said this that he was amazed that it conveyed no warning to Muller. Captain Muller, however, was already drinking heavily. He looked up when addressed and uttered a sound which might have been taken for an expression of polite acquiescence. Then he filled his glass again.

Mr. Snyder's parcel revealed a watch charm fashioned in the shape of a tiny candid-eye camera. "That," said Mrs. Pickett, "is a compliment to your profession." She leaned toward the captain. "Mr. Snyder is a detective, Captain Muller."

He looked up. It seemed to Mr. Snyder that a look of fear lit up his heavy eyes for an instant. It came and went, if indeed it came at all, so swiftly that he could not be certain. "So?" said Captain Muller. He spoke quite evenly, with just the amount of interest which such an announcement would naturally produce.

"Now for yours, Captain," said Oakes. "I guess it's something special. It's twice the size of mine, anyway."

It may have been something in the old woman's expression as she watched Captain Muller slowly tearing the paper that sent a thrill of excitement through Mr. Snyder. Something seemed to warn him of the approach of a psychological moment. He bent forward eagerly.

There was a strangled gasp, a thump, and onto the table from the captain's hands there fell a little harmonica. There was no mistaking the look on Muller's face now. His cheeks were like wax, and his eyes, so dull till then, blazed with a panic and horror which he could not repress. The glasses on the table rocked as he clutched at the cloth.

Mrs. Pickett spoke. "Why, Captain Muller, has it upset you? I thought that, as his best friend, the man who shared his room, you would value a memento of Captain Gunner. How fond you must have been of him for the sight of his harmonica to be such a shock."

The captain did not speak. He was staring fascinated at the thing on the table. Mrs. Pickett turned to Mr. Snyder. Her eyes, as they met his, held him entranced.

"Mr. Snyder, as a detective, you will be interested in a curious and very tragic affair which happened in this house a few days ago. One of my boarders, Captain Gunner, was found dead in his room. It was the room which he shared with Mr. Muller. I am very proud of the reputation of my house, Mr. Snyder, and it was a blow to me that this should have happened. I applied to an agency for a detective, and they sent me a stupid boy, with nothing to recommend him except his belief in himself. He said that Captain Gunner had died by accident, killed by a snake which had come out of a crate of bananas. I knew better. I knew that Captain Gunner had been murdered. Are you listening, Captain Muller? This will interest you, as you were such a friend of his."

The captain did not answer. He was staring straight before him. as if he saw something invisible in eyes forever closed in death.

"Yesterday we found the body of a dog. It had been killed, as Captain Gunner had been, by the poison of a snake. The boy from the agency said that this was conclusive. He said that the snake had escaped from the room after killing Captain Gunner and had in turn killed the dog. I knew that to be impossible, for, if there had been a snake in that room it could not have made its escape."

Her eyes flashed and became remorselessly accusing. "It was not a snake that killed Captain Gunner. It was a cat. Captain Gunner had a friend who hated him. One day, in opening a crate of bananas, this friend found a snake. He killed it, and extracted the poison. He knew Captain Gunner's habits. He knew that he played a harmonica. This man also had a cat. He knew that cats hated the sound of a harmonica. He had often seen this particular cat fly at Captain Gunner and scratch him when he played. He took the cat and covered its claws with the poison. And then he left the cat in the room with Captain Gunner. He knew what would happen."

Oakes and Mr. Snyder were on their feet. Captain Muller had not moved. He sat there, his fingers gripping the cloth. Mrs. Pickett rose and went to a closet. She unlocked the door. "Kitty!" she called. "Kitty! Kitty!" A black cat ran swiftly out into the room. With a clatter and a crash of crockery and a ringing of glass the table heaved, rocked, and overturned as Muller staggered to his feet. He threw up his hands as if to ward something off. A choking cry came from his lips. "Gott! Gott!"

Mrs. Pickett's voice rang through the room, cold and biting. "Captain Muller, you murdered Captain Gunner!"

The captain shuddered. Then mechanically he replied, "Gott! Yes, I killed him."

"You heard, Mr. Snyder," said Mrs. Pickett. "He has confessed before witnesses."

Muller allowed himself to be moved toward the door. His arm in Mr. Snyder's grip felt limp. Mrs. Pickett stopped and took something from the debris on the floor. She rose, holding the harmonica.

"You are forgetting your souvenir, Captain Muller," she said.

David Ely

Counting Steps

M r. Barrow awoke that morning with the suspicion that he was dying. Even so, being a man of habit, he performed his waking rite of counting the rows of figured squares in the wallpaper pattern between the ceiling and the top of the dresser. Having verified the existence of fourteen rows, as expected, Mr. Barrow sat up, and with slow deliberate movements swung first one leg and then the other over the edge of the bed and down to the floor, where his slippers were as usual pointed in the proper direction.

Once his feet were in the slippers, Mr. Barrow raised his head and saw his wife in the doorway with his tray. He smiled at her, not so much as a morning greeting as a test of his smiling capacity, for a stroke the month before had temporarily paralyzed all the workings on his left side, from head to toe.

The doctor had expressed optimism about the outcome of the case, but Mr. Barrow, being a lawyer, was professionally inclined to doubt, and had accepted only on a provisional basis the evidence of succeeding weeks, in which sensation and movement had returned. He could now get out of bed unaided, and go to the bathroom and back. He could also get dressed by himself, even though he was not yet strong enough to go downstairs.

What had reassured Mr. Barrow most of all was the sheer routine of being a patient. His regimen of medicine, rest, exercise, and nourishment was as regular as the daily schedule which he followed in his profession. Everything was timed to the minute; nothing was left to chance. Sick or well, Mr. Barrow was a prudent man. "If in doubt, don't," he was fond of saying to his clients. Likewise: "Look before you leap"—not that he would ever advise anything like a leap. He would no more go out for lunch ten minutes before the established time than he would attempt an impropriety with the girl who ran the switchboard.

So it was that, having counted the rows in the wallpaper, put on his slippers, and noted the presence of his wife in the doorway, Mr. Barrow was assured that the events of the day—pills, breakfast, exercise, naps—would unfold in their proper order and at their proper time. His death now seemed to him much less likely than it had when he awoke, if only because no provision had been made for such a deviation from his schedule.

At the same time, however, Mr. Barrow recalled with some uneasiness certain remarkable goings-on to which he had been subjected in the past two days. He had not mentioned this problem to his doctor or to his wife, supposing it to be a transitory phenomenon that would soon disappear. But it had not disappeared. He suspected that it was beginning to plague him again today as well, although he couldn't yet be sure, for what seemed to be taking place was confusing, in that it appeared to be part of his routine—or, more exactly, an exaggeration of his routine.

It was almost as if Mr. Barrow's routine had acquired a force and independence of its own, quite apart from his volition. He did not, for example, rise and dress himself until after breakfast, nor did he get dressed more than once a day, and yet he found that he was repeatedly imagining that he was rising, putting on his shirt and trousers, and standing in front of the dresser while he buttoned his cuffs, all so realistically that the first few times it happened he was amazed to discover that he was still in bed, still in his pajamas.

Likewise, he would have the sensation of drinking the water in the glass on the bed table—of drinking it over and over—and yet the glass remained full, and his wife, entering, would remind him to drink it. The actual drinking of the water seemed no more real to him, however, than his imaginary drinkings.

Similarly, he would envision himself turning on the lamp by the bed, or picking up a book, or executing the mild exercises counseled by the doctor—doing these things five, ten, a dozen times, and it was this very repetition that made him wonder if he was doing them at all. The entry of his wife into the room with his medicine or a tray of food also became subject to doubt, for it seemed to him that she entered too frequently, and that if he actually took all the medicine she presented to him, and ate all the food, he would be quite ill indeed.

Even at the present moment, while he sat on the edge of the bed, his feet in his slippers, a smile on his face directed toward his wife in the doorway, Mr. Barrow could not be absolutely certain that he was sitting where he seemed to be sitting, or that he was smiling, or that his wife was in the doorway.

Altogether, Mr. Barrow had the feeling that everything he was accustomed to had undergone a profound transformation while remaining in appearance quite the same as before. It was this treachery of the familiar that disquieted him. He belived that he was lucid in his mind, and that his basic sensory equipment was no longer impaired. Why, then, was there this troubling repetition of routine actions which surely for the most part he was imagining?

He did not want to think about it, and, as was his habit, he reminded himself that the world was a rational world by taking stock of certainties—in this case, he again counted the figured squares in the wallpaper and was gratified to find that there were still fourteen rows between the ceiling and the top of the dresser. But then he realized that he could not count the rows unless he were lying in bed in his waking position, whereas surely he was sitting on the edge of the mattress looking at his wife in the doorway.

To cover his confusion, he said the first thing that came into his mind: "Is it time for my medicine?" Immediately he was overtaken by doubt, for his question evoked no answer from his wife, nor did the expression on her face alter in any way, which indicated either that he had not spoken aloud, or that she hadn't heard him—or that she was not where she seemed to be.

Furthermore, even as he sat (or seemed to sit) on the edge of the bed, he was imagining himself standing at the dresser, buttoning the cuffs of his shirt and idly examining the keys and change that he would shortly slip into his trousers pocket. He was able to count the change: three quarters, a dime, and a penny. At the same time he was aware of his wife in the doorway. She was holding the usual tray, with two slices of toast, a small glass of orange juice, and a saucer on which rested his anti-coagulant capsule.

Mr. Barrow knew that one of these two visual effects was false. Undoubtedly it was the one at the dresser—and yet why hadn't his wife answered his question? And why was she still poised in the doorway? It seemed to him that she had been standing there far too long.

As a lawyer, Mr. Barrow was accustomed to analyze difficult problems by proceeding from one undisputed fact to the next, discarding whatever was irrelevant. But in his present circumstances, there seemed to be no undisputed facts—or rather, there were far too many of them—and he found himself in a tangle of contradictions, unable to determine what was relevant and what was not. He thought of asking his wife to answer the immediate question—what part of the bedroom did he happen to occupy?—and yet he realized that she was apparently part of the illusion problem, so he could not rely on her testimony.

The key to the matter, he reasoned, must be a distortion in his reckoning of time. All those glasses of water—he could very well have drunk every one, not in a matter of minutes (as he had supposed) but over an entire day. Likewise, the remarkable succession of meals and pills could be explained if the period involved were several days instead of the mere hour he had erroneously believed to be the case. Thus, time was slipping by him unnoticed.

On the other hand, his wife's immobility in the doorway suggested a contrary distortion, in which time had slowed or even stopped. Indeed, it seemed to him that her left shoe was very slightly raised off the floor, as though she were completing a step, although his observation of this detail was impaired by the fact (if fact it were) that he was also looking at his slippers to be certain that his feet were properly inside them. This, if true, indicated that he had not yet raised his head or smiled, or even seen his wife in the doorway. To wit, while in some instances he might be losing time, and in considerable quantities, in other cases time seemed to be stationary or, indeed, inching in reverse.

Disquieted by such reflections, Mr. Barrow tried to turn his thoughts to something that would soothe or distract him, and ease his mind. It was a pity he'd stopped collecting stamps. He couldn't even leaf through his old albums, for he'd given them to his nephew. Apart from pottering about in the yard on weekends, he had done nothing with his leisure time except read or watch television or think about his work.

On Sundays he and his wife had gone to church, where by habit he counted the number of fellow-worshippers and estimated the money in the collection plate when it came by. He paid little heed to the sermons except once when the word "judgment" had alerted him professionally, although of course the minister had been talking about the judgments of the Lord.

He was getting dressed again, apparently. There he was, buttoning his cuffs and examining the change and keys he would shortly put into his trousers pocket—except he never did manage to reach the point at which the change and keys were in fact pocketed. Instead, he would find himself back in bed counting the rows of wallpaper squares, or drinking that eternal glass of water, or smiling at his wife, or looking at his slippers, or taking his medicine, or doing all these things more or less simultaneously. It was, quite frankly, irritating in the extreme, and he finally closed his eyes to shut it out.

Thus shielded, Mr. Barrow decided to leave the bedroom, not in a physical sense—which seemed too risky—but in his thoughts, and so he pursued in his imagination the routine he had followed every workday morning for 33 years. He would pocket his change and keys at last, give his suit jacket a quick smoothing, walk out of the room, and descend the seventeen steps to the front hall. In the dining room, his wife would have his breakfast ready, the morning paper neatly folded beside the coffee cup. He always read while he ate.

At 8:23 on the dot he would go out to the curb, where the taxi he shared with a businessman down the block would be waiting. By nine o'clock he would be entering his office building. There were 83 steps through the lobby. He counted them every day in his mind (whenever he found that he took a step more or a step less, he adjusted the count on the next occasion). The elevator would take him sixteen stories up, and then there would be 21 steps along the corridor, fifteen more from the outer door past the switchboard girl to the desk where his secretary sat, and a final twelve paces into his own office.

Having thus abstractly arrived at work, Mr. Barrow proceeded to imagine his normal business day. He examined his mail, already sorted by his secretary, and called her in to dictate responses to the most important items. He then made and received telephone calls, studied various documents, dispatched his clerk to the law library for research, saw clients by appointment, ate his lunch in the little restaurant across the street, circled the block for exercise, and returned to his office for further dictation, telephone calls, and appointments. At 5:37 he presented himself at the corner for the taxi and his return ride home, where he ate supper, watched television, took his bath, and read a book until 11:15, when he turned off his bed lamp.

This evocation of his daily round afforded Mr. Barrow a certain relief. He opened his eyes, found himself lying in bed under the covers, imagined that he had just awakened, and proceeded to count the rows of figured squares in the wallpaper pattern again. There were fourteen rows, as expected, but his satisfaction at having confirmed this unvarying number was qualified by doubt. Hadn't he already awakened—and hadn't he already counted those rows?

He sat up and with slow deliberate movements swung first one leg and then the other over the edge of the bed and down to the floor, but as he inserted his feet into his slippers, he was perturbed by the recollection of having done that very thing just a few seconds before.

Either I was dreaming then or I am dreaming now, thought Mr. Barrow—but he didn't think he was dreaming.

Raising his head, he saw his wife in the doorway. "Is it time for my medicine?" he asked. But his wife was beside the bed now, and he had the glass of water in his hand. He drank it down. His wife had gone, and he was sitting on the edge of the bed again, putting his feet into his slippers.

This will not do, thought Mr. Barrow. Once more he closed his eyes, and in his mind he dressed, turned and left the room, and went down the seventeen steps to the front hall, and so into the dining room for his breakfast, following which he repeated his imaginary progression from taxi to office, pacing off the 83 steps across the lobby, rising the sixteen stories in the elevator, walking the 21 steps along the corridor, and arriving in the usual manner at his desk, where he again examined his mail, called in his secretary for dictation, and went through the other ordinary business of the morning as before.

This second conjuration of his working day was less soothing to Mr. Barrow, although it was exactly like the first, which was to be expected, as he never departed from his established routine. Still, he was vaguely disturbed by it, for he did not have the impression of controlling matters voluntarily. That is, he would have preferred to speed his progress from taxi to office, but it appeared that he had to take those 83 steps through the lobby, just as he felt obliged to remain at his desk until his regular lunchtime.

Mr. Barrow chafed under these apparent restrictions, which seemed excessive, as he was at work only in his imagination, and should be free, therefore, to do as he pleased—to go out to lunch early or fly to the moon, for that matter. He considered attempting to assert his independence, but caution forestalled him. Suppose he sought to leave his desk but could not do so? A pretty kettle of fish that would be, reflected Mr. Barrow. Better not try.

And so he remained where he had imagined himself to be, dutifully completing the rest of the day, which seemed to require hours, even though he supposed it was accomplished in a few seconds, for according to his best reckoning, in the space of time necessary for him to sit up in bed, swing his legs over the edge, put on his slippers, and smile at his wife, he had, in fantasy, drunk a gallon of water, got himself dressed six or seven times, and put in two full working days at the office.

He reopened his eyes. Yes, he was sitting on the edge of the bed, putting his feet into his slippers. He closed his eyes again—and immediately imagined himself pocketing his change and keys, ready to go downstairs for another breakfast. Mr. Barrow began to feel considerably vexed. Was he to have no peace from this? He wondered again, with some irritation, if he were dying—or if, in fact, this were his last instant of consciousness, in which shifting images were contending for his fading attention.

Unlikely, thought Mr. Barrow. A dying man would surely experience some sort of emotional profundity—awe, joy, perhaps terror—whereas he was more annoyed than anything else by the repetition of the trivial actions which he was (or was not) engaged in.

Besides, if he were dying, he would probably recall scenes of his formative years—his home, his parents, his childhood—and all he could force into his mind was a recollection of himself as a boy walking to school, counting the paces from one block to the next, being careful not to step on the cracks in the sidewalk. Mr. Barrow remembered that there were 137 steps on Grove Avenue between Pine and Walnut, and that in the middle of the block he had had to execute a complicated maneuver where the damaged pavement presented a network of cracks. In front of the church the sidewalk was paved with brick, so he'd had to do a sort of toe-dance there. Cracks were bad luck, especially in front of a church. Judgments of the Lord. And then from Walnut to Oak, there were 83 steps—no, it was 83 across the lobby, which he now seemed to be pacing off.

He was going to work again.

Mr. Barrow opened his eyes. His wife was no longer in the doorway. She was beside the bed, preparing to remove his tray. "Am I still alive?" Mr. Barrow said. He could hear his voice. It sounded fussy, as if he were asking why she hadn't brought the morning paper.

She didn't answer him. She was gone, and he was flexing his left leg the way the doctor had instructed him to do. He was walking around the room in his bathrobe. His wife was in the doorway with the tray. "Is it time for my medicine?" Mr. Barrow asked. He was at the dresser, buttoning his cuffs, and idly examining the change and keys that he would shortly slip into his trousers pocket. He closed his eyes, and descended the seventeen steps to the front hall.

"Am I still alive?" he asked. "Am I still? Am I?"

He sought to think of eternal things. Where was the awe, the terror? The taxi came at 8:23 every morning without fail. He stepped off the curb with care, look before you leap, avoid the cracks, the judgments.

He reached out for the glass of water on the bed table——his wife was in the doorway——he was at the dresser——21 steps along the corridor——his slippers were as usual pointed in the proper direction——swung first one leg and then the other over—drank the glass of water—called in the secretary for dictation—dispatched the clerk—sat up in bed and with slow deliberate the judgments of the Lord swung first one through the lobby to the elevator descended the seventeen sat up in bed the doorway the dresser the steps the judgments of the Lord of the Lord of the of

Mary   McMullen

Her   Heart's   Home

At ten o'clock on the sunny morning of that terrible day in March, Miss Rounce felt herself more than justified in taking ten minutes to relax at her desk with a cup of coffee.

Her world was in perfect order. Mr. Caudrey's great teak desktop was immaculately clear of papers, his telephone was serenely silent. He had flown off to his week in the sun in Jamaica—Miss Rounce smiled to herself as she mixed metaphors—on greased rails.

She had not only made all his travel arrangements, managed to get him in at his favorite hotel even though they said at first they were full; she had also, over a quiet lunch, made up Mrs. Caudrey's wavering mind for her.

Yes, much wiser to skip Jamaica this time, the sun did such disastrous things to the skin; better a week at that luscious spa in Texas . . . why, Mrs. Caudrey wouldn't know herself, and certainly Mr. Caudrey wouldn't know her, when they met again.

She had canceled and rebooked dentist's and doctor's appointments, as he had only made up his mind to go away last week. She'd had the lock on his alligator suitcase repaired, tracked down a pale-peach broadcloth shirt to replace the one with the collar just beginning to fray where it rubbed against his tie. She had filled his office flask with Canadian Club, from the hidden swinging bar in the teak paneling, and tucked it into his attaché case along with four paperbacks by his favorite mystery novelists, titles he hadn't read before. She had checked over his pills, added a big bottle of Vitamin E. And had deliberately not minded, had given him a brave cheerful smile, when he said a peculiar hasty goodbye, hardly even looking at her.

Excuses for this came readily to mind. He was being pressed on all sides. Philip Caudrey was president of Hope & Hayes Pharmaceuticals, still young, mid-forties, handsome, vital, popular. But being pushed, nevertheless, by that blowsy-haired boy Alec Mortimer, who was making such a big thing of the cosmetics division. And under attack from the board because of business conditions which certainly Mr. *Caudrey* had no control over. No wonder he wanted to get away, rest a bit, and regather his forces.

We'll get through, Miss Rounce thought, sipping her coffee. She had been his secretary for the past 13 of her 25 years with the company. Up with him, from District Sales Manager, to Vice President in charge of Sales, to President, the office he had held now for five years.

Perhaps another cup of coffee, and then the boy would be around with the 10:15 mail.

The door of Mr. Caudrey's office opened and two strange men walked in, one dark, one fair, both in Miss Rounce's opinion rather peculiarly dressed. She sat in her own small comfortable room off the big sunswept office. There were folding doors between, but he liked them kept open.

"Can't close the doors on my eyes and ears and memory, Maria, now can I?" he would say.

Feeling a little as if the privacy of her own home had been invaded, she rose from her desk and went over to the men.

"Yes? Can I help you?"

The dark one gave her an abstracted glance and continued in midsentence.

"—I see a magnificent dark-cave effect, aubergine vinyl walls, no daylight whatever—"

"I *beg* your pardon!" Miss Rounce commanded. She was a compact woman of medium height; her upright stance made her seem taller. Her pink face, going a bit to jowl, was pinker with indignation. "I am Mr. Caudrey's secretary. Will you please tell me what you are doing here?"

"Larrup Design Consultants, ma'am," the fair one said. "Doing over the office. Didn't your boss tell you? And your little room there"—he walked into it and looked over his shoulder at the other man—"all white? Crazy contrast? Think of it as a surprise extension of his office? A mirrored wall maybe with an etagère, tons of gorgeous green stuff, almost a conservatory effect?"

Her office. *Her* office, her place of being, bandied between these two strangers. Something began to beat in Miss Rounce's throat like a misplaced heart. The fair man's eyes, resting on her horn-rimmed glasses, gleaming little beaked nose, crisp curly graying hair, no doubt accurately figuring her age as 50 or thereabouts, thinking, *You* don't go with the mirror and the etagère . . .

It was a relief in a way when one of her two assistants, Minnie-May, who was in charge of the files, poked her lavender-blonde head in at the door.

"Mr. Fenelli would like to see you, Miss Rounce. At your earliest possible convenience, he said."

At any other time Miss Rounce would have said, "Indeed? Then tell him he knows where to find me." But better, for the moment, to get away from this upsetting silliness and try to sort things out. Would Mr. Caudrey have arranged for redecorating without consulting her?

Hardly. Fenelli might be able to enlighten her.

She glanced over her shoulder as she left, a loving look that stabbed her, at the fine old ivory and gold Kirman, the glow of teak, the soft rose brocade at the windows, the motionless swift white model under glass of Mr. Caudrey's sloop Valkyrie, the photographs in silver frames, one of them, the youngest girl, named Elizabeth Rounce Caudrey for her godmother. Was it all, then, to be violated, her heart's home?

Or maybe—with a delightful secret surge of feeling as she strode upright down the long bright corridor and around the corner—maybe he meant it as a great big marvelous surprise for her.

She knocked at the closed door, studying, during the annoying ten seconds she was kept waiting, the little white-lettered black label: Ronald Fenelli, Personnel Manager. Ronald indeed. Rocco more likely. Next thing you knew it would be Ronald Fennell. Just two more seconds and she would turn and go.

"Come in," Fenelli said, opening the door. "Sit down, Miss Rounce."

She thought afterward that she must have heard at the time every word he said to her, from his swift opening: "I have a most unpleasant duty to perform. I must tell you that effective immediately you are to be separated from the company . . ."

But, always, only faraway bits and pieces remained, like half-caught phrases carried by the wind from some distant hill. ". . . cutting back . . . long and honorable service . . . our executives putting themselves on a budget . . . after your position, naturally you wouldn't want to consider . . . pension on the basis of early retirement, not the larger sum, but . . ."

In the middle of the floating phrases the crystal vision striking. New office like "a magnificent cave," new secretary's office like a conservatory, new secretary, shining and young, to match . . .

". . . as of two weeks from today . . . of course, you may come in if you please and use the office—not Caudrey's, it's about to be torn apart, but I'm sure we can find you a cozy cubbyhole where you can use the phone and so on . . . on the other hand . . . embarrassment . . . Minnie-May can pack up everything of yours, bring it to your place . . ."

A tremor started deep inside Miss Rounce; then, to her horror, she began to shake. Her head shook. Her cheeks shook. Her voice shook. Her hands shook.

"But, what have I *done?* Twenty-five years—" It was not her voice at all.

Fenelli sighed and then smiled harshly.

"Don't make it hard for me, Miss Rounce. This is off the record, and don't quote me, and if you do I'll deny it. You're a woman of the world. Youth's the story today. We must make way. We must make way. You've had your turn, now haven't you? You said it yourself. Twenty-five years."

He stood up, warily eyeing her, waiting, she knew, for some awful, some shaming explosion. One thing that kept her from it, in addition to a quality of iron in her, was the cold knowledge that he was thoroughly enjoying himself.

She stood up, turned, walked out of the office, and closed the door behind her.

Around a corner, from the door of the typing pool, she heard a high young voice cresting on a giggle, "The Rounce has been bounced!"

Shortly before eleven o'clock Miss Rounce, pale, erect, a poisonous, dangerous bag of pain and hatred, went out for the last time through the revolving doors of Hope & Hayes Pharmaceuticals.

She lost the next three days more or less completely out of her life. She slept a lot, day and night, like someone recovering from, or contracting, some dreadful disease. She supposed later that she must have eaten and drunk now and then: the teacup in the sink, the soup can at the bottom of the brown paper bag in the little yellow garbage can.

Occasionally the telephone rang, unanswered.

There had been flashes of all-too-coherent thought. Of course, that was why Mr. Caudrey had suddenly decided to go to Jamaica. He didn't want to be around when his faithful secretary was dumped, canned, got rid of, fired. That was why he'd hardly looked at her when he said his nasty strange goodbye. He couldn't bear to regard poor doomed Miss Rounce. And it must—bite savagely at the aching tooth—must have been he who said she must go. New offices, new image, new man, to fight back at 29-year-old Alec Mortimer, the hairy terrier snapping at the heels of his glossy English shoes.

Was it dreaming, was it waking, that the darkness had rushed into her mind? *She would somehow fix Mr. Caudrey, Mr. President Philip Caudrey. She would fix Fenelli too, his willing, enjoying instrument. How?*

On the morning of the fourth day she got out of her tossed damp bed. She showered, combed her tangled hair, dressed, and remade the bed with taut immaculate white sheets and a fresh white blanket and a starched white eyelet bedspread. Maidenly, maidenly, she thought. Why did I work so hard all those years? Why did I never sin?

She made herself do an almost impossibly hard thing. It was something she had to know, before—

She called Hope & Hayes and asked for Mabel Ross in Accounting, an old and trusted friend. She cut across Mabel's where-have-you-been and I've-been-trying-to-reach-you.

"I can't talk now, Mabel, I'm on my way out—but tell me, what's my replacement like?"

Concerned, reluctant voice. "Oh, you know, the kind they stamp out by the thousands now. Long straight blonde hair. Ridiculous huge pink sunglasses. Legs like a—like a heron. I tell you, Maria, I'm in such a rage. I found out she'd been hired by *him,* Caudrey, last week and was just sort of waiting in the wings—"

"Call you soon," Miss Rounce said, hanging up. Her face was expressionless; there could be no further hurt when you hit the bottom of pain.

She found herself responding to a schedule that someone else seemed to have thought out for her. She went out and bought groceries. She bundled up the laundry and left it outside her apartment door. She washed, dried, and put away the few cups and dishes in the kitchen. She made a pot of hot strong tea and took it to the typing table she kept set up in her bedroom.

Often, on weekends, she did typing chores for Mr. Caudrey. Articles for trade newspapers—for which she did all the research—personal letters he didn't want to bother with, his address to the graduating class of Morningtown College. The machine on the table was new, bought only last month, an electric; it wouldn't do to have a comma the least bit out of alignment in anything she typed for Mr. Caudrey. She hadn't as yet, in fact, used the new machine. Good. Not that it could possibly come to that.

She closed her eyes in concentration, to collect the odds and ends. A half-heard telephone call to South Carolina, an order to the florist, an accidental glimpse of two figures ducking through the rain into his Mercedes. She hadn't been jealous, when to her all-seeing eye the odds and ends formed themselves into an unmistakable pattern; indeed, she felt a certain vicarious pleasure in the sheer brigandage of it, right under the nose of the Chairman of the Board, and his second wife at that, only married two years ago.

After pulling on a pair of thin white nylon gloves, she began typing. No formal salutation. Not in a letter like this.

"Dear Phillip (he always misspelled, on memos, Mr. Caudrey's first name): I will make this brief and to the point. Dossiers, you know, are more or less my business and I have a complete one on you and Cecelia Hayes—or shall we call her Cissie? Do you, for instance, recall a weekend in Charleston, South Carolina, at the Bluebird Motel? Six dozen white roses delivered to her house the day after Holy Joe Hayes left for the conference in the Virgin Islands? And so on, friend, and so on.

"You're feeling the hot breath of Mortimer and I'm feeling the same from Skillington, who questions some of my interviewing practices with young girls, quite unfairly, I may add. But as my tenure here may not be indefinite, I must make plans. I want from you, in exchange for my dossier, $50,000, which will be acceptable in five installments—cash, of course—the first to be placed in my mailbox at home no later than 6 o'clock on Monday. I'll let you know the dates for the other payments. As you may or may not know, I start my vacation Monday and will not be at the office; but I do assure you that your offering will be picked up. As ever, Ronnie F."

Miss Rounce did very well with the scrawled signature. She had had to learn to do Mr. Caudrey's, too, so that no one could tell the difference, the time he'd suffered from a pinched nerve and a resulting wrist malfunction. She addressed the envelope to Mr. Phillip Caudrey, 108 Chancery Road, stamped it, put it in her handbag, and reached thirstily for her now half-warm tea.

She would drop the letter, after business hours on Friday, through the mail slot of the main post office. On examination it could be seen not to have been typed on Fenelli's own machine in the office, but presumably on his typewriter at home. Not that it would come to that. Not if she knew Mr. Caudrey. The letter would be destroyed instantly. And then—

A man of powerful rages. And sudden, strong, unhesitating action.

In the meantime there was a little exploratory work to be done. It had been three years since she with most of the executive staff had gone to a large cocktail party at Fenelli's. She got her compact from the parking lot at the rear of the apartment and drove through the pleasant Pennsylvania city-town to a near southern suburb, just now beginning to be developed.

At the bend of a lane lined on both sides with birches was Fenelli's low white-brick ranch house, trim March-drab lawn in front, great shadowy groves of pine trees nodding in the wind on either side of the house and behind it. The lane angled at the house, turned left, and ambled past it to join a main road a quarter of a mile away.

Miss Rounce drove along it slowly, pleased with the anonymity of her sensible black car. That path, through the fir trees—glancing up it, she could see the wink of glass in a window, the edge of a low roof. A secret, silently pine-needled path.

Fenelli, she knew, kept no servants. A cleaning woman came in once a week—a woman he had got from Mabel Ross, and who enjoyed talking about one employer to another. There was no Mrs. Fenelli in the house among the pines; he was divorced. At the start of his vacation he would, if he followed past habit, spend Monday at home lazing, packing, and closing up the house, then leave on Tuesday morning for Vail. Fenelli was a dedicated skier.

His reservations were all in order for Tuesday, Miss Rounce learned, when she called to check with the airline.

Mr. Caudrey would be back on Sunday afternoon, late. He would have the house to himself; Mrs. Caudrey was not due back until Monday. He would change his clothes, pour a drink—call Cissie Hayes? Holy Joe Hayes had to go to Memphis for a weekend seminar he was addressing. Yes, call Cissie—then he would go leisurely through his mail.

I'd say between seven and eight, Miss Rounce thought. When it gets dark . . .

If Fenelli was out somewhere Sunday night, then Monday night.

Waiting for the three days to spend themselves, she felt odd, lightheaded. Torn from the routine of 25 years, she didn't quite know what to do with her hands and feet and body. Looking in the mirror, she felt an uncertainty as to who she was. If she was not Maria Rounce, Mr. Caudrey's invaluable executive secretary, the silently purring engine that ran his world, then who was she?

But now, on this thinly raining Sunday as darkness fell, this woman had plans, had things to do.

At six o'clock she made fresh coffee and put a vacuum container of it into her tote bag. She buttoned on a thick sweater under the lined all-weather black poplin coat with its enveloping hood. She pulled on zippered black rubber boots over comfortable shoes that would take a great deal of standing still in one place before her feet began to ache.

She wasn't really in her car, driving cautiously through the rain; she was looking over Mr. Caudrey's shoulder as he ripped open the white envelope—good thick paper, but nothing showy—and glanced at the opening: "Dear Phillip." She saw the slow purple which always seemed to surge down, not up—down from the thick creamy swoop of hair over the square forehead; and the veins, beside his large brilliant blue eyes, beginning to raise themselves ropily.

She saw his hands, with the beautiful long, strong, square-tipped fingers, reaching into the drawer of the bedside table where he kept his Colt .38. A raincoat donned in savage haste, the hand slipping the gun into the pocket. The sound of the Mercedes starting up, so real and near that she looked with panic into the driving mirror.

Not yet—the envelope was still sealed, the gun in the drawer, the raincoat in the closet, the Mercedes in the garage. Nothing at all had happened yet.

And Fenelli—what would he be doing? Waxing his skis, perhaps, sitting by his fire with a drink at his elbow. (*Well . . . you've had your turn, now haven't you?*) Thinking with relaxed anticipation about his two weeks in Colorado. She had been told that people felt freed, sprung, wonderful on vacation eve; she had always thought how difficult it was to get through the time away from her lovely job.

She approached Fenelli's house from the opposite direction this time, turning off the main road to the west of it into the ambling lane. About an eighth of a mile from the house in the pines was a stark little cottage she had noted on Thursday, empty, a FOR RENT OR SALE sign standing crookedly on its disheveled treeless front lawn. She drove her car behind the cottage and walked the rest of the way down the lane, her eyes adjusting to the wet blue darkness.

Here was the path. She moved along it, branches brushing her softly, rain dripping off the edge of her hood. Lights on in the house. As well as she could remember, his living room was at this end, its side windows looking into the woods, its front ones facing down the lane. Yes, they had gone to the right at the party, to leave their coats in the bedroom. Too soon to move up close to the window.

After a time she began to feel numb all over, with the cold and wet, and the waiting, and the immobility of her position against the bole of a tree, hiding her under a fall of branches.

The woman inside her, the thinker, the planner, the doer, watched what happened at 7:18 while poor bereft Miss Rounce cowered in the rain, appalled.

The sound of the car coming up the lane, slowly, stopping, at a guess, halfway up. The barest rumor of footsteps. The front doorbell ringing. Fenelli's windows were double-glassed and after he opened the door the two men faced each other, mouths moving, like a scene from a silent movie.

Mr. Caudrey, from a distance of about five feet, shot Fenelli. The other man stood for a moment, rocking a little back and forth as though he were considering some matter of grave importance. But his mouth was wide-open. Then he stumbled ungracefully backward and fell across a gold brocade armchair. He wore a dark suit and Miss Rounce saw no blood. The sound of the shot, muffled by the double-hung windows, seemed to linger in the pines.

Mr. Caudrey stood perfectly still, watching Fenelli. His face was a dangerous purpled red. Oh, do be careful, Mr. Caudrey. Go into the bathroom and take one of your pills.

He finally moved from his frozen stance. Brisk now, he felt Fenelli's pulse, looked for a moment into the open eyes. He scooped up a small portable television set, removed the watch from the dead man's wrist, then began ripping Fenelli's handsome room apart. Desk drawers out, contents in a wild flurry to the floor. A pair of curtains at a front window wrenched down, to lie in a golden heap. He kicked up a corner of the Bokhara rug, took an ornate pansy-painted porcelain clock off the mantelpiece and smashed it on the hearth. Then he went to the front door and let himself out.

The sound of the car starting up again. Not his Mercedes, but the softer sound of Mrs. Caudrey's Chrysler Imperial. Tiremarks—

An odd pride stirred in Miss Rounce. He had done it very well. Mrs. Caudrey wasn't back yet and he could say, if they ever got that close to the matter, that someone had stolen her car while he and she were away. In any case, the police would probably conclude, from the swift staging of it, armed robbery, a scuffle, and yet another sad meaningless death. Money for drugs, maybe.

The newspapers, radio, and television concurred the next morning. Hope & Hayes executive struck down in his home by an unknown assailant . . . armed robbery in quiet Morningtown suburb, the third in four months . . . police questioning known addicts.

Miss Rounce went again to her typewriter. She had slept badly, tossing and crying out warnings in her sleep, but she awoke feeling cleansed and empty.

She addressed the letter to the Morningtown Chief of Police. In it she detailed the name, the time, and the circumstances. The Chrysler Imperial, the Colt .38—"As I understand it, you will be able to match the bullet with the marks in the barrel. Don't look for fingerprints because he wore gloves—rough pigskin, but you might find a pigskin imprint here and there, it is a deeply marked leather. It was a wet night and I assume you check for footprints. He wore a pair of Blucher-style shoes, brown, with crepe rubber soles." At the end of the letter she wrote, "I was walking in the woods when I passed close to the house and saw all this happen. Don't trouble to contact me as I am leaving the state as soon as I mail this letter." She typed, for a signature, the name of the only dog she had ever owned, years and years ago when she was young, an Irish terrier, Shandy.

She got into her car and mailed the letter at the main post office a little after noon. They would have it by tomorrow morning. She wanted the confrontation to be, not in the privacy of his house, but in the full glare of day, with people around, people to see and hear.

At ten o'clock on Monday morning her telephone rang. Mabel? To tell her what had happened? I can't, I can't. I must. With shrinking fingers she picked up the cold black plastic.

"Rouncey!" His voice was warm and strong and rich. He only called her that on special, superspecial occasions. "I couldn't get you out of my head down there. My own invaluable, irreplaceable Rouncey."

Liar, she thought. *You're frightened. You want the old, old security of Miss Rounce to guard you from all harm, as she always had.*

But the chilled blood in her veins stirred and rioted.

"To hell with executive budgeting!" he said. "But in any case, the way things have worked out—you've heard about poor Fenelli?"

"Yes."

"There's the job for *you.* You'll make an absolutely magnificent personnel head. I talked to Holy Joe first thing and he thinks it's a great idea. Your tax bracket is going to take an almighty jump, but you can cope with that, Rouncey, right? And you'll be here on the scene, so I can always turn to you for help when my blonde knucklehead—"

There was the sound over the telephone of a door opening, of voices, commotion.

"Oh, God, the police—" His voice became a sort of gasping wail. "Rouncey, *Rouncey*—"

A click.

And then there was nothing but silence.

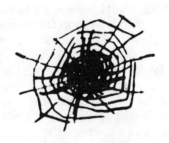

Barry Perowne

Raffles and the Unique Bequest

As it happened, I was with A. J. Raffles when he had occasion, one hot day in London, to call at a hotel in the aristocratic Mayfair neighborhood.

Grey-toppered and equipped with binoculars, we were on our way to Ascot Races, a fashionable event in the summer social calendar, and at the hotel reception desk we chanced to find the manager himself.

"Good morning," said Raffles. "Will you please have Miss Dinah Raffles informed that Mr. Manders and I are here to take her to Ascot?"

Immaculately frockcoated, the manager drew himself up with unexpected hauteur.

"I feel obliged to notify you, Mr. Raffles," he said, "that Miss Raffles has a person with her in her apartment."

"A person?" said Raffles.

"As you are Miss Raffles' brother," the manager said stiffly, "it were perhaps better that Miss Raffles herself account to you for the company she is keeping."

"Very well," Raffles said, with a frown, "we'll go up." He turned to me. "Come on, Bunny."

Not liking the hotel manager's tone, I felt rather uneasy as I accompanied Raffles upstairs. His sister Dinah had been in London only a week, and we knew as yet little about her. Seven years his junior, she had grown up under guardianship far apart from him, owing to their parents' early demise. Now twenty-one, and seeing her brother's name often in the newspapers, as he was currently England's cricket captain, she had grown so curious about him that she suddenly had taken it into her head to come to London and share his life.

There being a side to his life which she must not know about, let alone share, her unforeseen advent had been disturbing for him, and I knew that he planned to amass a dowry for her so that he could get her safely married into some good European family, well away from England, before he should be exposed as a criminal and the consequent scandal should damage Dinah's prospects. Meantime, as women were ineligible for residence in the Albany, where Raffles had his bachelor chambers, he had engaged a suite for Dinah in this irreproachable Mayfair hotel.

The suite was on the third floor and, being at the rear, was free of the constant harness-jingle of passing cabs and carriages.

Raffles knocked on the door. There was no answer. He tried the door-handle. The door was not locked. I followed him into Dinah's sitting-room. It was flooded with sunshine from the wide-open casement window. Dinah was not in the room. The door to the bedroom was closed. Raffles gave it a hard look.

"Dinah?" he called.

I heard movements in the bedroom. The door opened and Dinah emerged. Closing the door carefully, she turned to us. She was wearing a delightful dress that Raffles had bought her for the races at Ascot. Now that he felt himself responsible for her, nothing was too good for his young sister—and indeed, with her fair hair and grey eyes, she did him much credit. She moved to the window, beckoned us to join her.

"You see that little garden down there?" she said.

Open to the public, yet seldom frequented, the garden was one of those sylvan corners that abound in Mayfair. Butterflies were flickering in the noonday heatshine over the vivid flowerbeds.

"This morning, at about eight o'clock," Dinah told us, "as I was having my coffee at this table by the window, I noticed a young lady all alone in that garden. She was sitting on a seat near that camellia tree down there. It still has a few blossoms left on it, and she'd evidently picked one. She was elegantly dressed, and so lovely, with her dark hair and pale, exquisite profile, that she fascinated me. She seemed so alone, sitting there holding the flower loosely in her lap, and she sat so awfully still that I had a feeling she'd been there all night. And—she reminded me of someone."

"Who?" said Raffles.

"It didn't come to me," Dinah said, "until I went into my bedroom to dress. I kept thinking about her. And it dawned on me that what I was beginning to remember, because of the flower she was holding, was a novel I'd read. It was about a lady who had many lovers, but died young, all alone in a garden—with a flower in her hands."

"*La dame aux camélias*," Raffles said quietly, "by Alexandre Dumas *fils*."

"When I remembered the novel," Dinah said, "I felt rather worried.

I came back to this window and looked out. She hadn't moved. I hurried downstairs and went round to the garden gate, which is in a side turning. I sat down beside her on the seat and said, 'Good morning.' She didn't move or answer, so I—touched her hands."

"Did you now," Raffles said softly.

"She opened her eyes," said Dinah. "Oh, I was *so* relieved! But she was so pale and she looked at me so vaguely that I said I was afraid she was unwell and if she'd like to lie down for a while, I lived nearby. She murmured something about 'dinner,' so I thought she might be hungry. I asked her. She smiled faintly and said something about dinner waiting for her in London every evening at eight, or eighty-eight, or eight-to-eight—something like that, but she has a slight foreign accent, and she was so vague and weak, her mind seemed to be wandering. But I'm sure she *had* been on that seat all night—and her weakness *was* from hunger."

"How can you be sure?" Raffles asked.

"Because I brought her here," said Dinah. "I had to help her up the stairs. My breakfast-tray was still here, with some croissants on it. The coffee and the milk were still warm, and she was so glad of them that I could tell she was simply *starving!*"

"And now?" Raffles said.

"I made her lie down on my bed, and she's sound asleep," said Dinah. "This little purse and these white-lace gloves on the table are hers. I brought them up from the garden seat. She's Russian, her name's Lydia, and she's a ballerina."

"A ballerina?" Raffles and I exclaimed.

"I thought she wouldn't mind," Dinah said, "if I looked in her purse to see if I could find her address, in case somebody waiting anxiously there should be informed where she is."

"Sound thinking," said Raffles.

"But you see?" Dinah showed us the contents of the dainty little purse. "There are just her *maquillage* things, her handkerchief embroidered with the name *Lydia*, this cardboard ticket—"

"A pawn ticket," said Raffles, examining it, "for an article pledged in Nice."

"And there's this lovely photograph of her," Dinah said. "From the photographer's stamp on the back, it must have been taken in Moscow."

The small photograph was of a young ballerina held gracefully in mid-air by a handsome male dance partner strikingly virile in skin-fitting tights.

"I must stay and look after her, of course," said Dinah, "so I'm afraid I can't come to Ascot with you. But I insist that you two go. There's nothing you can do here."

"Except mollify the hotel manager," said Raffles. "He must have seen you helping the ballerina upstairs and he probably thought she was the worse for liquor. Never mind, Dinah, I'll have a word with him, book a room here for your guest to move into, and Bunny and I'll return this evening to see how she is."

When we dropped in at the hotel that evening, Dinah reported that her guest had wakened, taken a little nourishment, and gone to sleep again. Dinah had decided to stay at the bedside and have her own dinner sent up on a tray.

"She seems fascinated by her guest," Raffles said as we emerged from the hotel. "And Dinah may well be right in saying that some-body may be waiting for Lydia—waiting anxiously somewhere."

"Yes," I said, "but where?"

"Lydia made a strange remark, Bunny. She was near collapse from hunger," Raffles said, "yet she seems to have implied that every evening, somewhere in London, there's a dinner awaiting her—dinner at eight or something to that approximate effect. A mere hunger fantasy? Maybe. But if she really *has* such an appointment, doesn't it usually take two persons to make a dinner date? In which case, might not the other party to the nightly appointment be faithfully keeping it—and growing more and more anxious? So wouldn't the logical place for us to look for that anxious person be—the appointed rendezvous?"

"But we haven't a clue where it is."

"I wouldn't say that, Bunny. As a matter of fact, I always carry a number of cards in my wallet—cards that come my way, from time to time, from persons of influence. One never knows," Raffles said, giving me a wicked look, "when the right card, presented at the right place, may come in useful." He hailed a passing hansom. "Cab!"

The destination at which Raffles presently paid off the cabbie proved to be a tall, rather dilapidated house in one of those run-down old streets that huddle in the vicinity of Drury Lane Theatre and Covent Garden fruit-and-flower market. The cab jingled away along the otherwise deserted street, and from the nearby market an aroma of wilting blossoms was tainting the warm, mauve twilight as I followed Raffles up two worn stone steps to the door of the dilapidated house.

He beat a rat-a-tat with the iron knocker. Echoes clapped away along the narrow street. Peering at the shabby door, I made out on it the tarnished brass numeral: 88.

The door opened. Framed against gaslight from within stood an impeccably liveried footman.

"Good evening," said Raffles. "I have here the card of a gentleman known to you. He's kindly written a note of introduction on it."

"This gentleman," replied the footman, scrutinizing the card, "is certainly well known here at Eighty-Eight. If you care to step in, I will inquire if it is feasible to accommodate you at such short notice."

Thus invited, we stepped into a narrow hallway, oak-paneled and richly carpeted. To the left was a row of tall-backed, carven chairs. Indicating them to us, the footman went off, taking the card Raffles had presented, and disappeared between heavy curtains of crimson velvet that flanked a carpeted staircase leading up from the back of the hallway.

Two other men, who like ourselves appeared to be waiting, were standing before a Louis XVI marquetry table to the right. They were studying a large, gilt-framed painting on the paneled wall there.

"*Le Déjeuner sur L'Herbe*," the shorter of the men said. A platter-hatted priest of sturdy stature, he had a large, napkin-covered basket on his arm. "I'm told, Gilbert, that this painting is esteemed by competent critics, a masterpiece of the modern 'naturalistic' school."

"The fallacy of modern 'naturalism,' " objected the other man, who, though much younger than the priest, towered over him in height and conspicuously outdid him in girth, "is that it is highly unnatural."

Wearing a bohemian black cloak, and with a black slouch hat in one hand and a stout walking-stick hooked on his arm, the younger man had bushy hair of a chestnut hue. Studying the painting through ribboned eyeglasses held at a distance from his eyes, he pursed his lips disparagingly under the eaves of his moustache.

"Admittedly," he said, "the subject of this painting—this woodland picnic, with naked ladies seated on grass—is quite appropriate to Eighty-Eight here, where you tell me that gourmets foregather. But let me venture the modest suggestion that this alleged 'masterpiece' flouts plausibility. These ladies in the buff—saving your presence, Father—would not be, as depicted, tranquilly picnicking. Far from it! In reality, they would be tormented to the point of hysteria by the attentions of wasps, spiders, and hairy centipedes."

"I'm afraid, Gilbert," said the priest, with a smile, "that you have a tendency to disputation. I've often noticed it in our discussions of theology."

"As a mere amateur in that subject, Father," said the large bohemian, "I seek light from you. But art is another matter. Tchah, I snap my fingers at this decadent daub!"

He did so—with such scorn that the gesture dislodged the walking-stick from his arm. Raffles, in his courteous way, picked up the stick, and, restoring it to its owner, was rewarded with expostulations of gratitude—which were curtailed by the arrival of a footman who, liveried like the one who had admitted us, descended the staircase and addressed himself respectfully to the priest.

"The *patron*," said the footman, "presents his apologies for keeping you waiting, Father. His gout is troublesome tonight, but he would appreciate a word with you in his bureau abovestairs. Allow me to relieve you of your basket."

"Have you told the *patron*," asked the priest, "that I have a friend, a rising poet and journalist, with me this evening?"

"The *patron*," said the footman reassuringly, "will be charmed to make your friend's acquaintance."

"Come, then, Gilbert," said the priest, "and remember that I have your word to write nothing about the matter that brings me to this place."

"In London literary salons," declared the poet, plodding massively upstairs at the priest's heels, "my word is warranted sterling—I hope!"

The footman having made off somewhere with the priest's basket, the departure upstairs of the two theologians left Raffles and myself alone in the hallway, and Raffles murmured, "Bunny, does that huge, cloaked poet remind you of someone?"

"Porthos," I said, "in *The Three Musketeers*, by Alexandre Dumas *père*."

"Exactly," said Raffles, "and, oddly enough, that walking-stick of his weighs heavy in the hand. It's a swordstick!"

Just then the footman who had admitted us reappeared from between the crimson curtains and said he was pleased to announce that Monsieur Kash found it feasible to accommodate us. Bidding us leave our toppers on the marquetry table, where he said they would be seen to, the footman piloted us between the curtains, along a carpeted corridor, into a panelled dining-room.

Here its supervisor, Monsieur Kash, who was of a square shape and had black hair cut *en brosse*, conducted us to a table, where he would have placed menus in our hands but Raffles said that, this being our first visit to Eighty-Eight, we felt we would do well to leave the selection of our repast to Monsieur Kash himself.

"I shall hope, then," Monsieur Kash said with a gratified twinkle, "to prove worthy of your compliment."

As he withdrew, I scanned the dining-room. The diners at the other tables seemed for the most part to be in affluent middle age, the gentlemen expansive of shirtfront and rubicund of complexion, their ladies elaborately coiffured and graciously ample of flesh. Mastication largely precluded the flow of conversation, the diners seeming wholly absorbed in their enjoyment of a succulent gastronomy.

Nowhere among the dedicated *bon viveurs* could I see anybody dining alone with a worried expression and anxious glances toward the door. But Raffles touched me on the arm, murmuring, "The flowers on the table in the corner to your left are different from those on the other tables. Take a look."

I saw his point in a flash.

"Camellias," I breathed.

"Note the significant proceedings," said Raffles.

An uncanny performance was in progress at the corner table, which was set for one person. Though no person occupied the chair at the table, dinner was being served there. A waiter was pouring wine reverently from a cobwebbed bottle reclining in a wicker cradle. Beside the table stood a naperied trolley. At this a *sous-chef* in starched white tunic and yard-high hat was cooking a delicacy in a chafing-dish over the pulsating flame of a spirit-lamp.

The *sous-chef* exhibited the contents of the chafing-dish to the empty chair for approval, then transferred the delicacy to a plate. His colleague, the waiter, took up the plate and placed it before the invisible diner. After a moment the waiter took up the plate again, its contents in no way disturbed, and replaced it on the trolley, which was wheeled away by the *sous-chef*.

It was deftly done.

"Don't stare, Bunny," Raffles murmured.

Notwithstanding his admonition, I could not keep myself from watching, sidelong, the faultless service of successive courses and wines at the table with no visible diner. It haunted me. I was quite unable to give our own dinner the attention it merited—but when

Monsieur Kash came to inquire if everything was satisfactory, I tactfully echoed Raffles' commendations.

"Though we must admit, Monsieur Kash," Raffles added, "to a curiosity about what's been taking place at that corner table with the camellias on it."

"Ah, table twelve," said Monsieur Kash. "Our regular diners have been long accustomed to the sight you mention. In fact, they have seen it seven-hundred and twenty-nine times—counting this, the penultimate evening for it."

"Penultimate?" Raffles said.

Monsieur Kash seemed pleased by our interest.

"At a time," he told us, "when the Royal Nevsky Ballet, from Moscow, was visiting London, it played a limited season at Drury Lane Theatre, just around the corner. One of our regular diners, a well known London stockbroker, a bachelor of mature years and a notable gourmet, conceived an infatuation for a young dancer in the corps-de-ballet."

Raffles and I exchanged a glance.

"He married her," said Monsieur Kash, "and one night, not long afterward, he brought her here to dine. I was not on duty that night, but I knew that the gentleman had taken great pains about the dinner, specifying the dishes in advance—*his* favorite table to be reserved, *her* favorite floral decoration for it. Gentlemen, he had a purpose."

"Indeed?" said Raffles.

"It was to awaken her," Monsieur Kash explained, "to the importance of proper dining. His purpose was evident, I was told, in the detail with which he enumerated to her the courses they were about to eat, with particulars of the ingredients and preparation of the various dishes, and the provenance of the wines that would accompany them."

"Fascinating," said Raffles.

"Unfortunately," said Monsieur Kash, "the young ballerina seemed more fascinated by our regular diners. Accustomed as she was to the airy, twinkle-toed companionship of ballet persons, she seemed to feel herself out of place among solid, serious citizens dining substantially. She gazed around at them, I was told, with a kind of aloof wonder—and her husband noticed her inattention to his culinary discourse. He flushed with anger."

"Not unnaturally," said Raffles.

"He reproached her," said Monsieur Kash. "He was heard to say he was deeply disappointed in her for making no effort to share his interests in life. She murmured something to the effect that it was all so bourgeois. This infuriated him. He retorted that all she cared about was squandering the generous pocket-money he allowed her on her ruinous Russian passion for gambling. Gentlemen, it was a fatal remark."

"Fatal?" Raffles said.

"Her eyes flashed," said Monsieur Kash. "She took off a necklace and bracelet she was wearing—obviously gifts he had lavished on her in his infatuation. She removed even her diamond earrings. She placed the jewels on the table before him. The first course of their dinner was about to be served. She turned her back on it and walked out of this room—and out of his life."

"Good Lord!" said Raffles.

"A few months later," said Monsieur Kash, "he departed it himself—from natural causes. He left her a species of bequest. He seems to have been convinced that her passion for gambling would be her ruin and that, within a year or two, she would be humbly glad to eat such a dinner as the one she had scorned. Hence the late gourmet's bequest, which imposed upon our *patron* here at Eighty-Eight the obligation and necessary funds to serve nightly for the ballerina, for a period of two years, a dinner at table twelve identical with the dinner so carefully arranged for her on the night of her proud defection."

"Extraordinary," said Raffles. "So the bequest dinners are, in a sense, a repeated service of funeral baked meats—with the late gourmet lurking spectrally, as it were, every night at table twelve, with the conviction that sooner or later, inevitably, he would have the posthumous satisfaction of seeing the improvident ballerina obliged at last to consume the charming repast."

I glanced uneasily at the corner table.

"Tomorrow night's service of the dinner," said Monsieur Kash, "will be the last. The young lady has never yet come to claim her dinners. Only the priest has come for them."

"The priest?" Raffles and I said.

"By arrangement with our *patron* here at Eighty-Eight," Monsieur Kash explained, "the parish priest, who officiated at the gourmet's melancholy interment—which our whole staff attended as a mark of respect—collects the bequest dinners if unconsumed by the ballerina. The priest now has a slum parish of London's dockland, where he maintains a soup kitchen for the destitute. Every evening he either sends an urchin or comes in person with a basket to collect the table twelve dinner."

Monsieur Kash chuckled. "The priest drolly refers to the unconsumed dinners as 'the manna,' and he tells me," said Monsieur Kash, "that food and wine for one person, as served here at Eighty-Eight, can be stretched considerably when added to a gruel and then distributed to the needy on the principle of the miraculous loaves and fishes—a biblical reference, gentlemen."

"I recall it from my schooldays," said Raffles.

The platter-hatted priest and the large cloaked poet were not in evidence when we left the deceptive premises of Eighty-Eight, so shabby externally, so sybaritic within.

"To a proud, sensitive young artiste of the ballet, and Russian at that," Raffles said to me thoughtfully, as we walked away, "the necrophilic aspect of those dinners bequeathed to her may well seem morbid and repulsive. One can understand why she might prefer to starve rather than have anything to do with them. I look forward to meeting her tomorrow."

But when we called at the Mayfair hotel toward noon the next day we were told at the reception desk that Miss Raffles' guest had fully recovered from her indisposition and that the young ladies had gone out shopping.

"Miss Raffles left this note for you, sir."

"Very well," said Raffles, when he had read the note. "Please tell Miss Raffles that Mr. Manders and I will call again later in the day."

"Dinah and her guest," Raffles said outside, "seem to have arrived at terms of mutual confidence, Bunny. I infer from Dinah's note that Lydia, when she walked out of the gourmet's life, must have rejoined the Royal Nevsky Ballet—and subsequently, on the gourmet's demise, have married the Nevsky's leading dancer. Dinah says that his name's Igor Koslov and that he's the graceful, virile fellow who appears with Lydia in that photograph we saw, the one taken in Moscow."

"Temperamentally," I said, "he's no doubt much more congenial to her than the gourmet ever was. But how did she come to be in the plight in which Dinah found her?"

"It was her own fault, Bunny. Dinah says that Mr. Koslov's been touring North America recently with the Nevsky Ballet. Lydia had no role in the repertoire, so she stayed in Europe, living at a hotel in Nice. Mr. Koslov left her with ample money for her expenses during his absence, but, according to Dinah, Lydia was tempted by the roulette tables at Monte Carlo and had very bad luck."

"So she *is* an incorrigible gambler!"

"Aren't all Russians?" said Raffles. "Anyway, she'd got herself into a fix—penniless and with a big unpaid bill at the Nice hotel. But she knew that Mr. Koslov and the Nevsky Ballet were on the way back from Canada in the liner *Laurentian,* due to dock at Liverpool today, so she decided to come to London and be at the station to join Mr. Koslov when he arrives here this evening on the boat-train from the liner."

"She'd kept at least enough money, then, for her fare from Nice?"

"Apparently not, Bunny. Dinah says that Lydia had to pawn a ring she was wearing. It brought just enough for her fare, with nothing over for food on her journey. So she arrived in London, day before yesterday, in a famished condition—and as she hadn't dared ask the Nice hotel to release her luggage with her bill unpaid, she couldn't very well, devoid of money and luggage, expect a hotel here to take her in. But she'd lived in Mayfair when she was married to the gourmet, so she knew of the little garden—and as these June nights are pleasantly warm, she decided just to sit it out in the garden until it came time to go to the station to meet Mr. Koslov."

"But she arrived the day before yesterday, and he's not due till this evening!"

"She doesn't impress one, Bunny, as being an eminently practical person. If it hadn't been for Dinah, some gardener or constable would certainly have found Lydia in a hunger coma and had her removed to the nearest workhouse infirmary for admission to the ward for indigent females."

"What a fate!" I exclaimed, appalled.

"Instead, she's Dinah's guest," said Raffles, "and Dinah's taken her shopping for 'some necessary millinery, as Lydia has only the clothes she is wearing.'" He smiled a shade wryly. "As the bills for Dinah's kindly purchases will certainly come to me, and I'm overdrawn at the bank, we'd better go to Ascot again, Bunny, and see if we can back a winner or two."

In this we were unsuccessful. Our minds were not really on it. We were out-of-pocket when in the evening we returned to London and called again at the Mayfair hotel—only to be told that the young ladies had been in but had gone out again.

"I heard some mention between them, Mr. Raffles," said the reception-desk attendant, "of having a hairdressing appointment."

"We'll wait for them, then," Raffles said. "Let us know when they come in. Mr. Manders and I will be in the Billiard Room."

We had a whisky-and-soda or two and played a hundred-up on the hotel's excellent billiard table. Raffles seemed restless. Every time he chalked his cue, he took out his gold half hunter for a glance at it.

"Perhaps, Raffles," I ventured to suggest, as we finished the game and racked our cues, "the girls have gone on from the hairdresser's to meet Mr. Koslov and the Nevsky Ballet off the boat-train."

"I wonder," said Raffles. A thought seemed to strike him. He stood for a moment in frowning abstraction, then said abruptly, "Come on, Bunny."

"Where to?" I said.

"To Eighty-Eight," said Raffles.

Alighting presently from a hansom in the ill-lit old street near Drury Lane Theatre, we were admitted to Eighty-Eight by the same sleek footman who had opened the door to us on the previous night. After only a brief wait, we were told that Monsieur Kash would be able to accommodate us.

"You are later this evening, gentlemen," he said, as he welcomed us in the dining-room, "but a table fell vacant about half an hour ago."

"But this," said Raffles, seeing to which table Monsieur Kash was ushering us, "this is table twelve!"

"Madame," said Monsieur Kash, "has dined."

My scalp suddenly tingled.

"Yes, gentlemen," Monsieur Kash said, with an air of suppressed excitement, "finally, on the very last night of the bequest, the long-awaited ballerina has appeared, dined at this appointed table, and has gone her way."

"Was she alone?" Raffles said.

"Quite alone," said Monsieur Kash. "Would you care this evening, gentlemen, to select from the menu?"

"We're content," Raffles said, "to leave it to you."

As Monsieur Kash went off, I glanced questioningly at Raffles.

"What in the world," I said, "can have made her change her mind?"

"It just could be, Bunny," he said, "that it was the visit to the hairdresser's."

His brows knitted and he said no more. I was frankly baffled. At the tables around us, the *bon viveurs*, napkinned to their double chins, were devoting themselves with a minimum of irrelevant conversation to their absorbed enjoyment of a cleverly conceived and impeccably served alimentation.

For our part, we again failed to give our own dinner the undivided attention it deserved. Raffles, gazing absently at the delicate pink and creamy pale camellias in the cut-glass bowl on the table, was pursuing some train of thought which I strove in vain to divine. "Eat up, Bunny," he said suddenly, "and let's get a cab back to the hotel."

When we reached the Mayfair hotel, we were told by the reception-desk attendant that, yes, the young ladies were in Miss Raffles' suite.

"We'll go up," said Raffles.

As we turned away from the deck, a small man was coming at a run down the carpeted staircase. Though he was wearing a smart suit, light traveling ulster, and corduroy cap, so that his lithe figure and masculine virility were not now emphasized by skin-fitting tights, he was instantly recognizable from the Moscow photograph. From the pallor of his handsome face, the hectic glitter of his dark eyes, he seemed to be in a shaking rage as he raced across the lobby and out into the street, shouting for a cab.

"Koslov the dancer," said Raffles.

He started upstairs at the double, myself at his heels. He knocked on the door of Dinah's sitting-room. The door was opened by a svelte, elegantly dressed young woman with raven hair parted in the center and swept softly back to a knot at her nape. Her lips a shade over-rouged, she gazed at us with wide grey eyes, mascara-shadowed and startled.

Raffles said coldly, "I prefer less *maquillage* and your hair its natural color—fair. What have you been up to, Dinah?"

I followed Raffles into the sitting-room, closed the door, and turned, staring stupefied at his young sister, so subtly changed in appearance.

"You're going to be furious with me," she said to him. "I've caused an awful row between Lydia and Igor Koslov. You remember Lydia said something about a dinner being served for her every evening? Well, it's true. She's told me all about it. The dinners are a queer bequest from her first husband, a kind of food addict. Lydia would rather die than touch them. She said they'd been hanging over her, dragging at her like a kind of fate, for two whole years, and she was thankful that tonight would be the end of them. Well, I suddenly thought it'd be rather fun if she sent *somebody else* to eat the dinner! It would sort of turn the tables on the gourmet—and Lydia would have the last word, after all, d'you see?"

"In a way," said Raffles.

"Lydia was horrified when I first suggested it," Dinah told us, "but then she got as excited as I was. She said that the people at the dinner place had seen her only once, and that was nearly three years ago—but to be on the safe side we went to a famous hairdresser's salon in Mayfair and asked him to make me look as much like Lydia as possible. He went to great pains to do it."

"Evidently," said Raffles.

"It was quite late when we came out of the hairdresser's," Dinah went on. "So Lydia went off in a cab to the station to meet Mr. Koslov and the Nevsky Ballet off the boat-train, and I got a cab and went to the dinner place. It's called Eighty-Eight and only gourmets know of it."

"Is that so?" said Raffles, expressionless.

"It looked rather dilapidated," Dinah said, "but a proper footman opened the door to me. I put on a slight foreign accent, like Lydia's, and showed him the little Moscow photograph and said I understood that table twelve was reserved for me. He said he'd inquire and went off with the photograph, leaving me in a little hallway, then he came back and said that Monsieur Kash found it feasible, and took me to a dining-room, where this Monsieur Kash seemed quite excited to see me. He said he had despaired of ever doing so."

"Did he indeed?" said Raffles dryly.

"He was awfully kind," Dinah told us. "He took me to table twelve and made a great fuss over me. So did the waiters. They couldn't do too much. Even the chefs in the kitchen peered out at me through the service hatch, and they were all smiles. Only the diners at the other tables paid no attention—they just went on stuffing themselves—but the staff were wonderful, so delighted to see me at last and make me feel important. And the food was delicious, though I couldn't really eat much, I felt too excited—most of all when I finished dinner and Monsieur Kash escorted me to the little hallway and, as he helped me on with my mantle, told me that he had a cab waiting outside and the cabman had instructions to take me to an address where I'd find that I was expected."

"And you went off in that strange cab?" Raffles said, with a shock I fully shared.

"Oh, it was quite all right," Dinah assured us. "Monsieur Kash helped me into the cab, and shook hands with me, and said I needn't feel the least disquiet as the address in Thamescourt Street, where the cabman would take me, was the house of a priest."

"A priest?" Raffles and I exclaimed.

"Yes," said Dinah, "and it was just as Monsieur Kash had told me. When I got to the house and pulled the chain of the doorbell, it was a priest in a cassock who opened the door to me. He was awfully kind. He invited me into his study, where the window was wide open and the walls were lined with books, and he introduced a friend of his who was there, an enormous person who wore a cloak and ribboned eyeglasses but seemed quite nice. The priest asked me if I had enjoyed my dinner at Eighty-Eight. I said I had. He said he knew all about the bequest dinners, had come to regard them as 'manna,' and had been in the habit of collecting it, most evenings, to help feed the poor of his parish. But he said that when he'd called at Eighty-Eight this evening with his friend to collect the last of the manna, they'd been told that I was in the act of eating it all—and, from the doorway of the dining-room, they'd seen me doing it. I felt terribly embarrassed."

"As well you might," Raffles said grimly.

"But the priest and his friend just laughed," Dinah told us, "and the priest said he was delighted to meet me at last. He said he'd heard that I was fond of gambling and he asked what game of hazard especially interested me. So, remembering what Lydia had told me, I said I had a passion for roulette. Then the priest and his friend talked to me about roulette for a while, and it was all quite pleasant—until suddenly an awful thing happened. The priest opened a drawer in his desk and took out a little package. He said it was for me—and that he knew he spoke for his ex-parishioner, the late gourmet, in expressing the hope that I would think very seriously about what I found in the package, and take it to heart."

"Good Lord!" said Raffles.

"I felt simply dreadful," Dinah confessed. "The package was meant for Lydia, of course, not for me. But all I could do was accept the package, say goodnight to the priest and his friend, and hurry back here to the hotel to give Lydia her mysterious package. But when I rushed into my sitting-room here, I found both Lydia and Igor Koslov waiting for me, and they were having a fearful quarrel—because apparently Lydia had told Igor that she'd let me go to Eighty-Eight in her place, and he was furious with her for having anything to do, even indirectly, with the wretched bequest."

"A woman's second husband," Raffles said, "is understandably sensitive on the subject of her first husband—whether he's been disposed of by death, as in this case, or merely by legislation."

"Oh, I know," said Dinah. "Both Lydia and Igor are terribly Russian and sensitive—and Igor demanded to know everything that had happened. I had to tell him, just as I've told you and Bunny. And Igor snatched the package from me and demanded of Lydia what was in it. She said she hadn't the faintest idea. He ordered her to open it immediately, in his presence. She said she'd have nothing to do with it, in or out of his presence, and she rushed off to her own room—the one you booked for her—and locked herself in. And Igor Koslov tore open the package himself."

"What was in the package?" Raffles asked.

"A little cardboard box," said Dinah, "but there was nothing in it!"

"*Nothing?*" Raffles said.

"Well, nothing," said Dinah, "except a few words written on a half sheet of notepaper. I didn't see what the words were, but Igor Koslov went absolutely livid when he read them. He said, 'By God, I'll get to the bottom of this!' He could hardly speak for rage. He crammed the paper into his ulster pocket and rushed out."

"Very well," Raffles said. "I'll talk to you tomorrow about your imprudent escapade, Dinah. Meantime, do something about your hair. Come on, Bunny."

We went down the hotel stairs at a run.

"There's not much doubt where Koslov's going," Raffles said, as we emerged from the hotel. He hailed the first cab that hove in view and asked the cabbie if he knew where Thamescourt Street was.

"I works out of a yard just around the corner from it," said the cabbie. "It's out by the docks—North Quay."

"Drop us at your yard, and there's a fiver for you if you ginger your nag up," Raffles said, adding grimly, as we jingled off in the hansom, "Koslov the dancer has about five minutes' start on us, Bunny, and in the mood he's in he's capable of anything!"

It was quite a long ride out to the maze of dark, depressing streets of the dockland slums, where the cabbie reined his horse at last to a standstill outside a yard where hansoms and four-wheelers stood around haphazard with upflung shafts.

"Thankee, guv'," said the cabbie, as Raffles tipped him. "Thames-court Street's a 'undred yards on down—first turn to yer right—you can't mistake it, there's a bleedin' church on the corner. Us 'ackies often gives the priest a free lift when 'e goes up west, Drury Lane way, wiv 'is basket of an evenin'."

Walking on quickly, we turned to the right, around the railings of the corner churchyard. The stifling midnight air reeked of tidal flotsam. A silent flash of heat lightning momentarily illumined the modest spire of the old stone church. Its lychgate faced, across the narrow street, the endless, smoke-blackened brick wall of a riverside warehouse. Fifty yards or so beyond the church stood a stationary four-wheeler cab, its back to us.

"Koslov's cab," Raffles said. "It's standing in front of a house—almost certainly the priest's house. There's a lighted ground-floor window at the side of the house. That's probably the priest's study. Let's see if we can make our way to it through the churchyard and get a look in at what's happening."

The lychgate creaked slightly as Raffles opened it. Our eyes on that square of lighted window, we groped towards it through the churchyard of gravestones, tomb-slabs, weeds, laurel bushes. A ship's siren bayed distantly. The church clock sounded a single mellow chime. Heat lightning, silent, flashed again over the sky. Raffles jerked me down, crouching, into the shelter of a laurel bush. We were within a few yards of the wide-open window, could see right into the gaslit, book-lined room.

"The answer to your questions is affirmative, Mr. Koslov," the priest was saying. His voice clearly audible to us, he was standing, cassocked but hatless now, a slightly rustic figure with his round, ruddy face, behind a desk on which a breviary lay open with a rosary on it. "I didn't, as it happened, officiate at my late parishioner's marriage to Lydia, the young dancer of the Royal Nevsky corps-de-ballet. But yes, I knew the man reasonably well. And yes, I'm fully aware of the terms of his bequest to her."

"Bequest?" Koslov said harshly. Trim, well knit, capped, and ulstered, his handsome face white to the lips with anger, he stood facing the priest across the flat-topped desk. "Seven hundred and thirty calculated slaps of her face, *that* was the rejected man's bequest to Lydia! And now this—these words on this paper! You knew the man. Do you know, then, the motive for this message from his grave? I insist that you answer!"

"Certainly," said the priest.

He ignored the half sheet of notepaper held out to him by Koslov. The priest's student in theology, the bushy-haired, Porthos-like poet, stick hooked on his arm, ribboned eyeglasses held to his eyes, towered cloaked and huge over both the priest and the dancer and looked thoughtfully from one to the other.

"I've never had the pleasure," the priest was continuing, "of meeting the young ballerina who's now your wife, Mr. Koslov. But you must be aware, or you would not be here questioning me, that there came forward this evening a charming claimant to the last—the very last—of the bequest dinners."

"I learned of this—this claimant," Koslov said angrily, "when I arrived in London this evening!"

"You know, of course," said the priest, "that she was a false claimant. But when she was sent on to me from Eighty-Eight, as I'd instructed should be done, I had an open mind about her, though I needed to be quite sure that she was indeed Lydia. I couldn't test the claimant's knowledge of Russian, my own linguistic range being more or less limited to liturgical Latin. Nor did I consider it altogether politic to invite the claimant to prove herself a ballerina by performing here in my study, before my friend and myself."

"The conventions," said the large poet regretfully, "rob me of many simple pleasures."

"But I knew, Mr. Koslov," continued the priest, ignoring the interjection, "that the real Lydia is an incorrigible gambler, with a particular passion for roulette. So my friend and I engaged the claimant in a conversation about that costly pastime."

"Of which her knowledge," said the poet, "proved suspiciously flimsy."

"Poor Dinah," Raffles whispered in my ear, "she lacks worldly experience."

"Now, Mr. Koslov," the priest was saying, "many people know of the bequest dinners. There's always been a possibility that some mischievous young woman might think it quite a lark to present herself at Eighty-Eight one night as the missing ballerina, and eat the late gourmet's mysterious dinner. I've long been prepared for such a possibility. True, the claimant who presented herself here this evening failed the roulette test. But it was not conclusive. There remained a slight chance that she might nevertheless be the real Lydia. I therefore put the claimant to a further test. I gave her a small package. I'd prepared it nearly two years ago—placing a message on it."

The priest's voice rang suddenly loud and clear from the gaslit study.

"*'I will make darkness light before you, and crooked things straight.'* Are there not, in those eleven words from the Book of the Prophet Isaiah," said the priest, "both a promise and a warning?"

"A paradox!" exclaimed his huge student in theology.

"Paradox, Gilbert, is in the eye of the beholder," said the priest. "That is the point. If the claimant were genuine, would she not read the promise implicit in the *first* seven words of that message? Would she not be likely to come back here and ask me if I could explain why my late parishioner, the gourmet, had sent her such a promise?"

Heat lightning flashed silently, blinding bright over the churchyard.

"On the other hand," I heard the priest saying, "if the claimant were false, would she not read the warning implicit in the *last* four words of that message? Would she not wonder, pondering uneasily on the word 'crooked,' if her imposture had been detected? And wouldn't she, therefore, take very good care *not* to come back here?"

"So this," said the cloaked poet, "is why you said to me, 'Wait a while, Gilbert, let's see if she returns.' Father, you are a subtle man!"

"Not I," said the priest, "but Isaiah. *I* am merely surprised—for the message has brought the unexpected." He looked at Koslov the dancer. "It's brought *you*, Mr. Koslov. And you've adequately identified yourself as Lydia's husband. I accept that. You imply a right to speak on her behalf. Very well, I accept that, too. But, Mr. Koslov, you've come a little late."

Koslov said, with icy anger, "What do you mean by that?"

"In terms of the gourmet's bequest," said the priest, "I was entrusted with a small package which I was to give to Lydia if, in consequence of her availing herself of any one of the dinners served for her nightly at Eighty-Eight, she should appear before me. The last of the bequest dinners was served for her at table twelve this evening. As you are well aware, Lydia did *not* eat that dinner. And at midnight tonight the bequest, as far as Lydia is concerned, became null and void."

In the gaslit study the priest opened a drawer in his desk. He took out a small, brown paper package tied with string, the knot sealed with blue wax.

"The late gourmet's alternative instructions regarding this package," said the priest, "became applicable as from midnight. Just now, the clock of my church chimed. The clock is accurate by the

chronometers of Greenwich, just across the Thames there. The chime
you heard, Mr. Koslov, marked the quarter after midnight."

"For two years," Koslov said tautly, "her first husband's damnable
bequest has haunted Lydia's imagination. I am determined to ex-
orcise his ghost from her life—*and* from mine!"

"Exorcism, Mr. Koslov," said the huge poet, "is a matter for an
ordained priest."

But Koslov, ignoring the poet, said harshly to the priest, "Open
that package!"

"You cannot," the priest said mildly, "demand that as a *right*, Mr.
Koslov—although—"

"*This* is my right!" said Koslov, and suddenly, in his hand, was
a small revolver.

Involuntarily, Raffles and I started half up from our crouch among
the laurels, but there in the gaslit study a swordblade flashed from
the walking-stick of Porthos the poet and he would have struck
violently at the leveled revolver had not the priest's shout of "Stop!"
rung out with an authority that held both poet and dancer momentarily immobile.

"Gilbert," the priest said, "sheathe your romatic sword. Your pen
becomes you better. Mr. Koslov, put away your firearm. These wild
gestures are quite uncalled for. You cannot demand, as a right, that
I open this package, Mr. Koslov, *although*—as I was about to say
when I was so immoderately interrupted—I have no objection whatever to opening it. In fact, the late gourmet's instructions entitle
me—since midnight—to do precisely that."

Raffles' grip on my arm had drawn me down again and my heart
was thumping as I saw the priest don a pair of small-lensed, steel-
rimmed spectacles and take from a drawer of his desk a pair of
scissors.

"Mr. Koslov," he said, "while I'm opening this package, let me ask
you a question. What is your wife's favorite flower?"

"Camellias," said the dancer, perplexed.

"And when a man uses a woman's favorite flower to speak to her
for him," said the priest, "what is he probably trying to tell her?"

Koslov did not answer.

"By the expressed desire of the testator," said the priest, looking
over his lenses at Koslov, "camellias have appeared nightly on the
table reserved for Lydia."

Koslov stood rigid.

"In hearing confessions," said the priest, "one comes to realize that almost every human action of seeming irrationality is prompted by confused motives. Lydia deserted her first husband, and his dinner bequest to her was the act of an emotionally disturbed man. We can't know all that he felt of bitterness, regret, self-blame—for he was more than twice her age, yet had rushed her into marriage—but no doubt something of all this is implicit in his bequest. Yet, surely, the camellias on table twelve cry aloud the strongest of his motives—his very real concern for her, believing as he did that her passion for gambling would soon so reduce her circumstances that a time would come when she would be glad to eat the dinner she had scorned."

Raffles' grip was iron-hard on my arm as we saw the priest, unwrapping the package, disclose a small cardboard box.

"And if that time should indeed come," the priest continued, "then it might well be that Lydia would have learned the folly of her gambling and would be grateful, at last, not only for the dinner, but for something else she had scorned to accept from him that now might provide her with the means to make a fresh start."

Lifting the lid from the box, the priest removed from it a wad of cotton-wool, then took out and laid on his desk a gold bracelet set with gems, a necklace of sapphires, a pair of diamond earrings.

"When she left him, she left behind not only his dinner, but these, his other gifts to her. Mr. Koslov, Lydia took *nothing* from her first husband—nothing," the priest said quietly, "but his heart."

Mellowly, the clock of the adjoining church chimed twice.

"At midnight," said the priest, "the disposal of these articles became a matter for my discretion. I could use the proceeds of them to help subsidize a soup kitchen and night refuge for the needy of many nationalities who teem in this polyglot dockside parish. But these jewels were originally gifts to Lydia. I therefore, in the spirit if not in the letter of the gourmet's bequest, exercise my discretion when I say to you now, Mr. Koslov—take them to her."

"Never!" said Igor Koslov. "Even if she would accept them, which is unthinkable, she would merely gamble them away! No, no! One experience of hunger has no more cured Lydia of gambling than ruin at the card tables of Homburg Spa and exile to the tundras of Siberia cured our great Russian novelist Dostoievski! It's in the blood."

He drew in his breath, deeply.

"For me," he said to the priest, "you have exorcised the ghost of

Lydia's first husband. But—for Lydia herself? I wonder! Father, what should I tell her?"

"As a celibate," said the priest, with a smile, "I am no more an authority on the feminine mind than the late gourmet seems to have been when he imagined there was anything on earth that could make a woman eat a dinner she had set her mind against. So I can only say to you, Mr. Koslov, tell Lydia what your heart tells you to tell her."

"Sound advice, Mr. Koslov," said the priest's companion, the huge, cloaked poet. "By the way, if you're going in the West End direction, may I share your cab? I'd like to hear more about the novelist Dostoievski you mentioned. I don't think his works have been translated into English yet."

"I'll see you out, gentlemen," said the priest.

The two theologians and Koslov left the study. In the book-lined room, now unoccupied, the jewels on the priest's deck glittered invitingly in the gaslight. The window stood wide open. To have nipped into the room, seized the jewels, and slipped away unseen through the churchyard would have been so easy that, knowing Raffles' intention of amassing a dowry for his young sister Dinah, I was seized by a terrible surmise. My heart pounded and the hair stirred on my scalp, as I peered at his keen profile here in the darkling shrubbery.

But I should have known him better.

"No, Bunny," he muttered, as though he had sensed my fear, "theft has its limits. Those jewels are not for us. They're strictly the priest's swag now—the last of the manna."

His grip tightened on my arm.

"Listen!" he said.

Out of sight at the front door of the house, the theologians were talking. Their voices were clearly audible.

"You know, Father," I heard his friend Chesterton saying, "I feel in my bones that one day I shall write about a priest-detective. I shall base the character on what I know of you and on things I've learned from you."

"Go home," said the priest. "That poor cabbie's been waiting a long time. Goodnight, Mr. Koslov. Goodnight, Gilbert."

"Goodnight, Father O'Connor," said the poet.

I heard the cab rumble away. The hoofbeats of the horse, receding, echoed from the bleak warehouse walls of Thamescourt Street. I heard the front door of the priest's house close.

He came slowly into his study. He was taking off his spectacles.

His expression thoughtful, he put them into their case and pocketed it under his cassock.

Thunder clapped across the midnight sky. Raindrops began to tap on the leaves of the laurels. The priest came to the window, stood for a moment looking out, then closed and latched it and drew together the curtains, shutting in the light and the sparkle of the dead man's jewels.

"Let's go, Bunny," said Raffles.

As we stole away empty-handed through the churchyard, a tugboat hooted vibrantly, not far off, surging down London river on the tide.

Author's Note

Mr. Manders' narrative, found recently among his clandestine records of criminal experience, inevitably raises the question of his credibility factor. In this connection, the following points, established by latter-day research, may perhaps be of interest:

Mr. G. K. Chesterton did indeed state, when later he wrote his great series of tales of a priest-detective, that he had based the character on certain attributes of his friend, the late Father O'Connor.

Biographers of Mr. Chesterton are agreed that for many years he carried a swordstick. He is known to have set great store by it, though research has failed to discover any occasion—other than that allegedly observed by Mr. Manders—when the blade was bared in anger.

Mr. Manders mentions in his narrative a promise made by Mr. Chesterton to write nothing about the affair of the gourmet's bequest. Possibly corroborative of Mr. Manders' account of the matter is the fact that there is no mention whatever of it in Mr. Chesterton's monumental and most enduring literary achievement, *The Father Brown Stories*.

John Lutz

Something Like Murder

I was leaning slightly from my fifteenth-floor window in the Norwood Arms watering my geraniums when Mrs. Vixton passed by wearing a pink flower-print kimono of shimmering silk. She passed by vertically, you understand, not horizontally, which would have been much more conducive to her health, though not nearly so remarkable.

She saw me, I believe, though to her I was of only passing interest. Still, I'm sure I saw a slight inclination of her head in my direction. Whatever else might be said of Mrs. Vixton, she was never a snob. She was descending face down, her arms spread incredibly wide, a frozen, determined expression on her face, as if she might yet have time to catch the knack of flying. Startled, I overwatered the geraniums. I didn't look down; there was no doubt of the outcome.

My name, incidentally, is Cy Cryptic. Not my real name, of course. I'm a movie reviewer for one of the larger papers here in town, and Cy Cryptic sounds and looks more like show biz than Marvin Haupt.

I'd have forgotten completely about Mrs. Vixton's death, except that cinematically it might have been effective, when a week later in the lobby I overheard a chance remark between Mrs. Fattler of the third floor and Gates the doorman.

"From her window—" I heard Mrs. Fattler say, dragging out her vowels as women often do when discussing a tragedy.

I edged closer. "Mr. Cryptic," Mrs. Fattler said in greeting, and Gates gave his ridiculous little salute. I joined the conversation.

Mrs. Vixton had committed suicide, I was told, by leaping from the south window of her apartment while the horrified Mr. Vixton looked on. A typewritten signed note was found later, expressing Mrs. Vixton's despondency and her desire to leave this world. I did not mention that I had seen Mrs. Vixton resplendent in mid-air the morning of her death. I did not think it wise in light of the fact that the Vixtons lived on the fourteenth floor, in the apartment *below* mine.

The matter of Mrs. Vixton's gravity-assisted death kept creeping into my mind that afternoon as I sat through an advance showing of *Life's Slender Thread,* a French import about, believe it or not, a man who pushes his mistress from a high window rather than turn her over to a gangland czar. It was a happy-ending film of unlikely gimmickry, small consequence, and incoherent subtitles. Yet the movie did create a certain mood. When I left the theater I decided to call on Mr. Vixton before writing my copy.

Mr. Vixton was of medium-height, a pear-shaped man in his fifties with a sleek set to his neck and shoulders that suggested that once he might have been lean and muscular. We shook hands and he invited me into his apartment, a twin to my own but for Vixton's tasteless and mismatched furniture on a riotous green-and-black carpet. The carpet alone might have driven Mrs. Vixton to suicide. But I knew that it wasn't suicide.

"Sit down, Cryptic," Mr. Vixton invited, waving a compact arm toward a low sofa with clear lucite arms.

I sat, glancing at the south window. "I'm sorry about your wife," I said. "Are you?"

Vixton stood with his arms crossed; he cocked his head, then laughed. There was something froglike in his broad bespectacled features, his wide downturned mouth.

"I thought you might have seen me leaning out to water my geraniums," I said. "At any rate, I could never be sure you hadn't."

"And I could never be sure you didn't see my wife pass by you, Cryptic. Yours was the only window she had to pass above this fourteenth floor, after which it didn't matter. But as it happened, I did see your hand holding the watering can, some few seconds after Gloria's fall."

I leaned back in the gauche sofa and crossed my outstretched legs at the ankles. "I surmise that you pushed her from the roof."

"You surmise correctly. That way there would be no window frame for her to clamp onto, and no sign of a struggle in our apartment. I tricked her into signing the note I had typed, lured her onto the roof, then pushed her. None of it was difficult—certainly it was easier and more profitable for me than a divorce. What I'm curious about, Cryptic, is why you came down here and brought out in the open what both of us could only suspect—I that you did see Gloria pass your window, and you that I was aware that you had."

"I could never be sure you wouldn't kill me," I said candidly, "and if I went to the police with my story, they might not have believed me and you might have killed me out of revenge or to protect yourself, or possibly even sued me for libel."

"Truthfully," Mr. Vixton said, "I was considering the first alternative—to kill you. It was that glimpse of the watering can—" He frowned slightly, a toadlike contraction of his features. "But how does this visit improve the situation?"

"The situation, as I see it, is that we can't trust one another. You'll always feel I might go to the authorities, and I'll always feel you might do something drastic to preclude that eventuality. Now, what needs to be done is for circumstances to be arranged so that we *can* trust one another. Suppose you had something on me?"

Vixton puffed his cheeks and seemed to deliberate. "Something like murder?"

"There is a young woman named Alicia whom I often escort."

"I've seen her," Vixton said. "A charmer."

"Suppose I do away with Alicia in your presence, even let you photograph the event? That would make us even, so to speak, and we could be confident of each other's silence."

"It would be a standoff," Vixton said slowly, brightening to the idea. "Better than a standoff, actually, as I'd have absolute proof of your guilt. But what do you have against Alicia?"

"Absolutely nothing. She's merely convenient for our purpose."

I watched Vixton consider this, then saw his eyes darken at the sudden thought behind them. "I'm even more convenient than Alicia, Cryptic. Wouldn't it solve your problem if you"—he laughed a flat croaking laugh—"murdered *me?*"

"You're *too* convenient," I told him. "One: you're in the apartment below me; the police are bound to question me and suspect. Two: however deeply buried, I do have a motive. On the other hand, I'm only one of Alicia's many escorts, and she and I get along splendidly and always have."

Vixton nodded slowly. "It's crazy but it makes sense—if that makes sense."

"It does," I assured him. "Alicia lives in a west-side penthouse apartment on the thirtieth floor. I'll arrange things so we can go there together tomorrow night and she can meet the same fate as your late wife."

Vixton's broad face widened in a smile. He chuckled, then laughed aloud and went to the bar in the corner and poured us each a drink. We toasted tall buildings.

The next night Vixton and I took the elevator to the thirtieth floor of Alicia's building and walked down the deep-carpeted hall to the door labeled with her apartment number. She must have heard us coming, for as I raised my hand to knock, the door opened.

"Cryptic," she said, "how good to see you!"

But it was better to see her. She was slender and tan in a long pink dress, with honey-blonde hair cascading in carefully arranged wildness to below her shoulders. She wanted to be in films, and on looks alone she had a chance.

"This is Mr. Vixton," I told her, as Vixton and I stepped inside. "He's a film producer from Los Angeles here to consider some outdoor locales for a movie."

Alicia's eyes took on a special, harder light. "Which of the studios are you from?"

"I'm an independent producer," Vixton said smoothly. He regarded Alicia with what passed for professional interest. "According to Mr. Cryptic you're a talented young woman."

"All she needs," I said with a smile, "is a little push."

Vixton coughed as Alicia led us out onto the balcony for drinks.

The balcony was large, bounded by a low iron rail on the east side and a four-foot-high stone wall on the north and south. Along the base of the iron rail ran a trough of rich earth from which grew a dense wall of green exotic foliage, including even two small trees. Like many cliff dwellers, Alicia was addicted to what green she could squeeze into her steel-and-cement-dominated existence.

Vixton had a martini, as did I. Alicia, as usual, drank a whiskey sour. I hastened to mix the drinks, my plan being to drop several capsules of a depressant into each of Alicia's whiskey sours. "Dangerous when mixed with alcohol," I had said to Vixton earlier, showing him a handful of the tiny capsules. "Downers in the true sense of the word."

In the thin cool air of the balcony I heard Vixton's harsh voice rasp, "It's going to be a great movie." He actually seemed to be enjoying himself. Alicia was on him like wet clothes.

After the third whiskey sour Alicia's eyelids seemed unable to make it more than halfway over her beautiful blue orbs, and I nodded to Vixton. While he watched, I held Alicia by the waist and guided her toward the iron railing.

"Don' wanna dance," she protested.

Vixton readied his pocket camera as I positioned Alicia just so before the lush green wall of foliage beyond which was star-speckled night sky. "Cryptic!" she said, suddenly alarmed.

"Sorry, love," I said, and pushed with my right hand. There was a quick sharp flash.

Alicia disappeared between the dense green branches, tumbling backward. One high-heeled shoe flew off as her tanned ankles flicked through the thick green leaves and disappeared. I heard a trailing scream, punctuated by Vixton's, "Got it!"

I glanced through the branches and quickly turned my head. "Let's go!" I said to Vixton, but he was already at the door that led inside the apartment. We took our martini glasses with us and hastily wiped our fingerprints from whatever else we might have touched.

There was no one in the hall as we walked quickly along the spongy carpet to the elevator and punched the button. Within a few minutes we were descending to street level. Perspiration had boiled to beads on Vixton's flat forehead.

We left by the building's side exit, got in my car, and quickly, but not too quickly, drove away. As we rounded the corner and passed the front of the building we saw a knot of people and a bare tanned foot protruding from a fold of pink material on the sidewalk. I drove faster.

Two days later I gave Vixton the details of Alicia's funeral.

And that's how we accomplished it—the perfect crime. I got the idea from *Life's Slender Thread,* that abominable French film. Only instead of a thin nylon rope, as used in the movie, we used a net from which there was access to the open window of the vacant apartment below Alicia's. It's true that Alicia wants to break into movies, but as a stuntperson, as I suppose they're now called. As promised, I might be able to arrange something for her.

After being caught in the net, Alicia quickly climbed through the window below, then ran out into the hall where she took the service elevator to ground level with Vixton and me minutes behind her. She then faked a crowd-gathering fainting spell on the sidewalk directly below her balcony.

I no longer have anything to fear from Vixton—but, just in case, I've moved out of the Norwood Arms and will be extremely difficult to locate. There was no way I could bear to kill Alicia, or even Vixton. Seeing that sort of thing done constantly on film is one thing, actually doing it another. I'm not a violent person; I like musicals.

My one concern is that Vixton will go to see *Life's Slender Thread.* But that isn't likely. Not after the review I gave it.

Joyce Porter

Dover Without Perks

" A nd this is where the body was found, sir."
Detective Chief Inspector Dover, having with difficulty been induced to leave the shelter of the police car, stood shivering inside his overcoat. He tossed an indifferent glance at the site before transferring his disgruntled gaze to his surroundings.

'Strewth, what a dump! Like the back of the bloody moon!

He was standing on a short stretch of access road which led from the busy dual carriageway on his left to a new housing development, just beginning to spread its unloveliness over the hillside on his right. From this distance the development was a jumble of unmade roads, scaffolding, patches of raw earth, and a few demoralized houses poking up like sore thumbs into the cold sky. Beyond, as far as the eye could see, lay acres of deserted, frost-bitten fields with only the occasional windswept hedge to break the monotony.

Such desolation made it all the more surprising that the access road proudly sported a brand-new pedestrian crossing, complete with black and white stripes and flashing orange beacons. It was here, some fifty yards before the access road swung round to glide into the dual carriageway, that the dead man had been found at 5:25 that morning.

"Funnily enough, sir, it was his son-in-law who found him. He's a milk roundsman and he was cycling down to his depot. It was still dark then, of course, but he spotted the old chap in the light of the beacon." Even Inspector York, the local man who was doing the honors, was stamping his feet to warm them.

But Dover, who had been transported from London to the scene of the crime with what he considered unseemly haste, still hadn't got his bearings. "Where the hell are we?" he demanded crossly while his young, handsome, and long-suffering assistant, Detective Sergeant MacGregor, turned aside to hide his blushing.

Inspector York was a little disconcerted, too. It was his first encounter with Scotland Yard's famous Murder Squad and he didn't know quite what to make of it. Surely they couldn't all be like this?

"Well, this is Willow Hill Farm Housing Estate, actually, sir," he said, indicating the miserable clutch of dwellings on the hillside.

"Part of Bridchurch's slum-clearance scheme. Bridchurch is where you got off the train, sir. It's three miles away." He pointed down the dual carriageway. "Someday, sir"—this time he made a generous, encircling gesture—"all this will be covered with houses. Meantime, it's all a bit isolated. Still, that should make our job a bit easier, shouldn't it, sir?"

Dover's response might have been a belch or it might have been an encouraging grunt.

Naively, Inspector York plumped for the encouraging grunt. "There are not likely to be many people knocking about round here on a dark November night," he explained earnestly. "We've been working on the hypothesis that the murderer has some connection with the housing estate. In fact, he probably lives there. We found a lump of dried mud not far from the body and it probably came off the car that hit him. Now, we're pretty certain that the mud came from the housing estate—it's a proper quagmire when it rains, as you can imagine. It hasn't, however, rained for a fortnight. Well, if our chappie was on the estate a fortnight ago, the odds are that he lives there. Or, at the very worst, he's a frequent visitor."

Dover's habitual scowl deepened appreciably. "If it's a local case, why the hell fetch us into it?"

Inspector York quailed before such naked fury. "Our Chief Constable thought the Yard would want to handle it themselves, sir, since the dead man was one of yours."

"One of ours?"

"Malcolm Bailey, sir. He was an ex-Metropolitan policeman. We thought there might be—well—ramifications."

"Ramifications? Was he Special Branch or what?"

"No, sir." Inspector York wished the Chief Constable was there to do his own dirty work. "His last job before retirement was court usher at Ealing actually. Since then he's had fifteen years with the Corps of Commissionaires in the West End. He was a Londoner, you see. Nothing to do with Bridchurch at all."

But Dover's butterfly mind had already moved on to weightier problems. The murder of obscure superannuated coppers could wait. "Here," he said, trying to disappear into the depths of his overcoat, "where've you set up the Murder Headquarters? I'm getting bloody frozen out here. Got us a nice cosy pub, have you?"

To date, unfortunately, there were no pubs on the Willow Hill Farm Estate. Nor were there any shops, cinemas, or other amenities.

"We were going to use a caravan, sir, but it hasn't arrived yet. I've been trying to chase it up but—"

But Dover was already stumping back to the comparative warmth and shelter of the police car. After a moment's hesitation MacGregor and Inspector York followed him.

Once they were all in the car, MacGregor took charge of things since Dover appeared to have lost all interest and was sitting slumped in a corner with his bowler hat pulled well down over his eyes. If it hadn't been completely unthinkable, Inspector York might have been tempted to conclude that old Mastermind was having a bit of a snooze.

"If Bailey was a Londoner," said MacGregor, resting his notebook awkwardly on his knees, "what was he doing down here?"

"He'd come for a few days' holiday with his daughter. He arrived only yesterday."

"That's the daughter who's married to the milkman who found the body?"

"Yes. They're named Muldoon. Apparently, last night, the dead man decided to go out for a drink. Like I said, there aren't any pubs on the Estate, so he had to catch a bus out there on the main road and go into Bridchurch."

"The Muldoons didn't go with him?"

"No. They don't go out much at night in the middle of the week because of him having to be up so early in the morning."

MacGregor pondered. "The Muldoons didn't raise the alarm when Bailey failed to return home at a reasonable hour?"

"They didn't know. It's this milk business again. Both Muldoon and his wife go to bed early—about half past nine, they say. Last night they simply gave Bailey a key and told him to let himself in when he got back. They'd no idea, they claim, that he wasn't fast asleep in the spare room until Muldoon himself practically fell over the dead body on the pedestrian crossing."

Dover, roused by a crick in the back of his neck, joined in the conversation. "Damned fool place to stick a zebra crossing," he grumbled, massaging the offending spot. "Right out here in the back of beyond."

Inspector York risked a placatory smile. "It's supposed to be a mistake on the part of the Highways Department, sir. It should have been erected on another housing development on the other side of town."

" 'Strewth!" said Dover and surrendered himself once more to torpidity.

Inspector York, a novice at Dover-watching, waited to see if any more pearls of wisdom were going to drop from beneath that motheaten little black mustache, but luckily MacGregor knew a snore when he heard one.

"What about the medical evidence? Have we got a time of death yet?"

Inspector York dragged his eyes away. "Er—oh, yes, sorry, Sergeant! Time of death? About eleven last night. That fits with the supposition that Bailey would be on the last bus from Bridchurch which would drop him out there on the main road just before eleven. He wouldn't hang about on such a cold night and I reckon he simply walked from the bus stop to where he was found and was killed there. He wasn't robbed, by the way."

"And the cause of death?"

"Head bashed in with a blunt instrument. However"—Inspector York leaned forward so as to deliver his *bonne bouche* with maximum effect—"before that he'd been knocked down by a car. The doctor's absolutely sure about it. Bailey was severely bruised all down the left side, though it's unlikely the car was damaged. Still, you see what it means, Sergeant?"

"Oh, I think so," said MacGregor with a patronizing smile, the local bobby not having yet been born who could catch him napping. "It means that Bailey was probably knocked down by a car which was coming *from* the housing estate." He flapped a languid hand. "If Bailey got off the bus at that stop, he'd walk down there and cross this road here at the crossing with his left-hand side towards the housing estate. Interesting."

Inspector York suppressed an unworthy longing to sink his fist up to the wrist in a certain smug young face, then reminded himself that it was his job to be helpful. He got a couple of sheets of paper out of his pocket. "Luckily," he said, "there aren't many people on the estate who can afford to run a car these days. It takes some of 'em all they can manage to pay the bus fares. Anyhow"—he passed one sheet of paper over—"there's a list of those who have got cars. And here"—he held out the second sheet—"is a real bonus!"

"You don't say!"

Inspector York gritted his teeth. Much more of this and he'd leave the pair of 'em to stew in their own juice! "It's the name and address of an old lady who may narrow the field down even further. My lads had a chat with her earlier on and she seems bright enough. However, she's no chicken, so you'll have to use your own judgment."

"Your lads seem to have been very busy," said MacGregor as he accepted the second sheet.

Inspector York let some of the bitterness show through. "My lads," he muttered angrily, "could have had this case tied up a couple of hours ago if they hadn't been told to hang back and wait for you lot."

Mrs. Alice Golightly was 84 years old and still fighting back in spite of the fact that she had been sentenced to virtual solitary confinement by a caring community. The sheltered housing, into which she had been moved, was miles away from all her friends and relations and consisted of a drab row of two-roomed units built halfway up a steepish hill and fronting onto a block of communal garages.

"Bloody motor cars!" quavered Mrs. Golightly. "I'd ban 'em if I was prime minister, straight I would." She leaned across and gave Dover a poke in the paunch to gain his attention. "Nasty stinking things! They're more bloomin' bother than they're worth."

MacGregor smiled a kindly smile

Mrs. Golightly leered back. It had been a long time since she'd had two fine chaps like this hanging on her every word. "There's that young punk up at the back," she went on. "You know—What's-his-name." She rummaged around in her memory. "Miller—that's him! Woke me up at ten past seven this morning trying to start his car—grind, grind, grind! Well, that meant I had to go to the toilet, didn't it? I'd hardly got sat down when—damn me!—he finally gets it going and all these stinking, smelly petrol fumes come pouring in through the bathroom window where there's gaps you could drive a corporation bus through. It's a public scandal! There isn't a bloody window in this whole bloody row that fits proper."

Dover roused himself to recall his hostess to a sense of what was fitting and proper. "Don't you," he bellowed at her, "usually have a cup of coffee about this time, missus? And a butt and a few biscuits?"

Mrs. Golightly was not amused and MacGregor rushed in before she could start expressing her opinion of those who attempted to sponge on old-age pensioners. "Er—does this Mr. Miller often wake you up starting his car?"

"He'd better not! Next time I'll have the law on him. Bloody motor cars!" She looked up. "I remember when it was all horses," she boasted. "Not but what they hadn't got some disgusting habits, but at least they didn't go messing your telly up!"

"Ah," said MacGregor with heaven-sent inspiration, "your television, Mrs. Golightly! Is that how you know when the cars use the garages opposite?"

Mrs. Golightly nodded grimly. "They break my picture up something cruel," she grumbled. "Every last one of 'em! And don't talk to me about suppressors! They've all had 'em fitted and it doesn't make a ha'porth of difference. I've had them Post Office engineers round here," she went on savagely. "Endless. Nothing but kids, most of 'em, and about as much use as my old boot. I have to keep a bloody record for 'em now, you know." She snatched a small writing pad off the table and waved it contemptuously. "Like I told her from the Welfare—it's coming to something when a lady's word isn't good enough!"

MacGregor tried to unravel things, just in case Dover was still listening. "You keep a note of every time there's interference with your television picture," he said, "and that means every time a car enters or leaves those garages opposite."

Mrs. Golightly's sniff acknowledged that this was so.

"And you watch television all evening?"

"I watch it all day," came the forthright answer. "And so will you when you're my age, sonny! I'd have it on now if you lot weren't here putting me through the third degree."

"And last night?"

"None of them went in or out after six o'clock. Well, they never do on a Thursday, do they?"

"Don't they?"

"Everybody's skint on a Thursday." Mrs. Golightly appreciated a bit of company but you could have too much of a good thing. "Friday's payday. Nobody's got any money left to go gallivanting on a Thursday. I should have thought even you'd know that."

Dover heaved himself to his feet. Although, to the untutored eye, his role in the interview may have appeared completely passive, some information had evidently filtered through. "I'll just go and have a look at that toilet," he said.

MacGregor tried to pass the time in small talk, but Mrs. Golightly's aged ears didn't miss a thing. Eventually she raised her voice over the sound of rushing water. "That fellow who's been killed—"

"Malcolm Bailey?" asked MacGregor.

"I saw him when he arrived," said Mrs. Golightly. "A fine figure of a man." She paused spitefully to underline her point. "What I call a *real* policeman!"

So, if old Mrs. Golightly's evidence was to be believed, none of the cars habitually kept in the block of garages could have been involved in the murder.

"And that, actually, sir, leaves us with only three suspects." MacGregor gazed unhappily around at the wilderness of builders' rubbish and half finished houses. "The people who own cars but who leave them parked out on the road. Always assuming, of course, that Bailey was killed by whoever knocked him down. I wonder what the motive was. It can't be anything to do with his past life, surely. He's been retired for ages and he doesn't seem to have been exactly a ball of fire when he was in the Force. On the other hand, he's hardly been down here long enough to make enemies. Less then twenty-four hours and this was his first visit." MacGregor sighed. "I think we'll have to have a good long look at this daughter and her husband."

Dover was not the man for idle speculation. "For God's sake, let's get out of the bloody wind!" he growled. "It's enough to freeze a brass monkey!"

MacGregor, being MacGregor, knew where he was going. "Azalea Crescent, sir," he said as he led the way into a slightly curving, potholed stretch of road. "Mr. Jarrow lives here. And that, I imagine, is his car." Ever mindful that Dover's eyesight was something less than keen, MacGregor indicated an enormous black Humber parked by the curb and sparkling magnificently in the pale sunlight.

Sparkling?

"*Stop that!*" MacGregor leaped forward and screamed like a banshee.

The man with the soft duster jumped back as though stung. "Eh?"

"You're destroying evidence!"

"What?"

"Didn't the police tell you we might want to examine that car?"

The unfortunate perfectionist shook his head. "A couple of 'em had a good look at it earlier on," he said lamely.

"Didn't they tell you not to touch it?"

Bill Jarrow gesticulated feebly with his duster. "I was just passing the time, like."

It was Dover—he of the aching feet and the rumbling stomach—who moved the proceedings indoors. Bill Jarrow put his duster away and called to his wife to put the coffee on. He thus insured that, unless the evidence was *very* strong to the contrary, he'd be able to get away with murder where Dover was concerned. He further endeared himself by keeping his answers short and to the point, seemingly knowing by instinct that Dover valued brevity well above truthfulness.

Mr. Jarrow proved to be a taxi driver and the car he had been polishing belonged to the company for whom he worked. Most weekday evenings, when business was slack, he was allowed to bring the car home with him and answer any calls from his house. "It saves 'em keeping the office open," he explained.

"Did you get called out last night?"

"No. Me and the missus sat watching telly till it was time for bed."

"So your wife is the only witness?"

Bill Jarrow didn't seem unduly perturbed that his alibi was being questioned. "You can check the mileage if you like. They'll have a note at the office of what it was yesterday evening when I left. You can soon see if it doesn't tally."

Since Dover had got his National Health Service dentures inextricably sunk in Mrs. Jarrow's homemade treacle cake, MacGregor carried on with the questioning. "There's no meter on the taxi?"

"Not this one. We use this one for funerals, you see," said Mr. Jarrow, passing Dover's cup through the kitchen hatch for a refill. "Folk don't like to see a meter clicking away when they're following their loved ones to the crematorium."

MacGregor examined Bill Jarrow thoughtfully. "Anything to stop you getting a call, doing the job, altering the mileage reading, and pocketing the fare?" he asked pleasantly.

For the first time, Mr. Jarrow's occupational antipathy to the police showed through. "Trust you bloody cops!" he said disgustedly. "Look, mate, I've been a taxi driver for twenty years. I wouldn't last five minutes if I started pulling tricks like that. What do you think my boss is, stupid or something? Petrol consumption alone'd be a dead giveaway. And suppose I had a smashup? Or somebody saw me?"

Bill Jarrow continued to wax indignant for some time, but eventually he recovered his equilibrium sufficiently to direct MacGregor to Japonica Mount, their next port of call. It was so close at hand that even Dover didn't think it was worth demanding a police car . . .

"That chap might have run us there in his taxi," Dover observed sourly as he and MacGregor proceeded slowly on their way back past Mrs. Golightly's humble abode, "if you hadn't been so bloody rude to him. What got into you? Any fool could see he's too thick to be anything but honest."

MacGregor didn't agree. "You don't need much intelligence, sir, to alter a mileage reading. And he was giving that car a thorough cleaning. He could have been removing traces of incriminating evidence."

"Stuff!" puffed Dover, already finding the going hard. "Besides, where's the motive? He'd never even met What's-his-name."

"Bailey, sir." MacGregor was well used to Dover's inability to remember any name (including probably his own) for more than five minutes. "Besides, I don't think we're looking for that kind of motive."

"Oh, don't you?" sneered Dover in a poor imitation of MacGregor's refined accent. "Well, what kind of motive are we looking for, Smartie-boots?"

"I think the murder is tied up with the car accident, sir."

Dover paused to contemplate the young mountain which had suddenly loomed up in front of them. 'Strewth, if he'd realized that the "couple of hundred yards" was going to be straight up . . . "Of course it's tied up with the car accident," he growled, once he'd got his breath back. "The killer runs Whatd'yecall'im down and immobilizes him, and then gets out to finish him off with a tire lever or something. Gangsters in America are doing it all the time."

"It'll be just by that small red car, sir," said MacGregor, cringing as Dover grabbed his arm and hung on. As a 240-pound weakling, the Chief Inspector wasn't fussy about who shared the burden. "I was thinking of a slight variation, actually," MacGregor went on, failing to appreciate that aching feet were now looming larger in Dover's mind than violent death. "I was wondering if the murder had to be committed *because* of the accident. That would fit Jarrow, you see.

"Suppose he had been doing a job without his employer's knowledge, and during the course of it accidentally knocked Mr. Bailey down. Well, to report the accident in the normal way would expose what he'd been doing and he'd get the sack. So"—even MacGregor was beginning to sound unconvinced—"he finished Bailey off. I admit it sounds a bit thin, sir, but"—MacGregor cheered up—"plenty of murders have been done for less."

"This it?"

They had climbed almost to the top of the steep incline that was Japonica Mount and were now level with the small red car. According to its number plate it was fourteen years old and it was obvious why its owner wasn't paying out good money to rent a garage for it.

Dover turned thankfully through the little wrought-iron gate and waddled up the path. The curtains in the front room had twitched but he stuck his finger in the bell-push and rested his weight on it.

A woman opened the door and Dover was halfway inside before he discovered, to his undisguised chagrin, that it was the wrong house.

"No," said the woman, "I'm Mrs. Jedryschowski. The Millers live the next house down." She moved forward fractionally and pointed.

Dover's fury mounted as he realized that the Miller house was one they had already passed.

"You'll not find her there, of course," said Mrs. Jedryschowski, "but he's in. The police turned him back when he was going to work."

Dover wasn't prepared to let the matter rest there. It was MacGregor's fault for dragging him to the wrong address, of course, but this Mrs. Whatever-her-name-was must take some of the blame. "That his car?" he demanded, with menace.

"Mr. Miller's?" Mrs. Jedryschowski eyed Dover with some suspicion. "Yes, it's his car."

"Then why is it parked outside your house?"

Not for the first time MacGregor marveled at Dover's unerring ability to grasp at the inessential.

It was all one to Mrs. Jedryschowski, of course. "You might well ask," she said, leaning forward to stare at the vehicle in question. "He always leaves it there. We have spoken to him about it but it makes no difference. He says it's something to do with saving his battery."

MacGregor, of course, understood perfectly. "Oh, you mean he starts it by letting it run down the hill."

Mrs. Jedryschowski, something of an ignoramus where the internal combustion engine was concerned, nodded. "Something like that. If he leaves it outside his own front door, he doesn't get a long enough run or something." She watched her visitors go back halfway down the path before closing the door on them.

Henry Miller was a livelier character than his next-door neighbor, though not by much. He welcomed Dover and MacGregor into a house that was clearly lacking a woman's touch. Dover realized there was a fat chance of being offered any decent light refreshments here. He shoved a bundle of old socks out of the most comfortable-looking armchair and flopped down. This was going to be a bloody short interview.

Mr. Miller cleared a couple of dirty plates off another chair for MacGregor. "Bit of a mess," he mumbled in apology. "What with the wife being away—"

"Not ill, I hope?" asked MacGregor politely as he got his notebook out.

"Not exactly." Mr. Miller perched himself on the arm of the settee and looked hunted. Like everybody else on the housing estate, he knew all about the murder. He didn't, however, know Mr. Bailey or his daughter and her husband. "People keep themselves to themselves round here," he explained. "We don't want to impose. And this time of year you don't want to leave your own fireside, do you?"

Mr. Miller paused in the hope that somebody else might like to say something, but they didn't. "I work as a groundsman," he volunteered. "At Bridchurch Central Junior School. The police stopped me when I was driving off to work this morning and said I was to stay at home till somebody came and took a statement off me or something. They had a look at my car, too."

There was another pause. Mr. Miller mopped his brow. This time, however, MacGregor took pity on him and tossed a question.

Mr. Miller was grateful but unhelpful. "No, I didn't. I got back from work about four o'clock and I didn't leave the house again till this morning."

Even MacGregor was obliged to swallow a yawn. Dover, of course, wasn't even pretending to listen and was now resting his eyes against the light.

"You're alone in the house?"

Mr. Miller blinked. "Yes. With the wife being away like."

MacGregor looked at the layer of burnt crumbs which covered one corner of the table. "Has she been away long, sir?"

Mr. Miller sighed. "Only three days. I'm afraid I've been. letting the housework slip a bit."

Having been given MacGregor's solemn word that the home of the last car owner could be reached in three minutes and that it was downhill all the way, Dover reluctantly consented to walk.

Since it really was downhill, the Great Detective had breath to spare for an in-depth discussion of the case so far. "That milksop?" he questioned incredulously. "You must have lost your marbles! He couldn't say boo to a goose!"

"He hasn't got an alibi, sir."

"Innocent people never have alibis," retorted Dover, generously imparting the fruits of his many years of experience. "Besides, where's his motive? What's-his-name could hardly get *him* into trouble for driving his own blooming car."

"Miller might have come up against Bailey in a professional capacity, sir. Bailey might have nabbed him for something and this is a revenge killing."

"A revenge killing?" Dover's uninhibited hoot of mirth sent the sea gulls winging up from a nearby field. " 'Strewth, you've been at those detective-story books again! Revenge—on a clapped-out copper from Ealing who's been retired for twenty years?" Dover, seeing that MacGregor was about to correct his figures, rushed raucously on. "That Miller pouf would still have been in his cradle when Who's-your-father was pounding the beat."

MacGregor quietly resolved to check whether Miller had a police record and if there was any possible earlier connection between him and the deceased. "Ah, here we are, sir."

They had just turned into Viburnum Avenue and the car this time was a huge and very ancient Ford, liberally decorated with anarchistic slogans, Mickey Mouse stickers, pictures of nude ladies, and rust. Inside the appropriate house they found the owner of this vehicle—Lionel Hutchinson. He was a moronic-looking, slack-mouthed teenager, the epitome of a petty, unsuccessful crook. Lionel's mother, having let Dover and MacGregor into the house while her ewe-lamb remained lolling full-length on the sofa, returned wearily to her ironing.

Young Lionel was uncooperative. "You must be joking!" He removed neither his eyes from his comic book nor the cigarette from his mouth. "Drive that jalopy out there? Watcher trying to do—trap me?"

"I was merely asking if you went out in it last night," said MacGregor.

"Not last night and not for months!" said Lionel. "Because why? Because it hasn't passed its M.O.T. test, it isn't licensed, and it's not insured. Damn, I should have thought even you punks knew it was a criminal offense to take a car like that on the bleeding road. Besides"—he chucked his cigarette stub vaguely in the direction of the fireplace and reached for the packet on the floor at his side—"I can't affort the petrol."

Mrs. Hutchinson spoke up. "He doesn't get hardly anything from Social Security."

Dover looked hopefully at the packet of cigarettes, but it was not handed round. That was the trouble with these working-class crimes—no bloody perks! Dover vented his disappointment on Lionel. "You took that car out last night, didn't you?"

Lionel turned over the page. "Negative, Fatso."

"Just because it wasn't taxed and insured?" sneered Dover. "Try pulling the other one!"

Mrs. Hutchinson came galloping to the rescue again. "He's got to watch his step," she explained. "It's prison next time they catch him."

Lionel raised himself up and glared at his mother with less than filial affection.

Dover had another spot. "You took that car out last night and—"

"Stuff yourself!"

"—ran Bailey down because he was a copper and then—"

"Aw, get knotted!"

"—got out and finished him off as he lay there helpless."

Lionel Hutchinson struggled into a sitting position. "Without nicking his wallet?" Almost as exhausted by the effort as Dover would have been, he sank back. "I was home all evening. Ask my mum!"

Once they were safely outside, Dover waxed bolder. "I'll get that little bleeder!" he promised, looking fierce.

MacGregor took a more moderate line. "I doubt if he'd have the guts to kill a grown man, sir. Mugging old ladies for their pension books is about his limit."

"There's probably a gang of 'em," grunted Dover. He was bored, hungry, thirsty, and suffering from nicotine starvation.

"Perhaps forensic will turn up something on the murder weapon," said MacGregor hopefully. "And I think we must examine these cars again, too. I can't really believe that the car that knocked Bailey down would be completely unmarked."

They were walking slowly back up the hill and Dover was in no condition to contradict everything MacGregor said just for the hell of it.

"Oh, look, sir!" MacGregor pointed. "There's the caravan at last. Good! Now at least we'll have somewhere we can settle down to work in."

Dover shied like a nervous horse at the mere mention of work. "I want my lunch! I'm starving."

"Oh, there'll be coffee and sandwiches in the caravan for sure, sir."

By some miracle Dover found the puff to tell MacGregor what he could do with his coffee and sandwiches, interrupting his tirade only to stick his tongue out at old Mrs. Golightly who was peeping out from behind her curtains.

MacGregor hastened to make amends by giving her a cheery smile and raising his hat. "Poor old thing," he said when he could get a word in. "You'd think they could do something better for them than this, wouldn't you, sir? Sticking them out here miles away from anywhere and right on top of those noisy garages, to say nothing of having petrol fumes seeping in through your bathroom window. Good God!"

Afterward, both MacGregor and Dover claimed to have spotted it first but, since Dover had fewer inhibitions about bawling his head off on the public highway, he tended to hog the glory at the time.

He stopped dead in his tracks. "But there shouldn't have been any petrol fumes!"

By great good fortune there they were, standing right on the spot. Branching off on the left as they went up the hill was the row of houses for the old-age pensioners. And running up even higher behind them was Japonica Mount. Miller's small red car was clearly visible, not more than a couple of hundred feet away, still outside Mrs. Jedryschowski's house and still with its nose pointing down the hill.

Dover's brain nearly blew a gasket as he struggled to work it out. "How far," he panted, "on a cold morning would you have to let that car roll down the hill before you could start it?"

MacGregor was amazed at Dover's grasp of the technical problem involved. "Oh, right to the bottom, I imagine, sir. Certainly well past Mrs. Golightly's bathroom window."

"We've got him!" said Dover, and rested his case.

MacGregor felt they needed a little more than that. "Miller could have started his car on the starter this morning for some reason or other, sir."

"Why the hell should he? And even if he did, the fumes still wouldn't get into that old biddie's bog, would they?"

"Not if the car was parked outside Mrs. Jedryschowski's house where it is now, sir," agreed MacGregor. "On the other hand"—his eyes narrowed as he took in the topography of the area—"if he started the car on the starter outside his own house, old Mrs. Golightly would certainly have got the full benefit of both the noise and the smoke. He'd be hardly any distance away as the crow flies."

Dover had had his fill of the Willow Hill Farm Housing Estate. "Come on," he said with unwonted enthusiasm, "let's go get him!"

MacGregor was appalled. "But there could be dozens of perfectly innocent explanations, sir," he bleated anxiously. "I think it would be a big mistake for us to go off half cocked like this before we've—"

"You speak for yourself, laddie!" snorted Dover, already charging up the hill like a two-year-old tortoise. "Me, I've never gone off half cocked at anything in my whole bloody life!"

It was fortunate for the Cause of Justice that Henry Miller was one of Nature's losers.

"I knew I'd never get away with it," he said dejectedly as Dover lay panting like a stranded whale in one of the armchairs and MacGregor, getting his notebook out, issued the formal caution. "Oh, I don't mind making a statement. Why not?"

"Keep it short," advised Dover, cursing himself for not having had his lunch first. He accepted a cigarette from MacGregor, unaware that it was offered with the sole aim of stopping his mouth up.

But Miller had never been much of a talker in any case. "My wife left me a couple of days ago," he mumbled. "Just went. Late last night I got to wondering if she'd gone to stay with her sister. I thought I'd drive over and see."

"What time did you leave?"

Miller shrugged. "Latish."

"How did you start your car?"

"Like I always do—I let it roll down the hill."

"And you headed for the main road?"

"That's right. I wasn't going fast or anything. Then, just by the zebra crossing, he stepped out right in front of me and—bang!—I hit him. Not hard. I wasn't doing more than twenty. I stopped and got out. Well, he just lay there in the road, cursing me up hill and down dale. A right mouthful. Said I knocked him down deliberate on a pedestrian crossing and he'd have the Law on me.

"Said he'd charge me with dangerous driving and God knows what. I tried to calm him down a bit and ask if he was hurt, but he just kept on shouting. Said he was an ex-policeman and that he'd see me behind bars if it was the last thing he did. Well, he would have, wouldn't he? My word against his? I wouldn't have stood a chance. So I killed him."

"Just like that?" Dover didn't like to hear of policemen being disposed of so casually.

"I couldn't afford to be found guilty, you see," said Miller drearily. "Not on any charge. I've been in trouble before, you see."

"I'm not surprised," sniffed Dover. "Was it Bailey who nabbed you?"

"Oh, no, nothing like that. I didn't know Mr. Bailey from Adam."

"Then why kill him, for God's sake?"

Miller sighed heavily. "It was when I was still up north. I"—he cleared his throat and avoided looking at either of his two inquisitors—"well, it was sort of to do with sex."

"Oh, yes?" said Dover, on whom the mouth-stopping cigarette was not working too well.

Miller moistened his lips. "Children, actually," he muttered. "I got six months. But"—he raised his head with a faint show of defiance—"that was four years ago and I haven't been in trouble since. I pulled myself together, see? I moved down here and got myself a good job and got married and everything."

MacGregor understood. "You were afraid that if you were convicted on this motoring charge, your previous record would come out in open court?"

"They say they don't punish you twice for the same offense, but they do. I'd have lost my job straight off. I work at a school, you see. Kids everywhere. And then there's the wife. She'd have never come back if she knew I'd been in the nick for molesting kids. And then there's the neighbors." He appealed to the more sympathetic face confronting him. "You can see how I was fixed, can't you? I couldn't just do nothing and let him ruin my life. I didn't want to kill him, but he gave me no choice. I hit him with the wheel brace."

But Dover's heart was not made of stone. He saw how distressed

Miller was and was ready with solace. He addressed MacGregor. "Why don't you go and make us all a nice cup of tea, laddie?"

Miller raised his head. "There's a bottle of whiskey in the sideboard," he said shyly.

Dover beamed. "Even better! Where do you keep your glasses?"

Miller's statement was completed in an increasingly convivial atmosphere and he had to be asked several times about the parking of his car after the murder.

"Oh, that," he said. "Well, I forgot all about going after the missus and I come rushing back here. All I wanted was to get out of sight as quick as possible. That's why I left the car right outside instead of driving it to the top of the hill and turning it around ready for the morning like I usually do."

"So when you left for work today you had to start the car on the starter?" MacGregor, of course, didn't drink on duty and was as sober as a judge.

"That's right. I had the devil of a job with it. It really needs a new battery but what with one thing and another . . . Anyhow, I won't have to bother about that now, will I?"

"What did you do with the murder weapon?"

"It's under the coal in the shed. I was going to chuck it in the canal when things quietened down. Here"—for the first time Miller showed a flicker of curiosity—"how did you get on to me?"

"It was the break in the pattern, laddie!" said Dover, feeling he owed his host something for the whiskey. "If you'd turned your car and parked it like you always did outside the Jedryschowskis, you'd have got away with it."

MacGregor gawped. How on earth had the old fool managed to hang onto a name like Jedryschowski, for heaven's sake?

"You got cloth ears or something, laddie?"

MacGregor abandoned his disloyal speculations. "Sir?"

"I said, go and get somebody to take him away."

MacGregor hesitated. Leave Dover alone with a self-confessed murderer? "Will you be all right, sir?"

Dover winked wickedly and reached for the whiskey bottle. "Oh, I'll be fine, Sergeant!" he said. "Just fine now!"

"Q"

Nigel Morland

The de Rougemont Case

Jersey, the largest of Britain's Channel Islands, is not the sort of place where anything spectacular ever happens; but when it does it is always remarkable—as, for example, the de Rougemont case.

This occurred in the lonely northern parish of St. Jerome where the local inhabitants were mainly concerned with the growing of potatoes and tomatoes for the mainland markets.

To understand something of the official background, it is as well to explain that Jersey's only large town, St. Helier, possesses regular uniformed police. In all the outside parishes (each one a self-contained unit) the law is administered by a Constable through his Centeniers—civilians who work without pay but who hold full powers of office and, indeed, under the Law, supreme power; it is a system that goes back to Duke William of Normandy (William the Conqueror) from whose lands the Islanders originally came. And one of the obstinate Norman-French speaking peasants of Jersey was Jean Soustrelle.

Centenier Soustrelle was a peaceful man, a farmer who could trace his ancestry back a thousand years to Normandy. He was a Norman countryman to the life—short, stout, and rubicund, a bumbling man of remarkable amiability and an almost bovine look. And one still August morning, when France just across the waters of the bay looked as if it were only a mile away, Soustrelle was told that Richard de Rougemont wished to see him.

"De Rougemont—" Soustrelle ambled from the byre where he had been working when his housekeeper summoned him "—who has bought the new house on La Rochelle Point?"

"Veritably, m'sieu." The housekeeper spoke in the antiquated French common in the families of the old *Jersaise*. "He is deeply disturbed, that one."

"Hm." Soustrelle wiped his hands on his grimy jeans and slipped his bare feet into a pair of espadrilles. "Inform him I will be there within moments." He paused in the kitchen to take a quick swig from a jug of Calvados.

Richard de Rougemont was waiting in the stuffy parlor in the front of the Soustrelle farmhouse. He rose from his chair as Soustrelle entered—a tall, neatly dressed man.

"Good morning, Centenier." His voice was harsh and obviously he was no local product, for he spoke in the clipped English of the mainland. "I am sorry to disturb you. I have bad news."

"Yes?" Soustrelle's mild blue eyes were unsurprised. "It is of a truth that it is always bad news when I am called Centenier."

"I see." De Rougemont touched his forhead with a shaking hand. "Mr. Soustrelle, I was born in Jersey but left as a boy for England where I have since lived. Now that I have retired I returned here with my wife to live out my years in a peaceful place."

"Excellent. And?"

"Centenier, for a long time I have suspected she had a lover. I could not prove it. When we came here I rented a house in the west end of the island, in St. Michelet. To please her I have since bought a house on La Rochelle. We were to move in next week. Yesterday afternoon my wife did not return to tea, nor did she return during the night. I was alarmed but did not take any action because twice before she has spent the night at our new house to enjoy its atmosphere—she is an artist, an amateur, you see." Soustrelle nodded as if this explained such eccentricity. "I went to our house."

"And—she is there?"

"Yes. The house is filled with our furniture, ready for us to move in, but we were waiting a few days until the smell of new paint has vanished—I find it sickens me. Yes, she is there." De Rougemont paused. "She is on the bed in our room. A man is beside her—a man named Venning, who, my *dear* friends have hinted to me, was her lover."

"You mean, they are dead?"

"I smelled gas when I opened the front door. I tried the bedroom door; it was locked. There is a balcony and I went there, peering into the bedroom." De Rougemont shuddered, covering his eyes with one hand.

"We will go there immediately. You have a motor car?"

The de Rougemont car was as new and shining as was, Soustrelle observed, the de Rougemont house. It was a fine place on a promontory overlooking the sea and the distant beaches of France, shining whitely under the sun.

Inside the wide hall Soustrelle sniffed gently, admiring what he could see of this elegant house so far superior to his peasant's farmhouse. And with a peasant's interest in money he wondered what all this splendor had cost.

De Rougemont led the way upstairs, through a spare room to a balcony which ran the length of the house. He paused before an uncurtained French window.

Soustrelle peered through the glass, then made a small sound of distress. On the bed, fully dressed, lay a gray-haired man and beside him a good-looking woman of early middle age.

"You will go at once for the doctor, Mr. de Rougemont. It is the red house at the end of your road. Advise him and mention my name."

When the sound of a car moving away had reassured him, Soustrelle lifted one foot, ruthlessly kicking in the glass of the door and muttering when he bruised his big toe. The fresh breeze from the sea emptied the room of gas quickly, once the French windows had been opened. Soustrelle sniffed cautiously after some minutes, then entered.

Both bodies were cold; on the dressing table was a note signed *Agnes*, a brief heart-cry explaining that, devoted as she was to her husband, she and Venning could no longer face life in their separate worlds and had resolved to die together.

Soustrelle muttered angrily in French; he hated waste of any sort and here were two lives thrown away, to say nothing of de Rougemont's sorrow and, perhaps, that of Venning's family.

But there was work to do. The room had to be examined to satisfy Soustrelle's inborn sense of doubt and caution.

The hissing, unlighted gas-fire was turned off. The windows were checked; Soustrelle observed they were carefully sealed with wide Scotch tape. The typical pertinacity of suicides was revealed in the diligent way the crack round the door had also been completely sealed with tape. Even the keyhole was closed with a small sticky seal; the key lay on the dressing table, next to the letter.

When the doctor at last arrived and had confirmed what had happened, there was a curiously mulish expression on Soustrelle's round face. Against the doctor's objections that he was busy, that there was no need for it, Soustrelle insisted—which he was empowered to do—that a post-mortem should be done, and not until he was given the results of it did he visit the big white house where the Constable lived, with a brass plate on his front door which announced *Connétable*, a title meaning much more than its bald English translation.

The plump white-haired old man who was, as it were, the father, the councillor, the protector of his parish, listened to Soustrelle's story without speaking.

"I understand, my good friend. Then they died of gas poisoning?"

"Of that there is no doubt." Soustrelle's head moved from side to side in that odd Gallic gesture which can mean anything, and his shoulders came up. "There is present a mild sleeping drug, a barbiturate, which Dr. Mathieu says is not unusual—suicides do such things that they might die painlessly without knowing they die; the tablets we find on the table beside the bed."

"There remains a problem? Come, my good man, I recognize that stubborn look only too well."

"I am not content, you will understand, Michel. May I continue with my investigations?"

"Such a fine word! You mean, it is not suicide in a locked room, sealed from within? Come, Jean, you are not a man of imaginative fancies. There is no harder head on this island."

"Will you have patience with an old man, Michel? You permit?"

"Until tomorrow night. After that we must follow routine. We have enough harsh words about us from the Paid Police in St. Helier—I do not wish to give them more reason to say our antiquated system is also stupid."

Soustrelle went home and put on his good gray suit and the trilby hat that his long-dead wife had once bought for him on a trip to Verona. He summoned Pierre-Marc, who owned the decrepit village taxi, and bade him to drive to St. Helier, "And with care and caution, my friend, for much as we like the tourists who bring us prosperity, they always forget the narrowness of our twisting little roads."

St. Helier was packed with the hordes of holiday-makers who pour into Jersey every year for sunshine and tax-free tobacco and liquor. Through these throngs Soustrelle made his slow way, to spend an hour in a bistro near the harbor where visitors never went; but the place was popular with the native born, particularly the ancients with their remarkable knack of knowing supposedly hidden secrets which passed steadily as the small change of gossip.

Following that, Soustrelle visited several shops, finding what he wanted in the last of them. Then he returned with Pierre-Marc to St. Jerome and spent some minutes in the now-empty de Rougemont house. He delved through the rooms and peered interestedly in a broom closet where he found a portable hand vacuum-cleaner, the type used by good housewives for going over soft furniture.

Standing in the new and unused sitting room, staring through the windows at the gentle sea, Soustrelle was far away. He lighted his pipe and the rank aroma of the French tobacco he favored was all about him. His shrewd, always cynical peasant mind worried at the problem he was brooding over and gradually, piece by piece, he erected an edifice of deduction. He examined it with slow mental eyes from every conceivable angle and could find no flaw in it. He nodded at last, making a little jerking motion of one hand as if he were demonstrating the upper half of a ball.

The patient Pierre-Marc was waiting in his taxi. He was ordered to drive Soustrelle to the house of Prunier, the Constable of St. Michelet Parish where de Rougemont rented a house. There the story was told again and, eventually, Prunier sent for one of his Centeniers and they went to de Rougemont's home.

But there they learned he had left to stay at a hotel in St. Helier. This irritated Soustrelle because it meant complications, and more work. He thanked Prunier and went back to St. Jerome, where he carefully wrote out in his round schoolboy hand in its official form a deposition which he took to his Constable for an authorizing signature. It was given reluctantly and then only because of Soustrelle's written assurance that he knew what he was doing.

Pierre-Marc was required to journey back to town again, and there Soustrelle visited the Constable of St. Helier, then the Chief of the Paid Police; Soustrelle, two uniformed men, and the Constable of St. Helier now visited the hotel where they found de Rougemont and arrested him for murder.

The sensation was a big one, for Jersey seldom has capital crimes, and at the height of the season the States, which governed the island, did not know whether to be pleased at the inevitable influx of tourists which would follow or irritated at the necessity of working with the judicial system of Britain and its government, which would be automatic in such a crime. The sole evening paper had no doubts—its front page that evening dealt with little else.

It was a weary Soustrelle who eventually joined the Constable of St. Jerome for a verbal post-mortem.

"It is done, Michel. The wheels now turn and it is for law to proceed."

"De Rougemont presented no difficulties?"

"I have seldom seen a man so disturbed. He was so sure of his security that when he was arrested his control was broken. He has of a certainty confessed in full."

The Constable looked at the stolid man on the other side of his dining-room table, poured him another glass of Calvados, and waved one hand.

"Come, Jean, you are not on a stage. You shall disentangle this little mystery of yours and not behave like the dubious hero of a *roman policier.*"

Soustrelle's smile was a contraction of his features rather than an exhibition of mirth.

"It was not easy, Michel. I made some inquiries of friends and, it would seem, this de Rougemont has money difficulties, and in England before he left he ran up many large bills; he was also not *simpatico* with Madame de Rougemont. He had, however, become intimate with a woman of great wealth and few scruples who will solve his troubles at the price of marriage. But Madame de Rougemont, as a good daughter of the Church, would never for one little moment consider divorce."

"Ah!"

"Precisely. De Rougemont invented the story of the lover: the man Venning is simply a friend of the family. De Rougemont had them both round to the new house to drink wine to its success, a wine containing a mild sedative. When they were sleeping he carried them to the bedroom and there set the scene of the false suicide, even to the forgery of the little letter from his wife."

"And sealed the doors and the windows from the inside, and left the key on the dressing table." The Constable's voice held a note of mild reproof, and he looked sharply at Soustrelle's Calvados.

"Michel, you mock an old friend! He sealed the windows, and round the inside of the door while it was still open he placed an overlapping stretch of adhesive tape— *Ecossais*, is it not?"

The Constable chuckled.

"*Scotch* tape, my dear Jean; it is of America, a trade name that has become an ordinary descriptive term."

"Precisely. I am of course an ignorant man. However. He also placed a small square of tape on the inside of the keyhole, then closed the door. With a little vacuum cleaner moved round the crack of the door he sucked the tape, as you might say, so that it became a tight seal, securing the door. The lock? Simple! He had a duplicate key made, filed off a fraction from the nose, and locked the door from the outside—the nose of the key, being absent, thus did not break or even mark the little seal."

"Perfection! A locked and sealed room like something from a sensational *feuilleton* in a boy's magazine!"

"Just so. A clever plan, adroitly conceived."

"You are to be congratulated, my dear Jean. But—" and the Constable wagged a cautionary finger "—in future no more guesswork. It might have turned out unsuccessfully and we of the Parish would have looked foolish."

"Guesswork?" Soustrelle's large smile was roguish. "I forget!" He smote his forehead. "A sealed room, an air-tight room, Michel? De Rougemont on entering the house, he informed me, smelled gas. But when I entered all I could smell was new paint. A small thing, you understand, a very small thing, but we farmers are apt to notice such small things, for are we not small men?"

Hugh Pentecost

The Birthday Killer

The letter was quite explicit. It was handwritten in a bold script on plain white paper that could have been bought at a thousand newsstands or drugstores. The envelope was a thirteen-cent-stamped envelope attainable at any branch post office. It was addressed to John Jericho, Jefferson Mews #16, New York City. There was no salutation on the piece of plain paper, only the message.

You will not live beyond your birthday, 3/10/78.

Jericho, six feet four inches tall and 230 pounds of hard-muscled body, with thick red hair and a red beard that made him look like a Viking warrior, sat alone at the breakfast table in his Jefferson Mews studio-apartment. The letter lay open on top of other mail and the morning paper that had been in his mailbox. He was surrounded by the brilliant vital paintings that had made him famous, some finished, some still in the works. The coffee in the mug on the table beside him had turned cold. The pot-bowled pipe he had filled prior to reading his mail rested beside the coffee mug, gone out after the first lighting.

He had opened this letter first because it had no return address on it. He knew who the other mail was from. At any other time he would have thought of it as a crank letter, a bad joke. But he had already glanced at the front page of his newspaper as he brought it up from the mailbox. The headline on a follow-up story had attracted his attention.

POLICE REPORT NO LEAD TO THE BIRTHDAY KILLER

A year ago the city had been horrified by the Son of Sam, called the .44 killer, who had murdered the Lord-knows-how-many people in cold blood—young couples parked in cars after dark. Now there was The Birthday Killer.

At first there had seemed to be some sort of connection between The Birthday Killer's victims. First, there had been Frances Kelleher, a woman judge presiding in the criminal courts. Then there had been Lou Ducillo, an Assistant D.A., a prosecutor of criminal cases. Then George Armstrong, a crime reporter for *Newsview* magazine. Each of them had received exactly the same letter as the one that lay on Jericho's breakfast table except for the birthday date.

Each letter had been received about three days before the birthday date. Judge Kelleher had paid no attention to hers. She had received many threatening letters in her long and distinguished career. She was ill-advised to ignore the threat. She was shot to death in the self-service elevator in her apartment building a few hours before her birthday had passed. No clues. No witnesses.

Two months later Lou Ducillo, the Assistant D.A., got his letter just two days before his birthday. Exactly the same wording, except his birthdate, as the one Judge Kelleher had received. Same handwriting, according to the experts at the Homicide Bureau. Lieutenant Mark Kreevich of Homicide saw the glimmering of a motive, a possible connection. Someone was getting revenge for the prosecution and sentencing of a criminal But which criminal? Ducillo had prosecuted almost twenty cases in Judge Kelleher's court.

Ducillo decided to take an unplanned vacation out of the country. He didn't choose to wait for the Homicide detective to sort out all the possibilities. But the Assistant D.A. was shot to death in a men's room at Kennedy Airport twenty minutes before his plane was to leave for the Virgin Islands. No clues. No witnesses.

Three months passed and Kreevich hadn't run anything substantial to earth. Then George Armstrong, the crime reporter, got his letter, three days before his birthday. He hotfooted it to Lieutenant Kreevich. Same writing, same wording as the others except for the birthdate. Connection? Armstrong had covered thirteen of Ducillo's prosecutions in Judge Kelleher's court. That seemed to narrow the number of cases from twenty to thirteen.

Armstrong was offered police protection. He accepted—but he had to keep an appointment he had with a key person in a story he was covering. Kreevich's guards would pick him up an hour later at the Yale Club. They never caught up with him. He was found shot to death in his car in a parking lot. No clues. No witnesses.

Kreevich went about the grim business of tracking down everyone connected with the thirteen cases that linked Judge Kelleher, Ducillo, and Armstrong. Nothing tangible. And then the whole structure of Kreevich's case was jolted. There was a fourth killing.

Wu Sung, the proprietor of a Chinese Restaurant in Chinatown, was found shot to death in an alley between his restaurant and the parking lot behind it. In his pocket was a letter from The Birthday Killer. As far as Kreevich could determine, there was absolutely no connection between the dead Chinese and the three others. Wu Sung's people were certain that none of them—the Judge, Ducillo, or Armstrong—had ever been patrons of the restaurant. Wu Sung had never been involved in a criminal case, not as a witness, not even as a spectator. As far as they knew, he had never spoken of the now notorious Birthday Killer. Nor had he mentioned to anyone receiving a threatening note from the killer. The day he died was Wu Sung's birthday.

Now, a month later, a letter lay open on Jericho's breakfast table. Jericho had never met or had any communication with the four people who had received letters before him. The only possible connection Jericho had with the case was a long friendship with Lieutenant Mark Kreevich.

Kreevich was not a typical cop. He was a man with a law degree, a man with sophisticated tastes. He was a man dedicated to law and order, but not in the jargon sense of the phrase used by office-seeking politicians. People had a right to live without fear—crime should be prevented, not solved after the fact. Jericho, the artist, was involved in a lifelong crusade against man's inhumanity to man. His paintings were a perpetual protest against viciousness and violence. In his lifestyle he had become a protector of the underprivileged, of the underdog, the helpless innocents trapped by ruthless men. The similarity of their aims had drawn Kreevich and Jericho together.

Jericho reached for his telephone and dialed.

"I have a letter in the mail this morning that will interest you," he said, when Lieutenant Kreevich came on the line.

"Someone putting the arm on you for tickets to the policemen's ball?" Kreevich asked.

"It's one of your kind of letters," Jericho said.

"My kind?"

"The Birthday Killer."

There were a few seconds of silence, then Kreevich said, "You have to be kidding."

"The wording is the same as the others, if the newspapers have reported correctly," Jericho said. "You'll have to see it to be certain the handwriting is the same as the others, of course."

Kreevich's voice had turned cold and impersonal. "When is your birthday? Tomorrow? The next day?"

"That's an interesting variation," Jericho said. "This letter reads: *You will not live beyond your birthday, 3/10/78.* That is tomorrow. But March tenth isn't my birthday. My birthday is the tenth of August, which would make it 8/10/78, five months from now."

"Where are you?"

"In my studio, but not for long. I'm having a one-man show at the Cleaves Gallery, as you know if you received your invitation. The formal opening is at eleven this morning. I have to be there ahead of time. Cleaves is on 57th Street, just east of Fifth Avenue."

"I'll meet you there," Kreevich said. "Bring the letter." Concern crept into his voice. "Watch your step, Johnny. He looked you up in *Who's Who* and copied your birthdate wrong. Could be."

It was a cold March day. Courage, Jericho told himself, is a happy commodity to own, but a man is a fool who doesn't know fear when there's something to be genuinely afraid of. Some kind of psycho had him on a death list, a psycho who had already struck four times without leaving a scrap of evidence.

As he dressed in his brown Harris-tweed suit to go to the opening of his show, Jericho put together what he knew about the killer. He did his work at close range where there were no witnesses: Judge Kelleher had been shot in a self-service elevator, Ducillo in a men's room at an airport, Armstrong in his car in a parking lot, Wu Sung in a dark alley between buildings. Did this killer confront his victims at the last moment and let them know why they were to die?

There was nothing in the pattern to suggest a sniper on a rooftop. Open spaces appeared to be safe places. It occurred to Jericho that his greatest danger might lie just outside his apartment door, in the narrow hallway. The Birthday Killer obviously didn't work in crowds—there hadn't been a single witness to his four murders. People had seen Son of Sam run away from his victims; there had been descriptions of his getaway car. But no one had seen The Birthday Killer. He chose the precise moment when he could be alone with each victim.

Jericho took a handgun from the top drawer of his bureau and slipped it into the pocket of the sheepskin-lined topcoat he planned to wear. He had a license for the gun. He had been hunted before in his long crusade against violence, but before he had always known who was hunting him.

It was time to go. He felt an unaccustomed tensing of his muscles as he opened the door into the hallway. He didn't camouflage his gun. He held it at the ready. Sunlight streamed through a window at the far end of the hall. There was no dark place for someone to hide at this time of day.

He walked to the end of the hallway where there was a right-angle turn to the one flight of stairs that led down to the street. He edged around the corner. No one was in sight. At the foot of the stairs was a narrow hallway that went to a cellar door. If he walked straight down, there might be someone at his back when he reached the front door. He went halfway, then turned, and went the rest of the way backward, facing the cellar entrance.

No one. Nothing.

Coming out onto the street was like emerging from a dark underground tunnel into warm spring sunshine. People came and went through the Mews. They smiled at him. He was a familiar figure. A world of witnesses. The Birthday Killer wouldn't strike out here in the open. It wouldn't be in keeping with his pattern.

A taxi parked at the mouth of the Mews didn't appeal to Jericho. Alone in a vehicle with a driver who might be—? You're acting like a nervous old maid, he told himself. And yet the killer had struck four times without leaving a trace. No reason to think he might be less efficient on his fifth venture. Safety lay in crowds. Jericho decided to walk the two miles uptown to the Cleaves Gallery.

Kreevich was there ahead of him, slim, almost elegant, less like a cop than anyone he could imagine. The gallery was already well filled with painting enthusiasts. A little murmur of interest could be heard as the giant redbearded artist swept onto the scene. A hundred witnesses here.

Kreevich looked grim. He handed Jericho a brochure that the gallery had prepared for the show, listing the paintings by number and with a biography of Jericho.

"Here's the mistake in your birthdate," the detective said.

It was there: John Jericho, born 3/10/38, Lakeview, Connecticut.

Jericho located Tom Cleaves, the gallery's proprietor. "How come this error, Tom?" he asked.

Cleaves scowled at the brochure. "It's from your handwritten copy, Johnny," he said.

"I'd know my own birthday."

"Copy's in my office. Let me get it," Cleaves said, and departed for an inner room.

"What took you so long?" Kreevich asked. "I was beginning to worry about you."

"I walked. Crowds seemed safer," Jericho said. From his pocket he took the threatening note and handed it to Kreevich.

Kreevich frowned. "Same damned handwriting," he said. "It looks like the McCoy."

Cleaves came back from his office with a piece of paper torn from a yellow legal pad. "Just as you wrote it, Johnny," he said.

It was there—3/10/38. Jericho saw what had happened. He'd written it in a hurry with a ballpoint pen. The first stroke of the pen had been dry and the first 8 looked like a 3.

"It's not so serious, is it?" Cleaves asked. He was a cheerful, moon-faced man. The Jericho show was going to be a huge success. "We've already sold three paintings and we've only been open half an hour. The two things you did in Washington when those Muslims held those hostages in three office buildings. And the acrobats on the beach. You're twelve thousand five hundred dollars richer than when you got up this morning."

"You've just given these brochures out this morning?" Kreevich asked.

"By hand, yes," Cleaves said. "But hundreds of them were mailed out to potential customers two weeks ago."

Plenty of time for The Birthday Killer to have seen the incorrect birthdate and sent his warning.

They moved around, surrounded by Jericho's canvases in bright colors. They came to one titled *Beach Acrobats*. There was a SOLD sticker on the frame of the painting. Kreevich's hand closed on Jericho's wrist like a painful vise.

"My God!" Kreevich said.

"What's the matter?" Jericho asked.

Kreevich pointed with his free hand at the painting. It was a beach scene, with colored umbrellas, swimmers in the distant surf, sunbathers wearing dark glasses. In the foreground were two men involved in an acrobatic feat. One man was doing a headstand, arms spread out to steady himself. Balanced above him, actually standing on the soles of the headstander's feet, was a second man, grinning out at the world.

"Impossible!" Kreevich said.

"Difficult, but they did it," Jericho said.

"I'm not talking about the stunt," Kreevich said. "The man on top—the smiler—you know him?"

"No. I just saw him the day I made the original sketch."

Kreevich released his hold on Jericho's wrist. A little nerve twitched high up on his cheek. "His name is Fred Miller—or was Fred Miller," the detective said in a flat cold voice. "He killed a woman cop in a drug stakeout in Times Square. He later hanged himself in his jail cell. You didn't know who you were painting?"

"No idea. He was just a man on the beach."

"It's an extraordinary likeness."

"I have a photographic eye," Jericho said.

Kreevich looked straight at his friend. "He was prosecuted for Murder One by Lou Ducillo and the jury convicted. Judge Kelleher sentenced him to life. He was a heroin addict. He bought something from what he thought was a lady pusher in Times Square. She turned out to be a cop and he shot her dead. There was some outcry about police methods at the time, and George Armstrong wrote an article defending the police."

"So three of them were connected with this Fred Miller," Jericho said.

"And you painted his picture," Kreevich said. "What about the man on the bottom, the man standing on his head?"

Jericho tried to recall. "It's difficult to remember a face that's upside down."

"But they didn't stay there all day in that position. What about when they broke it up?"

"I don't remember," Jericho said, frowning.

Kreevich found Tom Cleaves and asked him who had bought the painting. The gallery proprietor shrugged. "An old man. It was rather odd, because he paid cash and wanted to take the picture with him. I told him he'd have to leave it here for the run of the show—two weeks. He didn't like it, but he finally agreed."

"He didn't give you his name?"

"No. But I gave him a receipt for his money so he could claim the painting later."

"Describe him."

"Old, frail-looking, thick white hair. He somehow didn't look like a man who could afford $2,500 for a painting. But he had it in cash."

Kreevich turned to Jericho. "One itch has been scratched, anyway," he said. "This birthday jazz. No reason for it until now."

"You know something I don't know?" Jericho asked.

"Fred Miller hanged himself in his jail cell—on his birthday!" Kreevich said. "Press made something of it. Now some psycho avenger is making everyone else pay at birthday time. Let's take a walk."

Half an hour later Jericho found himself in the office of a young lawyer named Herbert Goldsteyn. On the way there in a taxi Kreevich had explained that Goldsteyn had been Fred Miller's lawyer and

had fought a brilliant if losing battle for his client. Goldsteyn was
a dark, wiry little man with suppressed energy that kept him wriggling in his desk chair while he chain-smoked cigarettes.

Kreevich had talked to him before because of Fred Miller's connection with three of The Birthday Killer's victims. Now he handed
Goldsteyn the threatening note Jericho had received and a copy of
the gallery brochure which contained a black-and-white reproduction of *Beach Acrobats*.

"Tell Johnny what you told me about your financial arrangements
with Fred Miller," Kreevich said.

Goldsteyn exhaled a cloud of smoke. "People thought I was some
sort of legal-aid freak," he said. "As a matter of fact I was hired and
paid a substantial fee for defending him."

"By Miller?" Kreevich asked, obviously knowing the answer.

"I don't know who paid the bills," Goldsteyn said. "I would present
an accounting to Miller every couple of weeks—over the months of
the trial and the appeal. A couple of days after each presenting I
would get payment through the mail, in cash. A thousand dollars
or more in nice new bills each time. No letter, no nothing. The money
came in an ordinary stamped envelope, with an extra stamp or two
added according to weight."

"Do you happen to have one of those envelopes?" Kreevich asked
him.

Goldsteyn grinned. "Since you called me to tell me you were coming, Lieutenant, it just happens I do." From the drawer of his desk
he produced an envelope.

Kreevich placed Jericho's note beside the envelope.

"Same handwriting," Jericho said. His eyes narrowed. "The Birthday Killer paid Miller's legal bills?"

"So it would appear," Kreevich said.

"Something in the neighborhood of $30,000," Goldsteyn said.

"Have you been expecting one of these threatening notes, Mr.
Goldsteyn?" Jericho asked.

The lawyer shrugged. "Why should I? I tried to save Miller. Ducillo
was responsible for his conviction, the judge sentenced him, and
Armstrong urged the maximum punishment in his articles. What
did *you* do to him, Mr. Jericho?"

"It seems I painted a picture of him," Jericho said.

"I don't think so," Kreevich said. "You painted a picture of *another*
man—a man who was balancing Miller in that acrobatic act on the
beach."

"No face," Jericho said.

"But you could be expected to remember the face, and I think you'd better remember, friend," Kreevich said, "and fast. He thinks your birthday is tomorrow."

The human brain, Jericho told himself, is a computer, a memory bank. But like computers it is fed by man, and in the case of the brain, by the man whose brain it is. He had painted a picture of two men doing a balancing act on the beach. The one face had been clearly visible—Fred Miller's—and he had caught a perfect likeness. But the other man, his face hidden, was a zero. He'd had no reason to remember anything about him, no reason to store him in his memory bank.

He should have spent the day at the Cleaves Gallery, being charming to prospective buyers, but instead Jericho had gone back to his studio in Jefferson Mews. He had made dozens of sketches that day at the beach, the day of the balancing act. There might be a clue among them that would remind him of something that was presently lost, hidden.

Kreevich had offered, almost insisted, on providing a bodyguard for his friend. Jericho was perversely stubborn about it. All his adult life he had been involved with violence and danger. He had determined long ago that when his time came to confront death he wanted to do it alone. Quixotic? At any rate he was not careless. He double-locked the studio door and fastened the guard chain. He checked out the bedroom, the closets, No one was waiting for him.

He searched through file cabinets until he found the sketchbook he had used that day on the beach almost two years ago. He sat down in a big armchair opposite his easel, first taking the handgun out of his pocket and placing it on a table beside him. He was ready for any surprise. He couldn't shake the feeling that this room was where the final confrontation would take place.

The sketches stirred nothing in his memory. There had been brilliant sunlight, the waves foaming as they broke on the sand; scores of people were sunbathing, girls almost nude, men tanned a coffee brown—and that absurd balancing act, Fred Miller smiling his delight, and the upside-down man beneath him faceless. Nothing else. Absolutely nothing.

The day wore on and Jericho found himself exhausted from searching for something that wasn't there. He slept, slumped in the armchair.

It must have been a long time because when he woke, the room was dark except for the reflected light from a street lamp at the window and the bright stars visible through the skylight. Jericho glanced at the illuminated dial of his wristwatch. It was almost eleven o'clock. He had slept for nearly seven hours.

An odd thought occurred to him. If tomorrow had actually been his birthday there was only about one hour to go before it arrived.

He turned on a lamp and went to the sideboard where he poured himself a Jack Daniels on the rocks. Then back to trying to put it together. There was one thing missing, he told himself. There was still no connection to Wu Sung, the Chinese restaurateur.

It was like a flash of lightning illuminating his mind. He saw the balancing act on the beach. He saw Fred Miller finally topple down to the sand, laughing. Then the upside-down man somersaulted to his feet and for a moment his smiling face was there as he turned to Miller. The man was an Oriental!

Jericho picked up the gun from the table and slipped it into his jacket pocket. Now he would be the hunter and not the hunted. He went out into the hall, careful as before, then down to the street. At the end of the Mews was a waiting cab.

"There's a place called The China Palace somewhere near Mott Street in Chinatown," Jericho told the driver.

"They close up about this time down there," the driver said.

"Just the same," Jericho said.

The cab drove him deep into the city and eventually stopped outside The China Palace. Jericho paid and went to the door. Some customers were emerging and Jericho stood aside for them. Then he went in and found his way blocked, just inside, by a young Chinese.

Jericho felt his heart jam against his ribs. It was a well remembered face now, the face of the upside-down man in the balancing act on the beach.

"I'm sorry, sir, but we are no longer serving," the Chinese man said.

"I do not want to be served. I want to talk to you," Jericho said.

"We are closing now, sir."

"Your name?"

"I am Kim Sung, the proprietor."

"I think you know my name is Jericho."

Tiny beads of perspiration stood out on Kim Sung's forehead.

"If you care to sit down at a table while my waiters clear the place," Sung said.

Jericho saw that there was just one table occupied—four people preparing to leave. Sung led the way to a table some distance from the door. "You will excuse me while I arrange for someone else to stand at the door." He crossed the floor and spoke to a waiter at some length. He bowed politely to the departing customers. He came back to Jericho and sat down opposite him. "What can I do for you, Mr. Jericho?"

"I got tired of waiting for you," Jericho said.

"I don't understand."

"I think you do," Jericho said. "Let me tell you something, Mr. Sung. In my jacket pocket, just under the edge of the table, is a .38 police special. It is aimed directly at your stomach. If you make a move toward me I promise to blow a hole in you big enough to drive a truck through. I got your letter, so you see I know that you are The Birthday Killer."

Sung moistened his thin pale lips. "Look around you, Mr. Jericho. You will see that you have no chance in the world of leaving this place."

Chinese waiters, doing no cleaning up, guarded every exit from the large room.

"So we are both going to die," Jericho said flatly. "There's a joke about it, Sung. This isn't my birthday."

"It doesn't matter," Sung said. "I could not have waited till later. Your painting at the Cleaves Gallery. Someone finally told you the face you painted was Fred Miller's?"

"Lieutenant Kreevich."

"A clever man, but not quite clever enough."

"You bought the painting?"

"I had the painting bought. I hoped to have it removed from the gallery before someone asked questions and stirred your memory."

Jericho drew a deep breath. "Before this stalemate brings an end to both of us I'd like to know why. Why the killings? Why your own father? He was your father?"

Sung tilted back slightly in his chair. His eyes glittered in the light from the chandelier over his head. "Fred Miller was the best friend I've ever had," he said.

"So you embarked on a psychotic revenge scheme. I can understand your motive against the prosecutor, the judge, the crime writer. But why your father? He had no connection with the case."

Sung began to rock, very gently, back and forth in his chair. "Let me tell it," he said. "Let me tell it just once, because no one knows it all."

Jericho nodded, his finger tight on the trigger of his gun. One wrong move and Sung would never get to tell it all.

Nor, Jericho thought, would he ever get to hear it all if he made an overt move. The Chinese waiters seemed to have formed a kind of circle around the table, at a distance but with no effort to hide the fact that they were a trap.

"Vietnam—the Establishment's war, the politicians' war," Kim Sung said. "Fred Miller and I met there—in Vietnam. You ask what a Chinese was doing in the United States army in Vietnam?" His smile was bitter. "I am an American. Born here on Mott Street. Went to school here in the city. Graduated from the school of engineering at Columbia. This is the land of opportunity, you know. The only job a Chinese engineer could find was selling chop suey in his father's restaurant to American Americans who think it's a Chinese dish! But the army took me, not as an engineer but because I spoke languages that were useful in Vietnam."

Sung's bitterness cut at some vein of sympathy in Jericho. He went on.

"I met Fred Miller in Saigon. We were both on a short leave. On leave you drank and found women, and many soldiers found drugs. Fred was a sensitive, compassionate man. He had seen old men and women and children killed senselessly. He had seen crops and forests defoliated. He had seen isolated villages of no military significance bombed flat. Drugs helped him forget what he had seen. He wanted to break the habit but he couldn't. I tried to help him. I hated what drugs did to men and particularly to Fred. I stayed with him while he sweated with terrible hungers. Sometimes I thought he was winning the fight."

"Where did soldiers find drugs?" Jericho asked.

"Black market operated by other soldiers with gold bars on their collars. They got rich on it. That is the way of high command. Like everywhere else, the powerful feed off the helpless. Well—in an air raid Fred and I managed to rescue some high brass. We were wounded, decorated together, and honorably discharged together.

"Back home I had a job—here, selling chop suey. Fred could find nothing. He was still fighting drugs. I spent every free moment I had trying to help him. It is thought that for a man to love a man is evil, or sick. But I loved Fred. I would have given anything on earth to help him with his trouble—drugs. We spent all our free time away from sources, like the day you saw us on the beach. And then—then my father chose to send me on a business trip to San Francisco. I refused. Fred was going through a bad spell.

"But my father was made of iron. I could not help Fred without my job here. So I had to go. I made arrangements to call Fred on the telephone every day at a certain time. On the second day he didn't answer. I knew! I knew!"

Sung brought his fist down on the table. "I had to stay another few days. Fred never answered the phone. When I got back here it was all over. He had killed a policewoman who had been posing as a supplier."

Sung twisted, as if in pain, in his chair. "That is how we do things in this Land of the Free, Mr. Jericho. The police, the F.B.I., infiltrate criminal groups, invite the helpless into their webs, urge them to commit a crime, and when they do—in this case the possession of drugs—they throw them in the slammer."

"It was more than possession of drugs, Sung. He killed a policewoman," Jericho said.

"Only after she had tricked him! I heard of a highly recommended lawyer, a man named Goldsteyn. I persuaded Fred to hire him. Goldsteyn thought he had a chance to save Fred."

"You were the person who paid Goldsteyn's fee?"

"Yes. Goldsteyn's argument in court was a sound one. Fred was a sick man. The police had preyed on his sickness to drive him to kill, something he would never have done had he been himself. Goldsteyn made the point that Fred was a man who needed help, not a murderer who deserved punishment. The prosecutor didn't see it that way, the jury didn't see it that way, the judge threw the book at him. And Fred—poor Fred made a rope out of a bedsheet and hanged himself on his birthday! These people, without understanding, without compassion, had killed him."

"And so you went after them one by one?"

"Yes. One by one."

"But your father?"

Sung moistened pale lips. "He sent me to San Francisco against my will. If I had not been away I could have prevented what happened to Fred. I would have been with him, helping to fight his battle."

Jericho was speechless.

Sung's smile looked pasted on his face. "So here we are, Mr. Jericho. If you kill me you will never get out of this room alive. If you don't kill me—you will never get out of this room alive."

The room was so still that Jericho thought he could hear a faucet dripping in the kitchen. And then there was a roar of sound. Men came charging into the room through a door. The circle of waiters was broken. There was a gunshot.

Across the table from Jericho, Sung had suddenly risen. From his sleeve, as if by magic, appeared a glittering knife. He lunged at Jericho.

The artist dodged and fired, at a knee, not the stomach. Sung screamed and fell across the table.

"You damn fool!" Kreevich said. He was standing over Jericho, who had flattened himself on the floor. "Why couldn't you let us handle it?"

Jericho fought an absurd urge to laugh hysterically as he struggled to his feet. "How did you get here?" he asked.

"I got a report on Miller's war record. He and Kim Sung were decorated together. That tied it all up. It took hours to get a judge to sign a search warrant. The police have to work by the book. I tried to find you, you idiot, and I realized you must have remembered the face of the upside-down man and were playing the role of a silly dragon killer by yourself."

The laughter came. "Do you suppose a man can get himself a drink in this place?" Jericho asked.

Conrad S. Smith

Steffi Duna, I Love You!

None of us felt there was anything particularly sinister about Simon Atherton's nephew when we first met him. What could be sinister about a tall blondish youth, overly handsome—the kind of lad who went out of style with Troy Donahue?

"Rick's come out here to break into pictures," Simon explained to us.

"Although I'll start in television if I have to," Rick added with a lofty little smile.

Laughable, maybe. An egotistical kid who had a lot to learn. But hardly sinister. Yet soon after, the monthly invitations from Simon stopped coming and the ominous wall went up around him. He couldn't telephone or write to any of the five of us, and our calls and letters never got through to him.

If only we'd all tracked each other down and shared our suspicions sooner! But we had this slightly screwball relationship: Simon was the hub of our kinky little wheel, he did all the party-giving at his lush place in the Hollywood hills; the rest of us were like five spokes, all in phone contact with *him* but not with each other. And after each party we'd all scatter off to our separate tacky lives for another whole month.

In Los Angeles, I do mean scatter.

My little bachelor dump was in Venice. The Nortons lived with her folks 30 miles inland in El Monte. Adam Roth camped, as he put it, way down in Long Beach, near his cubbyhole shop aboard the *Queen Mary*. And as for Ruth Galloway—well, who knows where a fat lonely soul like Ruth would live?

The point is simply this: fond as we all were of each other once a month, with our mutual and very special interest as the magnet, we'd never got around to exchanging telephone numbers or addresses—and that's what delayed things so badly. We all feel terrible about that now. But I'm getting ahead of myself . . .

It all began two years ago when the six of us, then strangers, chanced to enroll in an evening adult course at UCLA. *"The Development of Films from 1930 to 1960"* was the juicy bait, and every old-movie buff in Southern California was lured out of his cage to devour it.

During the coffee break one night a funny little man with questionably dark hair and a sunlamped face started chatting cozily as though we were all old friends. Adam Roth had that rare knack of melding a mismatched bunch regardless of age or sex. In Adam's case you weren't certain about either. But who cared? What did matter was the crinkly laughter in his eyes. He splashed his small talk with giddy reminiscences.

"I was one of those mad autograph creatures who haunted all the premieres," he bubbled. "The Phantom of Grauman's Chinese! And let me tell you, I screamed when Randolph Scott stalked down that red carpet and whacked Louella on her behind! That was at *Navy Blue and Gold* in 1936."

Impulsively he narrowed his eyes. "Anyone know who played the girl in that?"

Without a second's hesitation the fat woman next to him said, "Florence Rice."

Adam squealed in ecstasy. "Now it's your turn, Miss Trivia," he challenged her.

Ruth Galloway hesitated only a moment. Then: "Rosemary, Lola, and Priscilla Lane played three of the *Four Daughters*. Who played the fourth?"

I flicked a bit of lint from my sleeve.

"Gale Page," I said.

We thought Adam would go into orbit. That fifteen-minute recess flew by on the wings of Jane Frazee, Cora Sue Collins, and El Brendel. No doubt about it, we were all movie-trivia freaks, including the long-haired Nortons—and even the older, expensively dressed man who was so far out of our bracket. After a shy start he pitched in with delight.

His specialty was obscure character actors: George Barbier, Henry Armetta, Franklin Pangborn, Grady Sutton. Now there's a collection of stars for you!

Simon Atherton was retired, it turned out, with a lot of free time to fill. From later conversations I gathered that he was by nature a loner. All his hobbies were solitary—collecting fine porcelain and glassware, old playbills, dabbling at prize orchids. But once in a while he felt impelled to sample the real world outside his luxurious shell.

After several weeks of our coffee-break mania we were ripe for his suggestion:

"Why don't we make an evening of this at my place? You must all come for dinner and a real game."

"Only if you invite Lona Andre and Dixie Dunbar too," quipped Adam.

Simon jotted down all our phone numbers, and so the next Friday evening found me chugging up a curved road lined with mansions. At the top, handsome iron gates opened into a courtyard fronting Simon's Spanish palace. ("Ramon Navarro built it," he confided.) I began to regret my scruffy Levis and desert boots. Three other shy little cars were there already, huddled far from the awesome Bentley and its license plate reading SIMON.

Simon had cooked up a special welcome. "Hello, Douglas Dumbrille!" he beamed as he swung open the massive carved door. I tried to top him with, "Good evening, Etienne Girardot!" Chuckling happily, he led me into a cavernous hallway.

I was relieved to see he had dressed casually too, though his tailormade jeans must have cost him sixty bucks compared to my ten-dollar swapmeet pair.

We moved into the elegant warmth of what would have been the family room if Simon had had a family. The other misfits were trying to thaw out their awkwardness around a crackling fire. The awkwardness hung over all of us despite Simon's disarming manner and attentive bartending. I saw that each of our crystal glasses had a star's name etched on it. Mine said Anna May Wong. Ah, so.

"Two drinks and then dinner," Simon announced. "We want to stay sharp for The Game. Then at 11:30 we'll catch Joan Crawford in *Rain* on the Late Show."

Thoughtfully, he'd sensed that having a servant around would inhibit us even more. So he gave his man the evening off after laying out a lavish buffet.

Then, over our gold edged platters of smoked turkey, shrimp salad, and creamed asparagus tips (fresh and very out-of-season), we were finally as relaxed as though we were sipping our paper-cup coffee at recess.

We learned that Edna and Bill Norton commuted to downtown office jobs (shedding their beads and denim in El Monte, I'm sure). But how their eyes glowed behind their granny glasses when they talked of their experimental film efforts! A two-reeler of theirs had just won a prize.

Adam sighed. "I do hope you don't wallow in all those dreary innovations? Hand-held cameras, crazy quick cuts—" He shuddered. "And really, you know, erotica is so *depressing*. That's why I stopped going to new movies. I only look backward now!"

His shop aboard the *Queen* offered old movie stills, posters, and fan magazines. He didn't make a dime, I'm sure, but he was in his own personal heaven.

Ruth was the most reticent that first night, but over the months I figured her out. During her teens she must have come to terms with her mirror and snailed inward, consoling herself with endless chocolates and movies. To her great credit, though, this lonely indulgence paid off. (The movies, not the chocolates.) She was now the invaluable right hand to a casting director with only one flaw—a terrible memory for names.

The Game made the evening really whiz along. Simon gave a miniature gold Oscar to the winner, and I'm proud to say it shared *my* Volkswagen seat on the way home. I'd finally stumped everybody when we varied the game by playing it with initials.

"S.D.—female star of the Thirties" was the only clue I gave. That drove them up the wall before they surrendered.

Steffi Duna, I love you!

Over the years the movies have given me a lot of blessed escape from a lot of deadly jobs. If I ever finally make it with my playwriting, maybe I'll enjoy telling interviewers: "I supported myself during the Long Struggle by working as a messenger, mail clerk, plumber's helper, truck driver . . ." But till then, forget it! That's what I loved about our group. Nobody gave a damn what you did; all that mattered was what you knew.

The happy times continued that way for well over a year. Whenever one of us feebly muttered something about passing around the hosting chores, Simon always showed the quality that's so rare in a wealthy man, his great sensitivity. He'd hush us up with the kind excuse that his location was the most central. Actually, he knew we couldn't afford it, none of us had the proverbial pot. (No, not that one, I mean the one of gold.)

Simon's gilded pot was the result of his Midas touch with investments. He'd begun with only the same modest inheritance as his brother. But his share multiplied dazzlingly compared to Richard's repeated fiascos. Through the years he'd kept financing Richard in one "sure-fire" scheme after another, but by now (in their early fifties) Richard—with his carbon-copy son—was still plodding away at some grubby deal back east, while Simon—who'd never married—had long since moved to California. They rarely kept in touch any more.

But suddenly one day Simon had to postpone our party. He was flying east for his brother's funeral. Richard had died falling off a ladder from a second-story window.

When he got back, Simon sprang the surprise on us—his nephew Rick. He must have answered one more plea for help by bringing the destitute boy along. Obviously they hadn't had time to go shopping yet because Rick's clothes were flashy and cheap-looking.

I really began to dislike him as soon as he found out what Ruth did for a living. He switched on his full wattage, hopped to refill her glass, piled her plate with seconds and thirds (how could he hope to wangle a job out of her if he killed her?), and hung dewy-eyed on her every word. Ruth, bless her, was past the stage where she could believe such nonsense, so the sudden infatuation was one-sided.

Things got much worse very quickly when we started to play The Game. Now, Movie Trivia is something you either go bananas over or you hate, depending a lot on what you bring to it. Rick came empty-handed. And his youth was no excuse—Edna and Bill were just a few years older. It's simply that he had no interest in anything that didn't bear directly on himself or his seedy ambitions.

When it was his turn, he led us down a tiresome dead end by insisting that Jane Fonda had played Scarlett O'Hara.

"Of course," purred Adam. "And didn't Tiny Tim make a divine Rhett Butler!"

We'd all have been very relieved if Rick had gone upstairs, but he wasn't about to leave Ruth's side. Happily, he found a mirror facing his chair, but once in a while I caught him staring at us as if we were beings from another world. Which I guess we were.

Simon tried to compensate for the stickiness by talking louder and laughing longer. But we all begged off earlier than usual, just as the Late Show started. As I got into my car I heard Rick's voice whining through the night, "Migod, Uncle Simon, who the hell are Joan Leslie and Dennis Morgan?"

Several of us were away for Thanksgiving, so the next party was our Christmas bash. Simon didn't look at all well. His ruddy cheeks were pale and his eyes lacked their familiar twinkle. He seemed

listless as he served our drinks. Thankfully, there was no sign or
mention of Rick.

Ruth drew me aside, though, to tell me what a laughing-stock
he'd already made of himself in his two-month attack on Hollywood.
Directors and agents all around town were chortling over the composite photo he'd sent out.

"He spent a lot of Simon's money having himself photographed
in twelve different costumes," she said. "They're all on one composite: D'Artagnan, a motorcyclist, Louis XV, a Nazi stormtrooper, an
astronaut—you name it."

She started to giggle.

"But every pose is shot from exactly the same angle—to show
Rick's good side. And he's flashing exactly the same inane grin. It
looks like one of those paper-doll sets where kids lay a lot of different
outfits over the same figure."

Her giggles were getting out of control.

"And then across the top in big bold letters he printed: RICK ATH-
ERTON, MAN OF A THOUSAND FACES!"

Simon was approaching us, but then he paused and glanced toward
the hall. He'd heard the descending footsteps before we had. His
expression was a curious blank.

Rick appeared in the archway. He was now sun-bronzed, and hand-
somer than ever in a magnificent leisure suit made of leather. He
favored us with a barely civil nod.

"A thousand and *one* faces," I murmured to Ruth.

Now another man joined him. He was somewhat older, about 30,
but with the same general type of good looks, vacuous yet arrogant.
He too wore an ensemble of shining leather. They stood there, creak-
ing and redolent.

Since they were obviously on their way out, Simon must have felt
that introductions all around were futile. He merely said, "Everybody, this is Dr. Jordan."

We were honored with another brief nod for our scrapbook of
memories. Then Rick said, "We won't be back till very late, Uncle
Simon. Don't forget to take your pills." And with that they rustled
off.

I bet Adam's thoughts were X-rated at that moment. He broke the
awkward silence.

" 'Back'? Is kindly old Dr. Marcus Horsehide your resident phy-
sician now?"

Simon managed a little smile. "He's staying here with us—not because I need him though. He's a friend of Rick's from the east."

Edna looked worried. "But Rick mentioned pills. Simon, are you all right?"

"Of course. Just a little digestion trouble. Otherwise, I'm fine."

But he didn't look fine and we noticed later that he only toyed with his food.

We were even more concerned the following month to find Simon propped up on the couch in his robe. He looked ill and he'd lost weight.

"Self-service tonight." He drifted an apologetic hand toward the bar. "And the boys left us a casserole in the oven."

It was hard to know which question to ask first. Bill Norton started.

"Isn't your man with you any more?"

"No," Simon murmured. "Rick told me he and Dr. Jordan caught Rogers padding the household accounts." He shook his head sadly. "He'd been with me for twenty years."

"What did Rogers say when you questioned him?"

"He was gone before I learned about it. I—I'm afraid I was out of things for a day or two."

"You mean unconscious?" Ruth gasped.

"Well—under sedation," Simon said reluctantly. "I hadn't been sleeping well and—"

"What does your doctor say?" Adam demanded. "I mean your own doctor, not that collar-ad quack."

Simon bristled a bit. "Dr. Jordan *is* my doctor. I've never needed one before."

"Obviously you need one now," I said. "The best you can find."

"Dr. Jordan's a specialist in my type of gastric problem. He has his own sanitarium in the east."

"But if you've always been in perfect health—" Edna Norton began.

Simon shrugged. "I'm not getting any younger. It's only natural that my wicked ways should begin to catch up with me."

"Oh, nonsense, you—"

Simon spoke with a quiet but definite firmness. "Please. I appreciate your concern—very much. But for the first time in my life I have someone of my own to worry about me. It's a good feeling. Rick's the only family I've got left now, and I don't want to do anything that might offend—" He winced. "Oh, let's get off this deadly subject. Mix your drinks and we'll have some fun."

We tried our best, but it wasn't the jolliest of evenings. Simon tired early. We didn't want to leave him alone, so we lingered until we heard the Bentley pull in. We missed seeing Rick and his whatever. They must have slipped in the back door as we went out the front.

The next day I got a temporary job driving a rig, filling in for a guy on vacation. That kept me out of town for a couple of weeks, but my first day back I gave Simon a ring. Rick answered.

"This is Rod Wilson," I said.

"Who?"

"One of the regulars at the monthly parties."

"Oh—yes."

"Can I speak to Simon, please?"

"No. He's resting."

"How is he?"

"Much better. He'll be glad to hear you called."

"But when—"

Too late, Rick had already hung up. So I sat down and wrote Simon a chatty letter, mentioning the play I was trying to write in my off hours on the road. The temporary job was developing into a permanent one, I told him, but I'd be home again for our end-of-the-month shindig.

I was wrong. They kept me hustling cross-country for a whole four weeks this time. I was so beat when I got back that I quit. The money was good but what's the point, I reasoned, if it left me with no time or energy for *my* work? I decided to gamble on myself, for the umpteenth time, and live off my savings till they ran out.

When I dragged myself home from the truck terminal, I found a big depressing stack of mail. Probably all bills. I shuddered, flopped on the couch with a beer, and began browsing through the mountain of newspapers I'd forgotten to cancel. (I can never bear to throw out an unread paper. It's a quirk of mine. I always fear I might be missing that one wonderful little fact I could use in a play sometime.)

Three beers later I'd caught up to two Sundays ago. For a newspaper addict like me, even the Real Estate section is worth at least a quick glance. I love to drool over all the "luxurious alternatives to my present lifestyle." Hah!

Suddenly my boots hit the floor. My eye was riveted on a picture with the heading:

Former Navarro Estate Offered

It was Simon's place all right. The ad was placed by a real-estate agency and the photo said the asking price was $500,000. No mention of Simon.

What the devil had happened? I grabbed the phone and called Simon. But before it started to ring, the operator cut in with that "disconnected service" jazz. My mind was in a turmoil. All my vague uneasiness of the past couple of months suddenly hardened into chilling suspicion.

If I phoned the real-estate agency, maybe they could tell me where Simon was. Not so easy. The girl at Maisons et Jardins, Inc. was a haughty one.

"Our Mr. Parkinson who handles that listing won't return from his luncheon for half an hour. And in any case we don't give out our clients' addresses over the telephone."

Half an hour. Just the time it would take me to drive to their Brentwood office. I hopped in the old love bug and headed north.

Not until I pulled up in front of a small-scale French chateau did it occur to me that I should have changed from my dirty work clothes. When I approached his Louis Quatorze desk, our Mr. Parkinson flared his nostrils. I guess he didn't like my Eau de Budweiser cologne.

I thrust out the newspaper. "I want to ask you about this."

Which was nastier, the five-second pause or the supercilious little simper?

"You were thinking of the Navarro property for yourself?"

"Oh, no," I said grandly, "I'm quite happy in the old Tyrone Power house."

(That's a bit of Hollywood snobbery: once a movie star has lived somewhere, even for a three-month sublet, it's forever after called the "so-and-so house." Believe it or not, I even know people who live in the "Eve Arden apartment.")

"I'm a friend of the owner," I went on, "and I—"

"You?" The old eyebrows climbed a few rungs. "A friend of Rick Atherton's?"

Rick. So it wasn't my lurid imagination.

"The owner," I snapped. "Simon Atherton."

"For the purposes of the sale young Atherton is the owner," sniffed Parkinson. "He's acting on his uncle's power-of-attorney."

Oh, poor Simon. What the hell was going on?

"They're not still living in the house?"

"Mercy, no. All the furnishings have been removed for sale at auction next week."

"Then where—"

"I'm afraid that's all I'm going to tell you." Mr. Parkinson's beady eyes were clamped on a particularly large grease stain on my T-shirt.

"Not quite," I said. "I want their address."

"Out of the question." An airy little laugh. "Unless of course you wish to enter purchase negotiations? We'd need a small deposit. Shall we say, $25,000? In cash."

I told him what he could do with the $25,000 and I stormed out.

My first impulse was to rush to the police. But with what? No evidence, just a horrible suspicion. A man has a right to get sick, they'd tell me, *and* to sell his house, *and* to give power-of-attorney to his nephew. No, I would need some definite proof, or maybe another person to back me up.

The group! But how to find any of them? I didn't know the name of Edna's parents. Ruth had mentioned once that she had an unlisted number. And Adam probably couldn't afford a phone. Wait a minute. Adam! His shop aboard the *Queen Mary!*

Like most locals who ignore their own tourist attractions, I'd never visited the beached whale. She loomed majestically over a phony English "village" of shops in the parking area. And two full decks of Her Majesty had been converted to more shops.

When I finally popped in Adam's door, I don't know who was more surprised—me to find Edna and Bill with him, or the three of them to see me. The Nortons, I discovered, were shooting a film about past and present transportation versus the energy crisis, and naturally the *Queen Mary* symbolized the past. Poor Adam's cluttered cubicle was bursting with all their camera gear and our four bodies. It was like that classic Marx Brothers scene in the ship cabin.

I cut the chitchat by whipping out the newspaper story. They were equally shocked. Their letters to Simon had also been ignored, and their phone calls got the same brushoff from Rick. But since they hadn't tried in a couple of weeks, the disconnected service was news to them.

"Show Rod the picture!" Adam said.

They handed me an 8 by 10 glossy. It was an enlargement, Bill explained, of a single movie frame—a traffic scene, cars waiting for the light to change, a Chevy, a Toyota—and a Bentley. Even blurred, you could make out SIMON on the license plate and identify Rick and Dr. Jordan in the car.

I was confused. "What—how—?"

"We were shooting some random traffic scenes last weekend from a high rooftop," Bill continued. "We used one of those super-zoom lenses which swoops you in real close, and it wasn't till we ran the film last night that we spotted this."

"We hoped it meant that Simon's better," Edna said doubtfully. "They look so happy."

"There could be another explanation for that," I said grimly.

"You really think—"

"Look. Rick's 'career' is a disaster, isn't it? But there's that fat inheritance! Very conveniently his doctor buddy appears on the scene to start administering drugs—to a man in perfect health. They dump good old Rogers, they isolate Simon, they force the power-of-attorney out of him—"

"But why wouldn't they just—just kill him right away?" Edna stammered.

"Rick would, but Jordan is smarter. They bide their time. They sell the house and furniture for their *first* installment while they figure out the safest way to haul in the big prize."

"Then they're holding Simon somewhere like a prisoner?" asked Bill.

I nodded. "My first thought was Jordan's sanitarium. But this picture would indicate they're incognito out here instead."

"In a small town nearby," Adam breathed eerily. "A grieving boy and his fatally ill uncle—nobody knows them—and then one day the poor man dies quietly—and nobody will question what Jordan writes on the death certificate."

Edna almost screamed, "Lordy, we've got to take this picture to the police right away!"

I shook my head. "It's not enough. It only proves that they're still around. And no one has questioned that."

"But—"

"Let's be honest," I argued. "Aren't we a fairly crumby-looking crew to go barging in yelling murder just because our millionaire Daddy Warbucks got bored with us?"

"That's utterly ridiculous!" Adam said. "You know very well Simon would contact us if they'd let him!"

"I'm only telling you what the cops would say. We must have something more concrete."

Adam turned to his bookshelves. "I wonder if Ruth has had a line on Rick lately?" He pulled out a ratty volume. "She's never mentioned the name of that man she works for, but maybe if we phoned around—" He handed it to me. "Here's a directory of all the major studios and agents."

"Oh, dandy," I groaned. "1952 Edition!"

Adam was still miffed at me. "They can't *all* be dead and gone," he said testily. "Do your thing, Ameche."

Two hours later my dialing finger was numb, my head was aching, and my throat was parched. Nobody seemed to know "a very fat girl" (sorry, Ruth) "with lovely brown eyes" (you're welcome, Ruth). Edna and Bill were back from some shooting and Adam was cooing over some lonely old nut who wanted a picture of Nita Naldi. It was nearly five and I'd just about given up hope. Then it happened.

"You mean that *real* big dame who works for Sam Cutler?" said the voice. "In Century City. Here's the number—"

Before calling Cutler's office, I had a good thought.

"I feel like company tonight," I announced. "Why don't we all buy some steaks and go back to my pad?"

They were delighted. They didn't want to be alone with their thoughts either. So I started dialing.

"I warn you, my digs are a far cry from Simon's, but—hello, Ruth?"

She was happily surprised. I sketched in the bare bones of the crisis, but suggested we'd all hash it out over dinner at my place if she was free. She told me not to buy the dessert, she'd pick up a chocolate torte.

I had a last notion. "Ruth, did you throw out Rick's composite? . . . Still on the bulletin board? Well, bring it along. We just might have to show it to the cops . . . Okay, about seven. The gray bungalow on the corner of Oakwood, and watch out for the broken front step."

My usual method of tidying up consists of piling all the miscellaneous debris from every chair onto one chair. But with my guests being so unexpected, naturally I hadn't done it. There were newspapers all over the joint, beer cans, laundry on the dining-room table—

Adam stared with glazed eyes.

"Gracious, we're not exactly Craig's Wife, are we?"

"Don't flaunt your ignorance," I chided him. "This is the old Three Stooges' house."

Edna steered me into the bedroom. "Stay there for twenty minutes, you slob. When you come back, you won't recognize this room."

They scurried around like three of the Seven Dwarfs while I made like Snow White. I emerged in a clean sports shirt and chinos to find the dump looking almost presentable.

Edna pointed apologetically. "I hope you don't mind. I moved all the stuff from all the chairs onto one chair."

I grinned. "Why don't you get rid of Bill and marry me?"

She'd doused the lights and had flattering candles glowing around the room. Judging by the savory aromas wafting in from the kitchen, Adam was in superb command out there, and Bill was making himself useful over the drinks. We had ourselves a very good atmosphere.

From the front steps came a horrendous thud.

"Ah, here's Ruth now!" I said.

All that was missing was one of us, a very dear one of us. We choked a little when we raised our glasses and Bill said softly, "Here's to Simon."

Ruth had been just as worried as we were, and feeling just as helpless. No, Rick hadn't been around the office for weeks. We looked at the composite and while it had sounded funny before, now it made us kind of sick. Adam flipped it over to read the personal note Rick had scribbled on the back: "Height 6′2″, weight 190, hair blond, eyes blue—the same shade as Paul Newman's. Experience: H.S. Senior Class Play, *They Knew What They Wanted*." Adam looked grim. "Don't they though!" Then he snorted. "And did you ever see such moronic handwriting? Pigeon tracks!"

Edna's eyes widened.

"That's odd—I said the same thing myself a half hour ago!"

Ruth was puzzled. "But you're just seeing this now for the first time."

"It was the same handwriting! I'm sure it was. On a letter for you, Rod—in that mess on the chair."

"For me—from *Rick?*" I yelped. In a minute I undid all of Edna's work. Bills, junk mail, bills—there it was! Sure enough, the same immature, almost illegible scrawl. No return address. Postmarked the fifteenth, two weeks ago Saturday, the day before the newspaper story appeared.

I ripped it open as we huddled around the table. There were three pages inside, on one a note from Rick, and on the others—hallelujah!—two pages in Simon's hand. Rick's note was brief:

"Dear Mr. Wilson:

Tell your freinds [sic] not to worry if you don't hear from Simon for a while. Dr. Jordan says he can give him better treetment [sic] back east, so we're all leaving tomorrow. Simon is very cheerful and he's been keeping busy writing you.

Yours truly,
Rick Atherton"

"He was lying!" Edna cried. " 'Back east'! That was just to throw us off the track!"

But Simon's letter provided a surprise:

"Dear All:

How I wish we could have another one of our good evenings together soon! But I agree completely with Rick and Dr. Jordan about the care I need, so I'll do what they advise. Don't worry about me, I'm fine!

I hope these game questions I'm enclosing will amuse you. It's been fun composing them. Have yourselves a party and see if you can get all 22 answers!

My fond regards until???
Simon"

And there was more:

"P.S. to Rod:

I still cherish the delight on your face when you won the Oscar. Remember how? Maybe next time we should make it tougher for you by using first names only!

S."

We stared at each other, fighting a sense of anticlimax. Simon was okay after all. We'd let our imaginations run berserk.

"Wouldn't we have felt like idiots," Edna said, "if we had rushed to the police and then found this!"

But Ruth wasn't completely sold. "Rick says they're taking Simon back east"—she picked up the enlargement—"but they're *here*."

"Simple enough," reasoned Bill. "They flew him to the sanitarium the next day, left him in good hands, and then flew back to L.A. to be around for the sale of the house and the furniture."

"That's another thing though—why would Simon be selling his beautiful home?"

Adam said gently, "He may know he's much more seriously ill than he wants to tell us."

That sobered everybody.

Then Bill said, "You know our trouble? We dislike that kid so much we *wanted* to think the worst."

I was rereading Simon's letter. His P.S. touched me. Imagine his remembering my screwy little triumph of two years ago—typical Simon thoughtfulness. On an impulse I grabbed Oscar from the mantel and centerpieced him between two candles on the dinner table. Then I held up the third page for everybody to see. It was Simon's list of twenty-one Movie Trivia questions.

"What do you say? Shall we play Simon's game now?"

Adam was aghast. "Over the cook's dead body. My potatoes are done and I just need to turn the steaks once more. We'll eat *first*, and then play The Game over coffee."

"And dessert," Ruth added.

So it was that half an hour later we filled our coffee mugs and sliced the luscious chocolate torte.

We decided that I should read the questions aloud and we'd each write our own answers. But after the first five or six we paused in dismay. Had Simon lost his marbles? The questions were far too easy for us hard-core fanatics. From him we'd expected sticklers about the likes of Luis Alberni, Nat Pendleton, Halliwell Hobbes. But these—!

"It's as if he *wanted* us to get them all," Bill said.

"We're just too smart," Adam sighed. "But at least there's one consolation. We know that naugahyde nitwit, Rick, wouldn't be able to guess even—"

He stopped abruptly. The same thought hit us all at the same instant.

Ruth gasped, "*Simon's trying to tell us something!*"

"You're right!" I shouted. "And I see what it is! Haven't you noticed? All the questions relate to crime and murder. We've never done that before—that's the clue!"

"It's surely a hint," cried Edna, "but would Simon leave it at that?" Ruth grabbed Simon's letter. "No, look! He says, 'See if you can get all twenty-*two* answers.' But he's given us only twenty-one questions. Doesn't that mean there's one more answer—a big one?"

"Oh, wonderful Simon!" Adam crowed. "He knew Rick wouldn't have the faintest idea of what he'd hidden in this quiz!"

"And Rick would surely mail *this* letter," I said, "because it tells us how well Simon's being treated."

Edna wailed, "But he wrote it over two weeks ago! What must he think of us by now? And what if we're too late?"

"That's no way to talk!" snapped Bill. "We can't be too late, we can't!"

"We're wasting precious time," I growled. So with a frenzy, we attacked the list.

GAME QUESTIONS

1. The night-club musician unjustly accused of murder in Hitchcock's *The Wrong Man*.
2. The grieving mother of the murdered child in *The Bad Seed*.
3. The silent-screen master of horror (*The Hunchback of Notre Dame*, etc.).
4. An ex-wife of the man who played the murderous *Monsieur Verdoux*, and who later married Erich Maria Remarque.
5. Hitchcock once stranded her at sea in a mink coat, but her final role was that of a homicidal maniac in *Die, Die, My Darling*.
6. "Sam Spade" in *The Maltese Falcon*.
7. Typed for years as a cruel Prussian officer, he also played the mysterious butler-chauffeur of a mad ex-cinema queen.
8. Often a villain, but best known for his role as a Far East potentate with no dandruff problem.
9. Grace Kelly's charming but lethal husband in *Dial "M" for Murder*.
10. The insurance-investigator nemesis of Fred MacMurray and Barbara Stanwyck in *Double Indemnity*.
11. The evil little sidekick of the "Fat Man" in *The Maltese Falcon*.
12. Current wife of the man who played the murderous *Monsieur Verdoux*; daughter of a noted playwright.
13. The murderess in *Ladies in Retirement*: off-screen wife of radio Sam Spade.
14. The "Fat Man" himself in *The Maltese Falcon*.

15. She tried to drive Bette Davis insane in *Hush, Hush, Sweet Charlotte.*
16. He was "Watson" to Rathbone's "Holmes."
17. Typed as a spy and adventuress, this Hungarian blonde once sang with Nelson Eddy.
18. She mourned her lover, William Holden, in *Sunset Boulevard.*
19. She murdered her lover, William Holden, in *Sunset Boulevard.*
20. She immortalized Agatha Christie's "Miss Marple."
21. *The Bride of Frankenstein* herself.

Now we were finished. But so what? We had a list of 21 movie celebrities, all involved in some form of celluloid murder, mayhem, or madness. But what was it supposed to tell us?

I gnawed on my pencil and stared at Oscar on the table in front of me. Then suddenly lightning struck. I clutched Simon's letter and read the P.S. again. I knew what he wanted me to remember!

While the others gaped at me in bewilderment, I started scribbling frantically on the bottom of my list. Then I took a deep breath and showed them the result.

A creepy tingle went through all of us. For a moment nobody could say anything. I stood up and gathered together Rick's composite, the enlargement of the Bentley, the newspaper story, and the letters from Rick and Simon.

"Come on, everybody," I said. "We're going to the police."

NOTE TO THE READER

Please turn to the next page for Rod's solution.

SOLUTION

1. Henry Fonda
2. Eileen Heckart
3. Lon Chaney
4. Paulette Goddard
5. Tallulah Bankhead
6. Humphrey Bogart
7. Erich von Stroheim
8. Yul Brynner
9. Ray Milland
10. Edward G. Robinson
11. Peter Lorre
12. Oona O'Neill
13. Ida Lupino
14. Sydney Greenstreet
15. Olivia de Havilland
16. Nigel Bruce
17. Ilona Massey
18. Nancy Olson
19. Gloria Swanson
20. Margaret Rutherford
21. Elsa Lanchester

This is what Rod remembered:
He'd won the original game by playing it with initials. Then Simon gave him a new hint: Use the first initials only.

And this is Rod's final note:
First initials in the order of Simon's list:

HELPTHEYREPOISONINGME

HELP THEYRE POISONING ME

H. R. F. Keating

Mrs. Craggs' Sixth Sense

It was a good thing that Mrs. Craggs had had her twinges. If she had not, and had not acted on them, the nasty little somthing-or-other that had developed just under the skin on her right slbow could not have been dealt with so easily; and more important, poor old Professor Partheman would have been in much worse trouble than he was. But twinges she did have, and the doctor she went to recommended a minor operation. With the consequence that Mrs. Craggs "did for" Professor Partheman that particular week on Wednesday and not on Thursday.

And so she set eyes on Ralph.

He was doing no more than mow the lawn in front of the professor's ground-floor flat and from time to time taking a boxful of clippings round to the compost heap behind the shrubbery. But that was enough for Mrs. Craggs.

"Excuse me for mentioning it, sir," she said to the professor as she tucked her wages into her purse, "but I would just like to say a word about that chap."

"What chap, Mrs. Craggs? I was not aware that we had discussed any chap."

The old professor was a bit spiky sometimes, but Mrs. Craggs liked working for him because, despite his great age, there he was always beavering away at his writing and papers, doing his job and no messing about. So she ignored the objection and went on with what she had to say.

"That feller what you've got in to mow your old bit of a lawn, sir."

"Ralph, Mrs. Craggs," said the professor. "A young man employed as domestic help over at Royal Galloway College and making a little extra on his day off. Now, what do you want to say about him?"

The professor glared, as if he already knew without realizing it that Mrs. Craggs had an adverse comment to make.

She took a good long breath.

"I don't think you ought to have him around, sir," she said. "I don't like the looks of him, and that's a fact."

"Mrs. Craggs," said the professor in the voice he had used to put down any number of uppish undergraduates, "that you do not 'like the looks' of Ralph may be a fact, but anything else you have said or implied about him most certainly is not. Now, do you know any facts to the young man's detriment?"

"Facts, I don't know, sir. But feelings I have. He'll do you now good and of that I'm certain sure."

"My dear good lady, are you really suggesting I should cease to offer the fellow employment just because of some mysterious feeling you have? What is it about his looks that you don't like, for heaves's sake?"

Mrs. Craggs thought. She had not up to that moment attempted to analyze her feeling. She had just had it. But overshelmingly.

After a little she managed to pin something down.

"I think it's the way he prowls, sir," she said. "Whenever he goes anywhere he prowls. Like an animal, sir. Like a—"

She searched her mind.

"A jaguar, sir. He prowls like one o' them jaguars. That's it."

"My dear Mrs. Craggs. You cannot really be telling me that all you have against the chap is the way he walks. It's too ridiculous."

But Mrs. Craggs was not so easily discouraged. She thought about the young gardener at intervals right up to the following Monday when she was next due at the professor's. She even was thinking about him during the minor operation which had been such a striking success. And when on the Monday she had been given her money she broached the subject again.

"That Ralph, sir. I hope as 'ow you've had second thoughts there."

"Second thoughts." The aged professor's parchment-white face was suffused with pinkness. "Let me tell you, my dear lady, I had no need for more than the swiftest of first thoughts. I have spent a lifetime dealing in facts, Mrs. Craggs, hard facts, and I'm scarcely likely to abandon them now. Not one word more, if you please."

Mrs. Craggs sighed. "As you like, sir."

But, though she said no more then, she made up her mind to do all that she could to protect the old professor from the jaguar she had seen prowling across hiw lawn carefully avoiding ever appearing to look in at the windows of the flat.

And, she thought, she had one way of perhaps obtaining some "facts." It so happened at that time that her friend of long standing, Mrs. Milhorne, was employed as a daily cleaner at Royal Galloway College. At the first oppotunity she paid her a visit at her home, though that was not unfortunately till the following Tuesday evening.

"Oh, yes, Ralph," said Mrs. Milhorne. "I always knew in my bones about him. Handsome he may have been, and sort of romantic, if you take my meaning, but I never tried to make up to 'im, no matter what they say."

"I'm sure you didn't, dear," said Mrs. Craggs, who knew her friend's susceptible nature. "But why do you go on about him as if he ain't there no more?"

"Because that's what he aidn't," said Mrs. Milhorne.

And then the whole story came out. Ralph had been dismissed about a fornight before, suspected of having brutally attacked a young Spanish maid at the college. The girl, Rosita by name, although battered about terribly and still actually off work, had refused to say who had caused her injuries. But, as Ralph had notoriously been attracted to her, no one really had had any doubt.

"'Spect he's back home now, wherever that is," said Mrs. Milhorne, and she sighed.

"No, he's not," Mrs. Craggs said. "I told you, dear. He's coming every Wednesday to mow old Professor Partheman's lawn, and the professor's got picture frames full of old coins, gold an' all. He's what's called one o' them new miserists. An' if that Ralph's just half o' what I think he is, he'll be planning to help himself there, 'specially now he's out of a job."

A red flush of excitement came up on Mrs. Milhorne's pallid face.

"We'll have to go to the rescue," she said. "Just like on telly. The United States Cavalry."

"Yes," said Mrs. Craggs. "Only when old Professor Partheman sees you a-galloping up, an' me come to that, you know what he'll do? He'll tell us to turn right roun' and gallop away again. Or he will unless we come waving somefacts on our little blue flags."

She stood considering.

"Rosita," she said at last. "She's got to be made to talk."

But since Rosita knew hardly a word of English and since she had obstinately persevered with her silence, Mrs. Craggs's plan seemed to run up against insuperable difficulties.

Only it was Mrs. Craggs's plan.

Introduced next morning to the room in which Rosita was resting, her fact still blotched with heavy bruises, Mrs. Craggs first gave her a heartwarming smile and then joined her in a nice cuppa, selecting from a plate of biscuits the sweetest and stickiest and pressing them on the Spanish girl with such hearty insistence that if the interview was to do nothing else it would at least add some ounces to Rosita's already deliciously buxom figure. But Mrs. Craggs had only just begun.

" 'Ere," she said, when she judged the moment ripe. "You know I works for an old professor?"

Rosita would hardly have understood this abruptly proffered piece of information had not Mrs. Craggs at the same time jumped to her feet and first mimed to a T the old professor, frail as a branch of dried twigs, and then had imitated herself brushing and dusting and polishing fit to bust.

"*Si, si,*" said the Spanish girl, eyes alight and dancing. "Work, *si, si.* Ol' man, *si, si.*"

"Ah, you're right, dear," Mrs. Craggs said. "But I ain't the only one what works fer 'im."

Another bout of miming.

"*Ah, si. Si. Jardinero.*"

"Yes," said Mrs. Craggs. "A gardener. Ralph."

And the vigor she put into saying the name sent at once a wave of pallor across the Spanish girl's plump and pretty face.

"*Ah, si,* Ralph."

"Yes, dear. You got it nicely. But, listen. That old prof, he's got a lot o' valu'ble coins in his study. His study, see."

In place of Mrs. Craggs there came a picture of an ancient scholar bent over his books, scribbling rapidly on sheet after sheet of paper and from time to time taking a rare and precious old coin and scrutinizing it with extraordinary care.

"*Ah, si.* He have *antigo dinero, si.*" And then suddenly a new expression swept over her face. "*Dios,*" she said. "Ralph!"

After that it was the work of only half a minute for Mrs. Craggs to be seated at the driving wheel of some vehicle capable of the most amazing speed, and then to reincarnate her picture of Professor Partheman and put onto his lips a stream of sound that could not have meant anything to anybody, but made it perfectly clear that the old man was a fluent speaker of Spanish. Rosita seized a coat and scarf and showed herself ready for instant departure.

"But, hurry," said Mrs. Craggs. "We ain't got much time to lose. That Ralph gets there by two o'clock."

They had not much time, but in theory they had enough. Buses from outside the college ran at twenty-minute intervals; the journey to the professor's took only half an hour or a little more, and it was only just 12:45.

But.

But bus services everywhere suffer from shortage of staff, and when they do they are apt simply to miss one particular run. The run missed that day was the one due to pass Royal Galloway College at 1:00 P.M. exactly. That need not have mattered. The 1:20 would bring them to within a couple of hundred yards of the professor's by 1:55 at the latest. And it arrived at the college on the dot. And in the words of its conductor it "suffered a mechanical breakdown" just five minutes later.

Mrs. Craggs posted herself plank in the middle of the road. In less than a minute a car pulled to a halt. An irate lady motorist poked her head out. Mrs. Craggs marched up to her.

"Life an' death," she said. "It may be a matter o' life an' death. We gotter get to Halliman's Corner before two o'clock."

The lady motorist, without a word, opened the car's doors. Mrs. Craggs, Mrs. Milhorne, and Rosita piled in. Once on the go, Mrs. Craggs explained in more detail. The lady motorist grew excited. But she was a lady who relied more on the feel of the countryside than on signposts or maps. And a quarter of an hour later all four had to admit they had no idea where they were.

"The telephone," suggested the lady motorist. "We shall have to go to a house and telephone your professor."

"No good," said Mrs. Craggs. "He don't never answer it when he's working. Rare old miracle he is like that. Ring, ring, ring, an' never a blind bit o' notice."

"I'd die out o' curiosity," put in Mrs. Milhorne.

"So would I, dear," said Mrs. Craggs. "But that ain't getting the United States Cavalry to the wagon train."

They resumed their progress then, eyes strained to catch the least sign of anything helpful. And it was Mrs. Craggs who spotted something.

"That old plastic sack on top o' that gatepost," she said. "I remembers it from the bus coming out. It's that way. That way."

The lady motorist, recognizing an infallible sign when she heard one, turned at once.

"We'll be there in five minutes," she shouted.

"Yes," answered Mrs. Craggs. "An' it's two minutes to two now."

There was a little argument about whose watch was right, but all agreed that two o'clock was bound to come before they reached their destination. And it did.

"Quick," said Mrs. Craggs, as at last they got to the familiar corner. "Up that way. We may not be too late. He may not've doen it yet."

But she could not see in her mind's eye that prowling jaguar carefully mowing the old professor's lawn before he struck. And she could see, all too clearly, the thornlike obstinate old man defending his property to the last. And she could see frail thorns, spiky though they might be, all too easily being crushed to splinters.

The car pulled up with a screech of brakes. Mrs. Craggs was out of it before it had stopped. She hurled open the gate. The graden was empty. Ominously empty. Mrs. Craggs tore across the unmown lawn like an avenging amazon. She burst into the professor's study.

The professor was sitting holding up an ancient coin, scrutinizing it with extraordinary care.

"Ralph!" Mrs. Craggs burst out. "Where's Ralph?"

Professor Partheman turned to her.

"Ah, yes, Ralph," he said. "Well, Mrs. Craggs, I happened to read in *The Times* this morning a most interesting article about research at Johns Hopkins University in America proving that women do have a particular skill in what is called nonverbal communication. Or, to put it in popular terms, their instinct is to be trusted. So with that fact at my disposal I decided to give credence to your—ahem—feeling and left a note on the gate telling Ralph I no longer required him. Yes, you can trust a woman's intuition, Mrs. Craggs. You can trust it for a fact."

"Yes, sir," said Mrs. Craggs.

Ross Macdonald

Gone Girl

It was a Friday night. I was tooling home from the Mexican border in a light blue convertible and a dark blue mood. I had followed a man from Fresno to San Diego and lost him in the maze of streets in Old Town. When I picked up his trail again, it was cold. He had crossed the border, and my instructions went no farther than the United States.

Halfway home, just above Emerald Bay, I overtook the worst driver in the world. He was driving a black fishtail Cadillac as if he were tacking a sailboat. The heavy car wove back and forth across the freeway, using two of its four lanes, and sometimes three. It was late, and I was in a hurry to get some sleep. I started to pass it on the right, at a time when it was riding the double line. The Cadillac drifted toward me like an unguided missile, and forced me off the road in a screeching skid.

I speeded up to pass on the left. Simultaneously, the driver of the Cadillac accelerated. My acceleration couldn't match his. We raced neck and neck down the middle of the road. I wondered if he was drunk or crazy or afraid of me.

Then the freeway ended. I was doing 80 on the wrong side of a two-lane highway, and a truck came over a rise ahead like a blazing double comet. I floorboarded the gas pedal and cut over sharply to the right, threatening the Cadillac's fenders and its reckless driver's life. In the approaching headlights his face was as blank and white as a piece of paper, with charred black holes for eyes. His shoulders were naked.

At the last possible second he slowed enough to let me get by. The truck went off onto the shoulder, honking angrily. I braked gradually, hoping to force the Cadillac to stop.

It looped past me in an insane arc, tires skittering, and was sucked away into darkness.

When I finally came to a full stop, I had to pry my fingers off the wheel. My knees were remote and watery.

After smoking part of a cigarette, I U-turned and drove very cautiously back to Emerald Bay. I was long past the hot-rod age, and I needed rest.

The first motel I came to, the Siesta, was decorated with a vacancy sign and a neon Mexican sleeping luminously under a sombrero. Envying him, I parked on the gravel apron in front of the motel office. There was a light inside. The glass-paned door was standing open, and I went in.

The little room was pleasantly furnished with rattan and chintz. I jangled the bell on the desk a few times. No one appeared, so I sat down to wait and lit another cigarette. An electric clock on the wall said a quarter to one.

I must have dozed for a few minutes. A dream rushed by the threshold of my consciousness, making a gentle noise. Death was in the dream. He drove a black Cadillac loaded with flowers. When I woke up, the cigarette was starting to burn my fingers. A thin man in a gray flannel shirt was standing over me with a doubtful look on his face.

He was big-nosed and small-chinned, and he wasn't as young as he gave the impression of being. His teeth were bad, the sandy hair was thinning and receding. He was the typical old youth who scrounged and wheedled his living around motor courts and restaurants and hotels, and hung on desperately to the frayed edges of other people's lives.

"What do you want?" he said. "Who are you? What do you want?" His voice was reedy and changeable like an adolescent's.

"A room."

"Is that all you want?"

From where I sat, it sounded like an accusation.

I let it pass. "What else is there? Circassian dancing girls? Free popcorn?"

He tried to smile without showing his bad teeth. The smile was a dismal failure, like my joke.

"I'm sorry, sir," he said. "You woke me up. I never make much sense right after I just wake up."

"Have a nightmare?"

His vague eyes expanded like blue bubblegum bubbles. "Why did you ask me that?"

"Because I just had one. But skip it. Do you have a vacancy or don't you?"

"Yessir. Sorry, sir."

He swallowed whatever bitter taste he had in his mouth, and assumed an impersonal obsequious manner.

"You got any luggage, sir?"

"No luggage."

Moving silently in tennis sneakers like a frail ghost of the boy he once had been, he went behind the counter, and took my name, address, license number, and ten dollars. In return, he gave me a key numbered 14 and told me where to use it. Apparently he despaired of a tip.

Room 14 was like any other middle-class motel room touched with the California-Spanish mania. Artificially roughened plaster painted adobe color, poinsettia-red curtains, imitation parchment lampshade on a twisted black iron stand. A Rivera reproduction of a sleeping Mexican hung on the wall over the bed. I succumbed to its suggestion right away, and dreamed about Circassian dancing girls.

Along toward morning one of them got frightened, through no fault of mine, and began to scream her little Circassian lungs out. I sat up in bed, making soothing noises, and woke up. It was nearly nine by my wristwatch. The screaming ceased and began again, spoiling the morning like a fire siren outside the window. I pulled on my trousers over the underwear I'd been sleeping in, and went outside.

A young woman was standing on the walk outside the next room. She had a key in one hand and a handful of blood in the other. She wore a wide multicolored skirt and a low-cut gypsy sort of blouse. The blouse was distended and her mouth was open, and she was yelling her head off. It was a fine dark head, but I hated her for spoiling my morning sleep.

I took her by the shoulders and said, "Stop it."

The screaming stopped. She looked down sleepily at the blood on her hand. It was as thick as axle grease, and almost as dark in color.

"Where did you get that?"

"I slipped and fell in it. I didn't see it."

Dropping the key on the walk, she pulled her skirt to one side with her clean hand. Her legs were bare and brown. Her skirt was stained at the back with the same thick fluid.

"Where? In this room?"

She faltered. "Yes."

Doors were opening up and down the drive. Half a dozen people began to converge on us. A dark-faced man about four and a half feet high came scampering from the direction of the office, his little pointed shoes dancing on the gravel.

"Come inside and show me," I said to the girl.

"I can't. I won't." Her eyes were very heavy, and surrounded by the bluish pallor of shock.

The little man slid to a stop between us, reached up, and gripped the upper part of her arm. "What is the matter, Ella? Are you crazy, disturbing the guests?"

She said, "Blood," and leaned against me with her eyes closed.

His sharp glance probed the situation. He turned to the other guests, who had formed a murmuring semicircle around us.

"It is perfectly okay. Do not be concerned, ladies and gentlemen. My daughter cut herself a little bit. It is perfectly all right."

Circling her waist with one long arm, he hustled her through the open door and slammed it behind him. I caught it on my foot and followed them in.

The room was a duplicate of mine, including the reproduction over the unmade bed, but everything was reversed as in a mirror image. The girl took a few weak steps by herself and sat on the edge of the bed. Then she noticed the blood spots on the sheets. She stood up quickly. Her mouth opened, rimmed with white teeth.

"Don't do it," I said. "We know you have a very fine pair of lungs."

The little man turned on me. "Who do you think you are?"

"The name is Archer. I have the next room."

"Get out of this one, please."

"I don't think I will."

He lowered his greased black head as if he were going to butt me. Under his sharkskin jacket a hunch protruded from his back like a displaced elbow. He seemed to reconsider the butting gambit and decided in favor of diplomacy.

"You are jumping to conclusions, mister. It is not so serious as it looks. We had a little accident here last night."

"Sure, your daughter cut herself. She heals remarkably fast."

"Nothing like that." He fluttered one long hand. "I said to the people outside the first thing that came to my mind. Actually, it was a little scuffle. One of the guests suffered a nosebleed."

The girl moved like a sleepwalker to the bathroom door and switched on the light. There was a pool of blood coagulating on the black and white checkerboard linoleum, streaked where she had slipped and fallen in it.

"Some nosebleed," I said to the little man. "Do you run this joint?"

"I am the proprietor of the Siesta motor hotel, yes. My name is Salanda. The gentleman is susceptible to nosebleed. He told me so himself."

"Where is he now?"

"He checked out early this morning."

"In good health?"

"Certainly in good health."

I looked around the room. Apart from the unmade bed with the brown spots on the sheets, it contained no signs of occupancy. Someone had spilled a pint of blood and vanished.

The little man opened the door wide and invited me with a sweep of his arm to leave. "If you will excuse me, sir, I wish to have this cleaned up as quickly as possible. Ella, will you tell Lorraine to get to work on it right away pronto? Then maybe you better lie down for a little while, eh?"

"I'm all right now, father. Don't worry about me."

When I checked out a few minutes later, she was sitting behind the desk in the front office, looking pale but composed. I dropped my key on the desk in front of her.

"Feeling better, Ella?"

"Oh. I didn't recognize you with all your clothes on."

"That's a good line. May I use it?"

She lowered her eyes and blushed. "You're making fun of me. I know I acted foolishly this morning."

"I'm not so sure. What do *you* think happened in Room Thirteen last night?"

"My father told you, didn't he?"

"He gave me a version, two of them in fact. I doubt that they're the final shooting script."

Her hand went to the central hollow in her blouse. Her arms and shoulders were slender and brown, the tips of her fingers carmine. "Shooting?"

"A cinema term," I said. "But there might have been a real shooting at that. Don't you think so?"

Her front teeth pinched her lower lip. She looked like somebody's pet rabbit. I restrained an impulse to pat her sleek brown head.

"That's ridiculous. This is a respectable motel. Anyway, father asked me not to discuss it with anybody."

"Why would he do that?"

"He loves this place, that's why. He doesn't want any scandal made out of nothing. If we lost our good reputation here, it would break my father's heart."

"He doesn't strike me as the sentimental type."

She stood up, smoothing her skirt. I saw that she'd changed it.

"You leave him alone. He's a dear little man. I don't know what you think you're doing, trying to stir up trouble where there isn't any."

I backed away from her righteous indignation—female indignation is always righteous—and went out to my car. The early spring sun was dazzling. Beyond the freeway and the drifted sugary dunes, the bay was Prussian blue. The road cut inland across the base of the peninsula and returned to the sea a few miles north of the town. Here a wide blacktop parking space shelved off to the left of the highway, overlooking the white beach and whiter breakers. Signs at each end of the turnout stated that this was a County Park, No Beach Fires.

The beach and the blacktop expanse above it were deserted except for a single car, which looked very lonely. It was a long black Cadillac nosed into the cable fence at the edge of the beach. I braked and turned off the highway and got out. The man in the driver's seat of the Cadillac didn't turn his head as I approached him. His chin was propped on the steering wheel, and he was gazing out across the endless blue sea.

I opened the door and looked into his face. It was paper-white. The dark brown eyes were sightless. The body was unclothed except for the thick hair matted on the chest, and a clumsy bandage tied around the waist. The bandage was composed of several blood-stained towels, held in place by a knotted piece of nylon fabric whose nature I didn't recognize immediately. Examining it more closely, I saw that it was a woman's slip. The left breast of the garment was embroidered in purple with a heart, containing the name *Fern*. I wondered who Fern was.

The man who was wearing her purple heart had dark curly hair, heavy black eyebrows, a heavy chin sprouting black beard. He was rough-looking in spite of his anemia and the lipstick smudged on his mouth.

There was no registration on the steeringpost, and nothing in the glove compartment but a half-empty box of shells for a .38 automatic. The ignition was still turned on. So were the dash and headlights, but they were dim. The gas gauge registered empty. Curlyhead must have pulled off the highway soon after he passed me, and driven all the rest of the night in one place.

I untied the slip, which didn't look as if it would take fingerprints, and went over it for a label. It had one: Gretchen, Palm Springs. It occurred to me that it was Saturday morning and that I'd gone all winter without a weekend in the desert. I retied the slip the way I'd found it, and drove back to the Siesta Motel.

Ella's welcome was a few degrees colder than absolute zero. "Well!" She glared down her pretty rabbit nose at me. "I thought we were rid of you."

"So did I. But I just couldn't tear myself away."

She gave me a peculiar look, neither hard nor soft, but mixed. Her hand went to her hair, then reached for a registration card. "I suppose if you want to rent a room, I can't stop you. Only please don't imagine you're making an impression on me. You're not. You leave me cold, mister."

"Archer," I said. "Lew Archer. Don't bother with the card. I came back to use your phone."

"Aren't there any other phones?" She pushed the telephone across the desk. "I guess it's all right, long as it isn't a toll call."

"I'm calling the Highway Patrol. Do you know their local number?"

"I don't remember." She handed me the telephone directory.

"There's been an accident," I said as I dialed.

"A highway accident? Where did it happen?"

"Right here, sister. Right here in Room Thirteen."

But I didn't tell that to the Highway Patrol. I told them I had found a dead man in a car on the parking lot above the county beach. The girl listened with widening eyes and nostrils. Before I finished she rose in a flurry and left the office by the rear door.

She came back with the proprietor. His eyes were black and bright like nailheads in leather, and the scampering dance of his feet was almost frenzied. "What is this?"

"I came across a dead man up the road a piece."

"So why do you come back here to telephone?" His head was in butting position, his hands outspread and gripping the corners of the desk. "Has it got anything to do with us?"

"He's wearing a couple of your towels."

"What?"

"And he was bleeding heavily before he died. I think somebody shot him in the stomach. Maybe you did."

"You're loco," he said, but not very emphatically. "Crazy accusations like that, they will get you into trouble. What is your business?"

"I'm a private detective."

"You followed him here, is that it? You were going to arrest him, so he shot himself?"

"Wrong on both accounts," I said. "I came here to sleep. And they don't shoot themselves in the stomach. It's too uncertain, and slow. No suicide wants to die of peritonitis."

"So what are you doing now, trying to make scandal for my business?"

"If your business includes trying to cover up a murder."

"He shot himself," the little man insisted.

"How do you know?"

"Donny. I spoke to him just now."

"And how does Donny know?"

"The man told him."

"Is Donny your night keyboy?"

"He was. I think I will fire him, for stupidity. He didn't even tell me about this mess. I had to find it out for myself. The hard way."

"Donny means well," the girl said at his shoulder. "I'm sure he didn't realize what happened."

"Who does?" I said. "I want to talk to Donny. But first let's have a look at the register."

He took a pile of cards from a drawer and riffled through them. His large hands, hairy-backed, were calm and expert, like animals that lived a serene life of their own, independent of their emotional owner. They dealt me one of the cards across the desk. It was inscribed in block capitals: RICHARD ROWE, DETROIT, MICH.

I said, "There was a woman with him."

"Impossible."

"Or he was a transvestite."

He surveyed me blankly, thinking of something else. "The HP, did you tell them to come here? They know it happened here?"

"Not yet. But they'll find your towels. He used them for bandage."

"I see. Yes. Of course." He struck himself with a clenched fist on the temple. It made a noise like someone maltreating a pumpkin. "You are a private detective, you say. Now if you informed the police that you were on the trail of a fugitive, a fugitive from justice . . . He shot himself rather than face arrest . . . For five hundred dollars?"

"I'm not that private," I said. "I have some public responsibility. Besides, the cops would do a little checking and catch me out."

"Not necessarily. He *was* a fugitive from justice, you know."

"I hear you telling me."

"Give me a little time and I can even present you with his record."

The girl was leaning back away from her father, her eyes starred with broken illusions. "Daddy," she said weakly.

He didn't hear her. All his bright black attention was fixed on me. "Seven hundred dollars?"

"No sale. The higher you raise it, the guiltier you look. Were you here last night?"

"You are being absurd," he said. "I spent the entire evening with my wife. We drove up to Los Angeles to attend the ballet." By way of supporting evidence, he hummed a couple of bars from Tchaikovsky. "We didn't arrive back here in Emerald Bay until nearly two o'clock."

"Alibis can be fixed."

"By criminals, yes," he said. "I am not a criminal."

The girl put a hand on his shoulder. He cringed, his face creased by monkey fury, but his face was hidden from her.

"Daddy," she said. "Was he murdered, do you think?"

"How do I know?" His voice was wild and high, as if she had touched the spring of his emotion. "I wasn't here. I only know what Donny told me."

The girl was examining me with narrowed eyes, as if I were a new kind of animal she had discovered and was trying to think of a use for.

"This gentleman is a detective," she said, "or claims to be."

I pulled out my photostat and slapped it down on the desk. The little man picked it up and looked from it to my face. "Will you go to work for me?"

"Doing what, telling little white lies?"

The girl answered for him. "See what you can find out about this—this death. On my word of honor, father had nothing to do with it."

I made a snap decision, the kind you live to regret. "All right. I'll take a fifty-dollar advance. Which is a good deal less than five hundred. My first advice to you is to tell the police everything you know. Provided that you're innocent."

"You insult me," he said.

But he flicked a fifty-dollar bill from the cash drawer and pressed it into my hand fervently, like a love token. I had a queasy feeling that I had been conned into taking his money, not much of it but enough. The feeling deepened when he still refused to talk. I had to use all the arts of persuasion even to get Donny's address out of him.

The keyboy lived in a shack on the edge of a desolate stretch of dunes. I guessed that it had once been somebody's beach house, before sand had drifted like unthawing snow in the angles of the walls and winter storms had broken the tiles and cracked the concrete foundations. Huge chunks of concrete were piled haphazardly on what had been a terrace overlooking the sea.

On one of the tilted slabs Donny was stretched like a long albino lizard in the sun. The onshore wind carried the sound of my motor to his ears. He sat up blinking, recognized me when I stopped the car, and ran into the house.

I descended flagstone steps and knocked on the warped door. "Open up, Donny."

"Go away," he answered huskily. His eye gleamed like a snail through a crack in the wood.

"I'm working for Mr. Salanda. He wants us to have a talk."

"You can go and take a running jump for yourself, you and Mr. Salanda both."

"Open it or I'll break it down."

I waited for a while. He shot back the bolt. The door creaked reluctantly open. He leaned against the doorpost, searching my face with his eyes, his hairless body shivering from an internal chill. I pushed past him, through a kitchenette that was indescribably filthy, littered with the remnants of old meals, and gaseous with their odors. He followed me silently on bare soles into a larger room whose sprung floorboards undulated under my feet. The picture window had been broken and patched with cardboard. The stone fireplace was choked with garbage. The only furniture was an army cot in one corner where Donny apparently slept.

"Nice homey place you have here. It has that lived-in quality."

He seemed to take it as a compliment, and I wondered if I was dealing with a moron. "It suits me. I never was much of a one for fancy quarters. I like it here, where I can hear the ocean at night."

"What else do you hear at night, Donny?"

He missed the point of the question, or pretended to. "All different things. Big trucks going past on the highway. I like to hear those night sounds. Now I guess I can't go on living here. Mr. Salanda owns it, he lets me live here for nothing. Now he'll be kicking me out of here, I guess."

"On account of what happened last night?"

"Uh-huh." He subsided onto the cot, his doleful head supported by his hands.

I stood over him. "Just what did happen last night, Donny?"

"A bad thing," he said. "This fella checked in about ten o'clock—"

"The man with the dark curly hair?"

"That's the one. He checked in about ten, and I gave him Room Thirteen. Around about midnight I thought I heard a gun go off from there. It took me a little while to get my nerve up, then I went back to see what was going on. This fella came out of the room, without no clothes on. Just some kind of a bandage around his waist. He looked like some kind of a crazy Indian or something. He had a gun in his hand, and he was staggering, and I could see that he was bleeding some. He come right up to me and pushed the gun in my gut and told me to keep my trap shut. He said I wasn't to tell anybody I saw him, now or later. He said if I opened my mouth about it to anybody he would come back and kill me. But now he's dead, isn't he?"

"He's dead."

I could smell the fear in Donny: there's an unexplained trace of canine in my chromosomes. The hairs were prickling on the back of my neck, and I wondered if Donny's fear was of the past or for the future. The pimples stood out in bas-relief against his pale lugubrious face.

"I think he was murdered, Donny. You're lying, aren't you?"

"Me lying?" But his reaction was slow and feeble.

"The dead man didn't check in alone. He had a woman with him."

"What woman?" he said in elaborate surprise.

"You tell me. Her name was Fern. I think she did the shooting, and you caught her red-handed. The wounded man got out of the room and into his car and away. The woman stayed behind to talk to you. She probably paid you to dispose of his clothes and fake a new registration card for the room. But you both overlooked the blood on the floor of the bathroom. Am I right?"

"You couldn't be wronger, mister. Are you a cop?"

"A private detective. You're in deep trouble, Donny. You'd better talk yourself out of it before the cops start on you."

"I didn't do anything." His voice broke like a boy's. It went strangely with the glints of gray in his hair.

"Faking the register is a serious rap, even if they don't hang accessory to murder on you."

He began to expostulate in formless sentences that ran together. At the same time his hand was moving across the dirty gray blanket. It burrowed under the pillow and came out holding a crumpled card.

He tried to stuff it into his mouth and chew it. I tore it away from between his discolored teeth.

It was a registration card from the motel, signed in a boyish scrawl: *Mr. and Mrs. Richard Rowe, Detroit, Mich.*

Donny was trembling violently. Below his cheap cotton shorts his bony knees vibrated like tuning forks. "It wasn't my fault," he cried. "She held a gun on me."

"What did you do with the man's clothes?"

"Nothing. She didn't even let me into the room. She bundled them up and took them away herself."

"Where did she go?"

"Down the highway towards town. She walked away on the shoulder of the road and that was the last I saw of her."

"How much did she pay you, Donny?"

"Nothing, not a cent. I already told you, she held a gun on me."

"And you were so scared you kept quiet until this morning?"

"That's right. I was scared. Who wouldn't be scared?"

"She's gone now," I said. "You can give me a description of her."

"Yeah." He made a visible effort to pull his vague thoughts together. One of his eyes was a little off center, lending his face a stunned, amorphous appearance. "She was a big tall dame with blondey hair."

"Dyed?"

"I guess so, I dunno. She wore it in a braid like, on top of her head. She was kind of fat, built like a lady wrestler, great big watermelons on her. Big legs."

"How was she dressed?"

"I didn't hardly notice, I was so scared. I think she had some kind of a purple coat on, with black fur around the neck. Plenty of rings on her fingers and stuff."

"How old?"

"Pretty old, I'd say. Older than me, and I'm going on thirty-nine."

"And she did the shooting?"

"I guess so. She told me to say if anybody asked me, I was to say that Mr. Rowe shot himself."

"You're very suggestible, aren't you, Donny? It's a dangerous way to be, with people pushing each other around the way they do."

"I didn't get that, mister. Come again." He batted his pale blue eyes at me, smiling expectantly.

"Skip it," I said and left him.

A few hundred yards up the highway I passed an HP car with two uniformed men in the front seat looking grim. Donny was in for it now. I pushed him out of my mind and drove across country to Palm Springs.

Palm Springs is still a one-horse town, but the horse is a Palomino with silver trappings. Most of the girls are Palomino too. The main street was a cross-section of Hollywood and Vine transported across the desert by some unnatural force and disguised in western costumes which fooled nobody. Not even me.

I found Gretchen's lingerie shop in an expensive-looking arcade built around an imitation flagstone patio. In the patio's center a little fountain gurgled pleasantly, flinging small lariats of spray against the heat. It was late in March, and the season was ending. Most of the shops, including the one I entered, were deserted except for the hired help.

It was a small shop, faintly perfumed by a legion of vanished dolls. Stockings and robes and other garments were coiled on the glass counters or hung like brilliant treesnakes on display stands along the narrow walls. A henna-headed woman emerged from rustling recesses at the rear and came tripping toward me on her toes.

"You are looking for a gift, sir?" she cried with a wilted kind of gaiety. Behind her painted mask she was tired and aging and it was Saturday afternoon and the lucky ones were dunking themselves in kidney-shaped swimming pools behind walls she couldn't climb.

"Not exactly. In fact, not at all. A peculiar thing happened to me last night. I'd like to tell you about it, but it's kind of a complicated story."

She looked me over quizzically and decided that I worked for a living too. The phony smile faded away. Another smile took its place, which I liked better. "You look as if you'd had a fairly rough night. And you could do with a shave."

"I met a girl," I said. "Actually she was a mature woman, a statuesque blonde to be exact. I picked her up on the beach at Laguna, if you want me to be brutally frank."

"I couldn't bear it if you weren't. What kind of a pitch is this, brother?"

"Wait. You're spoiling my story. Something clicked when we met, in that sunset light, on the edge of the warm summer sea."

"It's always bloody cold when I go in."

"It wasn't last night. We swam in the moonlight and had a gay time and all. Then she went away. I didn't realize until she was gone that I didn't know her telephone number, or even her last name."

"Married woman, eh? What do you think I am, a lonely hearts club?" Still, she was interested, though she probably didn't believe me. "She mentioned me, is that it? What was her first name?"

"Fern."

"Unusual name. You say she was a big blonde?"

"Magnificently proportioned," I said. "If I had a classical education I'd call her Junoesque."

"You're kidding me, aren't you?"

"A little."

"I thought so. Personally I don't mind a little kidding. What did she say about me?"

"Nothing but good. As a matter of fact, I was complimenting her on her—er—garments."

"I see." She was long past blushing. "We had a customer last fall some time by the name of Fern. Fern Dee. She had some kind of a job at the Joshua Club, I think. But she doesn't fit the description at all. This one was a brunette, a middle-sized brunette, quite young. I remember the name Fern because she wanted it embroidered on all the things she bought. A corny idea if you ask me, but that was her girlish desire and who am I to argue with girlish desires."

"Is she still in town?"

"I haven't seen her lately, not for months. But it couldn't be the woman you're looking for. Or could it?"

"How long ago was she in here?"

She pondered. "Early last fall, around the start of the season. She only came in that once, and made a big purchase, stockings and nightwear and underthings. The works. I remember thinking at the time, here was a girlie who suddenly hit the chips but heavily."

"She might have put on weight since then, and dyed her hair. Strange things can happen to the female form."

"You're telling me," she said. "How old was—your friend?"

"About forty, I'd say, give or take a little."

"It couldn't be the same one then. The girl I'm talking about was twenty-five at the outside, and I don't make mistakes about women's ages. I've seen too many of them in all stages, from Quentin quail to hags, and I certainly do mean hags."

"I bet you have."

She studied me with eyes shadowed by mascara and experience. "You a policeman?"

"I have been."

"You want to tell mother what it's all about?"

"Another time. Where's the Joshua Club?"

"It won't be open yet."

"I'll try it anyway."

She shrugged her thin shoulders and gave me directions. I thanked her.

It occupied a plain-faced one-story building half a block off the main street. The padded leather door swung inward when I pushed it. I passed through a lobby with a retractable roof, which contained a jungle growth of banana trees. The big main room was decorated with tinted desert photomurals. Behind a rattan bar with a fishnet canopy a white-coated Caribbean type was drying shot glasses with a dirty towel. His face looked uncommunicative.

On the orchestra dais beyond the piled chairs in the dining area a young man in shirt sleeves was playing bop piano. His fingers shadowed the tune, ran circles around it, played leap-frog with it, and managed never to hit it on the nose. I stood beside him for a while and listened to him work. He looked up finally, still strumming with his left hand in the bass. He had soft-centered eyes and frozen-looking nostrils and a whistling mouth.

"Nice piano," I said.

"I think so."

"Fifty-second Street?"

"It's the street with the beat and I'm not effete." His left hand struck the same chord three times and dropped away from the keys. "Looking for somebody, friend?"

"Fern Dee. She asked me to drop by sometime."

"Too bad. Another wasted trip. She left here end of last year, the dear. She wasn't a bad little nightingale but she was no pro, Joe, you know? She had it but she couldn't project it. When she warbled the evening died, no matter how hard she tried, I don't wanna be snide."

"Where did she lam, Sam, or don't you give a damn?"

He smiled like a corpse in a deft mortician's hands. "I heard the boss retired her to private life. Took her home to live with him. That is what I heard. But I don't mix with the big boy socially, so I couldn't say for sure that she's impure. Is it anything to you?"

"Something, but she's over twenty-one."

"Not more than a couple of years over twenty-one." His eyes darkened, and his thin mouth twisted sideways angrily. "I hate to see it happen to a pretty little girl like Fern. Not that I yearn—"

I broke in on his nonsense rhymes: "Who's the big boss you mentioned, the one Fern went to live with?"

"Angel. Who else?"

"What heaven does he inhabit?"

"You must be new in these parts—" His eyes swiveled and focused on something over my shoulder. His mouth opened and closed.

A grating tenor said behind me, "Got a question you want answered, bud?"

The pianist went back to the piano as if the ugly tenor had wiped me out, annulled my very existence. I turned to its source. He was standing in a narrow doorway behind the drums, a man in his thirties with thick black curly hair and a heavy jaw blue-shadowed by closely shaven beard. He was almost the living image of the dead man in the Cadillac. The likeness gave me a jolt. The heavy black gun in his hand gave me another.

He came around the drums and approached me, bull-shouldered in a fuzzy tweed jacket, holding the gun in front of him like a dangerous gift. The pianist was doing wry things in quickened tempo with the dead march from *Saul*. A wit.

The dead man's almost-double waved his cruel chin and the crueler gun in unison. "Come inside, unless you're a government man. If you are, I'll have a look at your credentials."

"I'm a freelance."

"Inside then."

The muzzle of the automatic came into my solar plexus like a pointing iron finger. Obeying its injunction, I made my way between empty music stands and through the narrow door behind the drums. The iron finger, probing my back, directed me down a lightless corridor to a small square office containing a metal desk, a safe, a filing cabinet. It was windowless, lit by fluorescent tubes in the ceiling. Under their pitiless glare, the face above the gun looked more than ever like the dead man's face. I wondered if I had been mistaken about his deadness, or if the desert heat had addled my brain.

"I'm the manager here," he said, standing so close that I could smell the piney stuff he used on his crisp dark hair. "You got anything to ask about the members of the staff, you ask me."

"Will I get an answer?"

"Try me, bud."

"The name is Archer," I said. "I'm a private detective."

"Working for who?"

"You wouldn't be interested."

"I am, though, very much interested." The gun hopped forward like a toad into my stomach again, with the weight of his shoulder behind it. "Working for who did you say?"

I swallowed anger and nausea, estimating my chances of knocking the gun to one side and taking him bare-handed. The chances seemed pretty slim. He was heavier than I was, and he held the automatic as if it had grown out of the end of his arm. You've seen too many movies, I told myself. I told him, "A motel owner on the coast. A man was shot in one of his rooms last night. I happened to check in there a few minutes later. The old boy hired me to look into the shooting."

"Who was it got himself ventilated?"

"He could be your brother," I said. "Do you have a brother?"

He lost his color. The center of his attention shifted from the gun to my face. The gun nodded. I knocked it up and sideways with a hard left uppercut. Its discharge burned the side of my face and drilled a hole in the wall. My right sank into his neck. The gun thumped the cork floor.

He went down but not out, his spread hand scrabbling for the gun, then closing on it. I kicked his wrist. He grunted but wouldn't let go of it. I threw a punch at the short hairs on the back of his neck. He took it and came up under it with the gun, shaking his head from side to side.

"Up with the hands now," he murmured. He was one of those men whose voices go soft and mild when they are in a killing mood. He had the glassy impervious eyes of a killer. "Is Bart dead? My brother?"

"Very dead. He was shot in the belly."

"Who shot him?"

"That's the question."

"Who shot him?" he said in a quiet white-faced rage. The single eye of the gun stared emptily at my midriff. "It could happen to you, bud, here and now."

"A woman was with him. She took a quick powder after it happened."

"I heard you say a name to Alfie, the piano player. Was it Fern?"

"It could have been."

"What do you mean, it could have been?"

"She was there in the room, apparently. If you can give me a description of her?"

His hard brown eyes looked past me. "I can do better than that. There's a picture of her on the wall behind you. Take a look at it. Keep those hands up high."

I shifted my feet and turned uneasily. The wall was blank. I heard him draw a breath and move, and tried to evade his blow. No use. It caught the back of my head. I pitched forward against the blank wall and slid down it into three dimensions of blankness.

The blankness coagulated into colored shapes. The shapes were half human and half beast and they dissolved and reformed. A dead man with a hairy breast climbed out of a hole and doubled and quadrupled. I ran away from them through a twisting tunnel which led to an echo chamber. Under the roaring surge of the nightmare music, a rasping tenor was saying:

"I figure it like this. Vario's tip was good. Bart found her in Acapulco, and he was bringing her back from there. She conned him into stopping off at this motel for the night. Bart always went for her."

"I didn't know that," a dry old voice put in. "This is very interesting news about Bart and Fern. You should have told me before about this. Then I would not have sent him for her and this would not have happened. Would it, Gino?"

My mind was still partly absent, wandering underground in the echoing caves. I couldn't recall the voices, or who they were talking about. I had barely sense enough to keep my eyes closed and go on listening. I was lying on my back on a hard surface. The voices were above me.

The tenor said: "You can't blame Bartolomeo. She's the one, the dirty treacherous lying little bitch."

"Calm yourself, Gino. I blame nobody. But more than ever now, we want her back, isn't that right?"

"I'll kill her," he said softly, almost wistfully.

"Perhaps. It may not be necessary now. I dislike promiscuous killing—"

"Since when, Angel?"

"Don't interrupt, it's not polite. I learned to put first things first. Now what is the most important thing? Why did we want her back in the first place? I will tell you: to shut her mouth. The government heard she left me, they wanted her to testify about my income. We wanted to find her first and shut her mouth, isn't that right?"

"I know how to shut her mouth," the younger man said very quietly.

"First we try a better way, my way. You learn when you're as old as I am there is a use for everything, and not to be wasteful. Not even wasteful with somebody else's blood. She shot your brother, right? So now we have something on her, strong enough to keep her mouth shut for good. She'd get off with second degree, with what she's got, but even that is five to ten in Tehachapi. I think all I need to do is tell her that. First we have to find her, eh?"

"I'll find her. Bart didn't have any trouble finding her."

"With Vario's tip to help him, no. But I think I'll keep you here with me, Gino. You're too hot-blooded, you and your brother both. I want her alive. Then I can talk to her, and then we'll see."

"You're going soft in your old age, Angel."

"Am I?" There was a light slapping sound, of a blow on flesh. "I have killed many men, for good reasons. So I think you will take that back."

"I take it back."

"And call me Mr. Funk. If I am so old, you will treat my gray hairs with respect. Call me Mr. Funk."

"Mr. Funk."

"All right, your friend here, does he know where Fern is?"

"I don't think so."

"Mr. Funk."

"Mr. Funk." Gino's voice was a whining snarl.

"I think he's coming to. His eyelids fluttered."

The toe of a shoe prodded my side. Somebody slapped my face a number of times. I opened my eyes and sat up. The back of my head was throbbing like an engine fueled by pain. Gino rose from a squatting position and stood over me.

"Stand up."

I rose shakily to my feet. I was in a stone-walled room with a high beamed ceiling, sparsely furnished with stiff old black oak chairs and tables. The room and the furniture seemed to have been built for a race of giants.

The man behind Gino was small and old and weary. He might have been an unsuccessful grocer or a superannuated barkeep who had come to California for his health. Clearly his health was poor. Even in the stifling heat he looked pale and chilly, as if he had caught chronic death from one of his victims. He moved closer to me, his legs shuffling feebly in wrinkled blue trousers that bagged

at the knees. His shrunken torso was swathed in a heavy blue tur-
tleneck sweater. He had two days' beard on his chin, like moth-eaten
gray plush.

"Gino informs me that you are investigating a shooting." His
accent was Middle-European and very faint, as if he had forgotten
his origins. "Where did this happen, exactly?"

"I don't think I'll tell you that. You can read it in the papers
tomorrow night if you are interested."

"I am not prepared to wait. I am impatient. Do you know where
Fern is?"

"I wouldn't be here if I did."

"But you know where she was last night."

"I couldn't be sure."

"Tell me anyway to the best of your knowledge."

"I don't think I will."

"He doesn't think he will," the old man said to Gino.

"I think you better let me out of here. Kidnaping is a tough rap.
You don't want to die in the pen."

He smiled at me, with a tolerance more terrible than anger. His
eyes were like thin stab wounds filled with watery blood. Shuffling
unhurriedly to the head of the mahogany table behind him, he
pressed a spot in the rug with the toe of one felt slipper. Two men
in blue serge suits entered the room and stepped toward me briskly.
They belonged to the race of giants the room had been built for.

Gino moved behind me and reached to pin my arms. I pivoted,
landed one short punch, and took a very hard counter below the
belt. Something behind me slammed my kidneys with the heft of a
trailer truck bumper. I turned on weakening legs and caught a chin
with my elbow. Gino's fist, or one of the beams from the ceiling,
landed on my neck. My head rang like a gong. Under its clangor
Angel was saying pleasantly, "Where was Fern last night?"

I didn't say.

The men in blue serge held me upright by the arms while Gino
used my head as a punching bag. I rolled with his lefts and rights
as well as I could, but his timing improved and mine deteriorated.
His face wavered and receded. At intervals Angel inquired politely
if I was willing to assist him now. I asked myself confusedly in the
hail of fists what I was holding out for or who I was protecting.
Probably I was holding out for myself. It seemed important to me
not to give in to violence. But my identity was dissolving and receding like the face in front of me.

I concentrated on hating Gino's face. That kept it clear and steady for a while: a stupid square-jawed face barred by a single black brow, two close-set brown eyes staring glassily. His fists continued to rock me like an air-hammer.

Finally Angel placed a clawed hand on his shoulder, and nodded to my handlers. They deposited me in a chair. It swung on an invisible wire from the ceiling in great circles. It swung out wide over the desert, across a bleak horizon, into darkness.

I came to, cursing. Gino was standing over me again. There was an empty water glass in his hand, and my face was dripping. Angel spoke up beside him, with a trace of irritation in his voice.

"You stand up good under punishment. Why go to all the trouble, though? I want a little information, that is all. My friend, my little girl friend, ran away. I'm impatient to get her back."

"You're going about it the wrong way."

Gino leaned close and laughed harshly. He shattered the glass on the arm of my chair, held the jagged base up to my eyes. Fear ran through me, cold and light in my veins. My eyes were my connection with everything. Blindness would be the end of me. I closed my eyes, shutting out the cruel edges of the broken thing in his hand.

"Nix, Gino," the old man said. "I have a better idea, as usual. There is heat on, remember."

They retreated to the far side of the table and conferred there in low voices. The young man left the room. The old man came back to me. His storm troopers stood one on each side of me, looking down at him in ignorant awe.

"What is your name, young fellow?"

I told him. My mouth was puffed and lisping, tongue tangled in ropes of blood.

"I like a young fellow who can take it, Mr. Archer. You say you're a detective. You find people for a living, is that right?"

"I have a client," I said.

"Now you have another. Whoever he is, I can buy and sell him, believe me. Fifty times over." His thin blue hands scoured each other. They made a sound like two dry sticks rubbing together on a dead tree.

"Narcotics?" I said. "Are you the wheel in the heroin racket? I've heard of you."

His watery eyes veiled themselves like a bird's. "Now don't ask foolish questions or I will lose my respect for you."

"That would break my heart."

"Then comfort yourself with this." He brought an old-fashioned purse out of his hip pocket, abstracted a crumpled bill, and smoothed it out on my knee. It was a five-hundred-dollar bill.

"This girl of mine you are going to find for me, she is young and foolish. I am old and foolish, to have trusted her. No matter. Find her for me and bring her back and I will give you another bill like this one. Take it."

"Take it," one of my guards repeated. "Mr. Funk said for you to take it."

I took it. "You're wasting your money. I don't even know what she looks like. I don't know anything about her."

"Gino is bringing a picture. He came across her last fall at a recording studio in Hollywood where Alfie had a date. He gave her an audition and took her on at the club, more for her looks than for the talent she had. As a singer she flopped. But she is a pretty little thing, about five foot four, nice figure, dark brown hair, big hazel eyes. I found a use for her."

"You find a use for everything."

"That is good economics. I often think if I wasn't what I am, I would make a good economist. Nothing would go to waste." He paused and dragged his dying old mind back to the subject. "She was here for a couple of months, then she ran out on me, silly girl. I heard last week that she was in Acapulco, and the federal Grand Jury was going to subpoena her. I have tax troubles, Mr. Archer, all my life I have tax troubles. Unfortunately I let Fern help with my books a little bit. She could do me great harm. So I sent Bart to Mexico to bring her back. But I meant no harm to her. I still intend her no harm, even now. A little talk, a little realistic discussion with Fern, that is all that will be necessary. So even the shooting of my good friend Bart serves its purpose. Where did it happen, by the way?"

The question flicked out like a hook on the end of a long line.

"In San Diego," I said, "at a place near the airport: the Mission Motel."

He smiled paternally. "Now you are showing good sense."

Gino came back with a silver-framed photograph in his hand. He handed it to Angel, who passed it on to me. It was a studio portrait, of the kind intended for publicity cheesecake. On a black velvet divan, against an artificial night sky, a young woman reclined in a gossamer robe that was split to show one bent leg. Shadows accentuated the lines of her body and the fine bones in her face. Under the heavy makeup which widened the mouth and darkened the half-closed eyes, I recognized Ella Salanda. The picture was signed in white, in the lower righthand corner: *To my Angel, with all my love, Fern.*

A sickness assailed me, worse than the sickness induced by Gino's fists. Angel breathed into my face: "Fern Dee is a stage name. Her real name I never learned. She told me one time that if her family knew where she was they would die of shame." He chuckled. "She will not want them to know that she killed a man."

I drew away from his charnel-house breath. My guards escorted me out. Gino started to follow, but Angel called him back.

"Don't wait to hear from me," the old man said after me. "I expect to hear from you."

The building stood on a rise in the open desert. It was huge and turreted, like somebody's idea of a castle in Spain. The last rays of the sun washed its walls in purple light and cast long shadows across its barren acreage. It was surrounded by a ten-foot hurricane fence topped with three strands of barbed wire.

Palm Springs was a clutter of white stones in the distance, dia-monded by an occasional light. The dull red sun was balanced like a glowing cigar butt on the rim of the hills above the town. A man with a bulky shoulder harness under his brown suede windbreaker drove me toward it. The sun fell out of sight, and darkness gathered like an impalpable ash on the desert, like a column of blue-gray smoke towering into the sky.

The sky was blue-black and swarming with stars when I got back to Emerald Bay. A black Cadillac followed me out of Palm Springs. I lost it in the winding streets of Pasadena. So far as I could see, I had lost it for good.

The neon Mexican lay peaceful under the stars. A smaller sign at his feet asserted that there was No Vacancy. The lights in the long low stucco buildings behind him shone brightly. The office door was open behind a screen, throwing a barred rectangle of light on the gravel. I stepped into it, and froze.

Behind the registration desk in the office a woman was avidly reading a magazine. Her shoulders and bosom were massive. Her hair was blonde, piled on her head in coroneted braids. There were rings on her fingers, a triple strand of cultured pearls around her thick white throat. She was the woman Donny had described to me. I opened the screen door and said, "Who are you?"

She glanced up, twisting her mouth in a sour grimace. "Well! I'll thank you to keep a civil tongue in your head."

"Sorry. I thought I'd seen you before somewhere."

"Well, you haven't." She looked me over coldly. "What happened to your face, anyway?"

"I had a little plastic surgery done. By an amateur surgeon."

She clucked disapprovingly. "If you're looking for a room, we're full up for the night. I don't believe I'd rent you a room even if we weren't. Look at your clothes."

"Uh-huh. Where's Mr. Salanda?"

"Is it any business of yours?"

"He wants to see me. I'm doing a job for him."

"What kind of a job?"

I mimicked her. "Is it any business of yours?" I was irritated. Under her mounds of flesh she had a personality as thin and hard and abrasive as a rasp.

"Watch who you're getting flip with, sonny boy." She rose, and her shadow loomed immense across the back door of the room. The magazine fell closed on the desk: it was *Teen-age Confessions*. "I am Mrs. Salanda. Are you a handyman?"

"A sort of one," I said. "I'm a garbage collector in the moral field. You look as if you could use me."

The crack went over her head. "Well, you're wrong. And I don't think my husband hired you, either. This is a respectable motel."

"Uh-huh. Are you Ella's mother?"

"I should say not. That little snip is no daughter of mine."

"Her stepmother?"

"Mind your own business. You better get out of here. The police are keeping a close watch on this place tonight, if you're planning any tricks."

"Where's Ella now?"

"I don't know and I don't care. She's probably gallivanting off around the countryside. It's all she's good for. One day at home in the last six months, that's a fine record for a young unmarried girl." Her face was thick and bloated with anger against her stepdaughter. She went on talking blindly, as if she had forgotten me entirely. "I told her father he was an old fool to take her back. How does he know what she's been up to? I say let the ungrateful filly go and fend for herself."

"Is that what you say, Mabel?" Salanda had softly opened the door behind her. He came forward into the room, doubly dwarfed by her

blonde magnitude. "I say if it wasn't for you, my dear, Ella wouldn't
have been driven away from home in the first place."

She turned on him in a blubbering rage. He drew himself up tall
and reached to snap his fingers under her nose. "Go back into the
house. You are a disgrace to women, a disgrace to motherhood."

"I'm not *her* mother, thank God."

"Thank God," he echoed, shaking his fist at her. She retreated
like a schooner under full sail, menaced by a gunboat. The door
closed on her. Salanda turned to me.

"I'm sorry, Mr. Archer. I have difficulties with my wife, I am
ashamed to say it. I was an imbecile to marry again. I gained a
senseless hulk of flesh and lost my daughter. Old imbecile!" he de-
nounced himself, wagging his great head sadly. "I married in hot
blood. Passion has always been my downfall. It runs in my family,
this insane hunger for blondeness and stupidity and size." He spread
his arms in a wide and futile embrace on emptiness.

"Forget it."

"If I could." He came closer to examine my face. "You are injured,
Mr. Archer. Your mouth is damaged. There is blood on your chin."

"I was in a slight brawl."

"On my account?"

"On my own. But I think it's time you leveled with me."

"Leveled with you?"

"Told me the truth. You knew who was shot last night, and who
shot him, and why."

He touched my arm, with a quick tentative grace. "I have only
one daughter, Mr. Archer, only the one child. It was my duty to
defend her, as best as I could."

"Defend her from what?"

"From shame, from the police, from prison." He flung one arm
out, indicating the whole range of human disaster. "I am a man of
honor, Mr. Archer. But private honor stands higher with me than
public honor. The man was abducting my daughter. She brought
him here in the hope of being rescued. Her last hope."

"I think that's true. You should have told me this before."

"I was alarmed, upset. I feared your intentions. Any minute the
police were due to arrive."

"But you had a right to shoot him. It wasn't even a crime. The
crime was his."

"I didn't know that then. The truth came out to me gradually. I
feared that Ella was involved with him." His flat black gaze sought

my face and rested on it. "However, I did not shoot him, Mr. Archer.
I was not even here at the time. I told you that this morning, and
you may take my word for it."

"Was Mrs. Salanda here?"

"No, sir, she was not. Why should you ask me that?"

"Donny described the woman who checked in with the dead man.
The description fits your wife."

"Donny was lying. I told him to give a false description of the
woman. Apparently he was unequal to the task of inventing one."

"Can you prove that she was with you?"

"Certainly I can. We had reserved seats at the theater. Those who
sat around us can testify that the seats were not empty. Mrs. Salanda
and I, we are not an inconspicuous couple." He smiled wryly.

"Ella killed him then."

He neither assented nor denied it. "I was hoping that you were
on my side, my side and Ella's. Am I wrong?"

"I'll have to talk to her before I know myself. Where is she?"

"I do not know, Mr. Archer, sincerely I do not know. She went
away this afternoon, after the policemen questioned her. They were
suspicious, but we managed to soothe their suspicions. They did not
know she had just come home, from another life, and I did not tell
them. Mabel wanted to tell them. I silenced her." His white teeth
clicked together.

"What about Donny?"

"They took him down to the station for questioning. He told them
nothing damaging. Donny can appear very stupid when he wishes.
He has the reputation of an idiot, but he is not so dumb. Donny has
been with me for many years. He has a deep devotion for my daughter. I got him released tonight."

"You should have taken my advice," I said, "taken the police into
your confidence. Nothing would have happened to you. The dead
man was a mobster, and what he was doing amounts to kidnaping.
Your daughter was a witness against his boss."

"She told me that. I am glad that it is true. Ella has not always
told me the truth. She has been a hard girl to bring up, without a
good mother to set her an example. Where has she been these last
six months, Mr. Archer?"

"Singing in a night club in Palm Springs. Her boss was a racketeer."

"A racketeer?" His mouth and nose screwed up, as if he sniffed
the odor of corruption.

"Where she was isn't important, compared with where she is now. The boss is still after her. He hired me to look for her."

Salanda regarded me with fear and dislike, as if the odor originated in me. "You let him hire you?"

"It was my best chance of getting out of his place alive. I'm not his boy, if that's what you mean."

"You ask me to believe you?"

"I'm telling you. Ella is in danger. As a matter of fact, we all are." I didn't tell him about the second black Cadillac. Gino would be driving it, wandering the night roads with a ready gun in his armpit and revenge corroding his heart.

"My daughter is aware of the danger," he said. "She warned me of it."

"She must have told you where she was going."

"No. But she may be at the beach house. The house where Donny lives. I will come with you."

"You stay here. Keep your doors locked. If any strangers show and start prowling the place, call the police."

He bolted the door behind me as I went out. Yellow traffic lights cast wan reflections on the asphalt. Streams of cars went by to the north, to the south. To the west, where the sea lay, a great black emptiness opened under the stars. The beach house sat on its white margin, a little over a mile from the motel.

For the second time that day I knocked on the warped kitchen door. There was light behind it, shining through the cracks. A shadow obscured the light.

"Who is it?" Donny said. Fear or some other emotion had filled his mouth with pebbles.

"You know me, Donny."

The door groaned on its hinges. He gestured dumbly to me to come in, his face a white blur. When he turned his head, and the light from the living room caught his face, I saw that grief was the emotion that marked it. His eyes were swollen as if he had been crying. More than ever he resembled a dilapidated boy whose growing pains had never paid off in manhood.

"Anybody with you?"

Sounds of movement in the living room answered my question. I brushed him aside and went in. Ella Salanda was bent over an open suitcase on the camp cot. She straightened, her mouth thin, eyes wide and dark. The .38 automatic in her hand gleamed dully under the naked bulb suspended from the ceiling.

"I'm getting out of here," she said, "and you're not going to stop me."

"I'm not sure I want to try. Where are you going, Fern?"

Donny spoke behind me, in his grief-thickened voice. "She's going away from me. She promised to stay here if I did what she told me. She promised to be my girl—"

"Shut up, stupid." Her voice cut like a lash, and Donny gasped as if the lash had been laid across his back.

"What did she tell you to do, Donny? Tell me just what you did."

"When she checked in last night with the fella from Detroit, she made a sign I wasn't to let on I knew her. Later on she left me a note. She wrote it with a lipstick on a piece of paper towel. I still got it hidden, in the kitchen."

"What did she write in the note?"

He lingered behind me, fearful of the gun in the girl's hand, more fearful of her anger.

She said, "Don't be crazy, Donny. He doesn't know a thing, not a thing. He can't do anything to either of us."

"I don't care what happens, to me or anybody else," the anguished voice said behind me. "You're running out on me, breaking your promise to me. I always knew it was too good to be true. Now I just don't care any more."

"I care," she said. "I care what happens to me." Her eyes shifted to me, above the unwavering gun. "I won't stay here. I'll shoot you if I have to."

"It shouldn't be necessary. Put it down, Fern. It's Bartolomeo's gun, isn't it? I found the shells to fit it in his glove compartment."

"How do you know so much?"

"I talked to Angel."

"Is he here?" Panic whined in her voice.

"No. I came alone."

"You better leave the same way then, while you can go under your own power."

"I'm staying. You need protection, whether you know it or not. And I need information. Donny, go in the kitchen and bring me that note."

"Don't do it, Donny. I'm warning you."

His sneakered feet made soft indecisive sounds. I advanced on the girl, talking quietly and steadily, "You conspired to kill a man, but you don't have to be afraid. He had it coming. Tell the whole story to the cops, and my guess is they won't even book you. Hell, you can even become famous. The government wants you as a witness in a tax case."

"What kind of a case?"

"A tax case against Angel. It's probably the only kind of rap they can pin on him. You can send him up for the rest of his life like Capone. You'll be a heroine, Fern."

"Don't call me Fern. I hate that name." There were sudden tears in her eyes. "I hate everything connected with that name. I hate myself."

"You'll hate yourself more if you don't put down that gun. Shoot me and it all starts over again. The cops will be on your trail, Angel's troopers will be gunning for you."

Now only the cot was between us, the cot and the unsteady gun facing me above it.

"This is the turning point," I said. "You've made a lot of bum decisions and almost ruined yourself, playing footsie with the evilest men there are. You can go on the way you have been, getting in deeper until you end up in a refrigerated drawer, or you can come back out of it now, into a decent life."

"A decent life? Here? With my father married to Mabel?"

"I don't think Mabel will last much longer. Anyway, I'm not Mabel. I'm on your side."

I waited. She dropped the gun on the blanket. I scooped it up and turned to Donny. "Let me see that note."

He disappeared through the kitchen door, head and shoulders drooping on the long stalk of his body.

"What could I do?" the girl said. "I was caught. It was Bart or me. All the way up from Acapulco I planned how I could get away. He held a gun in my side when we crossed the border; the same way when we stopped for gas or to eat at the drive-ins. I realized he had to be killed. My father's motel looked like my only chance. So I talked Bart into staying there with me overnight. He had no idea who the place belonged to. I didn't know what I was going to do. I only knew it had to be something drastic. Once I was back with Angel in the desert, that was the end of me. Even if he didn't kill me, it meant I'd have to go on living with him. Anything was better than that. So I wrote a note to Donny in the bathroom, and dropped it out the window. He was always crazy about me."

Her mouth had grown softer. She looked remarkably young and virginal. The faint blue hollows under her eyes were dewy. "Donny shot Bart with Bart's own gun. He had more nerve than I had. I lost my nerve when I went back into the room this morning. I didn't know about the blood in the bathroom. It was the last straw."

She was wrong. Something crashed in the kitchen. A cool draft swept the living room. A gun spoke twice, out of sight. Donny fell backward through the doorway, a piece of brownish paper clutched in his hand. Blood gleamed on his shoulder like a red badge.

I stepped behind the cot and pulled the girl down to the floor with me. Gino came through the door, his two-colored sports shoe stepping on Donny's laboring chest. I shot the gun out of his hand. He floundered back against the wall, clutching at his wrist.

I sighted carefully for my second shot, until the black bar of his eyebrows was steady in the sights of the .38. The hole it made was invisible. Gino fell loosely forward, prone on the floor beside the man he had killed.

Ella Salanda ran across the room. She knelt, and cradled Donny's head in her lap. Incredibly he spoke, in a loud sighing voice, "You won't go away again, Ella? I did what you told me. You promised."

"Sure I promised. I won't leave you, Donny. Crazy man. Crazy fool."

"You like me better than you used to? Now?"

"I like you, Donny. You're the most man there is."

She held the poor insignificant head in her hands. He sighed, and his life came out bright-colored at the mouth. It was Donny who went away.

His hand relaxed, and I read the lipstick note she had written him on a piece of paper towel:

"Donny: This man will kill me unless you kill him first. His gun will be in his clothes on the chair beside the bed. Come in and get it at midnight and shoot to kill. Good luck. I'll stay and be your girl if you do this, just like you always wished. Love. Ella."

I looked at the pair on the floor. She was rocking his lifeless head against her breast. Beside them, Gino looked very small and lonely, a dummy leaking darkness from his brow.

Donny had his wish and I had mine. I wondered what Ella's was.

"Q"

Robert L. Fish

Muldoon and the Numbers Game

A few of those who believed in the powers of old Miss Gilhooley
said she did it with ESP, but the majority claimed she had to
be a witch, she having come originally from Salem, which she never
denied. The ones who scoffed, of course, said it was either the percentages, or just plain luck. But the fact was, she could see things—in
cloud formations, or in baseball cards, or in the throwing of bottle
caps, among other things—that were truly amazing.

Muldoon was one of those who believed in old Miss Gilhooley
implicitly. Once, shortly after his Kathleen had passed away three
years before, old Miss Gilhooley, reading the foam left in his beer
glass, told him to beware of a tall dark woman, and it wasn't two
days later that Mrs. Johnson, who did his laundry, tried to give him
back a puce-striped shirt as one of his own that Muldoon wouldn't
have worn to a Chinese water torture. And not long after, old Miss
Gilhooley, reading the lumps on his skull after a brawl at Maverick
Station, said he'd be taking a long voyage over water, and the very
next day didn't his boss send him over to Nantasket on a job, and
that at least halfway across the bay?

So, naturally, being out of work and running into old Miss Gilhooley having a last brew at Casey's Bar & Grill before taking the
bus to her sister's in Framingham for a week's visit, Muldoon wondered why he had never thought of it before. He therefore took his
beer and sat down in the booth across from the shawled old Miss
Gilhooley and put his problem directly to her.

"The unemployment insurance is about to run out, and it looks
like nobody wants no bricks laid no more, at least not by me," he
said simply. "I need money. How do I get some?"

Old Miss Gilhooley dipped her finger in his beer and traced a
pattern across her forehead. Then she closed her eyes for fully a
minute by the clock before she opened them.

"How old's your mother-in-law?" she asked in her quavering voice,
fixing Muldoon with her steady eyes.

Muldoon stared. "Seventy-four," he said, surprised. "Just last
month. Why?"

"I don't rightly know," old Miss Gilhooley said slowly. "All I know is I closed my eyes and asked meself, 'How can Muldoon come up with some money?' And right away, like in letters of fire across the insides of me eyeballs, I see, 'How old is Vera Callahan?' It's got to mean something."

"Yeah," Muldoon said glumly. "But what?"

"I'll miss me bus," said old Miss Gilhooley, and came to her feet, picking up her ancient haversack. "It'll come to you, don't worry." And with a smile she was through the door.

Seventy-four, Muldoon mused as he walked slowly toward the small house he now shared with his mother-in-law. You'd think old Miss Gilhooley might have been a little more lavish with her clues. She'd never been that cryptic before. Seventy-four! Suddenly Muldoon stopped dead in his tracks. There was only one logical solution, and the more he thought about it, the better it looked. Old Miss Gilhooley and Vera Callahan had been lifelong enemies. And his mother-in-law had certainly mentioned her life-insurance policy often enough when she first used it ten years before as her passport into the relative security of the Muldoon ménage. And, after all, 74 was a ripe old age, four years past the biblical threescore and ten, not to mention being even further beyond the actuarial probabilities.

Muldoon smiled at his own brilliance in solving the enigma so quickly. Doing away with his mother-in-law would be no chore. By Muldoon's figuring, she had to weigh in at about a hundred pounds dripping wet and carrying an anvil in each hand. Nor, he conceded, would her passing be much of a loss. She did little except creep between bed and kitchen and seemed to live on tea. Actually, since the poor soul suffered such a wide variety of voiced ailments, the oblivion offered by the grave would undoubtedly prove welcome.

He thought for a moment of checking with the insurance company as to the exact dollar value of his anticipated inheritance, but then concluded it might smack of greediness. It might also look a bit peculiar when the old lady suffered a fatal attack of something-or-other so soon after the inquiry. Still, he felt sure it would be a substantial amount; old Miss Gilhooley had never failed him before.

When he entered the house, the old lady was stretched out on the couch, taking her afternoon nap (she slept more than a cat, Muldoon thought) and all he had to do was to put one of the small embroidered pillows over her face and lean his two hundred pounds on it for a matter of several minutes, and that was that. She barely wriggled during the process.

Muldoon straightened up, removed the pillow, and gazed down. He had been right: he was sure he detected a grateful expression on the dead face. He fluffed the pillow up again, placed it in its accustomed location, and went to call the undertaker.

It was only after all decent arrangements had been made, all hard bargaining concluded, and all the proper papers signed, that Muldoon called the insurance company—and got more than a slight shock. His mother-in-law's insurance was for $400, doubtless a princely sum when her doting parents had taken it out a matter of sixty years before, but rather inadequate in this inflationary age. Muldoon tried to cancel the funeral, but the undertaker threatened suit, not to mention a visit from his nephew, acknowledged dirty-fight champion of all South Boston. The additional amount of money Muldoon had to get up to finally get Vera Callahan underground completely wiped out his meager savings.

So that, obviously, was not what old Miss Gilhooley had been hinting at, Muldoon figured. He was not bitter, nor was his faith impaired; the fault had to be his own. So there he was with the numbers again. 74—74— Could they refer to the mathematical possibilities? Four from seven left three—but three what? Three little pigs? Three blind mice? Three blind pigs? He gave it up. On the other hand, four plus seven equaled—

He smote himself on the head for his previous stupidity and quickly rubbed the injured spot, for Muldoon was a strong man with a hand like the bumper on a gravel truck. Of course! *Seven and four added up to eleven.* ELEVEN! And—Muldoon told himself with authority—if that wasn't a hint to get into the floating crap game that took place daily, then his grandfather came from Warsaw.

So Muldoon took out a second mortgage on his small house, which netted him eight hundred dollars plus change, added to that the two hundred he got for his three-and-a-half-year-old, secondhand-to-begin-with car, and with $1,000 in big bills in his pocket made his way to Casey's Bar & Grill.

"Casey," he asked in his ringing voice, "where's the floating game today?"

"Callahan Hotel," Casey said, rinsing glasses. "Been there all week. Room Seventy-four."

Muldoon barely refrained from smiting himself on the head again. How dumb could one guy be? If only he'd asked before, he wouldn't have had to deal with that thief of an undertaker, not to mention the savings he'd squandered—although in truth he had to admit the small house was less crowded with the old lady gone. "Thanks," he said to Casey, and hurried from the bar.

The group standing around the large dismountable regulation crap table in Room 74 of the Callahan Hotel was big and tough, but Muldoon was far from intimidated. With $1,000 in his pocket and his fortune about to be made, Muldoon felt confidence flowing through him like a fourth beer. He nodded to one of the gamblers he knew and turned to the man next to him, tapping him on the shoulder.

"Got room for one more?" he asked.

"Hunnert dollars minimum," the man said without looking up from the table. "No credit."

Muldoon nodded. It was precisely the game he wanted. "Who's the last man?" he asked.

"Me," the man said, and clamped his lips shut.

Muldoon took the money from his pocket and folded the bills lengthwise, gambler-fashion, wrapping them around one finger, awaiting his turn. When at last the dice finally made their way to him, Muldoon laid a hundred-dollar bill on the table, picked up the dice and shook them next to one ear. They made a pleasant ivory sound. A large smile appeared on Muldoon's face.

"Seven and four are me lucky numbers," he announced. "Same as them that's on the door of this room here. Now, if a guy could only roll an eleven *that* way—"

"He'd end up in a ditch," the back man said expressionlessly. "You're faded—roll them dice. Don't wear 'em out."

Muldoon did not wear out the dice. In fact, he had his hands on them exactly ten times, managing to throw ten consecutive craps, equally divided between snake-eyes and boxcars. They still speak of it at the floating crap game; it seems the previous record was only five and the man who held it took the elevator to the roof—they were playing at some hotel up in Copley Square that day—and jumped off. Muldoon turned the dice over to the man to his right and wandered disconsolately out of the hotel.

Out in the street Muldoon ambled along a bit aimlessly, scuffing his heavy work brogans against anything that managed to get in his way—a tin can, a broken piece of brick he considered with affectionate memory before he kicked it violently, a crushed cigarette pack. He tried for an empty candy wrapper but with his luck missed.

Seventy-four! What in the bleary name of Eustace Q. Peabody could the blaggety numbers mean? (The Sisters had raised Muldoon strictly; no obscenity passed his lips.) He tried to consider the matter logically, forcing his temper under control. Old Miss Gilhooley had never failed him, nor would she this time. He was simply missing the boat.

Seventy-four? Seventy-*four?* The figures began to take on a certain rhythm, like the *Punch, brother, punch with care* of Mark Twain. Muldoon found himself trying to march to it. Seventy-four-zero! Seventy-four-zero-*hup!* Almost it but not quite. Seventy-four-zero-hup! Seventy-four-zero, *hup!* Got it! Muldoon said to himself, deriving what little satisfaction he could from the cadence, and marched along swinging. Seventy-four-zero, *hup!*

And found himself in front of Casey's Bar & Grill, so he went inside and pulled a stool up to the deserted bar. "Beer," he said.

"How'd you do in the game?" Casey asked.

"Better give me a shot with that beer," Muldoon said by way of an answer. He slugged the shot down, took about half of his beer for a chaser, and considered Casey as he wiped his mouth. "Casey," he said earnestly, really wanting to know, "what do the numbers seven and four mean to you?"

"Nothing," Casey said.

"How about seven, four, and zero?"

"Nothing," Casey said. "Maybe even less."

"How about backwards?" Muldoon asked in desperation, but Casey had gone to the small kitchen in the rear to make himself a sandwich during the slack time and Muldoon found himself addressing thin air. He tossed the proper amount of change on the counter and started for the door. Where he ran into a small man named O'Leary, who ran numbers for the mob. It wasn't what he preferred, but it was a living.

"Wanna number today, Mr. Muldoon?" O'Leary asked.

Muldoon was about to pass on with a shake of his head when he suddenly stopped. A thrill went through him from head to foot. Had he been in a cartoon a light bulb would have lit up in a small circle over his head. Not being in a cartoon, he kicked himself, his heavy brogan leaving a bruise that caused him to limp painfully for the next three weeks.

Good Geoffrey T. Soppingham! He must have been blind! *Blind?* Insane! What possible meaning could numbers have if not *that they were numbers?* Just thinking about it made Muldoon groan. If he hadn't killed the old lady and gotten into that stupid crap game, at this moment he could be putting down roughly fifteen hundred bucks on Seven-Four-Zero. $1,500 at five-hundred-to-one odds! Still, if he hadn't smothered the old lady, he'd never have come up with the zero, so it wasn't a total loss. But the floating crap game had been completely unnecessary.

Because now Muldoon didn't have the slightest doubt as to what the numbers meant.

"Somethin' wrong, Mr. Muldoon?" O'Leary asked, concerned with the expression on Muldoon's face.

"No!" Muldoon said, and grasped the runner by the arm, drawing him back into Casey's Bar & Grill, his hand like the clamshell bucket of a steam shovel on the smaller man's bicep. He raised his voice, bellowing. "*Casey!*"

Casey appeared from the kitchen, wiping mayonnaise from his chin. "Don't shout," he said. "What do you want?"

Muldoon was prying his wedding ring from his finger. He laid it down on the bar. "What'll you give me for this?"

Casey looked at Muldoon as if the other man had suddenly gone mad. "This ain't no hockshop, Muldoon," he said.

But Muldoon was paying no attention. He was slipping his wristwatch and its accompanying stretch band over his thick fingers. He placed the watch down on the bar next to the ring.

"One hundred bucks for the lot," he said simply. "A loan is all. I'll pay it back tonight." As Casey continued to look at him with fishy eyes, Muldoon added in a quiet, desperate voice, "I paid sixty bucks each for them rings; me and Kathleen had matching ones. And that watch set me back better than a bill-and-a-half all by itself, not to mention the band, which is pure Speidel. How about it?" A touch of pleading entered his voice. "Come on—we been friends a long time."

"Acquaintances," Casey said, differentiating, and continued to eye Muldoon coldly. "I ain't got that much cash in the register right now."

"Jefferson J. Billingsly the cash register," Muldoon said, irked. "You got that much and more in your pants pocket."

Casey studied the other a moment longer, then casually swept the ring and the watch from the counter into his palm, and pocketed them. From another pocket he brought out a wallet that looked like it was suffering from mumps. He began counting out bills.

"Ninety-five bucks," he said. "Five percent off the top, just like the Morris Plan."

Muldoon was about to object but time was running out. "Someday we'll discuss this transaction in greater detail, Casey," he said. "Out in the alley," and he turned to O'Leary, grasping both of the smaller man's arms for emphasis. "O'Leary, I want ninety-five bucks on number seven-four-zero. Got it? *Seven-Four-Zero!* Today!"

"Ninety-five bucks?" O'Leary was stunned. "I never wrote no slip bigger than a deuce in my life, Mr. Muldoon," he said. He thought a moment. "No, a fin," he said brightly, but then his face fell. "No, a deuce. I remember now, the fin was counterfeit."

"You're wasting time," Muldoon said in a dangerous voice. He suddenly realized he was holding the smaller man several inches from the floor and lowered him. "Will they pay off? That's the question," he said in a quieter voice, prepared for hesitation.

"Sure they pay off, Mr. Muldoon," O'Leary said, straightening his sleeves into a semblance of their former shape. "How long you figure they stay alive, they start welching?"

"So long as they know it," Muldoon said, and handed over the ninety-five bucks. He took his receipt in return, checked the number carefully to make sure O'Leary had made no mistake, and slipped the paper into his pocket. Then he turned to Casey.

"A beer," he said in a voice that indicated their friendship had suffered damage. "And that is out of that five bucks you just stole!"

Muldoon was waiting in a booth at Casey's Bar & Grill at seven o'clock P.M., which was the time the runners normally had the final three figures of the national treasury balance—which was the Gospel that week. Muldoon knew that straight cash in hand would not be forthcoming; after all, he was due a matter of over $47,000. Still, he'd take a check. If he hadn't gotten into that crap game, he'd have been rich—or, more probably, in a ditch like the man had mentioned this afternoon. Who was going to pay off that kind of loot? No mob in Boston, that was sure. Better this way. Forty-seven grand was big enough to be the year's best advertisement for the racket, but still small enough by their standards for the mob to loosen up.

It was a nice feeling being financially secure after the problems of the past few years, and Muldoon had no intention of splurging. His honest debts would be cleared up, of course, and he'd have to buy himself some wheels—a compact, nothing fancy—but the rest would go into the bank. At five percent it wouldn't earn no fortune, he knew, but it would still be better than a fall off a high scaffold onto a low sidewalk.

He reached for his beer and saw old Miss Gilhooley walking through the door. Had a week passed so quickly? He supposed it must have; what with the funeral, and one thing and another, the time had flown. He waved her over and called out to Casey to bring old Miss Gilhooley anything her heart desired.

Old Miss Gilhooley settled herself in the booth across from him and noted the expression on his face. "So you figured it out, Muldoon," she said.

"Not right off," Muldoon admitted. "To be honest, it just come to me this afternoon. But better late than never; at least it come." He leaned over the table confidentially. "It was the numbers, see? The seven and the four for her age, plus the zero at the end, because whether you heard or not, that's what the poor soul is now."

Old Miss Gilhooley sipped the beer Casey had brought and nodded. "That's what I figured," she said, "especially after seeing O'Leary in me dreams three nights running, and me old enough to be his mother."

"And I can't thank you enough—" Muldoon started to say, and then paused, for O'Leary had just burst through the door of the bar like a Roman candle and was hurrying over to them, brushing people aside. His eyes were shining.

"Mr. Muldoon! Mr. Muldoon!" O'Leary cried excitedly. "I never seen nothin' like it in all me born days! And on a ninety-five-dollar bet!"

Muldoon grinned happily.

"Only one number away!" O'Leary cried, still astounded at the closeness of his brush with fame and fortune.

Muldoon's world fell with a crash. "One number away?"

"Yeah!" O'Leary said, still marveling. "You bet Seven-Four-Zero. It come out Seven-Five-Zero. Tough!" O'Leary sighed and then put the matter from his mind. After all, life had to go on. "Wanna number for tomorrow, Mr. Muldoon?"

"No," Muldoon said in a dazed tone, and turned to old Miss Gilhooley, who was making strange noises. But they were not lamentations for Muldoon—to Muldoon's surprise the old lady was cackling like a fiend.

"That Vera Callahan!" she said triumphantly. "I always *knew* she lied about her age!"

Cornell Woolrich

Death Between Dances

E very Saturday night you'd see them together at the country-
club dance. Together, and yet far apart. One sitting back against
the wall, never moving from there, never once getting up to dance
the whole evening long. The other swirling about the floor, passing
from partner to partner, never still a moment.

The two daughters of Walter Brainard (widower, 52, stocks and
bonds, shoots 72 at golf, charter member of the country club).

Nobody seeing them for the first time ever took them for sisters.
It wasn't only the difference in their ages, though that was great
enough and seemed even greater than it actually was. There was
about twelve years' difference between them, and fifty in outlook.

Even their names were peculiarly appropriate. Jane, as plain as
her name, sitting there against the wall, dark hair drawn severely
back from her forehead, watching the festivities through heavy-
rimmed glasses that gave her an expression of owlish inscrutability.
And Sunny, dandelion-colored hair, blue eyes, a dancing sunbeam,
glinting around the floor, no one boy ever able to hold her for very
long (you can't make sunbeams stay in one place if they don't want
to). Although Tom Reed, until just recently, had had better luck at
it than the rest. But the last couple of Saturday nights he seemed
to be slipping or something; he'd become just one of the second-
stringers again.

Sunny was usually in pink, one shade of it or another. She favored
pink; it was her color. She reminded you of pink spun-sugar candy.
Because it's so good, and so sweet, and so harmless. But it also melts
so easily . . .

One of them had a history, one hadn't. Well, at eighteen you can't
be expected to have a history yet. You can make one for yourself if
you set out to, but you haven't got it yet. And as for the
history—Jane's—it wasn't strictly that, either, because history is
hard-and-fast facts, and this was more of a formless thing, a whispered rumor, a half forgotten legend. It had never lived, but it had
never died either.

Some sort of blasting infatuation that had come along and changed
her from what she'd been then, at eighteen—the darling of the dance

floors, as her sister was now—into what she was now: a wallflower, an onlooker who didn't take part. She'd gone away for a while around that time, and then she'd suddenly been back again.

From the time she'd come back, she'd been as she was now. That was all that was definitely known—the rest was pure surmise. Nobody had ever found out exactly who the man was. It was generally agreed that it wasn't anyone from around here. Some said there had been a quiet annulment. Some—more viperishly—said there hadn't been anything to annul.

One thing was certain. She was a wallflower by choice and not by compulsion. As far back as people could remember, anyone who had ever asked her to dance received only a shake of her head. They stopped asking, finally. She wanted to be left alone, so she was. Maybe, it was suggested, she had first met him, whoever he was, while dancing, and that was why she had no use for dancing any more. Then in that case, others wondered, why did she come so regularly to the country club? To this there were a variety of answers, none of them wholly satisfactory.

"Maybe," some shrugged, "it's because her father's a charter member of the club—she thinks it's her duty to be present."

"Maybe," others said, "she sees ghosts on the dance floor—sees someone there that the rest of us can't see."

"And maybe," still others suggested, but not very seriously, "she's waiting for him to come back to her—thinks he'll suddenly show up sometime in the Saturday-night crowd and come over to her and claim her. That's why she won't dance with anyone else."

But the owlish glasses gave no hint of what was lurking behind them; whether hope or resignation, love or indifference or hate.

At exactly 9:45 this Saturday, this Washington's Birthday Saturday, tonight, the dance is on full-blast; the band is playing an oldie, "The Object of My Affections," Number Twenty in the leader's book. And Jane is sitting back against the wall. Sunny is twinkling about on the floor, this time in the arms of Tom Reed, the boy who loved her all through high school, the man who still does, now, at this very moment—

She stopped short, right in the middle of the number, detached his arm from her waist, and stepped back from its half embrace.

"Wait here, Tom. I just remembered. I have to make a phone call."

"I no sooner get you than I lose you again."

But she'd already turned and was moving away from him, looking back over her shoulder now.

He tried to follow her. She laughed and held him back. A momentary flattening of her hands against his shirtfront was enough to do that. "No, you can't come with me. Oh, don't look so dubious. It's just to Martha, back at our house. Something I forgot to tell her when we left. You wouldn't be interested."

"But we'll lose this dance."

"I'll give you—I'll give you one later, to make up for it," she promised. "I'll foreclose on somebody else's." She gave him a smile, and even a little wink, and that held him. "Now, be a good boy and stay in here."

She made sure that he was standing still first. It was like leaving a lifesize toy propped up—you wait a second to make sure it won't fall over. Then she turned and went out into the foyer.

She looked back at him from there, once more. He was standing obediently stock-still in the middle of the dance floor like an ownerless pup, everyone else circling around him. She raised a cautioning index finger, shook it at him. Then she whisked from sight.

She went over to the checkroom cubbyhole.

"Will you let me have that now, Marie."

"Leaving already, Miss Brainard?" The girl raised a small overnight case from the floor—it hadn't been placed on the shelves, where it might have been seen and recognized—and passed it to her.

Sunny handed her something. "You haven't seen me go, though."

"I understand, Miss Brainard," the girl said.

She hurried out of the club with it. She went over to where the cars were parked, found a small coffee-colored roadster, and put the case on the front seat.

Then she got in after it and drove off.

The clubhouse lights receded in the indigo February darkness. The music got fainter, and then you couldn't hear it any more. It stayed on in her mind, though: still playing, like an echo.

"The object of my affection
Can change my complexion
From white to rosy-red—"

The car purred along the road. She looked very lovely, and a little wild, her uncovered hair streaming backward in the wind. The stars up above seemed to be winking at her, as though she and they shared the same conspiracy.

After a while she took one hand from the wheel and fumbled in the glittering little drawstring bag dangling from her wrist.

She took out a very crumpled note, its envelope gone. The note looked as though it had been hastily crushed and thrust away to protect if from discovery immediately after first being received.

She smoothed it out now as best she could and reread it carefully by the dashboard light. A part of it, anyway.

"—There's a short cut that'll bring you to me even quicker, darling. No one knows of it but me, and now I'm sharing it with you. It will keep you from taking the long way around, on the main road, and risk being seen by anyone. Just before you come to that lighted filling station at the intersection, turn off, sharp left. Even though there doesn't seem to be anything there, keep going, don't be frightened. You'll pick up a back lane, and that'll bring you safely to me. I'll be counting the minutes—"

She pressed it to her lips, the crumpled paper, and kissed it fervently. Love is a master alchemist: it can turn base things to gold.

She put it back in her bag. The stars were still with her, winking. The music was still with her, playing for her alone.

"Every time he holds my hand
And tells me that he's mine."

Just before she came to that lighted filling station at the intersection, she swung the wheel and turned off sharp left into gritty nothingness that rocked and swayed the car.

Her headlights picked up a screen of trees and she went around to the back of them. She found a disused dirt lane there—as love had promised her she would—and clung to it over rises and hollows, and through shrubbery that hissed at her.

And then at last a little rustic lodge. A hidden secret place. Cheerful amber light streaming out to welcome her. Another car already there, offside in the darkness—his.

She braked in front of it. She took out her mirror, and by the dashboard light she smoothed her hair and touched a golden tube of lipstick lightly to her mouth. Very lightly, for there would be kisses that would take it away again soon.

She tapped the horn, just once.

Then she waited for him to come out to her.

The stars kept winking up above the pointed fir trees. Their humor was a little crueler now, as though someone were the butt of it. And in the lake that glistened like dark-blue patent leather down the other way, their winking still went on, upside down in the water.

She tapped her horn again, more heavily this time, twice in quick succession.

He didn't come out. The yellow thread outlining the lodge-door remained as it was; it grew no wider.

An owl hooted somewhere in the trees, but she wasn't afraid. She'd only just learned what love was; how should she have had time to learn what fear was?

She opened the car door abruptly and got out. Her footfalls crunched on the sandy ground that sloped down from here all the way to the lake. Silly, fragile sandals meant for the dance floor, their spike heels pecking into the crusty frosty ground.

She went up onto the plank porch, and there they sounded hollow. She knocked on the door, and that sounded hollow too. Like when you knock on an empty shell of something.

The door moved at last, but it was her own knock that had done it; it was unfastened. The yellow thread widened.

She pushed it back, and warmth and brightness gushed out, the night was driven to a distance.

"Hoo-hoo," she called softly. "You have a caller. There's a young lady at your door, to see you."

A fire was blazing in the natural-stone fireplace, gilding the walls and coppering the ceiling with its restless tides of reflection. There was a table, all set and readied for two. The feast of love. Yellow candles were twinkling on it; their flames had flattened for a moment, now they straightened again as she came in and closed the door behind her.

Flowers were on it in profusion, and sparkling, spindly-stemmed glasses. And under it there was a gilt ice pail, with a pair of gold-capped bottles protruding from it at different angles.

And on the wooden peg projecting from the wall, his hat and coat were hanging. With that scarf she knew so well dangling carelessly from one of the pockets.

She laughed a little, mischievously.

As she passed the table, on her way deeper into the long room, she helped herself to a salted almond, crunched it between her teeth. She laughed again, like a little girl about to tease somebody. Then she picked up a handful of almonds and began throwing them one by one against the closed bedroom-door, the way you throw gravel against a windowpane to attract someone's attention behind it.

242 DEATH BETWEEN DANCES

Each one went *tick!* and fell to the floor.

At last, when she'd used up all the almonds, she gave vent to a deep breath of exasperation, that was really only pretended exasperation, and stepped directly up to it and knocked briskly.

"Are you asleep in there, or what?" she demanded. "Is this any way to receive your intended? After I come all the way up here—"

Silence.

A log in the fire cracked sharply. One of the gilt-topped bottles slumped lower in the pail, the ice supporting it crumbling.

"I'm coming in there, ready or not."

She flung the door open.

He was asleep. But in a distorted way, as she'd never yet seen anyone sleep. On the floor alongside the bed, with his face turned upward to the ceiling, and one arm flung over his eyes protectively.

Then she saw the blood. Stilled, no longer flowing. Not very old, but not new either.

She ran to him, for a second only, tried to raise him, tried to rouse him. And all she got was soddenness. Then after that, she couldn't touch him any more, couldn't go near him again. It wasn't him any more. He'd gone, and left this—this *thing*—behind him. This awful thing that didn't even talk to you, take you in its arms, hold you to it.

She didn't scream. Death was too new to her. She barely knew what it was. She hadn't lived long enough.

She began to cry. Not because he was dead, but because she'd been cheated, she had no one to take her in his arms now. First heartbreak. First love. Those tears that never come more than once.

She was still kneeling there, near him.

Then she saw the gun lying there. Dark, ugly, dangerous-looking. His, but too far across the room for him to have used it himself. Even she, dimly, realized that. How could it get all the way over there, with him all the way over here?

She began crawling toward it on hands and knees.

Her hand went out toward it, hesitated, finally closed on it, picked it up. She knelt there, holding it between both hands, staring at it in fascinated horror—

"Drop that! Put it down!"

The voice was like a whip across her face, stinging in its suddenness, its lashing sharpness. Then leaving her quivering all over, as an aftermath.

Tom Reed was standing in the doorway like a tuxedoed phantom.

Bare-headed, coatless, just as he'd left the dance floor and run out after her into the cold of the February night.

"You fool," he breathed with soft, suppressed intensity. "You fool, oh you little fool!"

A single frightened whimper, like the mewing of a helpless kitten left out in the rain, sounded from her.

He went over to her, for she was crouched there incapable of movement; he raised her in his arms, caught her swiftly to him, turned her away with a gesture that was both rough and tender at the same time. The toe of his shoe edged deftly forward and the gun slithered out of her sight somewhere along the floor.

"I didn't do it!" she protested, terrified. "I didn't! Oh, Tom, I swear—"

"I know you didn't," he said almost impatiently. "I was right behind you coming up here. I would have heard the shot and I didn't."

All she could say to that was, "Oh, Tom," with a shudder.

"Yes, 'oh, Tom,' after the damage is done. Why wasn't it 'oh, Tom' before that?" His words were a rebuke, his gestures a consolation that belied them. "I saw you leave and came right after you. Who did you think you were fooling, with your phone-call home? You blind little thing. I was too tame for you. You had to have excitement. Well, now you've got it." And all the while his hand stroked the sobbing golden-haired head against his shoulder. "You wanted to know life. You couldn't wait. Well, now you do. How do you like it?"

"Is this—?" she choked.

"This is what it *can* be like if you don't watch where you're going."

"I'll never—I'll never—oh, Tom, I'll never—"

"I know," he said. "They all say that. All the little, helpless purring things. After it's too late."

Her head came up suddenly, in renewed terror. "Oh, Tom, is it too late?"

"Not if I can get you back to that dance unnoticed—you've only been away about half an hour—" He drew his head back, still holding her in his arms, and looked at her intently. "Who was he?"

"I met him last summer when I was away. All of a sudden he showed up here. I never expected him to. He's only been here a few days. I lost my head, I guess—"

"How is it nobody ever saw him around here, even the few days you say he's been here? Why did he make himself so inconspicuous?"

"He wanted it that way, and I don't know—I guess to me it seemed more romantic."

He murmured something under his breath that sounded like, "Sure, at eighteen it would." Then aloud, and quite bitterly, he said, "What was he hiding from? Who was he hiding from?"

"He was going to—we were going to be married," she said.

"You wouldn't have been married," he told her with quiet scorn. She looked at him aghast.

"Oh, there would have been a ceremony, I suppose. For how long? A week or two, a month. And then you'd come creeping back alone. The kind that does his courting under cover doesn't stick to you for long."

"How do you know?" she said, crushed.

"Ask your sister Jane sometime. They say she found that out once, long ago. And look at her now. Embittered for all the rest of her life. Eaten up with hate—"

He changed the subject abruptly. He tipped up her chin and looked searchingly at her. "Are you all right now? Will you do just as I tell you? Will you be able to—go through with this, carry it off?"

She nodded. Her lips formed the words, barely audible, "If you stay with me."

"I'm with you. I was never so with you before."

With an arm about her waist, he led her over toward the door. As they reached and passed it, her head stirred slightly on his shoulder. He guessed its intent, quickly forestalled it with a quieting touch of his hand.

"Don't look at him. Don't look back. *He isn't there. You were never here either*. Those are the two things you have to keep saying to yourself. We've all had bad dreams at times, and this was yours. Now wait here outside the door a minute. I've got things to do. Don't watch me."

He left her and went back into the room again.

After a moment or two she couldn't resist: the horrid fascination was too strong, it was almost like a hypnotic compulsion. She crept back to the threshold, peered around the edge of the door-frame into the room beyond, and watched with bated breath what he was doing.

He went after the gun first. Got it back from where he'd kicked it. Picked it up and looked it over with painstaking care. He interrupted himself once to glance down at the form lying on the floor, and by some strange telepathy she knew that something about the gun had told him it belonged to the dead man, that it hadn't been brought in from outside. Perhaps something about its type or size that she would not have understood; she didn't know anything about guns.

Then she saw him break it open and do something to it with deft fingers, twist or spin something. A cartridge fell out into the palm of his hand. He stood that aside for a minute, upright on the edge of the dresser. Then he closed up the gun again. He took out his own handkerchief and rubbed the gun thoroughly all over with it.

Each time she thought he was through, he'd blow his breath on it and steam it up, and then rub it some more. He even pulled the whole length of the handkerchief through the little guard where the trigger was, and made that click emptily a couple of times.

He worked fast but he worked calmly, without undue excitement, keeping his presence of mind.

Finally he wrapped the handkerchief in its entirety around the butt so that his own bare hand didn't touch it. Holding it in that way, he knelt down by the man. He took the hand, took it by the very ends, by the fingers, and closed them around the gun, first subtracting the handkerchief. He pressed the fingers down on it, pressed them hard and repeatedly, the way you do when you want to take an impression of something.

Then he fitted them carefully around it in a grasping position; even pushed one, the index-finger, through that same trigger guard. He watched a minute to see if the gun would hold that way on its own, without his supporting hand around the outside of the other. It did; it dipped a little, but it stayed fast. Then very carefully he eased it, and the hand now holding it, back to the floor, left them there together.

Then he got up and went back to the cartridge. He saw her mystified little face peering in at him around the edge of the door.

"Don't watch, I told you," he rebuked her.

But she kept right on, and he went ahead without paying any further attention to her.

He took out a pocketknife and prodded away at the cartridge with it until he had it separated into two parts. Then he went back to the dead man and knelt down by him. What she saw him do next was sheer horror.

But she had only herself to blame; he'd warned her not to look.

He turned the head slightly, very carefully, until he'd revealed the small, dark, almost neat little hole, where the blood had originally come from.

He took one half of the dissected cartridge, tilted it right over it, and shook it gently back and forth. As though—as though he were salting the wound from a small shaker. Her hands flew to her mouth to stifle the gasp this tore from her.

He thrust the pieces of cartridge into his pocket, both of them. Then he struck a match. He held it for a moment to let the flame steady itself and shrink a little. Then he gave it a quick dab at the gunpowdered wound and then back again.

There was a tiny flash from the wound. For an instant it seemed to ignite. Then it went right out again. A slightly increased blackness remained around the wound now; he'd charred it. This time a sick moan escaped through her suppressing hands. She turned away at last.

When he came out he found her at the far end of the outside room with her back to him. She was twitching slightly, as though she'd just recovered from a nervous chill.

She couldn't bring herself to ask the question, but he could read it in her eyes when she turned to stare at him.

"The gun was his own, or the user wouldn't have left it behind. I had to do that other thing. A gun suicide's always a contact wound. They press it hard against themselves. And with a contact wound there are always powder burns."

Then he said with strange certainty, "A woman did it."

"How do you—?"

"I found this in there with him. There must have been tears at first, and then later she dropped it when she picked up the gun."

He handed it to her. There wasn't anything distinctive about it—just a gauzy handkerchief. No monogram, no design. It could have been anyone's, anyone in a million. A faint fragrance reached her, invisible as a finespun wire but just as tenuous and for a moment she wondered at the scent.

Like lilacs in the rain.

"I couldn't leave it in there," he explained, "because it doesn't match the setup as I've arranged it. It would have shown that somebody was in there, after all." He smiled grimly. "I'm doing somebody a big favor, a much bigger favor than she deserves. But I'm not doing it for her, I'm doing it for you, to keep even a whisper of your name from being brought into it."

Absently she thrust the wisp of stuff into her own evening bag, where she carried her own, drew the drawstring tight once more.

"Get rid of it," he advised. "You can do that easier than I can. But not anywhere around here, whatever you do."

He glanced back toward the inside room. "What else did you touch in there—besides the gun?"

She shook her head. "I just stepped in and—you found me."

"You touched the door?"

She nodded.

He whipped out his handkerchief again, crouched low on one knee, and like a strange sort of porter in a dinner jacket scoured the doorknobs on both sides, in and out.

"What about these? Did you do that?" There were some almonds lying on the floor.

"I threw them at the door, like pebbles—to attract his attention."

"A man about to do what he did wouldn't munch almonds." He picked them up, all but one which had already been stepped on and crushed. "One won't matter. He could have done that himself," he told her. "Let me see your shoe." He bent down and peered at the tilted sole. "It's on there. Get rid of them altogether when you get home. Don't just scrape it; they have ways of bringing out things like that."

"What about the whole supper table itself? It's for two."

"That'll have to stay. Whoever he was expecting didn't come and in a fit of depression aging Romeo played his last role, alone. That'll be the story it tells. At least it'll show that no one *did* come. If we disturb a perfect setup like that, we may prove the opposite to what we're trying to."

He put his arm about her. "Are you ready now? Come on, here we go. And remember: *you were never here. None of this ever happened.*"

A sweep of his hand behind his back, a swing of the door, and the light faded away—they were out in the starry blue night together.

"Whose car is that?"

"My own. The roadster Daddy gave me. I had Rufus run it down to the club for me and leave it outside after we all left for the dance."

"Did he check it?"

"No, I told him not to."

He heaved a sigh of relief. "Good. We've got to get them both out of here. I'll get in mine. You'll have to get back into the one you brought, by yourself. I'll lead the way. Stick to my treads, so you don't leave too clear a print. It will probably snow again before they find him, and that'll save us."

He went on ahead to his own car, got in, and started the motor. Suddenly he left it warming up, jumped out again, and came back to her. "Here," he said abruptly, "hang onto this until I can get you back down there again." And pressed his lips to hers with a sort of tender encouragement.

It was the strangest kiss she'd ever had. It was one of the most selfless, one of the nicest.

The two cars trundled away, one behind the other. After a little while the echo of their going drifted back from the lonely lake. And then there was just silence.

The lights and the music, like a warm friendly tide, came swirling around her again. He stopped her for a moment, just outside the entrance, before they went in.

"Did anyone see you leave?"

"Only Marie, the check girl. The parking attendant didn't know about the car."

"Hand me your lipstick a minute," he ordered.

She got it out and gave it to him. He made a little smudge with it, on his own cheek, high up near the ear. Then another one farther down, closer to the mouth. Not too vivid, faint enough to be plausible, distinct enough to be seen.

He even thought of his tie, pulled it a little awry. He seemed to think of everything. Maybe that was because he was only thinking of one thing: of her.

He slung a proprietary arm about her waist. "Smile," he instructed her. "Laugh. Put *your* arm around *my* waist. Act as if you really cared for me. We're having a giddy time. We're just coming in from a session in a parked car outside."

The lights from the glittering dance floor went up over them like a slowly raised curtain. They strolled past the checkroom girl, arm over arm, faces turned to one another, prattling away like a pair of grammar-school kids, all taken up in one another. Sunny threw her head back and emitted a paean of frivolous laughter at something he was supposed to have said just then.

The check girl's eyes followed them with a sort of wistful envy. It must be great, she thought, to be so carefree and have such a good time. Not a worry on your mind.

At the edge of the floor they stopped. He took her in his arms to lead her.

"Keep on smiling, you're doing great. We're going to dance. I'm going to take you once around the floor until we get over to where your father and sister are. Wave to people, call out their names as we pass them. I want everyone to see you. Can you do it? Will you be all right?"

She took a deep, resolute breath. "If you want me to. Yes. I can do it."

They went gliding out into the middle of the floor.

The band was back to Number Twenty in the books—the same song they had been playing when she left. It must have been a repeat by popular demand, it couldn't have been going on the whole time, she'd been away too long. What a different meaning it had now.

"But instead I trust him implicitly
I'll go where he wants to go,
Do what he wants to do, I don't care—"

That sort of fitted Tom. That was for him—nobody else. Sturdy reliability. That was what you wanted, that was what you came back to, if you were foolish enough to stray from it in the first place. Sometimes you found that out too late—sometimes it took you a lifetime, it cost you your youth. Like what they said had happened to poor Jane ten or twelve years ago when she herself, Sunny, had been still a child.

But Sunny was lucky, she had found it out in time. It had only taken her—well, the interval between a pair of dance selections, played the same night, at the same club. It had only cost her—well, somebody else had paid the debt for her.

And so, it was back where it had begun. And as it had begun.

At exactly 10:55 this Saturday, this Washington's Birthday Saturday, the dance is still on full-blast; the band is playing "The Object of My Affections," Number Twenty in the leader's book. Jane is sitting back against the wall. And Sunny is twinkling about on the floor, once more in the arms of Tom Reed, the boy who loved her all through high school, the man who still does now at this very moment, the man who always will, through all the years ahead—

"Here are your people," he whispered warningly. "I'm going to turn you over to them now."

She glanced at them across his shoulder. They were sitting there, Jane and her father, so safe, so secure. Nothing ever happened to them. Less than an hour ago she would have felt sorry for them. Now she envied them.

She and Tom came to a neat halt in front of them.

"Daddy," she said quietly. And she hadn't called him that since she was fifteen. "Daddy, I want to go home now. Take me with you."

He chuckled. "You mean before they even finish playing down to the very last half note? I thought you never got tired dancing."

"Sometimes I do," she admitted wistfully. "And I guess this is one of those times."

He turned to his other daughter. "How about you, Jane? Ready to go now?"

"I've been ready," she said, "ever since we first got here, almost."

The father's eyes had rested for a moment on the telltale red traces on Tom's cheek. They twinkled quizzically, but he tactfully refrained from saying anything.

Not Jane. "Really, Sunny," she said disapprovingly. And then, curtly, to Tom: "Fix your cheek."

He went about it very cleverly, pretending he couldn't find it with his handkerchief for a minute. "Where? Here?"

"Higher up," said Jane. And this time Mr. Brainard smothered an indulgent little smile.

Sunny and Tom trailed them out to the entrance, when they got up to go. "Give me your spare garage key," he said in an undertone. "I'll run the roadster home as soon as you leave and put it away for you. I can get up there quicker with it than you will with the big car. I'll see that Rufus doesn't say anything; I'll tell him you and I were going to elope tonight and changed our minds at the last minute."

"He's always on my side anyway," she admitted.

He took a lingering leave of her by the hand.

"I have a question to ask you. But I'll keep it until next Saturday. The same place? The same time?"

"I have the answer to give you. But I'll keep that until next Saturday too. The same place. The same time."

She got in the back seat with her father and sister, and they drove off.

"It's beginning to snow," Jane complained.

Thanks, murmured Sunny, unheard, *Thanks*, as the first few flakes came sifting down.

Jane bunched her shoulders defensively. "It gets too hot in there with all those people. And now it's chilly in the car." She stifled a sneeze, fumbled in her evening bag. "Now, what did I do with my handkerchief?"

"Here, I'll give you mine," offered Sunny, and heedlessly passed her something in the dark, out of her own bag.

A faint fragrance, invisible as a finespun wire but just as tenuous. Like lilacs in the rain.

Jane raised it toward her nose, held it there, suddenly arrested. "Why, this *is* mine! Don't you recognize my sachet? Where'd you find it?"

Sunny didn't answer. Something had suddenly clogged her throat. She recognized the scent now. Lilacs in the rain.

"Where did you find it?" Jane insisted.

"Hattie—Hattie turned it over to me in the ladies' lounge. You must have lost it in there—"

"Why, I wasn't—" Jane started to say. Then just as abruptly she didn't go ahead.

Sunny knew what she'd been about to say. "I wasn't in there once the whole evening." Jane disliked the atmosphere of gossip that she imagined permeated the lounge, the looks that she imagined would be exchanged behind her back. Sunny hadn't thought quickly enough. But it was too late now.

Jane was holding the handkerchief pressed tight to her mouth. Just holding it there.

Impulsively Sunny reached out, found Jane's hand in the dark, and clasped it warmly and tightly for a long moment.

It said so much, that warm clasp of hands, without a word being said. It said: I understand. We'll never speak of it, you and I. Not a word will ever pass my lips. And thank you, thank you for helping me as you have, though you may not know you did.

Presently, tremulously, a little answering pressure was returned by Jane's hand. There must have been unseen tears on her face, tears of gratitude, tears of release. She was dabbing at her eyes in the dark.

Their father, sitting comfortably and obliviously between them, spoke for the first time since the car had left the club.

"Well, another Saturday-night dance over and done with. They're all pretty much alike—once you've been to one, you've been to them all. Same old thing week in and week out. Music playing, people dancing. Nothing much ever happens. They get pretty monotonous. Sometimes I wonder why we bother going every week, the way we do."

John Ball

Virgil Tibbs and the
Fallen Body

The first thing Officer Frank Mitchell heard was a violent thud directly behind him; it was so powerful it seemed for a second that the very ground had shaken under his feet. He turned quickly, saw the body scarcely thirty feet away, and had a sudden, compelling desire to be sick. Only seven months out of the academy, he was still not used to the sight of sudden and violent death.

The body of the suicide, if that's what it was, had landed so hard the skull had split and what was revealed took all of Officer Mitchell's courage to face. Partly by reflex action he looked up, far up the side of the towering building in front of which he was standing. He saw an immensity of structure and glass that was totally unmoved by what had just happened. On Mitchell's first inspection, the building gave no clue to the point from which the now smashed body had been launched into the air.

When he had seen and noted that, Officer Mitchell turned to do his unwelcome but necessary duty. There were a few others who had witnessed the terrible death; they hung back in a kind of hypnotized horror, unwilling either to come closer or to go away. Then through the small ring of spectators a slender but well built black man came running forward, peeling off his coat at the same time. Because the man was headed straight toward the body on the sidewalk, Officer Mitchell held up his hands to stop him.

He could have saved himself the trouble; he was ignored. Instead, the intruder dropped to one knee and threw his coat over the head and shoulders of the fallen man. Then he looked up at Mitchell. "Tibbs," the man said. "Pasadena Police. Get some backup and an ambulance."

Mitchell came out of his near shock and responded by taking his small portable police radio out of its belt carrier. He raised it to his face and put out an urgent call. His immediate duty done, he walked the few steps to where the now covered body lay grimly still on the concrete. "Thank you," he said. "It got to me for a moment."

"Of course." The Pasadena policeman got to his feet and had his own look at the sheer face of the massive building. "He probably came from halfway up, or more. Did you note the condition of the skull?"

Mitchell swallowed and nodded. "Frank Mitchell," he introduced himself.

"Virgil Tibbs."

"What do you work?"

"Robbery-Homicide."

"Look, if you'd care to stick around until my backup—"

"Of course. This isn't my jurisdiction, but I'll do what I can." He took out his Pasadena ID and clipped it to his shirt pocket.

Mercifully, the gathering crowd showed no signs of wanting to come closer. A single young man armed with a small pocket camera started to move in, but retreated when Mitchell waved him away. After that the scene was static until a black-and-white patrol car coming Code Two pulled up with its roof lights still on. A sergeant got out; he was closing the car door when a second unit rolled in.

The sergeant took in the situation with a single careful look, then he too scanned the vast side of the huge building. He raised a hand to wave Virgil Tibbs away, then he saw the plastic identification clipped to his pocket. He came close enough to read it before he spoke. "You covered the body." It was a statement.

"Yes."

"Thank you. The ambulance will be here right away."

As he spoke, a red paramedic unit from the fire department rolled up. The two-man crew had already been notified what to expect; one man riding on the passenger side had a blanket ready on his lap. He jumped out, walked quickly to the body, took off Tibbs's coat, and satisfied himself that life was extinct. Then he snapped the blanket open and dropped it over the corpse. After that he picked up the coat once more and returned it to its owner. "It may be stained," he warned.

Tibbs checked it carefully, then put it back on. "It's all right," he said. "I'll have it cleaned."

Mitchell was talking to his sergeant, reporting on what he had seen. It took him only a few moments, then he introduced Tibbs.

The Los Angeles sergeant was obviously experienced, but unpretentious. "I'm glad you were here to give us a hand," he said. "Bob Opper."

"Anything else I can do?"

"If you've got the time, I'd like to get your account of this."

"Whatever you want."

"You work homicide?"

"Yes."

"It looks like a jumper, of course, but I want to check it out. You're welcome if you want to come along."

That didn't call for an answer; as the sergeant turned toward the entrance of the very high building, Tibbs fell in beside him. "Did you get a look at the body before it was covered with the blanket?" Virgil asked.

"Partially. Why, did you catch something?"

"Perhaps," Tibbs replied.

They walked together into the huge lobby. By that time there were blue uniforms everywhere; the L.A.P.D. was definitely efficient. Behind them a coroner's unit arrived and two men got out. It was hardly ten minutes since the body had hit the sidewalk, but the official machinery to clean up was already functioning smoothly.

There was a uniformed guard in the lobby; at the sergeant's instruction he rang for the building manager.

That done, Opper turned to his black colleague from Pasadena. "You said you caught something."

"The deceased had on a brand-new pair of shoes. The soles were hardly scratched."

"And you figure that a man wouldn't go and buy himself a new pair of shoes just before he killed himself."

"That's right. Buying a pair of shoes takes selection and fitting: if he was planning to take his life within the next hour, that wouldn't be a logical thing for him to do. From the condition of the soles he couldn't have walked more than two or three blocks at the most."

"He could have put on a new pair of shoes and then driven here."

"Agreed, but the percentages are against it; again, it wouldn't be logical unless his decision to kill himself was very sudden."

A patrolman came in with a wallet in his hands. "Here's the ID of the deceased," he said. "Robert T. Williamson, DOB 13 June 1932. His home address is in Orange County."

"Run him—see if he was in any trouble or had a rap sheet."

"Yes, sir." The patrolman reached for his radio.

A man was hurrying up to them. He was middle-aged and well dressed in an expensive business suit. His shoes were shined and his tie was a model of good taste. He turned his attention at once to the sergeant. "Excuse me, I've been on the phone," he said. "My name is Phillips, I'm the general manager of this building. Tell me how I can help you."

"You know what happened?" Opper asked.

"Yes, unfortunately. I presume it had to come at some time, but this is the first such—tragedy—we've ever had."

As the two men were talking, Virgil Tibbs stepped over to the building directory and looked over the posted entries. When he came back, he had a question of his own. "Mr. Phillips, I notice that only the first thirty-two floors of the building appear to be occupied. Can you tell us about that?"

Phillips noted the police ID now clipped on the outside of Tibbs's coat, then responded. "Yes, that's true, although we don't advertise that fact. You see, the higher floors, while very desirable from a tenant's point of view, haven't been finished yet. Frankly, we found that rentals were way below our expectations while the building was going up, so the builders decided to hold off on the expense of completing the upper floors until there was a demand for the space. In that way, they could be finished to suit the wishes of the tenants who lease them."

"The whole building is air-conditioned," Tibbs said.

"Yes, of course. There's a great deal of glass, you see."

"My point is, Mr. Phillips, do the windows open or are they all sealed shut?"

Opper looked at Tibbs and clearly approved the question.

"Most of the windows are sealed shut. A few do open, because the tenants wanted them that way."

"On a building this high, isn't that dangerous?" the sergeant asked.

"Yes, so we designed them as casement types and set the handles so that they will only open a little way."

"Could a determined man squeeze his body out of the opening?" the sergeant continued.

Phillips hesitated. "That would depend, of course, on the man. Offhand, I would say that it would be very difficult."

"Do you have a list of the personnel who work in this building?"

"No, you'd have to get that from the individual tenants."

"Do you know a Robert Williamson? About forty-five, medium build?"

"No, not as far as I know."

Virgil took over. "Mr. Phillips, suppose someone wanted to get onto one of the higher floors, even though they're unfinished. Could he do that easily?"

Phillips was prompt and emphatic with his answer. "I don't think he could do it at all. Since there are no tenants, the stairwells are blocked off above the thirty-second floor. The elevators are all in, but only one of them will go above the thirty-second floor, and it takes a key to operate it."

"You have the key, of course."

"Yes. Do you want to go up there?"

"First, can you tell us offhand whether or not any of the windows on the north face of the building above the occupied floors can be opened?"

"I'm almost certain they are all sealed. I can have it checked."

"How about the roof?"

"The maintenance people go up there regularly, and our resident building inspector. He works for us; his job is to keep a continual check on the building structure and all its systems. A building of this size—"

"I understand," Tibbs cut him off. "Now, sir, if you please, we'd like to see the roof."

At that point the patrolman who had been checking on the dead man reappeared; Sergeant Opper stepped aside to hear his report. As he did so, he motioned Tibbs to join him.

"No wants or warrants," the patrolman said. "Several traffic violations—nothing heavy. I also checked with Orange County sheriffs and they gave me a little more."

"Good work," Opper said.

"Williamson was apparently wealthy, but the source of his funds isn't known. He was hospitalized about a year ago; he fell down and cracked some ribs. In the course of treating him, they found some evidence of illegal narcotics use."

"How did they get hold of information like that?" Tibbs asked. "That's privileged."

"I know, sir, but they still knew about it, don't ask me how. Apparently he wasn't hooked or anything like that, but he had some kind of medical history of narcotics. No action was taken at the time."

"Probably the patient gave permission to have his chart seen," Opper said, "without realizing that the narcotics data was on there. Anyhow, it explains a lot. He could have dropped acid sometime back when it was still popular. Then, without warning, he went off on another trip—you know it works that way. Somehow he got to the roof and, like a lot of others, thought he could fly."

"Let's go up to the roof," Tibbs suggested.

On top of the building the height was terrifying anywhere near to the edge. The rooftop itself had many pieces of equipment installed—huge air ducts, antennae, and housings for elevator machinery. A sharp wind reminded all three men how high they were. When Tibbs looked up, the movement of the clouds overhead gave the illusion that the building was leaning. After he recovered himself, he walked carefully across the cement to the comparatively low parapet, judged the wind once again, and then began a meticulous examination of a section of the protective wall. He spent so much time doing it that his L.A.P.D. colleague began to show impatience. "Find anything?" he asked.

Tibbs looked back at him. "No," he answered, "and I'm strongly reminded of the dog in the nighttime."

"The dog did nothing in the nighttime," the sergeant responded.

"You have just increased my admiration of the L.A.P.D.," Tibbs said. "You know your Sherlock Holmes. If you're through, let's go back down. This place is a little awesome."

When they were back on the ground floor, Tibbs noticed a coffee shop set in one corner. After thanking Phillips for the trip to the roof, and the rest of his cooperation, Tibbs suggested that the L.A.P.D. sergeant join him for a cup of coffee. Sergeant Opper, who understood completely, accepted and saw to it that they were seated in a secluded booth. "Now, what have you got?" he asked after their order had been taken.

"You've got one of two things—accident or homicide. At the moment I like homicide better."

Opper was careful. "From the condition of the body, the victim came off the roof, because he wouldn't have landed that hard from a lower floor. At least I don't think so; I'm no expert on jumpers."

"He didn't jump," Tibbs said. "The PM may show a percentage of drugs in his body, and a careful check should be made for past acid use—that's the most likely thing if it was an accident. But this may help you a little—he definitely *didn't* come off the roof."

Opper was thoughtful. "If Phillips is right, none of the windows on the unoccupied floors open. We haven't checked yet for a broken pane."

"In a way we have. If Williamson had broken a window in order to jump, there'd be some glass on the sidewalk. Your man out there might have been hurt, or some innocent pedestrians. No, I'm sure he didn't break a window."

"How certain are you that he didn't come off the roof?"

"You felt the wind up there. Despite it there was some dust on the roof. It wasn't disturbed where he would have had to have gone over. And the parapet was unmarked."

"Plus which, of course, just anybody couldn't get up onto the roof without a key to the special elevator. And Phillips, the building manager, had never heard of the dead man."

"Which leaves only one possibility," Tibbs said. He stopped then and waited while the coffee was served.

"He couldn't have fallen out of the sky," Opper mused. "You can't get out of modern aircraft the way that—what was his name?—did. Over the English Channel, wasn't it?"

"Helicopter," Tibbs said, and stirred his coffee.

"Someone would have seen it."

"Twenty years ago, yes, but not now. Police and media helicopters fly over the city at low altitude all the time and they're commonplace. The fire department has some too. The point is, no one notices them or hears them any more, except under unusual circumstances. They don't look up just to see them fly by."

Sergeant Opper drank some coffee while he thought. "All right, he could have come out of a helicopter; and come to think of it, some of them don't even have doors, or the doors are very easily opened."

"True."

"But the pilot would have reported it."

Tibbs smiled, not very much, and it was a little grim.

"All the helicopters operating in the greater Los Angeles area have a special frequency for talking to each other: it's one two two point nine five. If it had been an accident, then the pilot would have gone on the air immediately, knowing that all the law-enforcement helicopters airborne in the area would hear him. But he didn't. That's why I think it was a homicide."

"Anything else?"

"Yes. Helicopters can fly at almost any speed they like, up to their maximum. They can turn on a dime, hover, and do lots of other things."

"Therefore?"

"Therefore I think that Williamson was dumped out of a helicopter just at the point where it would appear he had jumped from the building. Remember, a good helicopter pilot can maneuver his machine with great precision, even in a wind."

"One objection, Tibbs, and it's a strong one. Williamson would have struggled. He would have grabbed onto something. He was a well set up man and the pilot had to keep flying. Unless there were other people in the chopper. Even then, throwing a man out against his will would take a lot of doing. I wouldn't care to try it."

Tibbs nodded. "Let me put together a theory—you can check it easily enough. The man had traces of narcotics use, but he wasn't hooked. That suggests someone who handled the stuff, but who was too smart to use it himself. That's supported by his evident wealth with no obvious source for the money—you can check that too. If I'm right so far, then we're talking about some very ruthless people who are engaged in one of the most profitable forms of crime known."

Opper took out his inevitable notebook. "I'll check with our narcotics people. If they knew Williamson, or of him, you've got something."

"Do you want the rest?"

"By all means."

"I don't think the fall killed him. Or if it did, he was unconscious when he was tossed from the chopper. Suppose he was given a shot and taken out. Then he was dumped from the chopper so that he would appear to have jumped from the building. No one saw the helicopter for the reasons already given."

"Father Brown's postman."

"Exactly. Getting rid of an unconscious man, or a dead one, could be done without too much trouble. The cause of death would be so obvious that extensive tests probably wouldn't be run."

"Not everybody has a helicopter," Opper said.

"And that's the point where your investigation should begin. If you'll allow me."

Opper got up. "I'll call you tomorrow," he promised.

MR TIBBS:
   WHILE YOU WERE OUT SGT OPPER OF LAPD CALLED YOU. HE SAID CORONER DETERMINED CAUSE OF DEATH OD HEROIN, NOT FALL(???) CHECK WITH SHERIFF'S ARGUS PATROL AND FIRE DEPARTMENT CONFIRMS NO MESSAGE RECEIVED ON 122.95 AT TIME OF INCIDENT. HE SAYS ONLY A MATTER OF TIME UNTIL CHOPPER ID'ED. CASE DEFINITELY HOMICIDE, MANY THANKS YOUR COOPERATION, LETTER COMING TO CHIEF MCGOWAN RE YOUR HELP. HE ALSO SAID NARCO HAD FOLDER ON WILLIAMSON. —MARGE
   (Hey, Virg, what the hell happened, anyway?—M.)

Nan Hamilton

Too Many Pebbles

Lieutenant Sam Ohara, Robbery-Homicide, sat at his desk brooding over the photographs of Ricky Zalba, deceased, sprawled on his back like a discarded ragdoll. Police flashbulbs had preserved every grisly detail in sharpest outline, but the photographs added little to what the Lieutenant had observed on the scene at six o'clock that morning. The body lay, arms outflung, half on a driveway and half on the damp earth of a vacant lot. A blood-tipped switchblade was frozen into the right hand, while the left hand seemed to claw for life in agonized desperation.

The lab reports contributed what he had already surmised. Zalba's skull had been fractured, his larynx and chest crushed. It was almost as if he had been run over by a car. But there were no abrasions, his expensive sportscoat was not torn, and there were no tire marks. The only unusual marks near the body were two deep parallel indentations in the earth.

Lieutenant Ohara studied the pictures again and noted the measurements. The upper indentation was five inches long by one and one-quarter inches wide, the lower one was four and three-quarter inches long by one and one-half inches wide. They had been driven into the ground to a depth of almost two inches.

The remaining information was sparse. The body had been discovered by a milkman at 5:30 A.M. A canvass of the neighborhood shortly afterward had turned up no witnesses. The final notation on the lab report was a little more helpful. They had discovered a derivative of sesame oil on the victim's left hand, and shattered glass and metal fragments under the victim's heel that might have been the remains of a woman's watch.

Half heard voices in the hallway broke his concentration and Ohara sat back in resigned exasperation as he caught the words.

"This where I'll find Lieutenant O'Hara?" Evidently Reagan, the desk sergeant, was breaking in a new recruit. Bob Wiseman from Vice, next door, was helping things along.

"The Irishman, O'Hara? He's in there."

Seconds later a sandy-haired patrol officer glanced past the Lieutenant and around the otherwise empty room. Ohara looked up.

"Yes?"

"I'm looking for Lieutenant O'Hara. Sergeant Reagan asked me to drop off this file."

"I'm Ohara." The Lieutenant stood up, an impressive six feet tall with football shoulders.

"But you're a Jap—" Ohara's smooth ivory face was very still and his black eyes were hard. "I mean"—the young officer stammered his confusion—"you're not Irish, sir . . . are you?"

Ohara's eyes relented. "Nope. Ohara is a good old Japanese name. We just don't use the Irish apostrophe."

The patrolman looked miserable. "I'm sorry, sir."

"Don't be. Reagan likes to have his fun." Ohara took the manila folder and put it on his desk. The officer, still flushed with embarrassment was almost out the door when Ohara remarked, *"Arigato gozaimashita,"* and then erased the patrolman's startled expression when he added, "Just 'thank you,' in Japanese."

The little scene played out, Ohara sat down recalling how he had bristled the first time the boys had pulled it on him. As a third-generation Japanese-American, he was still sensitive to slurs. But he had come to realize the rough camaraderie in it and now went along good-naturedly with the department joke.

He recognized, too, that his sensitivity was a by-product of his background. He had come out of high school with the typical American imprint—a good athlete and as fond of hamburgers and hot dogs as of sukiyaki. He was too young to remember the internment camp during World War II, but he'd heard his parents and grandparents talk about it.

He spoke better Japanese than most Japanese-Americans simply because his family had always used both languages interchangeably.

Ohara had learned early in life that when you are one of the so-called "quiet" minorities, your only chance is to be better than good, or else take what's left. So after his service in Vietnam he'd used his GI bill for a Masters in Police Science and had eventually joined the L.A. Police Department.

He picked up the photos again and stared at the puzzling indentations. The answer was there, he was sure, but he couldn't grasp it. He considered the victim. Zalba's four-page rap sheet for assault and narcotics violations offered possibilities. But it wasn't that kind of killing, not that straightforward. Absently, Ohara looked at his watch. He was off duty and should be leaving, since he'd promised his wife, Peggy, that he would be home in time for an early supper.

Their son, Jim, was in his first football game and wanted his parents there.

Gathering the pictures and reports, Ohara put them into his desk, wondering how he was going to tell Peggy that he could not go to her grandfather's birthday celebration tomorrow. She would be very disappointed. He hated to miss it himself, since Grandfather Takahashi, Black Belt Aikido Master, had been his teacher in that powerful martial art. In fact, it had been in Takahashi's Aikido class that Ohara had (literally) fallen for his wife, Peggy.

As he got into his car in the parking lot, he decided to stop in and see his old teacher, though nowadays he thought of him as *Ojiisan* (grandfather). It wasn't too far to the small house in Crenshaw and before long he pulled up in front of the neatly fenced yard and went through the gate, taking the pebbled path around the house to the back. Ohara knew *Ojiisan* would probably be enjoying his quiet Japanese garden at this time of day. And he was, looking like a picture of old Japan in his favorite dark kimono, which seemed so right with his ascetic face and erect bearing.

Ojiisan greeted his favorite pupil with a welcoming smile. They exchanged the polite inquiries of civilized conversation and turned to admire the master's prize collection of bonsei trees. Ohara marveled that although the old man would be seventy-five tomorrow, he looked a vigorous fifty. He always enjoyed his company but today, despite the peace of the small garden, Ohara could not control his restlessness. His mind kept probing his puzzling new case. He must have let his accumulated tension show, for *Ojiisan* drew him finally over to the rock-bordered fishpond.

"Isamu"—the old man laid a gentle hand on his arm—"do you see how clear the pool is?"

Ohara looked down at the golden *koi*, flashing like bright jewels beneath the water. "Yes, *Ojiisan*, it is beautiful."

Stooping quickly, the master picked up a handful of pebbles and dropped them one by one into the pool. The glassy surface was convulsed with rippling circles that obscured the watery world beneath.

"You see, Isamu, the pool can no longer reflect a true image of what is there. It is like your mind. You, too, are restless and disturbed because you have dropped in too many pebbles. Come inside; we will have tea."

Ohara would have liked to protest that he could not stay for tea, but he could not find it in his heart to disappoint the old man. "Yes, *Ojiisan*, I should like that very much," he answered and followed his teacher into the house, pausing only to remove his shoes in the small hallway.

When he was led into the formal *tatami* room, Ohara knew that not only refreshment was intended, but the full treatment—the ritual tea ceremony. It was too late to back out now, so obediently he settled himself Japanese fashion on his knees. As he waited for *Ojiisan* to complete the prescribed preparations of the tea master, Ohara's eyes passed over the exquisite simplicity of the room which was used only for the *cha no yu* ceremony.

The beautiful simple utensils lay waiting on a small lacquer tray, to be handled with respect and love in the time-honored graceful movements. He admired the chrysanthemums in the *tokonomo* alcove, their flowery heads arranged to honor heaven, man, and earth. His gaze was drawn to the old Japanese print that adorned a side wall. Its glowing colors of blue and amber depicted two sturdy and bulging-calved bearers carrying a lady over a moon-arched bridge.

He had long ago been trained by *Ojiisan* in the proper responses of the tea guest, so he carried off his part in the ceremony adequately. As he turned the brown glazed tea bowl the required three times and suitably admired its rich luster, he wondered briefly what the boys in the department would think of "the Irishman" if they could see him now.

When it was over, Ohara found that the small perfection of time had calmed him and cleared his mind. As he put on his shoes and bowed a last *sayonara*, he felt new confidence that he would find the answers he needed.

That evening, still amazingly relaxed, he enjoyed the football game and was proud of young Jim. Peggy had taken his announcement that he would have to work tomorrow quite well. She had by now accepted the realities of being a policeman's wife. After the game they had indulged in a pizza and beer, and gone home.

Peggy was warm and loving, and as he drifted toward sleep, his arms holding her tightly, he thought drowsily that he had truly emptied his mind. The pool was clear. The therapists, he reflected, should give the Japanese tea ceremony careful consideration. He saw again *Ojiisan*'s calm, measured movements, the quiet peace of the little *tatami* room, the bowing grace of the chrysanthemums, the rich glow of the old print . . . Suddenly he was sitting upright in bed.

"That's it! It could be nothing else!"

Peggy, halfway between rude awakening and growing concern, touched his shoulder in alarm.

"What is it, Sam? What's wrong?"

"Not what's wrong—it's what's exactly right. Never mind, dear, go back to sleep. I'll explain later."

Knowing him well, Peggy snuggled down again. Sam was all right, she knew, the rest didn't matter. But Ohara lay awake mentally fitting new pieces into the jigsaw puzzle of his case.

The next morning he called into the department and asked his partner, Jake Woszinski, to recheck the residents of the neighborhood where Zalba's body had been found. He wanted to know about anything unusual they might have seen or heard as much as a week before the murder.

After a fortifying breakfast of ham and eggs, he went down to Little Tokyo and visited the largest of the Japanese department stores. The answers he found there seemed to please him. Next he stopped at the office of the Japanese-language newspaper, *Rafu Shimpo*, and talked with the editor.

Here he obtained a back copy of the issue he wanted. He had a quick bowl of noodles in a small café, then headed for Pacoima and the scene of Zalba's killing. He knew now how it had been done, but he still didn't know why. Instinct told him that the why of it was most important. Deliberately he turned his mind off, concentrating on his driving. As he turned the corner, a block away from where the body had been found, he suddenly stamped on the brakes and pulled his car to the curb.

He had almost forgotten the convalescent hospital that looked more like a ranch house than an institution. Jake had checked it, he was sure, but the question that had just occurred to him was a brand-new piece of the puzzle.

After the usual protocol he found himself in the office of the nursing supervisor, a Miss MacPherson, who did not appreciate the intrusion of murder into her well ordered domain.

When he had asked his question, she fairly bristled in defense of her staff.

"Our people are carefully screened, Lieutenant Oh—Ohara." She stumbled momentarily over the name and looked down at his card for reassurance.

"I'm sure they are, Miss MacPherson. I merely want to talk to anyone who came on or went off duty or left the hospital between eleven and midnight on that night."

"Well, you're out of luck then. Our staff shifts at three-thirty, ten, and six in the morning."

Ohara's heart sank. The times were wrong. He stood up and his good-looking face relaxed into a smile. "Thank you anyway, Miss MacPherson. I'm sorry to have taken up your time. But sometimes even negative information can be of help."

Discouraged, he walked down the long corridor to the exit and was just going out the door when he heard his name called, and turned to see Miss MacPherson hurrying after him.

"Oh, Lieutenant Ohara, I just remembered. We have two special nurses who have been coming on for the past three weeks. One of them, Ellen Murakami, comes on at midnight. I wrote down her address."

She handed him a slip of paper with a self-conscious smile brightening her angular features.

Ohara, grateful, sensed what would please her. *"Arigato gozai-mashita, Okusan,"* he said, then bowed low and went out the door. Miss MacPherson stood looking after him, her hand touching her cheek, which was pleasantly flushed. "So like James Shigeta in *Flower Drum Song,"* she sighed to herself and walked dreamily back to her office.

Ohara glanced at his watch—almost four o'clock. Ellen Mura-kami's address was close by, and she would be at home now if she went on duty at twelve. He decided to check first with Jake and find out if anything new had turned up. He stopped at a pay phone to make his call.

Jake's jovial response told Ohara that his partner was pleased with the results of his work.

"How did you know I'd get a hit?" Jake asked.

"I looked in a fortune cookie. What is it?"

"A Miss Parker, who suffers from insomnia, says she has been hearing clicking sounds around midnight for the past two weeks. She thought it might be kids scraping her picket fence and looked out the window. But there was nothing to call the cops about, just a big fat guy going by in baggy clothes, a cap, and sandals."

Ohara felt a surge of elation. "Thanks, Jake. That's a help."

"Well, you'll need another fortune cookie. She didn't hear it on the night of the murder. That everything?"

"What's her address? I think I'll drop in and see her. I need to kill a few minutes before I talk to another possible witness. Was there anything new on the oil on Zalba's hand?"

"Yeah, the lab says it's a special kind of hair dressing. They haven't run across it before." Then Jake gave him Miss Parker's address and hung up.

Ohara found the woman's house a block down and knocked at the door. The sleepless lady volubly informed him that of course she didn't hear or see anything on the night of the murder because she had gone to her sister's to play bingo, and had stayed overnight.

As soon as he could, Ohara disengaged himself and a few minutes later was standing in front of Ellen Murakami's door waiting for someone to answer the bell.

A frail grandmother type opened the door, and after showing his credentials Ohara asked to speak to Miss Ellen Murakami.

"No, Engrishu," the old lady muttered, looking scared. She began to shut the door, and he repeated his question in polite Japanese. At this she looked even more frightened, but she opened the door and reluctantly motioned him to come into the living room.

With a hurried bow she said she would find Murakamisan, and darted out of the room. Ohara heard muttering in the background, but could distinguish no words. One of the voices he was sure had been a man's. Moments later a girl came through the old-fashioned archway that led into the small living room.

Ohara stood up as she came toward him, studying her pale face, so like a Utamaro painting, under a lustrous sweep of black hair. She was dressed simply in a dark skirt and white blouse. The modest V of the neckline was filled in by a peach-colored scarf which was wrapped closely to her throat.

"I'm Ellen Murakami," she said softly. "You wanted to see me?"

Her hands tore nervously at a handkerchief and she seemed scarcely to breathe. Ohara sensed her fear and felt a momentary pity, but his hunter's instincts were alerted. She was very much on guard. He smiled reassuringly. "Just a few questions. May we sit down?"

He led her through routine questions as to her hours and what she might have seen or heard on the night in question. When she began to relax, Ohara asked suddenly, "What time is it, Miss Murakami? My watch has been running slow today and I do have another appointment."

She looked automatically at her wrist, whitened, and turned her head toward the clock on the mantel. "It is five o'clock, Lieutenant." The fear was back again and it showed in her voice.

At that moment the grandmother came in with two small cups of green tea. The girl smiled, relieved. "My *Obachan* thought you would like tea—" She paused, uncertain. Ohara murmured polite thanks as the old lady set down the tea tray and darted away.

"How long ago did you lose your watch, Miss Murakami?" Ohara asked as he picked up the fragrant cup of tea.

"I—I—don't know."

"I noticed that you looked first at your wrist, so it must have been fairly recently."

"Perhaps, I can't remember." Suddenly Ohara felt uneasy, sensing another presence, unseen, listening. In the silence the sibilant sound of breathing was barely audible.

As he drained the tiny teacup, Ohara deliberately let his notebook fall to the floor, along with his pen. Instinctively polite, Ellen Murakami dropped to her knees to retrieve it.

Profuse with apologies, Ohara switched to Japanese and she answered him. His eyes never left her face and as she reached under the chair for the pen, he saw what he had expected to see. The peach-colored scarf, pulled slightly askew with the reach of her arm, showed a jagged red line against the ivory skin of her throat.

As Ohara accepted the pen and notebook from her hands with grave thanks, he said, still in Japanese for the benefit of the unseen listener, "I have found your watch, Miss Murakami. It was under the body of the man who was murdered two nights ago, not far from the hospital." He was stretching a point, he knew, since the smashed fragments in the lab were barely identifiable, but she could not find words to deny it. Her eyes, filled with terror and despair, were all the answer he needed.

He pressed his advantage. "I notice that you have been injured." He indicated her throat. "Did the man attack you? Was that how you lost your watch?"

He hated to bully her, but he knew it was necessary. With a sob she broke, but her words were unexpected. "Not murder—not murder—"

"Will you tell me about it, Ellen?"

"Iie . . ." she sobbed, shaking her head; the brief Japanese negative seemed her only defense.

Ohara raised his voice and made it threatening, doing what he had to do.

"Then I will have to bring you into the station for questioning, Miss. You are implicated in a murder." The staccato Japanese hammered the words home.

The small cruelty to the girl did the trick. Suddenly the archway was filled with the figure of a man—immense and powerful. His head, with a high formal topknot of hair glistening with oil, barely cleared the curve of the entrance. Ohara caught his breath as his eyes took in the huge bulk of him, straining the dark-blue kimono that covered three hundred pounds or more. The man's hands hung loosely, ready at his sides, and beneath the kimono his bare calves showed like young tree trunks.

Ohara's eyes slid down to the feet and lingered. As he had known they would be, ever since he had remembered *Ojiisan*'s Japanese print of the litter bearers, the man's feet were thrust into a pair of Japanese *geta*. Heavy thongs between the toes held the sturdy wooden platforms secure on top of two parallel blocks which raised them a good two inches from the ground. The same blocks, Ohara knew, which had left the peculiar indentations in the earth beside Zalba's body.

The wooden *geta* clicked on the bare floor as the man moved to stand in front of Ellen.

The inherent menace in the huge figure made Ohara step back into the defensive Aikido stance, his body loose, his mind concentrated to anticipate the expected attack.

But there was no attack. Instead, strangely soft yet guttural Japanese spewed out at him from the man's throat. At the sound another piece of evidence fell into place—the man spoke with the bruised vocal chords of a Sumo wrestler.

"Taisho, Officer. You will not take her. She has done nothing. It is I who have done this thing."

Before Ohara could answer, Ellen Murakami spoke in rapid English, her hands outstretched in appeal.

"Oh, no, please. It is not what you think. Jiro"—she placed her hand gently on the huge arm of the man beside her. "Jiro was trying to save me. That—that man grabbed me as I passed the driveway and held a knife to my throat." She pulled the scarf aside to show the ugly wound. "He said he was going to—he meant to—but Jiro had followed me." The glance she turned toward her silent protector was rich with love, then she continued. "Jiro pushed the man's hands away and told me to run. But I didn't. Then—then—" She hesitated and the involuntary shift of her eyes told Ohara her next words would not be all truth. "You must believe me. It was an accident. Jiro fell against him—an accident—not murder."

Gently, but with a reproachful look, the giant moved Ellen aside. "This is not woman's business. I will speak," he said in Japanese.

Ohara became suddenly formal. He bowed low. "I am glad, Onamisan."

"How do you know my name?"

In answer Ohara drew from his pocket a folded page from *Rafu Shimpo* with the story of the great Sumo wrestler, Onami, and his visit to California.

The famous wrestler grunted and asked in his soft slurred voice, "How did you find me? Did someone see?"

Ohara, pocketing the newspaper clipping, shook his head and answered in the Japanese honorific style that befitted the man who stood before him.

"No one saw the struggle, Onamisan, but someone noticed you several times the week before, passing by near the place where it happened."

The big man almost smiled. "I did not wear kimono, but I am too big to hide much. It was very dark. Do Americans not sleep at night?"

Ohara gestured toward Onami's feet. "The sound of your *geta* on the sidewalk woke someone who noticed you. Then, too, beside the dead body, I found the marks the *geta* make. When I knew what the marks were, I knew the man I was seeking was Japanese. No *gaijin* walks in *geta* on the street. When I saw how deep the marks were, I knew he must be a very heavy man."

"There are many such heavy men," Onami said impassively.

Ohara smiled. "True, Onamisan, but the oil on the victim's hand we found to be a kind of hair oil used only in Japan, only by Sumo wrestler." He allowed his eyes to glance at Onami's oiled topknot of hair.

"You are right, *Taisho*," Onami acknowledged, "but how did you come to this house?"

"The hospital told us Miss Murakami arrived about midnight that night. We found the remains of a woman's watch under the body. These two facts pointed here."

Onami moved suddenly and Ohara was on his guard again.

"Taisho, I have killed this animal, but I did not intend to kill him. Miyuki—" The wrestler turned to Ellen and gently wiped the tears from her cheek with one huge finger. "Miyuki is my friend's sister. I came from Japan to visit her. I have asked to marry her. I do not

like that she goes to work at night, so I follow her. That night I saw the man and what he tried to do. I pulled Miyuki from his hands. Then with his knife he ran against me.

"I am Sumo. I know only one way to fight." The dignity of the simple statement said it all, but Onami continued, "So I charge him and he goes down. When I charge this way in the Sumo ring no one dies. I am thrown down myself sometimes, yet I am alive."

Ohara could visualize the bulletlike launch of that massive body, the shoulder thrusting into Zalba's scrawny throat until the momentum of Onami's three hundred pounds bore him down, until his skull cracked like an egg on the concrete driveway.

Onami looked down at Ellen reproachfully. "I have told her to run away, but she is not yet obedient. She did not go. She came and touched the man and said he was dead. She warned me we must not say anything or I would be sent away and we could not marry."

Ohara, American as he was, felt his ancestral Samurai blood stir. It was like a tale out of old Japan. It seemed almost impossible that it could have happened on a quiet residential street in California. He looked at Onamisan, whose name meant Great Wave, waiting quietly for him to pass sentence. He kept his feelings out of his voice and used the polite formal phrases of Japanese officialdom which he knew were expected.

"Onamisan, I believe you did not intend to kill this man. Miss Murakami's testimony and the other evidence will show this. There will be some formalities, but you will not be detained longer than necessary."

He would not soon forget the look of pure joy on Ellen Murakami's face.

"Tomorrow you must come to the station and make a statement." Ohara almost smiled as he thought of the impact Onami would have on the department.

A short time and many bows later Ohara left the modest house where a modern-day Samurai stood protectively by his promised bride. As he drove away, his mind was undisturbed by the least ripple of doubt. Someday he would tell *Ojiisan* the story. Ohara felt he had a right to know.

"Q"

Ellery Queen

The Halloween Mystery

The square-cut envelope was a creation of orange ink on black notepaper; by which Ellery instantly divined its horrid authorship.

Behind it leered a bouncy hostess, all teeth and enthusiastic ideas, who spent large sums of some embarrassed man's money to build a better mousetrap.

Having too often been one of the mice, he was grateful that the envelope was addressed to *Miss Nikki Porter.*

"But why to me at your apartment?" wondered Nikki, turning the black envelope over and finding nothing.

"Studied insult," Ellery assured her. "One of those acid-sweet women who destroy an honest girl's reputation at a stroke. Don't even open it. Hurl it into the fire and let's get on with the work."

So Nikki opened it and drew out an enclosure cut in the shape of a cat.

"I am a master of metaphor," muttered Ellery.

"What?" said Nikki, unfolding the feline.

"It doesn't matter. But if you insist on playing the mouse, go ahead and read it."

The truth was, he was a little curious himself.

"*Fellow Spook,*" began Nikki, frowning.

"Read no more. The hideous details are already clear—"

"Oh, shut up," said Nikki. "*There is a secret meeting of The Charmed Circle of Black Cats in Suite 1313, Hotel Chancellor, New York City, Oct. 31.*"

"Of course," said Ellery glumly. "That follows logically."

"*You must come in full costume as a Black Cat, including domino mask. Time your arrival for 9:05 p.m. promptly. Till the Witching Hour.* Signed —*G. Host.* How darling!"

"No clue to the criminal?"

"No. I don't recognize the handwriting."

"Of course you're not going."

"Of course I *am!*"

"Having performed my moral duty as friend, protector, and employer, I now suggest you put the foul thing away and get back to our typewriter."

"What's more," said Nikki, "you're going, too."

Ellery smiled his Number Three smile—the toothy one. "Am I?" he said.

"There's a postscript on the cat's—on the reverse side. *Be sure to drag your boss-cat along, also costumed.*"

Ellery could see himself as a sort of overgrown Puss-in-Boots plying the sjambok over a houseful of bounding tabbies all swilling Scotch. The vision was exhausting.

"I decline with the usual thanks."

"You're a stuffed shirt."

"I'm an intelligent man."

"You don't know how to have fun."

"These brawls inevitably wind up with someone's husband taking a poke at a tall, dark, handsome stranger."

"Coward."

"Heavens, I wasn't referring to myself!"

Whence it is obvious he had already lost the engagement.

Ellery stood before a door on the thirteenth floor of the Hotel Chancellor, cursing the Druids.

For it was Saman at whose mossy feet must be laid the origins of our recurrent October silliness. True, the lighting of ceremonial bonfires in a Gaelic glade must have seemed natural and proper at the time, and a Gaelic grove fitting rendezvous for an annual convention of ghosts and witches; but the responsibility of even pagan deities must surely be held to extend beyond temporal bounds, and the Druid lord of death should have foreseen that a bonfire would be out of place in a Manhattan hotel suite, not to mention disembodied souls, however wicked.

Then Ellery recalled that Pomona, goddess of fruits, had contributed nuts and apples to the burgeoning Halloween legend, and he cursed the Romans, too.

There had been Inspector Queen at home, who had intolerably chosen to ignore the whole thing; the taxi driver, who had asked amiably: "Fraternity initiation?"; the dread chorus of miaows during the long, long trek across the Chancellor lobby; and, finally, the reeking wag in the elevator who had tried to swing Ellery around by his tail, puss-pussying as he did so.

Cried Ellery out of the agony of his mortification: "Never, never, *never* again will I—"

"Stop grousing and look at this," said Nikki, peering through her domino mask.

"What is it? I can't see through this damned thing."

"A sign on the door. *If You Are a Black Cat, Walk In!!!!!* With five exclamation points."

"All right, all right," Ellery grumbled. "Let's go in and get it over with."

And, of course, when they opened the unlocked door of 1313, Darkness.

And Silence.

"Now what do we do?" giggled Nikki, and jumped at the snick of the door behind them.

"I'll tell you now what," said Ellery enthusiastically. "Let's get the hell out of here."

But Nikki was already a yard away, black in blackness.

"Wait! Give me your hand, Nikki."

"*Mister* Queen. That's not my hand."

"Beg your pardon," muttered Ellery. "We seem to be trapped in a hallway."

"There's a red light down there! Must be at the end of the hall—*eee!*"

"Think of the soup this would make for the starving." Ellery disentangled her from the embrace of a number of articulated bones.

"Ellery! I don't think that's funny at all."

"I don't think *any* of this is funny."

They groped toward the red light. It was not so much a light as a rosy shade of darkness which faintly blushed above a small plinth of the raven variety. The woman's cornered the Black Paper Market, Ellery thought disagreeably as he read the runes of yellow fire on the plinth: TURN LEFT!!!!!!!

"And into, I take it," he growled, "the great unknown." And, indeed, having explored to the left, his hand encountered outer space; whereupon, intrepidly, and with a large yearning to master the mystery and come to grips with its diabolical authoress, Ellery plunged through the invisible archway, Nikki bravely clinging to his tail.

"Ouch!"

"What's the matter?" gasped Nikki.

"Bumped into a chair. Skinned my shin. What would a chair be doing—?"

"Pooooor Ellery," said Nikki, laughing. "Did the dreat bid mad hurt his— *Ow!*"

"Blast this— Ooo!"

"Ellery, where are you? Ouch!"

"Ow, my foot," bellowed Ellery from somewhere. "What is this—a tank trap? Floor cluttered with pillows, hassocks—"

"Something cold and wet over here. Feels like an ice bucket . . . Owwwww!" There was a wild clatter of metal, a soggy crash, and silence again.

"Nikki! What happened?"

"I fell over a rack of fire tongs, I think." Nikki's voice came clearly from floor level. "Yes. Fire tongs."

"Of all the stupid, childish, unfunny—"

"Oop."

"Lost in a madhouse. Why is the furniture scattered every which way?"

"How should I know? Ellery, where *are* you?"

"In Bedlam. Keep your head now, Nikki, and stay where you are. Sooner or later a St. Bernard will find you and bring—"

Nikki screamed.

"Thank God," said Ellery, shutting his eyes.

The room was full of blessed Consolidated Edison light, and various adult figures in black-cat costumes and masks were leaping and laughing and shouting: "Surpriiiiiise!" like idiot phantoms at the crisis of a delirium.

O Halloween.

"Ann! Ann Trent!" Nikki was squealing. "Oh, Ann, you fool, however did you find me?"

"Nikki, you're looking wonderful. Oh, but you're famous, darling. The great E.Q.'s secretary . . ."

Nuts to you, sister. Even bouncier than predicted. With that lazy, hippy strut. And chic, glossy chic. Lugs her sex around like a sample case. The kind of female who would be baffled by an egg. And looks a good five years older than she is, Antoine and others notwithstanding.

"But it's not Trent any more, Nikki—it's Mrs. John Crombie. Johnnnny!"

"Ann, you're *married?* And didn't invite me to the wedding!"

"Spliced in dear old Lunnon. John's British—or was. Johnny, stop flirting with Edith Baxter and come here!"

"Ann darlin'—this exquisite girl! Scotch or bourbon, Nikki? Scotch if you're the careful type—but bourbon works faster."

John Crombie, Gent. Eyes of artificial blue, sunlamp complexion, Olivier chin. British Club and Fox and Hounds—he posts even in a living room. He will say in a moment that he loathes Americah. Exactly. Ann Trent Crombie must have large amounts of the filthy. He despises her and patronizes her friends. He will fix me with the superior Mayfair smile and flap a limp brown hand . . . *Quod erat demonstrandum.*

"I warn you, Nikki," Ann Crombie was saying, "I'm hitched to a man who tries to jockey every new female he meets." Blush hard, prim Nikki. Friends grow in unforeseen directions. "Oh, Lucy! Nikki, do you remember my kid sister Lu—?"

Squeal, squeal.

"Lucy Trent! This isn't *you?*"

"Am I grown up, Nikki?"

"Heavens!"

"Lucy's done *all* the party decorating, darling—spent the whole solid day up here alone fixing things up. Hasn't she done an *inspired* job? But then I'm so useless."

"Ann means she wouldn't help, Nikki."

Uncertain laugh. Poor Lucy. Embarrassed by her flowering youth, trying hard to be New York . . . There she goes, refilling a glass—emptying an ashtray—running out to the kitchen—for a tray of fresh hot pigs-in-blankets? . . . the unwanted and gauche hiding confusion by making herself useful. Keep away from your brother-in-law, dear; that's an attractive little body under the Black Cat's skin.

"Oh, Ellery, do come here and meet the Baxters. Mrs. Baxter—Edith—Ellery Queen . . ."

What's this? A worm who's turned, surely! The faded-fair type, hard-used by wedlock. Very small, a bit on the spready side—she'd let herself go—but now she's back in harness again, all curried and combed, with a triumphant lift to her pale head, like an old thoroughbred proudly prancing in a paddock she had never hoped to enter again. And that glitter of secret pleasure in her blinky brown eyes, almost malice, whenever she looked at Ann Crombie . . .

"Jerry Baxter, Edith's husband. Ellery Queen."

"Hiya, son!"

"Hi yourself, Jerry."

Salesman, or advertising-agency man, or Broadway agent. The life of the party. Three drinks and he's off to the races. He will be the first to fall in the apple tub, the first to pin the tail on Lucy or Nikki instead of on the donkey, the first to be sick and the first to pass out. Skitter, stagger, sweat, and whoop. Why do you whoop, Jerry Baxter?

Ellery shook hot palms, smiled with what he hoped was charm, said affably, "Yes, isn't it?" "Haven't we met somewhere?" and things like that, wondering what he was doing in a hotel living room festooned with apples, marshmallows, nuts, and criss-crossing crepe-paper twists, hung with grinning pumpkins and fancy black-and-orange cardboard cats, skeletons, and witches, and choked with bourbon fumes, tobacco smoke, and Chanel No. 5.

The noise was maddening, and merely to cross the room required the preparations of an expedition, for the overturned furniture and other impedimenta on the floor—cunningly plotted to trap the groping Black Cats on their arrival—had been left where they were.

So Ellery, highball in hand, wedged himself in a safe corner and mentally added Nikki to the Druids and the Romans.

Ellery accepted the murder game without a murmur. He knew the futility of protest. Wherever he went, people at once suggested a murder game, apparently on the theory that a busman enjoys nothing so much as a bus. And, of course, he was to be the detective.

"Well, well, let's get started," he said gaily, for all the traditional Halloween games had been played, Nikki had slapped Jerry Baxter laughingly once and British Johnny—not laughingly—twice, the house detective had made a courtesy call, and it was obvious the delightful evening had all but run its course.

He hoped Nikki would have sense enough to cut the *pièce de résistance* short, so that a man might go home and give his thanks to God; but no, there she was in a whispery, giggly huddle with Ann Crombie and Lucy Trent, while John Crombie rested his limp hand on Nikki's shoulder and Edith Baxter splashed some angry bourbon into her glass.

Jerry was on all fours, being a cat.

"In just a minute," called Nikki, and she tripped through the archway—kitchen-bound, to judge from certain subsequent cutlery sounds—leaving Crombie's hand momentarily suspended.

Edith Baxter said, "Jerry, get up off that floor and stop making a darned fool of yourself!"—furiously.

"Now we're all set," announced Nikki, reappearing. "Everybody around in a circle. First I'll deal out these cards, and whoever gets the ace of spades *don't let on!*—because you're the Murderer."

"Ooh!"

"Ann, you stop peeking."

"Who's peeking?"

"A tenner says I draw the fatal pasteboard," laughed Crombie. "I'm the killer type."

"*I'm* the killer type!" shouted Jerry Baxter. "Gack-gack-gack-gack!"

Ellery closed his eyes.

"Ellery! Wake up."

"Huh?"

Nikki was shaking him. The rest of the company were lined up on the far side of the room from the archway, facing the wall. For a panicky moment he thought of the St. Valentine's Day Massacre.

"You go on over there with the others, smartypants. You mustn't see who the murderer is, either, so you close your eyes, too."

"Fits in perfectly with my plans," said Ellery, and he dutifully joined the five people at the wall.

"Spread out a little there—I don't want anyone touching anyone else. That's it. Eyes all shut? Good. Now I want the person who drew the ace of spades—Murderer—to step quietly away from the wall—"

"Not cricket," came John Crombie's annoying alto. "*You'll* see who it is, dear heart."

"Yes," said Edith Baxter nastily. "The light's on."

"But I'm running this assassination! Now stop talking, eyes closed. Step out, Murderer—that's it . . . quietly! No talking there at the wall! Mr. Queen is *very* bright and he'd get the answer in a shot just by eliminating voices—"

"Oh, come, Nikki," said Mr. Queen modestly.

"Now, Murderer, here's what you do. On the kitchen table you'll find a full-face mask, a flashlight, and a bread knife. Wait! Don't start for the kitchen yet—go when I switch off the light in here; that will be your signal to start. When you get to the kitchen, put on the mask, take the flashlight and knife, steal back into this room, and—pick a victim!"

"Oooh."

"Ahhhh!"

"Ee!"

Mr. Queen banged his forehead lightly against the wall. How long, O Lord?

"Now remember, Murderer," cried Nikki, "you pick anyone you want—except, of course, Ellery. He has to live long enough to solve the crime."

If you don't hurry, my love, I'll be dead of natural causes.

"It'll be dark, Murderer, except for your flash, so even I won't know what victim you pick—"

"May the detective inquire the exact purpose of the knife?" asked the detective wearily of the wall. "Its utility in this divertissement escapes me."

"Oh, the knife's just a prop, goopy—atmosphere. Murderer, you tap your victim on the shoulder. Victim, whoever feels the tap, turn around and let Murderer lead you out of the living room to the kitchen."

"The kitchen, I take it, is the scene of the crime," said Mr. Queen gloomily.

"Uh-huh. And Victim, as soon as Murderer gets you into the kitchen, scream like all fury as if you're being stabbed. Make it realistic! Everybody set? Ready? . . . All right, Murderer, soon's I turn this light off go to the kitchen, get the mask and stuff, come back, and pick your victim. Here goes!"

Click! went the light switch. Being a man who checked his facts, Ellery automatically cheated and opened one eye. Dark, as advertised. He shut the eye, and then jumped.

"Stop!" Nikki had shrieked.

"What, what?" asked Ellery excitedly.

"Oh, I'm not talking to you, Ellery. Murderer, I forgot something! Where are you? Oh, never mind. Remember, after you've supposedly stabbed your victim in the kitchen, come back to this room and quickly take your former place against the wall. Don't make a sound; don't touch anyone. I want the room to be as quiet as it is this minute. Use the flash to help you see your way back, but as soon as you reach the wall turn the flash off and throw flash and mask into the middle of the living room—thus, darling, getting rid of the evidence. Do you see? But, of course, you *can't.* Now even though it's dark, people, *keep your eyes shut.* All right, Murderer—get set—*go!*"

Ellery dozed . . .

It seemed a mere instant later that he heard Nikki's voice saying

with incredible energy, "Murderer's tapping a victim—careful with
that flashlight, Murderer!—we mustn't tempt our Detective *too*
much. All right, Victim? Now let Murderer lead you to your
doom . . . the rest of you keep your eyes closed . . . don't turn ar . . ."

Ellery dozed again . . .

He awoke with a start at a man's scream.

"Here! What—"

"Ellery Queen, you asleep again? That was Victim being carved
up in the kitchen. Now . . . yes! . . . here's Murderer's flash
back . . . that's it, to the wall quietly . . . now flash *off!*—fine!—toss
it and your mask away . . . Boom. Tossed. Are you turned around,
face to the wall, Murderer, like everybody else? Everybody ready?
Llllllights!"

"Now—" began Ellery briskly.

"Why, it's John who's missing," laughed Lucy.

"Pooooor John is daid," sang Jerry.

"My poor husband," wailed Ann. "Jo-hon, come back to me!"

"Ho, John!" shouted Nikki.

"Just a moment," said Ellery. "Isn't Edith Baxter missing, too?"

"My wiff?" shouted Jerry. "Hey, wiff! Come outa the woodwork!"

"Oh, darn," said Lucy. "There mustn't be two victims, Nikki. That
spoils the game."

"Let us repair to the scene of the crime," proclaimed Miss Porter,
"and see what gives."

So, laughing and chattering and having a hell of a time, they all
trooped through the archway, turned left, crossed the foyer, and
went into the Crombie kitchen and found John Crombie dead on the
floor with his throat cut.

When Ellery returned to the kitchen from his very interesting
telephone chat with Inspector Queen, he found Ann Crombie being
sick over the kitchen sink, her forehead supported by the greenish
hand of a greenish Lucy Trent, and Nikki crouched quietly in a
corner, as far away from the covered thing on the floor as the ar-
chitect's plans allowed, while Jerry Baxter raced up and down weep-
ing, "Where's my wife? Where's Edith? We've got to get out of here."

Ellery grabbed Baxter's collar and said, "It's going to be a long
night, Jerry—relax. Nikki—"

"Yes, Ellery." She was trembling and trying to stop it and not
succeeding.

"You know who was supposed to be the murderer in that foul

game—the one who drew the ace of spades—you saw him or her step away from the living-room wall while the lights were still on in there. Who was it?"

"Edith Baxter. Edith got the ace. Edith was supposed to be the murderer."

Jerry Baxter jerked out of Ellery's grasp. "You're lying!" he yelled. "You're not mixing my wife up in this stink! You're lying—"

Ann crept away from the sink, avoiding the mound. She crept past them and went into the foyer and collapsed against the door of a closet just outside the kitchen. Lucy crept after Ann and cuddled against her, whimpering. Ann began to whimper, too.

"Edith Baxter was Murderer," said Nikki drearily. "In the game, anyway."

"You lie!—you lying—"

Ellery slapped his mouth without rancor and Baxter started to weep again. "Don't let me come back and find any other throats cut," said Ellery, and he went out of the kitchen.

It was tempting to assume the obvious, which was that Edith Baxter, having drawn the ace of spades, decided to play the role of murderer in earnest, and did so, and fled. Her malice-dipped triumph as she looked at John Crombie's wife, her anger as she watched Crombie pursue Nikki through the evening, told a simple story; and it was really unkind of fate—if fate was the culprit—to place Edith Baxter's hand on John Crombie's shoulder in the victim-choosing phase of the game. In the kitchen, with a bread knife at hand, who could blame a well bourboned woman if she obeyed that impulse and separated Mr. Crombie's neck from his careless collar?

But investigation muddled the obvious. The front door of the suite was locked—even bolted—on the inside. Nikki proclaimed herself the authoress thereof, having performed the sealed-apartment act before the game began in (she said) a moment of "inspiration."

Secondly, escape by one of the windows was out of the question, unless, like Pegasus, Edith Baxter possessed wings.

Thirdly, Edith Baxter had not attempted to escape at all: Ellery found her in the foyer closet against which the widow and her sister whimpered. Mrs. Baxter had been jammed into the closet by a hasty hand, and she was unconscious.

Inspector Queen, Sergeant Velie & Co. arrived just as Edith Baxter, with the aid of ammonium carbonate, was shuddering back to life.

"Guy named Crombie's throat slit?" bellowed Sergeant Velie, without guile.

Edith Baxter's eyes rolled over and Nikki wielded the smelling salts once more, wearily.

"Murder games," said Inspector Queen gently. "Halloween," said Inspector Queen. Ellery blushed. "Well, son?"

Ellery told his story humbly, in penitential detail.

"Well, we'll soon find out," grumbled his father, and he shook Mrs. Baxter until her chin waggled and her eyes flew open. "Come, come, madam, we can't afford these luxuries. What were you doing in that closet?"

Edith screamed, "How should I know?" and had a convulsion of tears. "Jerry Baxter, how can you sit there and—?"

But her husband was doubled over, holding his head.

"You received Nikki's instructions, Edith," said Ellery, "and when she turned off the light you left the living room and went to the kitchen. Or started for it. What did happen?"

"Don't third-degree me, you detective!" screeched Mrs. Baxter. "I'd just passed under the archway, feeling my way, when somebody grabbed my nose and mouth from behind and I must have fainted because that's all I knew till just now and Jerry Baxter, if you don't get up on your two feet like a man and defend your own wife, I'll—I'll—"

"Slit his throat?" asked Sergeant Velie crossly, for the Sergeant had been attending his own Halloween Party with the boys of his old precinct and was holding three queens full when the call to duty came.

"The murderer," said Ellery glumly. "The real murderer, Dad. At the time Nikki first put out the lights, while Edith Baxter was still in the room getting Nikki's final instructions, one of us against that wall stole across the room, passed Nikki, passed Edith Baxter in the dark, and ambushed her—"

"Probably intended to slug her," nodded the Inspector, "but Mrs. Baxter obliged by fainting first."

"Then into the closet and away to do the foul deed?" asked the Sergeant poetically.

"It would mean," mused Inspector Queen, "that after stowing Mrs. Baxter in the foyer closet, the real killer went into the kitchen, got the mask, flash, and knife, came back to the living room, tapped John Crombie, led him out to the kitchen, and carved him up. That part of it's okay—Crombie must have thought he was playing the game—but how about the assault on Mrs. Baxter beforehand? Having to drag her unconscious body to the closet? Wasn't there any noise, any sound?"

Ellery said apologetically, "I kept dozing off."

But Nikki said, "There was no sound, Inspector. Then or at any other time. The first *sound* after I turned the light off was John screaming in the kitchen. The only other *sound* was the murderer throwing the flash into the middle of the room after he . . . she . . . whoever it was . . . got back to the wall."

Jerry Baxter raised his sweating face and looked at his wife.

"Could be," said the Inspector.

"Oh, my," said Sergeant Velie. He was studying the old gentleman as if he couldn't believe his eyes—or ears.

"It could be," remarked Ellery, "or it couldn't. Edith's a very small woman. Unconscious, she *could* be carried noiselessly the few feet in the foyer to the closet . . . by a reasonably strong person."

Immediately Ann Crombie and Lucy Treni and Jerry Baxter tried to look tiny and helpless, while Edith Baxter tried to look huge and heavy. But the sisters could not look less tall or soundly made than Nature had fashioned them, and Jerry's proportions, even allowing for reflexive shrinkage, were elephantine.

"Nikki," said Ellery in a very thoughtful way, "you're sure Edith was the only one to step away from the wall while the light was still on?"

"Dead sure, Ellery."

"And when the one you thought was Edith came back from the kitchen to pick a victim, that person had a full mask on?"

"You mean after I put the light out? Yes. I could see the mask in the glow the flash made."

"Man or woman, Miss P?" interjected the Sergeant eagerly. "This could be a pipe. If it was a man—"

But Nikki shook her head. "The flash was pretty weak, Sergeant. And we were all in those Black Cat outfits."

"Me, I'm no Fancy Dan," murmured Inspector Queen unexpectedly. "A man's been knocked off. What I want to know is not who was where when, but—who had it in for this character?"

It was a different sort of shrinkage this time, a shrinkage of four throats. Ellery thought: They *all* know.

"Whoever," he began casually, "whoever knew that John Crombie and Edith Baxter were—"

"*It's a lie!*" Edith was on her feet, swaying, clawing the air. "There was nothing between John and me. Nothing. Nothing! Jerry, don't believe them!"

Jerry Baxter looked down at the floor again. "Between?" he mumbled. "I guess I got a head. I guess this has got me." And, strangely, he looked not at his wife but at Ann Crombie. "Ann . . .?"

But Ann was jelly-lipped with fear.

"Nothing!" screamed Jerry's wife.

"That's not true." And now it was Lucy's turn, and they saw that she had been shocked into a sort of suicidal courage. "John was a . . . a . . . John made love to every woman he met. John made love to *me*—"

"To you?" Ann blinked and blinked at her sister.

"Yes. He was . . . disgusting. I . . ." Lucy's eyes flamed at Edith Baxter with scorn, with loathing, with contempt. "But *you* didn't find him disgusting, Edith."

Edith glared back, giving hate for hate.

"You spent four weekends with him. And the other night, at that dinner party, when you two stole off—you thought I didn't hear—but you were both tight . . . You begged him to marry you."

"You nasty little blabbermouth," said Edith in a low voice.

"I heard you. You said you'd divorce Jerry if he'd divorce Ann. And John kind of laughed at you, didn't he?—as if you were dirt. And I saw your eyes, Edith . . ."

And now they, too, saw Edith Baxter's eyes—as they really were.

"I never told you, Ann. I couldn't. I couldn't . . ." Lucy began to sob into her hands.

Jerry Baxter got up.

"Here, where d'ye think you're going?" asked the Sergeant, not unkindly.

Jerry Baxter sat down again.

"Mrs. Crombie, did you know what was going on?" asked Inspector Queen sympathetically.

It was queer how she would not look at Edith Baxter, who was sitting lumpily now, no threat to anyone—a soggy old woman.

And Ann said, stiff and tight, "Yes, I knew." Then her mouth loosened again and she said wildly, "I knew, but I'm a coward. I couldn't face him with it. I thought if I shut my eyes—"

"So do I," said Ellery tiredly.

"What?" said Inspector Queen, turning around. "You what, son? I didn't get you."

"I know who cut Crombie's throat . . ."

They were lined up facing the far wall of the living room—Ann Crombie, Lucy Trent, Edith Baxter, and Jerry Baxter—with a space the breadth of a man, and a little more, between the Baxters. Nikki stood at the light switch, the Inspector and Sergeant Velie blocked the archway, and Ellery sat on a hassock in the center of the room, his hands dangling listlessly.

"This is how we were arranged a couple of hours ago, Dad, except that I was at the wall, too, and so was John Crombie . . . in that vacant space."

Inspector Queen said nothing.

"The light was still on, as it is now. Nikki had just asked Murderer to step away from the wall and cross the room—that is, towards where you are now. Do it, Edith."

"You mean—"

"Please."

Edith Baxter backed from the wall and turned and slowly picked her way around the overturned furniture. Near the archway she paused, an arm's length from the Inspector and the Sergeant.

"With Edith about where she is now, Nikki, in the full light, instructed her about going to the kitchen, getting the mask, flash, and knife there, coming back in the dark with the flash, selecting a victim, and so on. Isn't that right?"

"Yes."

"Then you turned off the light, Nikki—didn't you?"

"Yes . . ."

"Do it."

"D-do it, Ellery?"

"Do it, Nikki."

When the darkness closed down, someone at the wall gasped. And then the silence closed down, too.

And after a moment Ellery's voice came tiredly, "It was at this point, Nikki, that you said 'Stop!' to Edith Baxter and gave her a few additional instructions. About what to do after the 'crime.' As I pointed out a few minutes ago, Dad—it was during this interval, with Edith standing in the archway getting Nikki's afterthoughts, and the room in darkness, that the real murderer must have stolen across the living room from the wall, got past Nikki and Edith and into the foyer, and waited there to ambush Edith."

"Sure, son," said the Inspector. "So what?"

"*How did the murderer manage to cross this room in pitch-darkness without making any noise?*"

At the wall Jerry Baxter said hoarsely, "Look, I don't have to stand here. I don't have to!"

"Because, you know," said Ellery reflectively, "there wasn't any noise. None at all. In fact, Nikki, you actually remarked in that interval, 'I want the room to be as quiet as it is this minute.' And only a few moments ago you corroborated yourself when you told Dad that the first sound after you turned off the light was John screaming in the kitchen. You said that the only other sound was the sound of the flashlight landing in the middle of the room after the murderer got back to the wall. So I repeat: How did the murderer cross in darkness without making a sound?"

Sergeant Velie's disembodied bass complained from the archway that he didn't get it at all, at all.

"Well, Sergeant, you've seen this room—it's cluttered crazily with overturned furniture, pillows, hassocks, miscellaneous objects. Do you think *you* could cross it in darkness without sounding like the bull in the china shop? Nikki, when you and I first got here and blundered into the living room—"

"In the dark," cried Nikki. "We bumped. I actually fell—"

"Why didn't the murderer?"

"I'll tell you why," said Inspector Queen suddenly. "*Because no one did cross this room in the dark.* It can't be done without making a racket, or without a light—and there was no light at that time or Nikki'd have seen it."

"Then how's it add up, Inspector?" asked Velie.

"There's only one person we know who crossed this room, the one Nikki saw cross while the light was on, the one they found in the closet in a 'faint,' Velie. *Edith Baxter!*"

She sounded nauseated. "Oh, no."

"Oh, yes, Mrs. Baxter," the Inspector went on. "It's been you all the time. You did get to the kitchen. You got the mask, the flash, the knife. You came back and tapped John Crombie. You led him out to the kitchen and there you sliced him—"

"No!"

"Then you quietly got into that closet and pulled a phony faint, and waited for them to find you so you could tell that cock-and-bull story of being ambushed in the foyer—"

"Dad," sighed Ellery.

"Huh?" And because the old man's memory of similar moments was very green, his tone became truculent. "Now tell me I'm wrong, Ellery!"

286 THE HALLOWEEN MYSTERY

"Edith Baxter is the one person present tonight who couldn't have killed John Crombie."

Edith moaned.

"Nikki actually saw somebody with a flash *return* to the living room after Crombie's death scream, go to the wall, turn off the flash, and she heard that person hurl it into the middle of the room. Who was it Nikki saw and heard? We've deduced that already—the actual murderer. Immediately after that, Nikki turned up the lights.

"If Edith Baxter were the murderer, wouldn't we have found her *at the wall with the rest of us* when the lights went on? But she wasn't. She wasn't in the living room at all. We found her in the foyer closet. So she *had* been attacked. She *did* faint. She *didn't* kill Crombie." —They could hear her sobbing.

"Then who did?" barked the Inspector.

"The one who was able to cross the room in the dark without making any noise. For if Edith is innocent, one of those at the wall must be guilty. And that one had to cross the room."

"But how, son, how?" bellowed his father. "It couldn't be done without knocking *something* over—making *some* noise!"

"Only one possible explanation," said Ellery tiredly; and then he said, not tiredly at all, but swiftly and with the slashing finality of a knife, "I thought you'd try that. That's why I sat on the hassock, so very tired. That's why I staged this whole . . . silly . . . scene."

Velie was roaring, "Where the hell are the lights? Miss Porter, turn that switch on, will you?"

"I can't find the—the damned thing!" wept Nikki.

"The rest of you stay where you are!" shouted the Inspector.

"Now drop the knife," said Ellery, in the slightly gritty tone of one who is exerting pressure. "Drop it . . ." There was a little clatter, and then a whimper. "The only one who could have passed through this jumbled maze in the dark without stumbling over anything," Ellery went on, "would be someone who'd *plotted a route through this maze in advance of the party* . . . someone, in fact, who'd plotted the maze. In other words, the clutter in this room is not chance confusion, but a deliberate plant. It would require photographing the details of the obstacle course on the memory, and practice, plenty of practice—but we were told you spent the entire day in this suite *alone*, fixing it up for the party."

"Here!" sobbed Nikki, and she jabbed the light switch.

"I imagine," said Ellery gently to the girl in his grip, "you felt *someone* had to avenge the honor of the Trents, Lucy."

ABOUT ELLERY QUEEN

Ellery Queen is the pseudonym of Frederic Dannay and his cousin the late Manfred B. Lee, both of whom were born in Brooklyn, N.Y., in 1905. In 1928, attracted by a $7,500 prize in a mystery-novel contest sponsored by *McClure's* magazine, they worked nights and weekends for six months, producing the novel which won the contest.

They celebrated by buying each other a Dunhill pipe monogrammed EQ, then learned that the magazine was going bankrupt and they would not collect the prize after all. Frederick A. Stokes Company, however, took on the novel—*The Roman Hat Mystery*—and its publication (in 1929) was a major historical event in the genre.

For this first collaboration they decided on Ellery Queen as their pseudonym as well as the name of their detective, writer Ellery Queen, hoping readers would find it easier to remember one name than two. Queen's genius for weighing the clues, timetables, motives and personalities in a complicated murder case until he has discovered the only possible solution dazzled his fans book after book.

For a while his creators lectured, masked, crosscountry, Dannay challenging Lee with intricate crime puzzles. Along with the Queen novels they also wrote four novels as by Barnaby Ross, three classic critical works on the mystery genre, *The Detective Short Story, Queen's Quorum,* and *In the Queen's Parlor,* and two collections of true-crime articles, *Ellery Queen's International Case Book* and *The Woman in the Case.*

In 1940 they interested publisher Lawrence E. Spivak of Mercury Press in the idea of *Ellery Queen's Mystery Magazine,* which first appeared in the fall of 1941. From the beginning, Dannay was its active editor. Davis Publications, Inc., was founded on August 1, 1957, with the purchase of *EQMM* from Mercury Press.

The Ellery Queen books have sold, in various editions published by approximately 100 publishers around the world, a total of more than 150,000,000 copies. Queen's books have been translated into every major foreign language except Chinese.

Ellery Queen popularized the mystery drama on radio in a program called *The Adventures of Ellery Queen,* which was on the air for nine years, and in 1950 *TV Guide* gave the Ellery Queen TV program its national award for the best mystery show on television. In 1975–1976 the most recent TV program starred Jim Hutton as Ellery and David Wayne as Inspector Queen.

Ellery Queen has won five Edgars (the annual Mystery Writers of America awards similar to the Oscars of Hollywood), including the prestigious Grand Master award (1960), three MWA Scrolls and one Raven, and twice Queen was runner-up for the Best Novel of the Year award. He also has won both the gold and silver Gertrudes awarded by Pocket Books, Inc. Mystery Writers of Japan gave Ellery Queen their gold-and-onyx Edgar Allan Poe ring, awarded to only five non-Japanese detective-story writers. In 1968 Iona College honored Queen with its Columba Prize in Mystery. In 1978 *And On the Eighth Day* won the Grand Prix de Litterature Policière.

The late Anthony Boucher, distinguished critic and novelist, described Queen best when he wrote: "Ellery Queen *is* the American detective story."